THREADED FOR TROUBLE

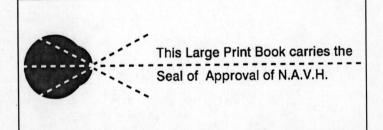
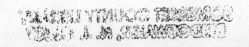

THREADED FOR TROUBLE

JANET BOLIN

WHEELER PUBLISHING
A part of Gale, Cengage Learning

GALE
CENGAGE Learning®

Detroit • New York • San Francisco • New Haven, Conn • Waterville, Maine • London

GALE
CENGAGE Learning®

Wheeler Publishing Large Print Cozy Mystery.
The text of this Large Print edition is unabridged.
Other aspects of the book may vary from the original edition.
Set in 16 pt. Plantin.

LIBRARY OF CONGRESS CATALOGING-IN-PUBLICATION DATA

Bolin, Janet.
   Threaded for trouble / by Janet Bolin. — Large Print edition.
      pages cm. — (Wheeler Publishing Large Print Cozy Mystery)
   "This is part of A Threadville Mystery series."
   ISBN 978-1-4104-5438-6 (softcover) — ISBN 1-4104-5438-X (softcover) 1. Embroidery—Fiction. 2. Murder—Investigation—Fiction. 3. Large type books.
I. Title.
PS3602.O6534T47 2013
813'.6—dc23   2012040958

Published in 2013 by arrangement with The Berkley Publishing Group, a member of Penguin Group (USA) Inc.

Printed in the United States of America
1 2 3 4 5   17 16 15 14 13

*To volunteer firefighters —
past, present, and future*

ACKNOWLEDGMENTS

Welcome to Threadville!

And thanks to Lorna Barrett, who coined the slogan.

Thanks also to mystery aficionados Jan and Bill Mustard, who served the meal and the wine that night (and others) and also helped brainstorm the original proposal. And Bill suggested a "killer" sewing machine . . .

As always, my incredible critique partners, Krista Davis and Avery Aames, helped hone and tweak this manuscript. What's it been now, eleven years that we've critiqued each other? You two deserve special badges for putting up with me this long! In addition, Avery got me thinking about the embroidery project at the back of the book.

My editor, Faith Black, amazes me with the magical way she knows what needs to be fixed and turns a manuscript into a book.

And my agent, Jessica Faust of BookEnds,

is always there for me.

A lot of credit goes to my cover artist, Robin Moline, for painting scenes that make me want to walk into them. In her case, a picture is worth eighty thousand words. Thanks to Annette Fiore Defex, who is responsible for the great cover design, and Tiffany Estreicher, who designed the interior text.

Thanks to Joyce of Joyce's Sewing Shop in Wortley Village, Ontario, for the first tip at the end of the book.

I appreciate the camaraderie of the Sisters in Crime, especially the Guppies and Toronto chapters. And thank you to Crime Writers of Canada — more camaraderie from very helpful people.

As always, my family and friends have cheered me on.

Last but not least, thanks to everyone who read *Dire Threads* and is returning to see what Willow and her friends are up to now. And to new readers, too.

Welcome to Threadville!

1

First, Felicity banished my dogs.

Naturally, I objected. "When In Stitches is open, Sally-Forth and Tally-Ho always stay in their pen." They could wag their plumelike tails at shoppers or trot downstairs to the apartment whenever they wanted a nap, snack, or drink.

Felicity glanced at my name tag, embroidered in willowy green script on white. "Willow —" She scrunched up her nose as if my name smelled. "Our guests may have allergies."

Most of *our* guests would be *my* usual customers, ladies who came on the Threadville tour bus four days a week to shop and take classes in all of the crafty stores. Threadville tourists loved my dogs and had never complained about allergies.

However, Felicity was my guest — sort of — and I would have to put up with her only during the first part of the morning. Hiding my annoyance, I gave in and herded my two active dogs, a brother and sister, one of whose parents must have been a border collie, into the stairway to the apartment and closed the door.

That's when the real reason for their banishment became clear. Felicity informed me that their vacant pen would be a perfect stage for our speeches.

Speeches? True, I had memorized a short one about how happy I was that someone from this corner of Pennsylvania — not that I'd ever met her — had won a top-of-the-line sewing and embroidery machine in a national contest. I supposed Felicity might want to say a few words as she presented the carton to the winner.

But no. Felicity was not handing over a *carton.* "Why is our Chandler Champion not yet unpacked?" she demanded. "Did you not test it as instructed?"

I attempted a smile, but my teeth clenched together, which could not have looked either friendly or professional. "We checked it thoroughly. It works well. It's a great machine. I got up early and packed it —"

"No, no, no, no, no!" Felicity didn't really need to say no that many times. I caught the gist before the second one. "It must be seen and admired. We do want to sell more of them, don't we." It was a command, not a question.

I gestured to the row of sewing machines behind me, which included a Chandler Champion exactly like the one in the carton, and two other, more modest Chandler models.

Felicity gasped. Actually, it was more like a shriek. "We must, simply must, hide all of your machines except the Chandlers. *Before* our audience arrives. We wouldn't want them looking at Chandler's competitors, would we." Another command.

But not one I was about to take. "They'll want to compare," I pointed out, "feature for feature."

She folded her arms and tapped the toe of one scuffed brown shoe against my shop's beautiful walnut floor. "And price for price. Okay, they can stay. Our business plan at Chandler is to make the best machines for the best price." Yes, it was also their motto, printed in huge red letters on the white plastic banner she'd had me string above my display of natural fabrics. Call me snooty, but if I had been in charge of making that banner, I would have used my machines to embroider it. On canvas or ripstop nylon.

She marched toward the front of the store.

"Let's bring that small table . . ." She shoved aside my two cute bistro chairs, then lugged my round metal table, complete with the tablecloth I'd embroidered, toward the back of the store. She was careful not to clank against the Chandlers, but I had to steer the table's legs past the other sewing machines and racks of dazzling embroidery threads.

She banged the table down in the middle of the dog pen, wadded up my tablecloth, and thrust it in my direction. "Get rid of that. Those aren't Chandler motifs."

I had designed those autumn leaves myself, using photos I'd taken and software from another manufacturer, one of my favorites. "Is Chandler planning to produce digitizing software?" Best software at the best price? That would be good.

"That's for me to know." A trade secret — fine. "Now, unpack that machine and put it here for everyone to admire." For the first time, she seemed to notice the chairs I had lined up for our audience. Another little scream. "You'll have to put most of those chairs away. Fewer chairs filled with people will make a better impression than lots of unoccupied chairs, and Mr. Chandler should already be here." She looked about to go into a panicked tailspin.

12

Mr. Chandler? The owner of the company? Felicity should have warned me. Not that I would have arranged my embroidery boutique differently or cooled a magnum of champagne, but it would have been nice to know what to expect. What other surprises did this woman have up her brown polyester sleeve?

I didn't give her a chance to tell me. I said, "Many of the women from the Threadville tour will attend the presentation."

"Why do you call this town Threadville? The maps call it Elderberry Bay."

"Everyone, locals and tourists, started calling the village Threadville when fabric and needlework shops opened here."

"Threadville." Sarcasm dripped from her voice. *"Tourists."*

She'd see. I wasn't about to argue with her, but I also wasn't about to put the chairs away, only to need to set them up again. I pointed out, "We should move the prize Chandler Champion closer to an outlet."

She looked to her left as if she had a friend beside her who would agree that I was impossible. "Fine, if you can't be bothered to dig up an extension cord. But hurry. Our winner is due any minute." She rummaged in a large vinyl bag.

Her last name, Ranquels, pronounced

13

"rankles" without irony on her part, suited her, but her first name didn't. A Felicity should have been . . . bubbly. Not only was she dour, she was short and thick, with ankles like tree stumps.

I'd expected a Chandler Sewing Machine Company representative to be decked out in the latest techniques of sewing and machine embroidery. Felicity's skirt and blouse were polyester, off the rack. Maybe she thought their muddy hues would hide the dirt. Maybe she didn't know she had dribbled toothpaste down her front.

Her jacket did look homemade. Not handmade, homemade. She'd used one of those sew-it-in-an-evening patterns. No cuffs, collar, buttons, or pockets. It did have lapels, the type that fold back to show the facing. It wasn't a bad pattern if done right, but she hadn't trimmed or clipped her seams. They were bunchy, and what should have been corners appeared to have been stuffed with balled-up candy wrappers. The front plackets stood out stiffly, as if she had used cardboard instead of interfacing. She had embroidered a bouquet of flowers, all in brown, where the right front pocket would be, if the jacket had pockets. I recognized the bouquet. It was one of the embroidery motifs that came with the Chandler Champion.

I hoped my outfit looked better than hers did. I loved playing with my embroidery software and machines. Luckily I had a good excuse for wearing embroidered clothing — I wanted to inspire my students and customers to buy machines and supplies from me, and to try new techniques. I was proud of the touches of embroidery on the T-shirt, fitted jacket, and denim miniskirt I'd worn for the morning's presentation. Yes, I was tall and my legs were, like the rest of me, willowy, but skirts that ended below mid-thigh never quite suited me.

I moved the table close to an outlet and began unpacking the Chandler Champion. It was the heaviest sewing machine I had ever lifted.

Felicity pulled a cell phone from her bag. She turned her back to me, but I heard every word. "Mr. Chandler has not arrived. When will he be here?" Silence, then, "I arranged for a limo to pick him up at the Cleveland airport. So what's the problem?"

By now, my friends in their shops across the street could probably hear her, too.

"You call me the minute you find out." Steam was practically puffing out her ears. "The ceremony is scheduled to begin in a half hour."

I plugged in the Chandler Champion. Felicity elbowed me aside and turned it on. The machine contained a powerful computer, complete with a color, high-definition touch screen.

Felicity fingered the screen. "You've been using this."

"Yes, we tested it." I didn't mean to let my irritation show, but at least I didn't add, *as you ordered.* It was true that testing a new machine was fun, but still . . . couldn't she be nicer?

Apparently not. "You put ten hours on it."

I defended myself. "It already had more than a hundred." Closer to two hundred, actually.

"That's different. Factory testing. We have to make certain that each machine is perfect. However, our manufacturing standards are high, and we have not encountered a flaw during the entire year since we first went to market."

Well, whoop-de-do. "I guessed the machine had been a floor model, or perhaps used and returned, before you offered it as a prize."

"Mr. Chandler would never do that."

He might not, I thought uncharitably, but

16

someone on his staff might, and I suspected I was looking at that person.

She glared at one of the pot lights in my shop's ceiling. "You need to re-aim that light. Lucky thing you didn't put your ladder away like I told you to."

"My ladder doesn't go up that high."

"You're tall. You hung the banner."

"The ceiling's much higher."

"Stand on the top step."

And fall off and break seventeen bones. What a superb idea. "I'll bring a floor lamp to the machine, instead." Not that we needed it. Morning sunshine poured through the shop's rear windows, backlighting the Chandler Champion. Besides, Threadville tourists tended to be enthusiastic about sewing machines. They wouldn't fail to notice this one perched on a table in the middle of the pen where my dogs usually were.

"Don't you know someone with a better ladder? What about the other shopkeepers? I see a fabric store across the street. At least I *assume* that's what The Stash means. We simply *must* re-aim that light."

The light chose that moment to burn out. With a pop.

Great.

Felicity paled as if about to faint, but her

voice didn't lose a decibel of its frantic volume. "Find a ladder!"

It was a perfect excuse. If I didn't talk to one of my friends that very minute, I would either explode or collapse in a giggling fit. I ran out the front door. The other Threadville shops were across the street on the ground floor of a gorgeous Victorian building. Its red brick and limestone exterior had stayed fresh and bright all these years in this sweet little village on Pennsylvania's Lake Erie shore. Next to Haylee's fabric shop was the yarn shop, then the notions shop, then the quilting shop. The proprietors lived in apartments above their stores.

There's nothing quite like the sense of anticipation a fabriholic feels when entering a fabric store, and The Stash never disappointed me. Haylee was arranging autumn-toned stretch poplins near her front door. People often mistook us for sisters. Her hair was blond, though, while mine was light brown. Her face was rounder than mine, and her eyes were a purer blue than my grayish ones. Today, she wore a navy linen shift she'd made. She always said that since we were the same size, I could borrow the outfits she hand tailored for herself. I would never dare. My strong desire to decorate everything with thread usually overcame my fondness for elegant simplicity.

As soon as I was certain that Felicity had not followed me across the street, I did explode. In a giggling fit. "You have to come to the presentation in my shop this morning," I managed.

One of Haylee's many sterling qualities is that she laughs with me, even when she doesn't know what's funny. "Why?"

"You'll see." I was almost out the door before I remembered the real reason for my visit. "Do you have a taller ladder than the one I've seen you use?"

Her eyes widened as if she thought the need for a ladder could be part of the joke. "No."

"That's okay. I wasn't the one who wanted it."

Haylee contemplated my grin, which had to hint at mischief. "Want me to tell the other Threadville store owners to come to your presentation?"

"Yes, please. And bring your customers. They'll enjoy the show." Still giggling at the impression Felicity's histrionics would make on the Threadville community of creative yet sensible textile artists, I headed back across the street.

I felt a thrill of pride whenever I approached In Stitches. The shop was on the main floor of a converted Arts and Crafts–style bungalow, with deep eaves and a homey roof sheltering its wide front porch. My customers often sat on that porch, in comfy handcrafted rocking chairs next to tables sporting books, magazines, and pots of flowers. The women discussed their projects, the homework I had assigned, and life in general while sipping fresh lemonade or iced tea. Often, while out there admiring Threadville shops, they realized they needed to purchase a few more crafting necessities, even when they lived in the village or were returning to it the next day.

Today, no one was on the porch, and the most prominent displays in my twin front windows were the linen banners I had embroidered with the words *Welcome, Winner!* The front door, glass surrounded by metal, clashed with the architectural style of the building, but the shop was homey, especially after I turned the sign in the door from *Closed,* embroidered in red satin stitches over puffy foam on white linen, to *Welcome,* embroidered in green letters with three-dimensional vines and flowers twining through them. I opened the door, setting my pretty sea-glass chimes jingling.

"Where's that ladder?" Felicity bellowed.

Hiding impending giggles with a nonchalant expression, I strolled around the folding chairs toward her. "Nobody has one tall enough."

The chimes jangled. A teenaged boy slouched in and plunked himself on a chair in the back row. With his long forelock and practiced sneer, he looked like a fifties rock star. I tossed him a welcoming smile.

"What are you doing here?" Felicity demanded. Did she know him?

The boy blushed. "My mom said I had to come."

"Shouldn't you be in school?" she asked.

I reminded her, "School doesn't start until after Labor Day." Why was a teenager spending a morning of his last two weeks of summer vacation in an embroidery boutique? He could be with friends, perhaps exploring the riverside trail or enjoying the village's wide, sandy beach. He obviously didn't want to be here.

He ducked his head. "I dropped out."

"Well," Felicity snapped, "did you learn enough before you dropped out to change a light bulb?"

The boy looked at the floor as if hoping it would open up and swallow him.

I tried to take the pressure off the poor kid. "That light's too high," I said. "I won't be able to find a tall ladder before the

21

presentation." Felicity was the one who had been harping about being ready for the winner's arrival.

The boy jumped out of his chair, which promptly folded onto the floor. Apologizing, he set the chair up again. "I know where to get a ladder." Pushing buttons on a cell phone, he bolted out the front door. Maybe I was lucky that Felicity had insisted on moving my bistro table away from the door. If she hadn't, the teenager might have swept the table ahead of him out onto the porch, and it could be rolling around, banging into rocking chairs and flower pots.

Minutes later, a red pickup truck parked beside the curb in front of In Stitches. A tall, athletic man got out and began pulling a long extension ladder from the truck bed.

Uh-oh. Clay Fraser.

2

Clay had renovated this building before I bought it. Whenever I had a problem, I called him, and he always came. For a while, I'd thought we might become friends, or maybe more than friends; then I'd made some rather rash accusations, and though he'd seemed understanding, my embarrassment over my behavior had kept me more or less away from him. Lately, I hadn't needed his help, which was just as well.

He and the boy carried the ladder into the shop. Clay was wearing jeans that were just tight enough. The sleeves of his light blue shirt were rolled up, revealing tanned and muscular forearms. The hair on them was the same dark brown as the hair on his head.

The Chandler Champion with its embroidery attachment looked ridiculous and top-heavy on a too-small table in the dog pen. My dogs whined from the other side of my apartment door. Unlike me, Sally-Forth and Tally-Ho weren't shy about showing their desire to be near Clay. He frowned toward the dogless pen and the closed apartment door.

Penning the dogs in the back of my shop where they could be with me and my customers without causing problems had been Clay's idea, and he'd designed and built the pen, a railing with a gate, in dark-stained oak that matched shelves he'd constructed for my shop. It all worked perfectly for me and the dogs. Would Clay think I no longer liked him and that was why I'd stopped using the pen for the dogs?

The color of his eyes reminded me of melting chocolate, and the concern in them made me consider just plain melting. "What's wrong, Willow?"

"Light bulb." Such astounding wit caused my face to flame. I gestured toward the ceiling and reached even greater heights of conversational ability. "Burned out."

Felicity was in the ladder's way. She had dragged one of my bistro chairs to the sewing machine and was adding yet more minutes to its run time. With maddening slowness, she turned off the machine and stood up.

The boy asked Clay, "Can I climb the lad-

24

der, Mr. Fraser?"

Clay bit back a grin. "Maybe we should get a new bulb, first, Russ. You steady the ladder. I'll run next door to The Ironmonger. Be right back."

Russ and I both said, "I'll go."

Clay glanced from me to Felicity and back again. "It looks like you have your hands full." He turned to Russ and asked, "Do you know which bulb to ask for?"

Russ blushed. Hair fell over his eyes, but he was holding the ladder with both hands and couldn't do anything about it. "No," he admitted. He tossed his head, but the lock of hair stubbornly went back to hang in his face.

Poor kid. I was tempted to trim his hair. I had lots of scissors, pairs I owned and even more pairs for sale. None of them were meant for haircutting, but I'd make do. "Me, neither," I admitted, smiling at Russ.

The boy stared straight ahead, at his hair, no doubt.

Clay left.

Felicity informed me, "You have to do something about those dogs."

I was used to hearing Tally's lonely whimper when he wanted something, so it hadn't dawned on me that his whining was accelerating and beginning to resemble the

25

honking of geese. Sally added yips of distress. "They'll settle down after Clay leaves," I answered. If they'd been in their pen where they could have greeted Clay properly instead of on the wrong side of a door, they wouldn't be fussing.

Clay returned with a new bulb. He gripped the base of the ladder while Russ climbed up and changed the bulb.

Felicity went out onto the porch, left the door open, and hollered into her cell phone, "What do you mean he's not coming? He has a speech to give."

Almost hidden by a tower of cookie tins, Susannah arrived. She peered around the tins at Felicity, saw me watching her, and broke into a bigger smile than I'd seen from her in a long time.

I ran to help her carry the tins to the refreshment table I had set up on one side of the store. In her early thirties, Susannah was reeling from a difficult divorce. She had been the star pupil in all the Threadville courses and workshops, so when the other four proprietors and I had decided to share an assistant, we'd offered her the job. She helped each of us one day a week and also went from store to store around lunchtime, giving us breaks. She was certified to repair machines made by every manufacturer represented in the Threadville shops. Today, Wednesday, she would work with Haylee in The Stash. She whispered, "Haylee said something amusing must be going on over here. That woman's outfit must be it — her sewing skills are hilarious."

"So," I murmured in my darkest, most ominous murmur, "is she. Stick around." We peeked into tins the other Threadville proprietors had contributed. "Wow," I said. My friends had made T-shirt-shaped cookies and embellished them with icing to imitate intricate embroidery.

The Threadville tour bus rumbled down Lake Street. The driver usually parked a couple of blocks away, in the lot down the hill near the beach. In a few minutes, our audience would arrive.

Clay and Russ carefully shortened the ladder and carried it outside to the truck, barely missing Felicity's flailing arm as they passed her. A piece of cardboard fell out of her jacket. She swooped down and stuck it back inside her lapel. For interfacing, she really had used cardboard, corrugated cardboard, clumsily folded where the lapels should have rolled smoothly, and she'd added it after she completed the jacket. What an odd construction method for a sewing professional to use.

Stifling giggles, Susannah and I and arranged napkins, plates, and glasses.

Her face redder than ever, Felicity stomped into the store. Frizzy might have been a more appropriate name for her. Maybe Mr. Chandler had stayed away because of a fear of home perms gone awry.

Felicity dug around in her shiny store-bought bag and handed me an index card. "Here, memorize this. You'll have to give my speech. I'll give Mr. Chandler's. He's unable to make it. A death in the family." Usually, people didn't look quite that angry when speaking of death.

She'd written almost exactly what I'd planned to say. I had a sudden and very fierce desire to rebel.

Clay drove away. Hair still over his eyes, Russ slunk into the store. Felicity glared at him.

"Thanks for your help, Russ," I said.

He mumbled, "Yeah." After undergoing a personality transplant around Clay, he had reverted to being a sullen teenager.

Felicity stumped off and stationed herself by the front door. Locals and Threadville tourists ran up onto my porch and brushed past her. Gabbing about the homework they'd done since yesterday's class, they surrounded Susannah and me. Several of them mentioned that they hoped this presentation would be short so they could get to work.

Felicity performed a good imitation of a volcano about to bubble over.

She didn't look happier when they gravitated to the gleaming new Chandler Champion. Maybe she had insisted we should use the dog pen as a pseudo stage because it could be closed off. But neither of us had shut the gate, and if Felicity wanted to shoo the throng of admiring women away from the sewing machine, she was welcome to try.

Russ slumped forward in his chair, elbows on his thighs, hands dangling between his knees. Why would a mother tell her teenaged son he had to attend a presentation with a bunch of chattering women?

Haylee and the other Threadville shopkeepers followed their students into my shop. Mona from the home décor shop came, too, showing a surprising amount of cleavage for an event in a thread art boutique on a Wednesday morning. Rumor had it that she was once again on the hunt for a man. But even before she'd sent her most recent husband packing, she'd dressed in clothes that neither fit nor flattered.

She thrust a flyer into my hands. "This

would be a good thing for you and your little friend to do," she whispered. Mona always shook her head no, even when she was being, in her own way, encouraging. Little friend? I tilted my head in confusion. She flapped a hand toward Haylee, who was at least a head taller than Mona. "It is the citizenly duty of the Threadville shopkeepers to help out in this effort."

The page's title was *Application to Volunteer with the Elderberry Bay Fire Department.* The subtitle was *Come Join Us — We Always Need New Firefighters.*

Always? How alarming. What happened to the old ones?

Suppressing a shudder, I told Mona, "I can't join the volunteer fire department. Firefighting requires skill and strength. And knowledge that I don't have."

"Nonsense," Mona countered, shaking her head. "They'll train you and your little friend."

"Haylee," I corrected her.

"You both must be strong from heaving bolts of fabric around."

Is that all she thought we did? "Are you joining?" I asked her.

She gave me a smile like I was just too, too cute. "I'm not big and strapping like you two."

First Haylee was my "little friend," and now she was big and strapping? No one had ever described either of us that way before. Both of us were tall and thin, and some people actually saw us as fragile, which wasn't true, either. I suspected that Mona's real reasons for refusing to become a volunteer firefighter had a lot to do with not wanting to wear a big clumsy outfit, mix soot in her makeup, or break a nail on a fire hose. I suppressed a grin at a mental picture of her shaking her head at a fire in hopes of encouraging it to extinguish itself.

Women milled around the Chandler Champion. Felicity crowded me. "Tell them to stop touching that machine. They'll destroy it."

I started to shake my head, thought of Mona, and settled for looking stern. "They're all careful around machines. And respectful. They would never harm a sewing machine."

"Do you know every single one of those women?"

"Most of them." I didn't recognize a few of the women poking at the Champion, but they probably attended classes in the other Threadville shops, and my friends could vouch for them.

"Can't you tell them to sit down?"

I flicked the lights to get everyone's attention.

Despite Felicity's predictions, we didn't have enough seats, and many of us remained standing near the door, including Felicity. She had backed out of my personal space but was still glowering, maybe because of the large crowd I'd drawn. "We can't start until our winner arrives," she whined. "Go say something."

Leaving Susannah near the door to greet latecomers, I folded the fire department flyer into a pocket and walked away from the door, past rows of excited Threadville regulars, to the back of the store.

Beside the dog pen's open gate, I turned and faced the audience. Most of the people were my students, or had been at one time or another. They beamed at me, and I forgot my annoyance with Felicity and spoke directly to them and to my friends standing by the front door. I couldn't make eye contact with Russ. He was still studying the floor. He probably felt odd being the only male in the room. To make matters worse, no one sat within two chairs of him.

A siren interrupted my ad-libbed welcoming speech.

3

A red SUV marked with the words *Fire Chief* stopped in front of In Stitches. Recruiting volunteers?

"Aha," Felicity announced from the front door. "Better late than never. Here comes our guest of honor." But instead of staying there to greet the winner of the sewing and embroidery competition, Felicity clomped up the aisle and stood beside me at the railing enclosing the prize Chandler Champion.

The SUV's doors opened, and children poured out. They arranged themselves and processed — that was the only word for it — into In Stitches.

Everyone in the chairs craned around as if to see a bride. Everyone except Russ, that is. He slumped lower.

A little girl came first. A chorus of oohs and aahs burst from the audience. The child was about three and looked adorable in a pale blue dress under a ruffled white organdy pinafore. The pinafore was embroidered with blue flowers and birds to match the dress. Golden curls tumbled to her shoulders. She was wearing stage makeup.

The next child was about eight. Her dress and the machine-embroidered flowers on her pinafore were pale yellow. Her hair was darker, but curled like the first girl's, and she also wore makeup. She gasped for breath, and no wonder. That pinafore was so tight it wrinkled across her middle.

The third girl scowled. She appeared to be about twelve. Her dress was candy pink. It and the pink-embroidered white pinafore over it were much too short, showing off bony knees, coltish legs, and pink ankle socks teamed with black patent leather Mary Janes matching the younger girls' shoes. The twelve-year-old's makeup was a slash of purple lipstick that she must have slapped on without the aid of a mirror, possibly during the ride in the fire chief's SUV. Her hair was dark and straight, and a lock fell across her forehead, like Russ's.

Exactly like Russ's.

Felicity called out, "Come right up here, girls, and let everyone see your mother's winning entry in the Chandler Challenge!" The two younger girls followed her orders, but the bigger girl climbed over two Thread-

34

ville tourists, fell into the chair next to Russ, and glared. Elbows on knees, Russ hid his face in his rawboned hands.

More children followed the first three. A girl who looked about fifteen came inside in jeans and a tank top. Showing what I was beginning to think of as the family sneer, she held hands with two little boys, one about four and the other about five, each wearing white cowboy shirts. The yokes of the shirts were piped in pastels and decorated with embroidery motifs matching the designs on the little girls' pinafores. The fifteen-year-old let the two boys go, gave them shoves that propelled them to follow the two youngest girls, then clambered over her sister and Russ to sit on Russ's other side.

Another boy, a slightly younger replica of Russ, complete with the sneer, torn jeans, T-shirt, and uncombed hair, slouched in behind his siblings. With a sardonic toss of the head, he held up a white cowboy shirt trimmed in mint green for the audience to see, then bunched it between his hands and stumbled into the row to sit beside the girl in the unfortunately tiny dress.

"And now," Felicity announced in her nasal voice, "the winner of the Chandler Challenge, Darlene Coddlefield!"

It should have been a proud moment for Darlene Coddlefield, but as she marched into my shop, she frowned down the row of seats at her older offspring. She tossed what looked like a white cowboy shirt trimmed in candy pink onto Russ's lap. I couldn't hear her words, but the meaning in her attitude was obvious. "Put it on."

Darlene Coddlefield was nearly as wide as she was high. Her eyes were bloodshot and baggy, as if she'd spent the night finishing her beautifully tailored ivory silk pants suit and ironing the children's dresses and shirts. She trundled up the aisle and straightened the smallest boy's collar before shaking hands with Felicity and me. Darlene's hands were clammy.

"My, my," Felicity said with a brightness I didn't expect, "now we understand why Darlene won Mother of the Year back in — when was it, Darlene?"

Darlene waved her hand in front of her face as if driving smoke away. "Many years, and six children ago." The audience laughed. "It was easier to be a good mother with only two babies." I guessed that would be Russ and the scowling older girl.

With a grunt of disgust, Russ stood, threw the pink-trimmed shirt into the lap of the sister wearing the matching dress, and climbed over the back of his chair, which folded and slammed down onto the floor. He flung himself out the front door. My sea-glass wind chimes banged and clattered.

Together, the owners of the yarn, notions, and quilting boutiques turned to watch him stride off the porch and out of sight down Lake Street.

I couldn't help comparing Darlene Coddlefield to these Threadville colleagues. Opal, Naomi, and Edna had met each other in kindergarten and had immediately become closer than many sets of sisters. By the end of junior high, after reading *Macbeth,* they'd started calling themselves The Three Weird Sisters. Then, at sixteen, Opal had become pregnant, and her folks kicked her out of their home. Edna and Naomi had teamed up to help look after Opal's fatherless child. The three women had lived together and taken turns working and going to school. They'd all ended up with degrees and professions. They'd also ended up with a clever, polite, kind, and sensible daughter whom they all adored.

Naturally, that daughter, Haylee, called them The Three Weird Mothers. When I'd moved to Threadville to open In Stitches, The Three Weird Mothers had figured out that my mother was distant in more ways than one. Opal, Naomi, and Edna had adopted me, and Haylee seemed glad to share them.

Haylee's mothers didn't divulge their ages, but Haylee was my age, thirty-three, so the math was easy — her mothers must be nearing or had quietly celebrated their big five-oh. Often, the rambunctious and enthusiastic women acted like they were still seventeen, and Haylee and I had to keep them out of mischief.

I had a sinking feeling that The Three Weird Mothers were considering ways of helping Darlene Coddlefield with all eight of her children. I would hate to see Haylee's mothers hurt if their good intentions were rejected. Always tenderhearted, Naomi looked about to cry in sympathy with the twelve-year-old in the baby dress and shoes.

I was behind the four younger children, close enough to admire Darlene's careful stitching and neat buttonholes. The girls' pinafores strained across their backs. The eight-year-old's wouldn't button at the waist, and the bow in the sash didn't hide the gap. Darlene must have planned and cut out these dresses, pinafores, and shirts a while ago. Meanwhile, her children had grown.

She was obviously an excellent seamstress,

but I couldn't help a teensy bit of jealousy on behalf of some of my customers and students who were every bit as talented but didn't possess top-of-the-line sewing and embroidery machines like the one that must have helped Darlene win the Chandler Challenge. Darlene had never shopped in my store, so I didn't know what kind of machine she already owned, but judging from the outfits she'd made, it was a good one. And now she was going to take home another.

I gave my speech, following my own impromptu script, not Felicity's. Although she was a yard away from me, the heat of her fury at my disobedience radiated from her. I concluded with, "I will be privileged to display Darlene's excellent handiwork, all these dresses and shirts that won her the challenge, in my shop for the rest of you to admire."

Felicity elbowed me aside and stepped in front of me. "It certainly would be a *privilege* for Ms. . . . um" — she consulted her notes — "Ms. Vanderling to display these garments, but they're scheduled to go on tour throughout the U.S., and after I spend the afternoon in the Coddlefield home, giving Darlene the free lesson she earned as part of her prize, I'm leaving for Cleveland and taking the prize-winning garments with me." She turned around and gave me a prissy and obviously fake version of an apologetic smile. "So sorry."

She was planning to leave the vicinity this afternoon. My mood suddenly improved.

The women in the audience nodded sympathetically. I could almost feel pats on my shoulder. Still smiling, I held my hands out in the age-old what-can-I-do-about-it manner. Haylee winked. Her three mothers frowned and whispered to each other.

Naomi beckoned to me. I made my way past rows of Threadville tourists to her.

We were behind the audience. She murmured, "We can lend those children clothes to wear home." Why wasn't I surprised?

Naomi's shop, Batty About Quilts, displayed quilted clothes in addition to bed coverings and wall hangings. In Tell a Yarn, Opal showed off scads of hand-knit and crocheted garments. Edna had some highly decorated outfits in Buttons and Bows, and Haylee's shop was full of clothes in different sizes, examples of what people could make using fabrics they bought and skills they learned in The Stash.

Garments embellished with thread art hung in my store, but at the moment, I wanted to lend that embarrassed, purple-mouthed twelve-year-old a pair of jeans, which she'd have to roll up, and a T-shirt. Sneakers, too, though mine would be too big for her.

I squeezed Naomi's arm in appreciation and turned my attention to the dog pen in front of us. The Chandler Champion glowed like a gem, spotlighted underneath the bulb that Russ had installed. Felicity droned on about how Mr. Chandler had hoped to make the award presentation himself. She turned to Darlene. "While you're at home washing, starching, and ironing these lovely outfits before I take them on tour" — Darlene gasped and leaned against the railing — "Ms. Um and I will pack this sewing machine for you."

Great. Another chance to work with Felicity. I'd have preferred to give each of Darlene's children an outfit to keep.

In a voice made breathy by nervousness, or perhaps by the thought of repeating all the washing, starching, and ironing that must have kept her up most of the night, Darlene asked Felicity to bring the sewing machine with her when she went to the Coddlefield farm to give the free lesson.

Felicity paled. "I'm expecting important phone calls. *Mr. Chandler* may call. Besides, I have a bad back. I can't lift it." With great

41

drama, she announced that she would now present the certificate. Darlene made a frowny signal toward the row of chairs holding her older children. Prolonging a handshake, Felicity gave Darlene a sheet of paper.

A printed paper certificate, not an embroidered silk one. It figured.

The oldest Coddlefield daughter, the one with the practiced sneer, shot up, took a flash picture, and plunked back into her chair. The back of her neck reddened. The brother who resembled Russ snickered. The young photographer slapped him while the twelve-year-old in frilly pink hissed at them to stop because everyone was staring. The poor kids. Being a teenager, or almost one, wasn't easy.

Darlene thanked Felicity, then turned to the audience and flashed us a triumphant smile.

Beside me, Naomi and Haylee stiffened. That smile had been more than triumphant. It had been gloating to the point of maliciousness, as if Darlene had been saying to someone in the audience, "Winning is the best revenge."

4

I wasn't the only one who thought that. Darlene's mean glance had been directed at one of us standing near the door. "Well," Edna huffed, her sweet brown eyes wide in amazement. During the summer, she'd gone overboard on coloring her hair. What was left of it resembled short stalks of platinum straw.

"Who was that nasty look aimed at?" I murmured.

Haylee's brow furrowed. "One of us, I thought. But I can't imagine why. I've never seen her before."

Russ's brother, the one who looked about fourteen, slouched out the door and down the street in the direction Russ had taken, toward the beach. Frowning, Darlene gathered the shirts the two boys had discarded and told Felicity she'd return later to collect her machine and lead Felicity to the Coddlefield farm. Darlene and the rest of

43

her children clambered into the fire chief's red SUV. I only knew the fire chief by his nickname, Plug. Was he also Darlene's husband?

Naomi patted my arm. With worried looks at each other and at me, Haylee and her mothers returned to their shops.

The look of hateful triumph that Darlene had thrown toward us was still creeping me out. I felt like I needed to protect someone. Haylee? Her three mothers? Susannah? Mona had gone back to her home décor store, but she'd been at the back of the audience with us, as had other locals, plus Threadville tourists who hadn't found seats in the crowded shop.

Susannah stayed in my shop a little longer to help serve refreshments. Most of the Threadville tourists hung around, too, vying for a closer look at the Chandler Champion. I poured lemonade. Susannah, bearing plates of cookies, mingled among our guests.

Felicity could have seized the opportunity to demonstrate the Champion's many fine features. Instead, she stationed herself at the refreshment table and gobbled cookies straight out of their tins. What a strange way to promote her company's star product.

Finally, she noticed the excitement swirling around the Chandler Champion.

Crumbs cascading down her front, she fumed, "Willow, you need to shoo those people away from Darlene's machine so you can pack it up."

After following her commands earlier, I had to be stubborn. "Packing it will only take a few minutes."

"Darlene could be back anytime. It's not like Elderberry Bay is very big."

Darlene had said she lived on a farm. Wouldn't that be out in the country? "I don't think Darlene lives in the village."

"That's her address," Felicity snapped.

I turned away without arguing. Felicity had a point. The Coddlefields had arrived in a vehicle belonging to the fire department and could conceivably come roaring back into Threadville at great speed.

Susannah and I tidied away the refreshments, then Susannah left for The Stash.

I needed to pack Darlene's Champion, but women were still experimenting with it. I guided them to the other Chandlers in my shop, a Champion and two machines that didn't have as many features, but were attractive anyway.

Felicity became frantic, pointing up at the ceiling. "I need to take that banner back with me."

I retrieved my ladder. Georgina, an avid

and very artistic customer who lived in Elderberry Bay, gravitated to my side. She made all of her own clothes, and I'd never seen her wear more than one color at a time. Today, her pants and long tunic were a yellowy gold she'd obviously chosen for this sunny August day. Always helpful, she had given Susannah loads of emotional support during Susannah's marriage breakup. Georgina steadied the ladder while I took the banner down. Maybe Felicity would learn something about cooperation from the helpful Threadville women. Georgina and I rolled the banner. Felicity reminded us to smooth out the wrinkles.

I tried to unplug Darlene's new sewing machine. The plug was stuck. Jiggling it, I pulled harder.

All of the lights in the back of the store went out.

Felicity shrieked, "What have you done to the Champion? Your electricity's faulty."

How could that be? Clay had renovated the building, turning a century-old bungalow into a gorgeous shop over an equally appealing apartment. He had installed two electrical panels, one up here, and another downstairs for my apartment. I charged into the storeroom and opened the shop's panel. None of the circuit breakers appeared to need resetting. I pushed the one for the rear of the store to its off position, then back on. The lights stayed off.

Perplexed, I returned to the dog pen. With Felicity shadowing me and muttering threats about what Mr. Chandler might do to me if I destroyed his pride and joy, I yanked the plug out of the outlet, lugged Darlene's super-heavy Champion to an outlet near the front of the store, and plugged it in. The machine powered on perfectly. Threadville tourists cheered.

I brought the carton, accessories, manual, and packing material out of the storeroom.

Georgina offered to check the electrical panel. Another customer, a wiry woman with a dandelion fluff of platinum hair, accompanied Georgina into the storeroom.

Felicity fussed about my ill treatment of the Chandler Champion.

Georgina emerged from the storeroom and interrupted Felicity's tirades. "We couldn't see anything wrong with the circuit breakers."

"Thanks, Georgina," I said, "and . . ." I looked at the woman with the fluff of blond hair.

"Mimi Anderson," Georgina supplied. "She's renting a cottage near the beach. She loves to sew."

Mimi cleared her throat. "I'm renting a cottage in Threadville *because* I love to sew. And all three of my children went off to college orientation this week, leaving me with an empty nest. So I flew the coop. And then I got here and discovered that I could have come on the tour bus from Erie every day! But I am enjoying my month in a beach house."

The village's fame was spreading. I welcomed her to Threadville. "And after the month's up and you go back home, you can come on the tour bus whenever you like."

"I love Threadville. And your shop." She appeared to be enraptured by the lined-up machines, natural fabrics, and embroidery threads and supplies. To sewing and machine embroidery fans, In Stitches was a treasure trove.

Georgina asked, "Mind if we borrow one of the lamps near your sewing machine display?"

"Sure, that's fine." With difficulty and no help from the hovering Felicity, I maneuvered the Champion into its carton. What had Chandler used to weight the bottom of the machine, lead? If they'd added a couple more pounds, I'd have needed a forklift to move it.

Georgina and Mimi took a lamp to the

back of the shop and plugged it into the outlet where the Champion had been. Nothing happened. Georgina wiggled the plug. All of the lights in the rear of the store flickered and flashed. She pulled the plug out. The lights stayed on.

Astonished, I gaped at the two women.

Georgina explained, "I had a similar problem with an outlet at home. It turned out to have a loose connection. You'd better have your electrician check it."

I managed not to sigh. I would have to ask Clay for help. Again.

Georgina and Mimi put the lamp back. I continued packing the Chandler Champion and its accessories. Glowering like I couldn't possibly do it right, Felicity supervised.

My students folded most of the chairs away in the storeroom, leaving only enough for the class to gather around the machine where I usually did my demonstrations.

"You didn't give the speech I told you to give," Felicity complained. "If you couldn't remember it, you could have read it."

I counted to ten, probably too fast. "I'd already memorized one. It said the same thing."

"I don't see how you can hope to be a reasonable seamstress if you don't follow instructions explicitly."

Wishing that Susannah or Haylee could have heard Felicity's latest criticism, I pointedly did not look at the bulky seams and bunchy corners of the jacket she'd interfaced with corrugated cardboard. I taped the Chandler Champion's carton shut. Darlene wasn't back, I was antsy to begin the morning's already shortened class, and my dogs were whining to return to the shop. I let them out of the apartment and into their pen. Wagging their tails, they accepted greetings from my students. Felicity sniffed like someone scheduling an allergic attack.

I showed my students how one type of digitizing software created shapes that could be arranged to form embroidery designs. Felicity smirked, obviously ready to pounce if I said anything wrong.

Darlene returned, with Russ behind her. Finally, Felicity would leave. She magnanimously led Darlene to the sealed carton. I offered a wheeled dolly, but Russ refused.

"He can carry it," his mother said, marching out my front door. "He's only sixteen, but he's strong."

She was right.

His face taut and his muscles straining, Russ hauled the box outside and set it carefully into the back of an old pickup truck, maroon with a wide white band around it.

But that was the end of the boy's caution. As soon as his mother climbed into his passenger seat, he peeled away, tires spewing billows of smoke.

In a small black sedan, Felicity pulled out behind Russ's truck. I hoped she'd be able to keep up. If she got lost, she might return to In Stitches.

"Good riddance," said Rosemary, one of my hardest-working students and also the Threadville tour bus driver. "That Felicity was unpleasant."

Mimi, who had stayed to attend my embroidery class, hid a cough in her elbow. "I hope she does corners better in her car than she does in her sewing."

Everyone laughed, and I felt fine again. Life in Threadville could go back to normal.

My students paid rapt attention to the rest of my lesson, then trooped out for lunch at Pier 42.

Shortly after one, Susannah came back so I could have my break, and the dogs and I went downstairs to our apartment. The building was on a steep slope, one story in the front, but two full stories in the back, so most of the apartment was above grade, and very bright and airy. Side yards let light into the bedroom windows.

I hadn't entertained any guests in my

51

second bedroom yet. Maybe, eventually, my parents would make the trek from South Carolina, but my mother, who had given up her practice as a physician to go into politics when I was a teenager, was now a member of the South Carolina House of Representatives, and claimed she needed to stay near her constituents. My father was content with his puttering and inventions. They hadn't visited me when I'd lived in New York City, and the northwestern corner of Pennsylvania was even farther away.

My guest room was ready, though, just in case, and decorated in embroidered white-on-white linens. Each bedroom had its own bathroom and walk-in closet sandwiched between the bedrooms. A small laundry room faced the other half of the apartment — one large room with kitchen, dining, and living areas. Floor-to-ceiling windows overlooked the sloping backyard and the quaint little house known as Blueberry Cottage. Someday, I would renovate the cottage. I hoped that Clay would keep his promise to be my contractor.

I ate my lunch outside while the dogs played in carefree joy. Tall cedars hedged both sides of the yard. The entire area, including Blueberry Cottage, was fenced for the safety of the dogs. At the top of the hill, a gate led to my front yard. At the bottom of the hill, another gate led to a hiking trail on the banks of the Elderberry River. Leaves on trees prevented a good view of the river and the state forest on the far bank.

The dogs and I returned to In Stitches. The afternoon class went well, too, and then I was free to spend the evening romping with the dogs and fiddling with embroidery.

Like many of my students, I wanted to enter a contest for machine embroidery, the International Machine Embroidery Competition, known fondly as IMEC, which we all pronounced "I make." Recently, I'd won an honorable mention with my machine-made version of a centuries-old method of embroidery known as stumpwork.

Next, I wanted to emulate another type of antique embroidery, candlewicking, named for the candlewick cord substituted for embroidery floss to add texture. Often, the wicks were knotted, creating largish bumps. Several sewing machine manufacturers provided "candlewicking" stitches, but they were almost flat. I wanted to create something thicker and more authentic. The contest deadline was looming.

And before that, I wanted to display my students' and my entries at the Harvest Festival. The Threadville proprietors were going to rent a corner of the handcrafts tent. We were to set up our booth in only eight days. I needed to get to work.

First, though, I had to buy some supplies.

5

I phoned Edna and asked if I could join her in Buttons and Bows for a little after-hours shopping. Of course she said yes. I grabbed my wallet, locked In Stitches, and ran across the street.

Edna opened her door, setting off a jaunty tune that she claimed was "Buttons and Bows," but supposedly was actually "Buttons and *Beaux,*" an old Vaudeville favorite that should have been called "*Un*buttons and Beaux," and couldn't be sung in polite company. Clay had renovated her store, too. Pot lights in the ceiling lit shelves of buttons to the left and a wall of trims to the right. They dazzled.

Edna opened her hand to show me gleaming amethyst beads. "I'm trying to get these to stick in my hair and hide the shaggy ends, but they're not staying."

"Edna," I said gently, "that pixie look suits you."

"Pixie haircuts went out when I was a baby. Besides, this is more like a haystack. You tall women keep finding a way to point out my lack of stature." It wasn't a real complaint. She loved to tease and be teased.

"Maybe you should let your hair rejuvenate before you mess around with it, or it will keep breaking."

"I suppose you're right." She brightened. "Maybe I'll try glitter glue instead. You know what this village needs?"

"I can think of a few things . . ." Another policeman or two. A paid fire department.

"A hairdresser."

"Maybe one will come. But she probably won't tell you to stick your hair together with glue."

"You're no fun."

I told her I needed trims and cords that could be made to look like candle wicks, and she helped me find several widths of rayon- and polyester-covered cord, some puffy cording for insertion into wide piping, and a couple of different types of braid. She led me into her back room with its gadgets and packaged trims and offered me white rickrack. I bought that in several widths, too.

"You have to see the projects Naomi and Opal have begun," she said. First, she took me to Naomi's shop, Batty About Quilts. Naomi's front room was an art gallery. White walls showed off work that she and her students had done. This week, in addition to two king-sized quilts, she displayed potholders, placemats, tea cozies, and other kitchen linens, all of them quilted in fall colors, and all of them fabulous.

Naomi was leaning over a large cutting mat in her back room. She wore a pretty sun dress she had pieced together using quilting methods and summery pastel cotton batiks, with no backing or actual quilting. All around her were bolts of quilting fabric in zillions of shades and prints, but the strips she was cutting out with her sharp roller were all in pure, bright colors, as if conjured from a rainbow. She was using more colors than the red, orange, yellow, green, blue, and purple that often represented a rainbow, though. She'd stacked up bolts of several of the hues between each of those colors, so that the transition from red to purple was gradual.

"Show Willow what you're doing," Edna demanded.

With one of her generous smiles, Naomi handed me a sheet of graph paper. She'd used colored pencils matching the fabrics to map out a quilt on the paper. The rectangles of color would be placed in rainbow order, but they'd be different heights, stepped up and down to create a sort of wavy rainbow effect.

"Bargello," I said. "I've seen it in needlepoint, but not in quilts."

Edna looked at me expectantly. "What's another name for this type of stitching in needlepoint?"

I clutched my purchases tightly as if she might take them away if I didn't answer correctly. Finally, I had to admit that I didn't know.

"Flame stitch!" she crowed. She pointed at the bag in my hands. "You're working on candlewicking, and Naomi's working on a flame stitch quilt."

"And Opal is —" Naomi began.

Edna interrupted her. "We're going there, next. Bring your grid and come along, Naomi."

All three of us charged out of Batty About Quilts, past Buttons and Bows, and into Tell a Yarn. The walls of Opal's shop were lined with diamond-shaped niches that Clay had constructed from light pine, the perfect background for Opal's yarns.

Lucy, Opal's gray tabby with the Siamese voice, met us near the door. The cat's welcoming speech outdid Opal's. I picked

Lucy up and cuddled her. The yowling stopped and the purring began.

Edna's eyes gleamed with excitement. "Opal, show Willow the afghan you're making!"

Opal brought out the beginnings of a perfectly crocheted afghan in the same shades and grid that Naomi was using.

Edna nearly danced in her excitement. "Opal's afghan and Naomi's quilt will match! They're going to hang them in our booth at the Harvest Festival and raffle them for charity. Aren't they wonderful?"

I agreed that they were. "And you're doing something similar in ribbons, buttons, and beads, Edna?"

"Just ribbons and beads. A sofa pillow."

With a devilish grin, Opal teased her. "No one would rest on it. All those beads — ouch."

Edna looked shocked. "Of course not. It will be a work of art." She winked. "But isn't it an odd coincidence that Willow is working on candlewicking? Flames, candles . . ."

"What's Haylee making?" I asked. "A banner for our Harvest Festival booth that says 'Fanning the Flames of Needlecraft'?"

Lucy's fur was softer against my cheek than Edna's proposed pillow would be.

Opal reached out and scratched Lucy's chin. "There's an idea."

Wrinkles appeared between Naomi's eyebrows. "Flames and candles. Why does the fire siren go off every night?"

"We've had such a dry summer," Edna said. "It's no wonder."

"But it's very worrisome," Naomi persisted. "Think of those wildfires in Texas last summer."

We tried to convince ourselves that it couldn't happen in this part of Pennsylvania.

Guessing that Opal, Edna, and Naomi would soon be having supper, I gave Lucy back to Opal, who cuddled and murmured to her. I ran back to my apartment.

The dogs and I ate outside, then I played with embroidery software — there were always new things to learn — until nearly bedtime. I took the pups outside for their last exercise, which involved a lot of charging up and down the hill, ears and tails up, mouths open in tongue-lolling grins. Sally acted like she might grab my hand, but, in her gentle way, she didn't let her teeth touch me. When I figured the dogs were tired enough to sleep, we all went inside to bed.

My bedroom was tucked mostly into the

hillside. I seldom heard street noises at night.

But I couldn't sleep through the sounds of tires squealing and people yelling.

Sally-Forth and Tally-Ho set up a frenzy of barking.

With that frightened, muzzy, heart-racing alert of being awakened from a deep sleep, I sat up, pushed my embroidered summer-weight duvet off, fiddled my feet into my slippers, threw on a robe, and rushed to the steps leading up to the shop, the only part of my building that looked out on Lake Street. The dogs went with me. None of us made it upstairs quickly or efficiently.

Without turning on lights, I ran to the big shop windows. No one was out there.

Tires screeched again. A pickup truck roared up Lake Street from the beach. I couldn't be certain of the truck's main color because the streetlights weren't bright enough, but the wide band around it was white, and I was fairly certain the rest of it was maroon. Russ Coddlefield's truck? Barking, Sally and Tally stood up with their front paws on the glass door.

I caught only a glance of the driver. Russ, I thought. He let out a yell. Passengers shouted with laughter. The truck bounced away.

With any luck, those kids were on their way home and wouldn't harm themselves or others. Listening for noises, I took the dogs back downstairs.

I'd barely drifted off to sleep when another noise awakened me, a siren, the one attached to Elderberry Bay's fire station. Its wail was distinct and very loud, and should call volunteer firefighters no matter how deeply they were sleeping. If I'd been one of the volunteers like Mona had suggested, I could have jumped out of bed again. Glad that I didn't have to, I snuggled deeper underneath my duvet and slept until warm sunshine awakened me again.

I dressed in a tank top and miniskirt, both featuring tiny, tasteful sprigs of embroidered leaves. While the dogs played outside, I enjoyed an alfresco breakfast under a cloudless blue sky. When I'd lived in New York City, a lack of rain seemed inconsequential, but in this small village surrounded by farmland, I'd learned to thirst for rain.

We went upstairs to open In Stitches. More classes today, more fun with embroidery . . .

More fun with Felicity Ranquels, as it turned out. The phone rang.

Felicity growled, "You killed that woman."

6

I killed a woman? I stared at my phone with the same amazement I'd have turned on Felicity if she'd been with me, instead of on a long-distance call. I finally managed to ask, "What woman?"

"Darlene Coddlefield. The winner of the Chandler Challenge. They're saying her Chandler Champion killed her." Between words, Felicity exhaled frantic bursts of air. "A Chandler machine would never do that."

"How," I asked sensibly, "could a sewing machine *kill* someone?"

"You should know. You're the one who played around with it all week, chalking up hours. You ruined the machine, and you killed Darlene. I will not let anyone shred Chandler's reputation." She banged the phone down.

Dr. Wrinklesides, the village's popular elder statesman of a doctor, sometimes assisted the coroner's office. He should know if anyone had died of mysterious causes during the night.

His receptionist answered. I asked her to have him phone me.

"What's this about?"

I didn't want to explain the whole thing. "Darlene Coddlefield."

She put me on hold, and to my surprise, Dr. Wrinklesides came on the line and boomed, "Willow!" He was a tad hard of hearing. "What seems to be the problem?"

Hoping no one out on the street could hear me, I hollered, "I've just been accused of tampering with a sewing machine and causing a death. Did you . . . Were you . . . I mean, you often help the coroner's office investigate local deaths, right?"

"Listen, Willow, don't you worry about a thing. It looked like an accident. The police are still investigating. Meanwhile, don't you be afraid of your sewing machines. I heard that she won that sewing machine from you."

So it was true. Darlene Coddlefield had died, and the sewing machine I'd presented to her yesterday was involved. The breakfast I'd eaten began to feel as heavy as that Chandler Champion.

"Your machines won't hurt you, Willow," Dr. Wrinklesides shouted. "You'll be safe."

Safe from my machines, yes, but safe from being accused of murder by people like Felicity Ranquels? My breakfast weighed even more. Hoping that my anxiety wouldn't force me to his office for treatment, I thanked Dr. Wrinklesides and let him get back to his patients.

A thread holding one of the banners celebrating Darlene's win had snapped, leaving the banner dangling by one corner in my front window. How could the poor woman have died, and what, if anything, had her sewing machine done to harm her? I put the banners away. Would I ever need them again, and if I did, would they bring back this sense of uncomprehending loss and grief?

I didn't want to be alone. Although it was almost time to open In Stitches, I ran across the street to The Stash.

Haylee's door was open. "Haylee!" I called.

She peered around a display of fabrics. "Hey, Willow, look at this shipment of tartans that just arrived from Scotland." She must have noticed the goose bumps on my bare arms, like zillions of tiny needles trying to work themselves out through my skin. "What's wrong?" she asked.

"Darlene Coddlefield is dead, and the

sewing machine she collected from In Stitches yesterday is being blamed." I couldn't help sounding hysterical.

"That's impossible." She ran a hand through her long blond hair. "I mean not impossible that someone would *blame* a machine, only that a sewing machine could kill someone."

I thought about Darlene's son's joyriding through the streets last night. "Unless someone clobbered her with it. It weighed a ton, but her oldest son, Russ, managed to lift it."

Haylee closed her eyes as if looking into the future. She opened her eyes wide. The future must have been shocking. "My mothers were already worried because some of the Coddlefield children seemed miserable yesterday. If those children have lost *their* mother, *my* mothers will end up raising the little terrors in their apartments."

"They wouldn't go that far," I protested.

"You know them."

"Yes, but Darlene's children still have a father."

"They're going to want to do *some*thing, probably inappropriate." As if to distract us both from the death of a woman we'd met the day before, Haylee stroked the bolt of wool beside her. "Check out the gorgeous winter fabrics I'm unpacking."

The tartans were tightly woven, the plaids precise, in colors that would make anyone claim Scottish heritage. I touched luminous corduroys, too. Unlike cords from only a few years ago, these were soft and would drape beautifully. Many of them had a little stretch woven in, making them easy to wear. And fleece seemed to improve every autumn. I couldn't stick around to admire it all, though. The Threadville tour bus rumbled into the village.

I rushed across the street to In Stitches. I was incredibly lucky to own this dream of a shop and live where every needlework supply I might need was either right here or across the street. I reminded myself that Darlene Coddlefield had been lucky, too, but her good fortune had ended suddenly and tragically.

Saddened, I ran inside to the dog pen. Sally and Tally stretched, wagged their tails, and looked up at me adoringly. I knelt and buried my face in their fur.

Most mornings, Threadville tourists dashed inside, chattered about their homework, and thrust it at me. This morning, they dragged in behind Rosemary, two by two, almost as if they were mimicking yesterday's procession of Coddlefield offspring. I'd never seen Rosemary so solemn. Her mouth was one thin line, and her smile wrinkles were shadows. She held her bag close to her side and walked hesitantly. "Willow," she said, "we heard something terrible about that woman who won the sewing machine. It was on the radio. They said her new machine killed her."

I reassured them with what Dr. Wrinklesides had told me. "She probably died from an accident."

Georgina and Mimi had followed the tourists in. Georgina shook her head as if to dispel grim horror. "She died doing what she loved."

Mimi cried, "But she had such young children!"

Rosemary suggested that some of the big siblings could help their father look after the little ones. Imagining Darlene's rambunctious teenagers taking charge of the little ones, I shuddered.

Had Russ gone on his wild ride after his mother died? Grief could do strange things. He was, his mother had said, sixteen. Hardly more than a child.

To show that the Chandler Champion for sale in my store was not a killer, I connected it to my computer and used it for the morning lesson. The Champion worked well

68

enough, though I preferred models from my trusted manufacturers, maybe because those sewing machines were solid and reliable. Besides, as far as I knew, none of them had ever been accused of killing anyone.

I'd begun using computers, software, and embroidery machines to create thread art when I lived and worked in New York City. People had not only bought the designs I'd offered on my website, they had commissioned me to create new ones. I had been quite happy to switch from working in New York to living in Threadville and owning a machine embroidery boutique, where my enthusiastic students inspired and encouraged me. In addition, customers from all over the world e-mailed me photos of their pets, homes, and in one case, a broken baseball bat that had been instrumental in winning a Little League semifinal, all to be immortalized in thread. Customers who owned their own embroidery machines downloaded my designs and stitched them in colors they chose. Others bought finished products. The baseball bat motif had embellished a wall hanging.

I demonstrated how different brands of software turned photographs into embroidery designs. We all loved the way the software showed how the designs should look when stitched. Rosemary and Georgina, who owned their own digitizing software, attempted it first and were pleased with the computerized depictions of their designs.

Mimi, still battling a dry cough, tried next, and had great luck, but the next woman's groans of dismay gave me the teaching opportunity I'd wanted. "Experiment with the number of colors," I suggested. "Sometimes more colors will help, but often, simpler is better. Try fewer colors."

"It means fewer thread changes," Rosemary added, "unless you own a commercial embroidery machine." None of us did. Our embroidery machines were accessories that went with amazing sewing machines like the Chandler Champion. We could sew with our machines or connect our embroidery attachments and stitch professional-looking designs. Our machines were versatile, and scads of fun.

Everyone gathered around and offered suggestions until the woman was satisfied with her design. After that, most of the students figured it out on their own. We saved the designs to stitch another day.

The afternoon class, composed of women who had spent the morning shopping or attending lessons at other Threadville shops, was similar, except that no one got it right the first time. They were good-natured about it, though. It helped that a few hours had passed since we'd found out about Darlene. Seeing a woman alive, right here, the day before, and hearing that she was dead less than twenty-four hours later had shocked all of us.

I looked forward to a quiet dinner with my dogs and an evening of working on my candlewicking project. However, the minute the Threadville tour bus disappeared up Lake Street, my phone rang. "Willow, it's Edna." I knew from the lowered tones of her usually chirpy little voice that she wanted something.

That could mean trouble . . .

7

My hand tightened on the phone. What did Edna want, and how could I keep her out of mischief?

"I made an extra lasagna," Edna said.

My breathing steadied. How much difficulty could Edna get into with a lasagna?

Plenty, apparently. She went on, "I'm going to take it to the Coddlefield children, since they just lost their mother and may not have anything to eat . . ." She stopped as if waiting for me to finish for her.

I managed, "Mmm-hmm."

"And I was wondering if you'd come along with me to drop it off, since you know the family better than I do."

Well, hardly, but Edna's proposal was a nice one, and the thought of eight motherless children dragged at my heart. Besides, Felicity had accused me of rigging a sewing machine to kill Darlene. Maybe we could get a look at that sewing machine.

I took a deep breath. "I'll bring cookies." I baked cookies every Monday, the one day of the week that none of the Threadville stores were open. It was only Thursday, and I still had lots of cookies in my freezer.

"Your molasses cookies, Willow? Yum, those are soooo good. Shall we drive out to the Coddlefields' after your dogs have their outing? You probably haven't had time to give them one since your customers left."

"Okay." Although Opal and I were the only Threadville proprietors to own — or be owned by — pets, all of Haylee's mothers were thoughtful about what others had to do for their pets. And for their kids.

I let Sally and Tally play outside, then settled them in our apartment and grabbed a tin of cookies — molasses, as Edna had suggested. What could I possibly say to children whose mother had just died? I patted the dogs good-bye, then dawdled across the street to Buttons and Bows.

Edna's store, as always, cheered me. I walked past the gleaming array of buttons, ribbons, and trims. Edna's back room overflowed with more notions and gadgets than anyone could ever use. Well, maybe. We could *try.* I called toward an open door at the back of the shop, "Edna?"

She pattered down the stairs from her

apartment and popped through the door-way. I smelled tomatoes, garlic, oregano, and cheese.

Mouth watering, I pointed at the elaborate quilted casserole carrier. "Did Naomi quilt that for you?"

"I made it." She lifted her chin. A dimple showed in one cheek.

"I should have known." Pastel satin bows decorated each quilt square. If the ribbons hadn't tipped me off, the sequins and rhinestones should have. "It matches your blouse." Edna had created a top by sewing satin ribbons together by their edges, then adding sequins and rhinestones.

Edna cocked her head. "Too much? I thought it would show that the casserole carrier wasn't part of the gift."

"Maybe you should leave the carrier in the car when we get there? But people usually return casserole dishes, don't they? So maybe they'll return the carrier, too."

She raised her shoulders in a just-between-us-girls gesture. "They won't return these. I used two disposable aluminum pans, one inside the other, so I wouldn't have another disaster."

"Disaster?"

"Well, it didn't actually *wreck* my dinner party. The restaurant we went to was fine.

74

These pans simply do *not* hold up to heavy lasagna with loads of cheese and tomato sauce. I had quite a mess to clean up after I got home." She pointed with her chin. "My car's out back."

Her sedan was small, but big enough for her and her best friends. They'd scrimped and saved while living together during their school years, sometimes doing without a car, sometimes sharing an old beater. Now, in addition to owning shops and apartments, they each had a vehicle, and none of them believed that Haylee needed one. Haylee, however, loved her new cherry red pickup truck. And her independence. Her shop was the largest in Threadville.

If birds could drive, they might drive like Edna did. Wobbling to whichever side of the lane caught her attention, she headed south, out of Elderberry Bay. "It's not far," she said.

Nodding her head toward fields on my side of the car, she drifted dangerously close to them. "Those soybeans are gone. Shriveled up. Hardly any rain all summer." Pointing at fields to our left, she nearly crossed the center line. Fortunately, a cornfield on the right came into view. "Those cornstalks shouldn't be so brown in the end of August." A mailbox threatened my window. I flinched.

We couldn't tell what crop had been beyond the line of trees on the left. That field was black, flattened, and acrid with the smell of burned vegetation. Edna crossed the center line. "Maybe that's where the fire was last night. Did you hear the siren?" Turning her head toward me, she nearly plowed into the ditch on my side.

I gripped the edge of my seat. "I heard it."

She shook her head, which had nearly catastrophic results for the car. And for us. "Everything's so dry, all it takes is one cigarette carelessly tossed out a car window. Ah, here we are." Beside a mailbox that said Coddlefield, a gravel driveway wound between trees to a clearing. A lawn dotted with colorful children's toys surrounded a three-story Victorian farmhouse.

The fire chief's SUV was parked in the driveway beside the maroon and white pickup truck I'd seen Russ driving. My earlier guess was confirmed. Plug must be Darlene's husband. I hadn't known our fire chief's last name. People just called him Plug. He said it was because he'd wanted to be a fireman all his life. His buddies joked that they'd given him the nickname in grade school because he was plug ugly, and built

76

like a fireplug, besides. Both were believable.

We got out of the car. After driving around with the windows open, Edna's bleached and broken-off hair stood up all over her head. That and the glitter glue she'd added gave her a rakish look of good cheer. She lifted the aromatic lasagna from her casserole carrier. Although she held the foil pan-within-a-pan with care, her lips thinned as if she were being burned.

I thrust my tin toward her. "Let's balance your lasagna on this. Maybe it will help thaw the cookies."

Together, we stacked the lasagna in its nestled pans on the tin. To keep our unwieldy donations steady, we walked sideways, facing each other with our hands under the tin and the hot edges of the disposable pans grazing our bare arms.

The front door banged open. "What are you doing here?"

I looked up into the red and angry eyes of Russ Coddlefield. "Russ, I'm sorry . . ."

He bounded down the porch steps and raced past us. "Leave me alone. Leave all of us alone."

He slammed himself into his truck, backed up, nearly hit Edna's car, then tore off, spewing gravel.

I don't think I moved during that entire time, except for a shudder.

"We should leave," I tried. "Russ doesn't want us here."

"He's too young and grief-stricken to know what he wants." Her deep brown eyes soft with sympathy, Edna watched the truck bounce down the driveway and disappear. "That poor boy." Haylee could be right. Her mothers might be planning to take on Russ, and perhaps all the other Coddlefield children, too, as their next do-good project. Uh-oh.

Edna backed up the porch steps. Not wanting to drop the food, I had to follow her.

She pressed the doorbell with her elbow. Deep inside the farmhouse, Westminster chimes sounded.

No one came. The front door stood open, with only a screen keeping us from walking right in. We couldn't see or hear anyone inside the house. Maybe we could retreat.

No such luck. Edna rang the doorbell again. More Westminster chimes.

"Coming," a sweet feminine voice called. Smiling, a girl who looked barely older than Russ strode down the hall and opened the screen door. Her blue-gray eyes were clear, her face rosy with heat. The only sign that things weren't quite right was her uncombed blond hair. Lank on this muggy day, it would be flyaway in the middle of winter. My hair gave me similar problems.

"We're so sorry about your mother," Edna began.

The girl shook her head. "She's not, she *wasn't* my mother. I'm the au pair."

"Who is it, Tiffany?" A man called. "Can't you get rid of them?" He sounded downright surly.

Tiffany blushed more, and frown wrinkles deepened between her pale eyebrows. I adjusted my estimate of her age upward into the mid-twenties. She jerked her head toward the back of the house. "Sorry about that. Plug . . . Mr. Coddlefield is not himself. Understandably."

"We thought you might be able to use a casserole," Edna said.

Awkwardly, we edged it, balanced on the tin, toward her.

"And some cookies," I added. "They're underneath the casserole."

"Lasagna," Edna explained. "It's hot."

Tiffany started to reach for it, then whisked her hands behind her back. "That's nice. Leave it out there, and I'll go get oven mitts."

"Tiffie?" Plug was apparently working up a rage.

"In a minute!" She fluted it over her shoulder in a placating, yet strangely flirtatious way.

Somewhere behind her, a child started crying, inconsolably, wails that could go on and on, for a lifetime, probably.

Tiffany's chin quivered. She lowered her head.

We were only making things worse. Maybe we should have obeyed Russ and left the family alone.

Edna squared her shoulders, a sure sign that she was fortifying herself with her particular brand of stubborn determination. "Is there anything we can do?"

She was only milliseconds away from barging inside, hunting down that child, and picking it up. Was it the littlest girl from yesterday, or one of the two small boys, proud of their cowboy shirts? Either way, I was about to cry, too. I tugged at the cookie tin and casserole combo we were carrying together. Edna, however, didn't budge, so I couldn't flee.

"You've done enough," Tiffany said. "Absolutely. Thank you. I totally appreciate it." She jerked her head back as if indicating something in the depths of the house. "He will, too, really. They all will. It's just that . . ." She heaved a ragged sigh. "It's hard, you know, so hard. But if you leave it on the table over there" — she pointed at a table next to an old-fashioned porch swing hanging from the white-painted wooden ceiling — "I'll take care of it."

Edna shuffled toward the open screen door. "We can bring them in."

I had to shuffle with her.

Tiffany shook her head quickly. "I've got to go." She released the screen door. It slammed in our faces, leaving us with no polite option besides following Tiffany's instructions and leaving the food on the porch.

I pulled toward the table beside the swing, but Edna planted her feet on the old floorboards. "A raccoon or cat could get it. Maybe a skunk." She shuddered.

If Haylee had known about our mission, she would have come along to keep Edna out of mischief, but Haylee wasn't here, so it was up to me to bring Edna safely home.

"The others will be expecting you," I tried. Most nights, Opal, Edna, and Naomi gathered together for dinner, taking turns in each others' apartments.

"Not until seven."

"I'd like to finish my IMEC project before

81

the Harvest Festival . . ." And I hadn't figured out yet exactly what I was going to do.

"It will only take a second to find the kitchen," she assured me. "Hang on while I open the door."

"Edna," I whispered, drawing her name out like a kid might on a playground.

Keeping one hand underneath the tin of cookies, she used the other to ease the screen door open. The foil pan slanted. I caught it with my forearm. The crimped aluminum edge didn't burn, but who needed a hot pan touching skin on a sweltering evening?

"Careful," Edna warned. She backed against the door to keep it open and slid her hand underneath the tin again.

I could have yelled or resisted or grabbed the pan and tin, heat and all, but the child's howling pulled at my heart, too. Steadying my side of the casserole and cookie tin, I sidled with Edna into a bright entryway.

All around us were touches of handmade needlework, projects that Darlene must have lovingly crafted. It appeared that she had also collected antique and vintage samplers and linens, and had decorated her walls with them. She'd been fond of the sorts of things I loved. I wished I'd gotten to know her. In her house, surrounded by her belongings, I understood some of the loss her family must be feeling.

We needed to set the casserole and tin of cookies down, then leave.

Edna must have seen my speculative glance at the spindle-legged antique table beside a stairway leading upward. "The hot pan might mar the wood," she warned.

Darlene's hand-crocheted doily would have prevented that, but Edna would only come up with another excuse, like the pan might scorch the doily. Her motherly instinct was much stronger than mine, which, I feared, was rapidly becoming stronger. More children joined the chorus of screams.

With marching-band precision, we sidestepped together down the hall past open doors leading to two former parlors, one now a playroom overflowing with books and toys, and the other a living room with soft couches and chairs and a wide-screened TV over a fireplace. From the outside, the house had appeared to ramble, with new sections built every few years. I hoped I wouldn't have to hobble, facing Edna and jointly lugging food, through all those additions to find a place to set the tin and the casserole. Edna was going to insist on locating those grief-stricken children before she would leave. And I still harbored hopes of getting a good look at Darlene's sewing machine. How could it have killed her?

We started past a doorway to the dining room. A peculiar, tuneless humming came from inside the room. I turned my head to see who was making the noise.

In the far corner, beside a glass-doored china cabinet, Tiffany was in the arms of a much older man — Plug Coddlefield, widowed for approximately twenty-four hours.

8

Tiffany was leaning into Plug, kissing him on the lips, moaning with apparent pleasure. The tips of his fingers were in the back pockets of her jeans.

Deeper in the house, his motherless children bawled and blubbered.

Edna had her back to the tableau in the dining room, but my dropped jaw must have alerted her. Plus my feet seemed to have forgotten how to move.

Edna glanced into the room and did a classic double take. Her mouth opened to match mine. I managed to be silent.

Edna, however, let out a gasp.

Tiffany and Plug jumped away from each other as if a firecracker had exploded at their feet.

Edna whipped around to face me and gave her head a jerk toward the back of the house. She tugged on the tin and casserole.

My feet had to come unglued, or hot,

gooey lasagna would cascade all over them.

We were still in view through the doorway. "What's going on?" Plug demanded.

Edna made a very plausible jump and turned toward him. "Oh!" Maybe she wasn't acting. Maybe she really was startled. Or embarrassed, like I was. "I didn't see you there!" Right. But to give her credit, she sounded sincere.

Then again, maybe *credit* wasn't quite the right word, and it was certainly not one that Haylee would have used under the circumstances. I was doing a less-than-stellar job of looking after Haylee's most headstrong mother.

"This casserole is hot," Edna chirped, "so we're just taking it to the kitchen." She was really good at playing innocent.

Tiffany knew that she'd told us to leave the food outside, but she didn't give us away. Her face a brilliant red, she brushed past us. "Stay right there. I'll get potholders."

Arms folded across his chest, Plug stared at us from the back corner of the dining room. He didn't seem conscious of his children's very vocal sorrow.

Edna mouthed, "Come on," and slid her feet quickly in the direction Tiffany had gone.

I managed to go with her.

Ahead of us, Tiffany cooed, but the children cried louder. Before we could catch up and see for ourselves that they were okay, Tiffany rushed toward us with a pair of oven mitts.

"Careful," Edna warned. "These pans are hot, and not very sturdy."

Biting her lip, frowning, Tiffany removed the casserole from our grasp, revealing the tin of cookies. "There's more?" She flicked a glance toward the dining room. "Bring it in, I suppose. I gotta see about those kids." She toted the casserole toward the back of the house.

Edna marched along after her. Her worry about the children, whose father hadn't emerged from the dining room, was contagious. With my tin of cookies, I brought up the rear.

I barely took in the exquisitely crafted kitchen curtains and tablecloth with their gorgeous machine embroidery, and I didn't have time to dwell on the loss of the talented Darlene Coddlefield. Her three youngest children appeared to be inconsolable. The little girl and smallest boy sat at the table. Still sobbing, the five-year-old boy had abandoned his seat to stand between his siblings and pat their shoulders. They hadn't finished their cookies and milk.

Edna swooped to them. "Oh, you poor dears!" She grabbed napkins from a yellow holder shaped like a duck and patted the kids' faces. The crying subsided into sniffles and hiccups.

Tiffany plucked the smaller boy out of his seat and stood him on the floor. "Now, now," she said. "I told you I was coming, and here I am. Come on, be a man." She lifted the little girl out of her booster seat and set her on the floor beside her brothers.

Misty-eyed, Edna looked ready to hug anyone who needed it, but Tiffany grasped Edna's wrist and pulled her toward a screen door. "Thank you two for your help, but it would be better for all of us if you left us to mourn our own way." She opened the door to a covered wooden porch sheltering bikes and trikes in every possible size. "Follow the walkway to the right, and you'll come out near your car."

Edna was not going silently. Still in Tiffany's grip, she smiled down at the children shadowing Tiffany. "You were all very grown up yesterday, showing off your beautiful dress and your handsome shirts."

The girl wrapped her arms around Tiffany's leg and buried her face in the side of Tiffany's skin-tight jeans. "I want my dwess back! That nasty lady took it!" The child must have meant Felicity, who had said she was taking the prize-winning outfits on tour after Darlene washed and ironed them again.

Tiffany let go of Edna's arm and picked up the little girl. "I'll make you more dresses," she murmured.

Edna swallowed and opened her mouth. Before she could think of another reason to stay, like promising new dwesses embellished with buttons and bows, I pulled her out the door.

"Ouch," she murmured when we were beside the house on a walkway between zinnias and petunias, their reds, oranges, and purples neon-bright under the August evening sun. "That Tiffany has *claws,* not fingers." Angry marks blazed on Edna's wrist.

"Maybe I did it," I said. "I'm sorry. But let's get out of here before she chases after us. Or Plug does."

Edna came, dusting her arm as if she could brush off the claw marks or prevent them from turning black and blue. "You didn't do it, Willow. She did. She was vicious." Rounding the corner, she stopped. Edna was seldom speechless. Her mouth opened, but only a little hiss came out.

Hands on hips, feet spread, Plug stood with his back to us, right in front of her car, like he was about to open the hood.

Or had just closed it.

Edna was, for once, as still as a statue. Head up, I kept walking.

I heard Edna run toward me. I put my hand behind my back and spread my fingers out like an inverted gesture to halt.

She grasped my hand. Her breathing became a thin, high whistle.

Squeezing her suddenly icy hand, I spoke to Plug. "We're sorry about your wife." *And for barging into your house and seeing you kissing the hired help.*

He whipped around to scowl at me.

Steadfastly, I went on, "We knew how . . . guessed how . . ." All I could think of was this middle-aged man groping a woman who looked less than ten years older than his firstborn son.

Edna came to my rescue. "We figured your household would be in an uproar and no one would be able to cook. At least not . . . Well, we figured you'd be too distracted . . ." Now it was her turn to break off, undoubtedly remembering what, rather *who,* his distraction had been.

I took up the narration of excuses, not that we should have needed to excuse ourselves.

Our intentions had been good. We hadn't meant to snoop. Not *that* much, anyway. I blundered on. "We own some of the sewing stores in town, and met your children yesterday. They're wonderful."

Behind my back, Edna crossed my fingers for me. If I hadn't been trying to appear sympathetic, I might have laughed. Plug's older children had been far from wonderful. The little ones, however, seemed sweet. That five-year-old trying to comfort the toddlers had been especially heart-wrenching.

Plug moved to the red SUV in his driveway and leaned against it. He could have been bracing himself, but one of his hands managed to rest beneath the words *Fire Chief.* "I know who you are." His voice was genial, and he managed a lip quirk that might have been a smile, but his eyes were sly. And chilling.

I tried to look like someone who would never dream of scolding a recently widowed man for grabbing a kiss.

Pulling her car keys from a pocket, Edna stalked around me, past him, and to her driver's door. I strode to the passenger side and shut myself in.

"Take it easy driving," I whispered. "We don't know what he could have done to your car."

She turned the car around. "Nothing *feels* wrong with it." She drove down his driveway and out onto the road. "But . . ."

How long had Plug been near her car? Five minutes, tops. What could he have done, slashed a few tires? I peered into the mirror on my side. "Both tires on this side look okay."

"I'll pull off so we can check everything, but I don't want to stop near Plug's house. He might follow us." Now she had no trouble staying in her lane. "That man." The anger in her voice was enough to set fire to the field beside us. "With a girl that young."

"She could be twenty-five," I pointed out. "And she didn't appear to mind." I fiddled with the window button. "But, how terrible! His wife died last night."

Edna threw me a knowing look, her eyebrows arched high. "Kind of makes you wonder, doesn't it?"

"Dr. Wrinklesides said Darlene's death appeared to have been an accident."

"Maybe she saw her husband with Tiffany and had a heart attack." She tightened her hands on the steering wheel and gasped.

A vehicle was racing toward us.

In our lane.

9

Edna and I were about to be crunched into a metal sandwich.

Her knuckles white, she swerved her car onto the shoulder.

Russ Coddlefield's pickup zipped past, only inches from us.

Russ veered back into his own lane and sped down the highway. His laughter blew back on the hot, dry wind.

His mother had died the night before, and now he was amusing himself by forcing us off the road. Last night, he had driven recklessly around Elderberry Bay. What other dangerous pranks could Russ have pulled?

Muttering choice phrases that I'd never heard from her before, Edna turned off the engine. "Let's see if that boy's father damaged my car." She got out. I did, too.

We met at the rear bumper. "Nothing looks out of place." The usual cheer was gone from her voice. We each continued our own circle, then Edna reached into the driver's side and popped the hood. I lifted it. Together we peered underneath it. I understood sewing machines, but the workings of a car baffled me.

Edna seemed equally perplexed. "I'm not sure I'd know if anything has changed, but it looks okay to me."

She slammed the hood. If Plug had closed it, he had done it more quietly. Then again, we hadn't heard much besides the children's anguish.

We climbed back into the car. Edna was probably as eager as I was to return to the safety of Threadville.

Ahead, Lake Erie and the sky above it were hazy blue, a perfect contrast with the golden fields, the dark green evergreens, and the yellowing leaves of late summer.

Edna asked, "Was Plug threatening us another way, besides acting like he might harm my car? If one of our shops caught fire, would the fire department take its time arriving?"

"Our shops won't catch fire. Our apartments, either. We're careful. But let's make certain that our smoke and carbon monoxide detectors have fresh batteries. We'll have to tell the others to check their batteries, too — Haylee, Opal, Naomi, and Susannah.

And Mona, also, in case he lumps her in with the rest of us."

Mona. I hadn't taken the application she'd given me seriously, but maybe, for the sake of all of us with textile shops, Haylee and I should become volunteer firefighters. I wasn't going to tell Edna, Opal, or Naomi, though. They'd try to dissuade us.

"Plug may think that Mona's shop resembles ours," Edna said. "I don't. The rest of us give classes twice a day, four days a week. She doesn't offer even one class a week. Nearly everything in Country Chic is already finished and decorated."

"She sells home décor fabrics," I said.

"She hasn't a clue how to make draperies or upholstery. And do people hop off the Threadville tour bus and head to Country Chic? No. They divide themselves among In Stitches, The Stash, Tell a Yarn, Buttons and Bows, and Batty About Quilts." She tapped out a rhythm on her steering wheel. "Still, you may have a point. Our philandering fire chief could simply ignore calls from any of us, including Mona."

And what about Sam the Ironmonger's hardware store, between my shop and Mona's? I would hate to see Sam come to harm. Maybe he wouldn't. He had owned that hardware store since long before Plug was born, and everybody loved him. "We're probably being silly," I said.

"Silly can save lives."

"Sounds like a motto. I'll embroider it in a candlewicking stitch for the Harvest Festival." That broke the tension. We laughed, and she pulled into Threadville.

While the dogs wrestled in my backyard, I dug out the fire department's flyer. Mona had thoughtfully given me two applications. I shut Sally and Tally into my apartment and ran across the street to Haylee's.

She was sewing in the huge classroom on one side of her shop. I handed her an application. "Here's a new way for us to have fun."

She glanced at it and understood immediately. "What a great way to learn more about Plug Coddlefield and the death of his wife!"

I told her about Plug's possible threat to all of us. She said she'd remind everyone to make sure they had fresh batteries in their smoke and carbon monoxide detectors. I described Plug and his young nanny.

Haylee wrinkled her nose. "Ewwww. Two people who might have wanted to murder Plug's wife."

"Dr. Wrinklesides said Darlene's death was an accident."

"What if it wasn't? What if a murderer is running around loose? We should catch him, or them, before they kill someone else. Like us."

It was as good a justification for joining the fire department as any, which was to say it wasn't very good.

The applications didn't require much information besides our names, addresses, and phone numbers. Small print warned of exams that would test our firefighting knowledge and physical fitness. "Push-ups," Haylee guessed.

"Ugh. I'd better practice, though Mona is convinced that you and I must be strong from heaving bolts of fabric around."

Haylee flexed her muscles. She had substantial biceps.

I copied her. To my surprise, I had substantial biceps, too. "Wow." I squeezed my right arm with my left hand. "Running a store really is better exercise than an office job was."

"It's better than everything about that office job." She never tired of reminding me that I'd been reluctant to give up the security of a salary and bonuses for the uncertainties of retail sales. Security hadn't been quite the right word for our jobs at Quinlan Financial Management, though.

Together, we had investigated our boss and had been instrumental in putting him behind bars for stealing money from his — and our — clients.

Haylee had started the first of the Threadville shops shortly after Jasper Quinlan was arrested, and her mothers had joined her and opened their own shops. I'd stubbornly continued working at Jasper's old firm, under new management, until after his trial and incarceration. Then, thanks to those bonuses and to my growing online embroidery business, I'd moved to Threadville and opened In Stitches. New customers discovered us every day. Best of all, Haylee and I both loved living and working here.

We finished filling out our applications. I went home, leashed the dogs, then walked them down Lake Street and around the corner to the fire station. It was closed up tight. I dropped our applications in the mail slot.

After a quick supper on the patio while the dogs played around me, I examined the cords and trims I'd purchased from Edna.

One way to create more authentic candlewicking stitches would be to zigzag over the trims with matching thread so the stitches would hardly be discernible, but I really wanted to find a way of forcing my embroidery machine to do the work, or most of it.

Unable to come up with a method I liked, I went to bed.

The inevitable siren from the fire hall woke me up in the wee hours. What was burning this time, another dry field?

Fortunately, I didn't belong to the fire department yet and didn't have to race off into the darkness, even if it might mean riding on a fire truck. I allowed myself to lie comfortably, imagining different ways of representing candlewicking. Drifting off to sleep, I pictured using the puffiest of the cording I'd bought from Edna, and satin stitching over it every quarter inch to squish it down. The unsquished parts would be similar to the lumps in knotted candle wicks.

In the morning, freshly confident with my nighttime idea, which, though labor-intensive, might work, I felt ready to tackle almost anything, including becoming a volunteer firefighter. I flopped down on the floor and tried push-ups. I could have done more if I hadn't been laughing at Sally's determination to lick my face. I collapsed in a heap with my two wriggling dogs, then took them upstairs and began sweeping the shop floor.

Susannah helped in my shop on Fridays,

and came in wearing an orange linen shirt. I complimented her on it. Before she'd assembled it, I'd helped her embroider the fabric in an allover design of small, pretty flowers.

"I love working with linen." Shadows under her eyes showed that she'd probably spent another night grieving over the death of her marriage.

I knew something that might cheer her up a little. "We've received another shipment of linen, heavier for fall and winter."

She ran to the storeroom and dragged out a bulky package of multihued bolts, all shrink-wrapped together.

A lanky man ambled in and introduced himself as Isaac Sonnenberg, deputy fire chief. "Congratulations, Willow," he said, his long face a picture of earnest solemnity. "We've accepted your application to join the fire department." His straight brown hair seemed to grow every which way. That, combined with the questioning pale blue eyes and the long arms and legs made him charmingly boyish, though I suspected he was in his mid-thirties at least.

"Haylee, too?" I asked.

He nodded. "Both of you."

Susannah straightened from unwrapping the bolts of linen. Her lips and forehead puckered. I wished Isaac had brought the news when I was alone. Susannah might tell Haylee's three moms that Haylee and I were joining the fire department. They wouldn't approve.

Isaac tilted his head. My reaction was apparently too slow.

"That's great," I lied. "We have physical fitness and written exams to pass first, don't we, before it's official?"

He flapped his big, bony hands toward the floor as if my concerns could be swept away with my broom. "You'll do fine." He pulled a folded sheaf of papers from the back pocket of his jeans. "Here's the manual. It covers all the questions that will be on the test, like 'What is a fire truck?' " His gave his head a shake to show he was joking. "Training's Tuesday evening. I'm sorry it's such short notice, but if you can't make it, maybe another time?"

He was offering me a way out. I told myself to snatch it.

"I can make it." I was never very good at heeding my own warnings.

Isaac was as tall as I was, maybe taller. I could look directly into his eyes. He gave me the manual and told me to go to the old ball field near the state forest at six on Tuesday evening. "Will you need a ride?"

he asked.

"I have a car." I raised my chin. "It will get me to fires, too." Or Haylee and I could ride together in her appropriately red pickup truck.

He blushed. "That wasn't part of the test. I figured you wouldn't have applied if you had to run to fires." He scuffed his shoes against the floor like I'd forced him to stay after school. "Or walk," he added. He reached into his chest pocket and pulled out a business card. "Here, in case you need to get in touch with me without phoning 911."

He was barely off my porch when Susannah asked, "What are you doing applying to the volunteer fire department? That could be dangerous."

Susannah used to be full of fun. Her caution since her divorce saddened me.

"I'll stay out of danger." Slipping the card like a bookmark into the manual, I dislodged a bright pink flyer for a flea market during the Harvest Festival.

Laughing, I showed Susannah the ad. "Now I understand why they're recruiting new members. They're raising funds for new fire-fighting equipment and need volunteers to run the flea market."

"Fine," Susannah retorted. "Help with

that. But don't go fighting fires. It's not safe."

"I've heard that by the time the fire trucks arrive in rural areas, there's hardly anything to do besides watch."

She stepped back. "There've been lots of fires lately. People are saying they may have been set."

"We've had barely a drop of rain all summer. The fields are tinder dry. Anything sets them off, including the lightning that zaps out of thunderclouds without bringing us any water." The story was the same all over the Midwest. "I want to help. Don't worry. I'll be careful."

Susannah looked down at her hands, which were clutching each other in seeming desperation. "It's just that —" She raised her head and met my gaze. I was certain I saw the remnants of fear in her eyes. "Our house burned down when I was eight. I don't think people realize how powerful and terrifying fires are. They scare me just thinking about them."

The day's students came pounding into the shop, eager to start our lesson. Susannah, who was a very accomplished seamstress, was still learning about embroidery. She helped wherever needed, but like the other students, she took her turn on one of our wondrous machines and stitched the design she'd created during the week.

She must have been silently fretting about fires all afternoon. Before she left for the evening, she pointed at the outlet in the dog's pen, the one that had malfunctioned on Wednesday. "Did you get that outlet fixed?"

I hid a sigh. "Not yet. I guess I should."

"Definitely. Call Clay Fraser. It could start a fire." Then as if a fire were beginning that very moment, she ran outside.

Great, call Clay and act needy again. I liked him, but I'd had a chance with him and lost it.

Besides, I never used that outlet, and everything had worked fine since that one glitch. *Witch-glitch,* I thought, picturing Felicity. She'd probably put a curse on the outlet.

The phone rang. Dr. Wrinklesides wanted me to visit him in his office.

That was odd. Usually, patients phoned doctors and asked to be seen, not the other way around. And Dr. Wrinklesides wasn't my official doctor. His fresh-out-of-med-school colleague was, and I hadn't seen her recently or gone for tests that would require a doctor to ask me to visit him. Especially not after work on a Friday.

10

At seven, Opal would hold her weekly storytelling night in Tell a Yarn, but that was more than an hour from now. I told Dr. Wrinklesides I'd be there in a few minutes.

His office was three blocks from In Stitches, so I leashed the dogs and walked down Lake Street. We passed the other Threadville shops, Sam's hardware store with its old wrought-iron sign, *The Ironmonger,* and Mona's Country Chic. At The Sunroom, the new, upscale restaurant, diners sat on a glassed-in balcony where they could watch both the Elderberry River and the beach. Across the intersection, cottagers and year-round residents thronged the outdoor patio of Pier 42, the village's popular restaurant and pub.

Folks fresh from a day at the beach lined up for treats at the hamburger truck and ice cream stand on Cayuga Avenue. The bakery, bank, library, and post office were closed for the evening. No vehicles were outside the fire station, and its big doors were rolled all the way down. Through trees beyond the fire station, I caught a glimpse of the sun, a red ball close to the northwest horizon where sky met lake.

The dogs and I turned south onto Jefferson Avenue, lined with Victorian and Arts and Crafts homes. Both architectural styles featured capacious front porches, and people were lounging on porch swings, sipping from tall glasses, watching children play, reading, working on needlecrafts, calling to each other, and waving at me and the dogs.

Outside Dr. Wrinklesides's office, I fastened the leashes to a sturdy railing. I'd be able to see Sally and Tally through the waiting-room window.

Dr. Wrinklesides was alone, sitting at the receptionist's desk. He stood and belted out an Italian aria. I assumed the words were welcoming, because he held out his arms like a father joyful at the return home of a long-lost daughter. I couldn't help smiling.

He broke off and bowed. He loved opera. And he had a great voice.

He had an operatic build, too, though he was shorter than I was. He held out a hand for me to shake. "Glad you could make it,

Willow. I wanted your advice."

Outside, Tally whined.

Dr. Wrinklesides gazed toward the door. "What's that?"

"My dogs."

"Bring 'em in. The janitors will be along later. They'll disinfect and sterilize everything."

He was probably exaggerating, but I brought the dogs inside and held on to their leashes. They didn't seem inclined to make pests of themselves, though. They leaned against my knees. Maybe they thought that Dr. Wrinklesides, in a white coat with a stethoscope draped around his neck, was a vet.

"Come see this, and tell me what you think." Dr. Wrinklesides led the dogs and me into an examination room, snapped off the light, and showed me an X-ray in a light box. He'd placed a piece of paper with a hole cut out of the middle over the X-ray. He pointed to a thin white object. "That white thing is metal," he told me. "What's it look like to you?"

He handed me a magnifying glass, but I didn't need it. "It's the pointy end of a sewing machine needle. There's its eye."

"Why does it bulge like that on both sides of the eye? Did someone pound it flat?"

"It was made that way on purpose. It's called a wing needle. It's like a double-edged sword, with blades on both sides that cut into the fabric to make holes beside the stitching."

He opened his eyes wide as if I'd amazed him, but I could see a teasing glimmer in their pale blue depths. "Holes! What would my patients think if I sewed them up and left big holes beside my stitches?"

I laughed. "Not much, probably." His patients adored him. "Unless they wanted a new sort of embellishment. In sewing, we make those holes for decoration. People who embroider by hand widen gaps in the weave. They pull out threads running one way . . ."

"The warp," he said.

"And they wind embroidery floss around the threads running the other way . . ."

"The WOOF," he shouted to the dogs. They wagged their tails and licked his fingers.

I heaved a hugely fake sigh. "I'll *dog*gedly continue my explanation. The process of eliminating warp threads and tying woof threads together makes neat rows of little holes. It's called hemstitching. You often see it on linens."

He gazed toward the wall, but that was

obviously not what he was seeing. "Yes," he murmured. "I remember. My grandmother's linen napkins."

"Some of us like the effect, but are too lazy to do all that stitching and thread-pulling by hand. So we fit our machines with wing needles and they make tiny holes, fooling the casual observer into believing we painstakingly tied embroidery floss around threads in the fabric."

Dr. Wrinklesides tapped the X-ray viewer. "I got this X-ray from the coroner's office. How did this needle get into Darlene Coddlefield's arm?"

I took an involuntary step back, bumped into Tally, then bent to pat him. His warm fur comforted me. I managed, "Is that what killed her?"

"No, not at all. Her sewing machine fell on her."

"*Fell* on her?"

"It appeared that she crawled underneath her sewing table, and it collapsed under the weight of the machine."

"What was she doing underneath her sewing table?"

"Attempting to unplug the sewing machine, apparently. It was too heavy for the table it was on. It really was a killer sewing machine." After years of helping county coroners, he deserved his dark sense of humor. "But it doesn't explain how the needle got into her arm."

"That's only half of the needle. It must have broken," I told him. "The other part, the shaft that gets clamped into the machine, is missing. Maybe she sewed over a pin, and the needle snapped. The sharp fragment pierced her."

"Where's the other fragment?"

"She probably left it in the machine. She could have been distracted by the piece in her arm."

Dr. Wrinklesides pulled the corners of his mouth down in a skeptical frown and glowered at the X-ray. "Instead of going for help, she crawled underneath her sewing table?"

"That does seem odd," I agreed. "Maybe she heard some of that thunder that seems to come every night. She may have wanted to protect her machine from electrical surges, and would have called for help with the needle if she'd lived. She took better care of her machine than she did of herself." I probably would have done the same thing.

"She couldn't have known that her sewing machine was about to land on her neck."

On her *neck*?

Dr. Wrinklesides gave me time to get over my shock. He knelt and crooned to my

dogs. Apparently, they were opera aficionados, too. Or maybe they liked the way he
ruffled their ears.

"I have wing needles for sale in my shop,"
I said when he paused to take a breath and
I'd regained mine. "If you ever want to see
one."

Using the base of the examination table as
a lever, he rose. "I could come now, if it's a
good time for you."

"Sure."

He shed his white coat and stethoscope,
double-checked doors and windows to
make certain they were locked, then reached
for a leash. I handed him Sally's, since Tally
was more likely to lunge. If one of us was
going to be knocked off our feet and end up
with a broken leg, it made sense for it *not*
to be the doctor.

Strolling along in his lemon yellow polo
shirt and khaki chinos, he could have been
on his way to play golf. "A beautiful
evening," he said, "beautiful dogs, and . . ."
He burst into song.

He was older than my father, and charming, and I enjoyed being with him. I had a
feeling that if I understood Italian or knew
more about opera, I'd be blushing. He sang
all down Jefferson, and all along Cayuga.
Still no signs of life at the fire department,

but his singing did turn heads at the hamburger truck and the ice cream stand. On the patio at Pier 42, people waved frosty mugs and hollered, "Hi, Doc!" A man and a woman in The Sunroom gazed at each other over candles on their table. It would take more than an operatic aria to divert their attention.

I was serenaded all the way up Lake Street. Windows opened in Naomi's, Edna's, and Opal's apartments. Dr. Wrinklesides stopped singing after we entered my shop.

I led him to the display of needles, opened a packet of wing needles, and showed him one.

He peered at it. "Yep, sure looks like the X-ray."

"You can keep that."

"Sure. I'll put it in my shirt pocket and it'll puncture me and all the hot air will come out. Pfffft. Then how will I tell my patients what to do?"

He was an odd sort of doctor. I could be silly, too. "How do your patients speak after you give them a shot?"

"That's different."

I had a feeling I was being set up, but I fell for it, anyway. "How?"

"Hot air rises. I insert their inoculations

farther down." He held an imaginary syringe in his fist, ready to plunge it into an imaginary patient. "Don't you know the old saying? 'Bend over and touch your toes. I'll show you where the needle goes.' "

I covered my mouth to prevent a snort of laughter. Dr. Wrinklesides no longer shocked me, but he could still surprise me. "I'll give you a *picture* of a wing needle. It won't puncture you and let out all that hot air." I tore a photo from a catalogue and gave it to him.

He left with the picture, not a needle, in his shirt pocket.

The dogs and I had a quick dinner, then I kissed them good-bye and ran across the street for storytelling, undoubtedly mixed with a bit of gossip, at Tell a Yarn.

11

Meowing, Opal's cat, Lucy, greeted me at the door of Tell a Yarn. The gray tabby usually had so much to say that I often wondered if she thought it was *her* job to tell the stories.

Loving the feel of her warm, silky fur, I gathered her into my arms. She revved up her purring.

The cat and I discussed the tempting yarns, hand-dyed in wintry colors, on Opal's diamond-shaped shelves. Opal must have heard us. She trotted out of the room she used both as a dining room and as a comfy place to gather with her students while she taught knitting and crocheting. As usual, Opal wore a handmade outfit. She'd used white cotton and a shell stitch to crochet tonight's knee-length skirt and matching top. Both featured scallops around their hems. The outfit was very pretty, and I told her so. She gave me a big hug. "Finish your scarf, and I'll teach you how to start something else."

Certain that I didn't need another reason to accumulate more fibers to make into things, I'd been reluctant to try knitting, but Opal had overruled my objections, in the nicest sort of very insistent, Opal-ish way. She had given me needles and a skein of alpaca yarn, and then had patiently taught me the basics. Every Friday I brought the same scarf to storytelling and increased it by a few more stitches. If I ever finished it, maybe I'd let her show me how to crochet.

Opal led me to her dining room, where open windows showed off her wildly colorful flower garden. Some of her sunflowers were taller than I was. The crowd around the table jostled their chairs to make room for me at the table.

Edna, Haylee, and Naomi were knitting. Susannah was crocheting lace from thin white cotton. Georgina was sewing buttons on a jacket she'd just made. New to storytelling night, Mimi worked some sort of magic with a ball of very fine cotton and something that resembled a hair barrette. Every few seconds, she cleared her throat.

The barrette-like shuttle and the intricate lace she was creating clued me in. "Is that tatting?" I asked her.

"Yes." She looked justifiably proud. "My grandmother taught me, but I only learned this one pattern before she died, so all of my lace looks alike."

Opal studied the lace Mimi had already made. "Don't apologize. It's beautiful. I wish I could do that. Maybe you could teach a class in my shop sometime?"

Mimi bit her lip. "I'm not sure I'm doing it right. Books might tell more . . ." She trailed off, looking sad.

Naomi filled the silence. "Crafts learned from grandmothers are the very best kind." Then she glanced at Haylee, who had never met her grandparents, and blushed furiously.

Haylee dropped her knitting and gave Naomi a squeeze. "Or from mothers."

Naomi smiled but looked appalled at what she undoubtedly perceived as her own thoughtlessness.

Mona shook her head, her way of agreeing. She never worked on a hobby during storytelling. Haylee and I weren't sure which would win, Mona's resolve not to do anything or Opal's commitment to teach everyone to love yarn along with the stories we heard every week.

Jane had come all the way from Erie to be

the evening's storyteller. An expert on southern folk tales, she kept us all spellbound.

I knit another stitch — actually, I was purling, which was the only stitch I knew — then another and another. Karen, the librarian that Elderberry Bay shared with other villages, stuffed plush teddy bears. Beside her, our postmistress, Petal, knit another row of the periwinkle blanket she had been making for years. The infamous blanket was big enough to cover a king-sized bed, and weighed so much that Petal loaded it into a bright red wagon for the several-block walk to and from Opal's shop. She joked that she'd soon need a pickup truck. Opal, of course, encouraged her to bind off and start something new, but Petal had bought scads of that periwinkle yarn cheaply at a yard sale and wasn't about to stop until she used every inch of it, on one project.

Jane had barely finished her last tale when Mona brought up Darlene's death. "What a tragedy — all those motherless children." She shook her head.

"And all that charitable work," Susannah said.

The information plus the hint of sarcasm in her voice piqued my interest. "What did she do?"

Susannah inspected her crocheted lace. "She volunteered for a children's charity. Fund-raising, I think."

Mimi sighed. "The good die young."

Susannah opened her mouth as if to say something, then clammed up and ripped out the last few stitches she'd made, though they'd looked fine to me. Had she been about to deny that Darlene was good?

Opal touched Susannah's arm. "Why are you ripping out so much? Your stitches are perfect."

Susannah's only response was a small, "Oh." She jabbed her crochet hook into her work and made more loops, but even I could tell that these new ones were too big and sloppy.

"How old was Darlene?" I asked.

"The obituary said thirty-nine," Karen said.

That was a surprise. Darlene had appeared to be in her mid to late forties.

Mona must have thought the same thing. "All those children must have aged her. Did she have others besides the ones who came to the ceremony?"

None of us knew.

Susannah ripped out the loose loops.

Opal eyed Susannah's work, but all she said was, "The older children didn't seem happy." Her usually strident voice was soft with sympathy.

"Poor things," Naomi agreed. "It looked like they were having typical teenager problems with their mother. Now they'll always be bothered because they'll never be able to work those problems out with her."

Haylee cocked an eyebrow and asked Naomi in a teasing voice, "Typical teenager problems?"

Naomi patted Haylee's arm. "You never had them. You were perfect."

Opal put down her knitting. "Or we refused to see any problems."

Haylee giggled. "I *was* perfect."

Edna bobbed her head up and down. "Perfect for us, and you still are."

Naomi looked dreamily toward the vase of showy dahlias eclipsing Opal's fireplace. "What could we do to help Darlene's children cope?"

Haylee obviously didn't want them coming up with one of their impulsive schemes. She asked, "What did you all think of the sewing machine company rep, especially her sewing skills?"

Petal, Karen, and Jane hadn't seen Felicity, but by the time we described her personality and lack of sewing skills, they were laughing as hard as the rest of us.

It felt good to laugh at something, even if it was at Felicity's expense. With any luck, none of us would ever see the poor woman again, and I had no plans to order more Chandler sewing machines anytime soon. Everyone roared when I told them I'd seen proof that Felicity had interfaced her jacket with corrugated cardboard. Even Susannah smiled, and her stitches looked even again.

When I got home, my scarf had grown by almost another row.

Tally woke me up in the wee hours with a prolonged and mournful howl. I hopped out of bed to comfort him. He snored and twitched as if chasing something.

I went back to bed and the next thing I knew, it was light. None of the three of us had any more sad dreams, and if the seemingly nightly fire siren had sounded, we'd all slept through it.

The day was supposed to be hot. I put on a blue linen top and a matching miniskirt that I'd made and sprinkled with embroidered daisies. I pinned my long hair up off my neck.

Upstairs, feet thumped on the floorboards of the front porch.

Sally and Tally yelped out a warning and dashed up the stairs toward the shop. Heart beating, I charged after them. Still barking, the dogs pawed at the door at the top of the stairs. The minute I unlatched it, they dashed, yipping, into the shop. I ran after them. They put their front feet up on the glass door and barked with even more urgency.

A cardboard carton was on my porch, just beyond the door. I'd last seen it, or one like it, on Wednesday. Big green letters across it said, *Another Fine Chandler Champion.*

12

Who had left a Chandler Champion carton on my porch? I looked up and down Lake Street. No one was out there.

I maneuvered the two excited dogs into their pen in the back of the store, shut the gate, then ran back to the porch.

A note was taped to the box. *Please look after me.*

Suddenly, I couldn't breathe.

What could be inside? This had to be the carton from Darlene's prize sewing machine. Who in her household was fond of dangerous mischief?

Her oldest son, Russ.

If I opened the carton, would something explode in my face?

Please look after me.

Me.

Like something inside the carton was alive? If I *didn't* open it, would a tiny, helpless animal suffocate?

Pressing my hand against my mouth so hard that it hurt, I shifted from foot to foot. In Stitches was scheduled to open in a half hour. I had to find out what was in this carton.

I could call Elderberry Bay's one and only police officer. Chief Smallwood had taken over after our previous chief left. Unfortunately, Smallwood had two personalities. On the phone, she was sometimes friendly and helpful, but in person, she could be cold and accusing. Besides, her previous career as a state trooper might have trained her to blow up the parcel.

Please look after me.

What if the carton contained a sleeping puppy, kitten, or — I didn't want to think about another possibility — a baby? I didn't dare phone Chief Smallwood.

The village was silent except for waves breaking on the beach at the foot of Lake Street.

I clenched my fist and exhaled into it. Unless I failed the written or physical exam, I was about to become a firefighter. I had to think like one. I should call in the experts. Not Plug. I didn't trust him.

Isaac was deputy chief, and his card was in my apartment with the manual he'd given me.

I left the carton on the porch. As if locks could prevent damage from an explosion, I locked the front door.

I took the dogs downstairs, through my apartment, and outside. I shut them in Blueberry Cottage, far from any possible blast. Back in my apartment, I phoned Isaac and explained that I'd found a mysterious parcel on my front porch and was afraid it might explode.

"We'll be right there!" He banged the receiver down.

Did he have to sound so enthusiastic? *We?*

With visions of fire trucks barricading each end of the block, I ran upstairs and looked out my front windows.

Plug's SUV rocketed up the street and stopped, lights flashing, in front of my shop.

Plug and Isaac started up my walk. Maybe it was a good sign that Plug wasn't afraid of the carton. I went out to the porch. What should I say? *Hi, Chief, can you make certain that no one planted a bomb in the carton that once contained your late wife's sewing machine?* If he had brought me a bomb, he wasn't likely to tell me.

His face was as red as his truck. He stopped at the base of my steps. "What's wrong *now*?" As if I called him every day.

I gestured at the carton at my feet. "This parcel showed up outside my door and . . . aren't we supposed to report suspicious parcels?"

Isaac nodded encouragingly. His hair stuck out as if my call had gotten him out of bed. Then again, he'd looked like that the only other time I'd seen him, too.

Plug planted his fists at the sides of his more-than-ample waist. "Ma'am, you *sell* sewing machines. Are you planning to call the fire department each time one's delivered?" In a gesture reminiscent of his son, he flicked a lock of hair out of his eyes.

Up on my porch, I towered over both men. "Not if I expect a delivery. This was a surprise. And I don't know *what's* in this box. It could be a bomb."

My warning didn't faze Isaac. He jogged up the steps and stared at the box. "Chief!"

The excitement in his voice made me edge back toward my door.

"What?" Plug thundered, the threads of his temper clearly fraying.

Isaac pointed at the note taped to the box. "This looks like your printing."

Plug folded his arms across his chest and slid his feet farther apart. "All printing looks alike."

Isaac shook his head. "Yours is different.

See, here, the way . . ."

Swearing, Plug marched up the steps, ripped the tape off the carton, and pushed the flaps back.

The carton contained exactly what it said. A sewing machine.

Not just any sewing machine, either. A Chandler Champion.

Plug swatted at one of the flaps and turned on Isaac. "Listen, dolt. This woman" — he pointed at me — "gave this sewing machine to my wife. My late wife. This woman can have the machine back. She can give it to someone else. She can sell it. She can bury it in her backyard. I don't give a flamin' fireplug *what* she does with it. But *I* don't want it. I don't want to see it. I don't want it in my house. I don't want to talk about it. I don't want to be reminded of it. I don't want to know it exists. Ya got that, dolt?"

Isaac's mouth had gaped open the first time Plug called him a dolt, and I wasn't sure he comprehended anything else until Plug repeated it. Veins in Isaac's neck bulged like piping. If anything was flamin', it was his eyes. He stood tall, making it obvious how short Plug was.

Plug stormed down the steps. He called over his shoulder, "Carry the thing into her

126

store for her." He got into his SUV and roared away.

Muttering, "I guess I'm walking back," Isaac stooped to pick up the carton.

"I can take it inside," I said. "I have a dolly."

He hefted it easily to his shoulder, something I would never, no matter how many bolts of cloth I hauled around, be able to do. "I'm in no hurry to join him at the fire station." His voice came out flatter than usual, as if he were trying to tamp down his anger, or at least hide it. "Where do you want it?"

I unlocked the storage room. "Here, until I figure out what to do with it."

He set it on a shelf. "How much do these things cost?" He swallowed. His Adam's apple bobbed. He was beginning to look genial again.

I told him the list price for a fully loaded Chandler Champion.

"That much? You could buy a used pickup for that."

I led him out of the storeroom. "Pickup trucks don't sew."

He laughed. "True. But they haul more than a sewing machine could." He pivoted and waved his hand at my tidy row of sewing machines. "The rest of these machines, are they that expensive, too?"

"That's the most expensive one. They do more than just sew." *The one we just put away killed someone.* I hoped the thought didn't show on my face. "They embroider, too."

He whistled. "Whoa. You've got a fortune in here. You got it all properly insured?"

Where was he heading with that? "Of course." It was true.

He cocked his head and rubbed his chin. "So the chief could've sold that sewing machine and made a lot of money."

"Yes." I pictured the little girl's face, tear-streaked from crying about missing her mother. And wanting her dwess back. I could sell the machine and start a fund for Darlene's kids.

Isaac gazed into the distance beyond my shop's front porch. "I always thought Plug was missing a gallon from his water tank. Now I know it." With a grim smile, he shambled out of In Stitches.

I had a feeling that the conflict I'd witnessed between the two men wasn't their first and wouldn't be their last.

I ran down the hill to Blueberry Cottage and released Sally-Forth and Tally-Ho from their temporary prison. They were, as always, overjoyed to see me and happy to be taken upstairs to their pen where they could "help" in the shop. I wanted to go tell Haylee about the morning's surprising events, but the Threadville tour bus had already arrived, and women were marching up my sidewalk.

Georgina, dressed all in shell pink, wanted to embroider a design all over gleaming white satin for her daughter's wedding gown, but she sensibly didn't want to start on the satin without practicing first. I gave the class pointers on hooping and rehooping fabric to make a design continuous without gaps or overlaps. Larger hoops and the latest software made it easier, but not everyone owned such luxurious machines, so we practiced with more basic machines, too.

Rosemary had great luck making various sizes of dots appear random. Mimi's cough must have been bothering her more than she let on. She kept clearing her throat, and no matter how many times she placed her embroidery in the hoop, her stitching ended up off center.

Georgina liked Rosemary's dots, but her daughter had requested the sorts of curlicues that might appear in a medieval manuscript.

Rosemary picked up the candlewicking

I'd dreamed up while drifting off to sleep. I had fastened thick, soft piping cord to the fabric, then had satin stitched over short sections of it in white, leaving alternate sections puffy. "What about putting this all over a wedding gown?" she asked.

Lucky thing I wasn't taking a sip of iced tea. I'd have spewed it over everyone. "I don't think brides want to look poufy. Besides, once it's washed, it will probably resemble drenched wooly caterpillars."

Everybody laughed. "I don't know about you," Rosemary said, "but I don't wash my wedding gowns. I take them to the cleaners."

"Husbands, too?" Georgina teased.

Rosemary smiled happily. "Them, too." I'd met Rosemary's husband. They'd been married for almost twenty years and obviously adored each other. If another husband had predated him, she'd been a child bride.

It was Saturday, so Susannah wasn't in my shop, which was just as well, since I didn't think she was quite ready to joke about ex-husbands. She was helping Edna in Buttons and Bows all day, except for giving the rest of us our midday breaks. When it was my turn, I enjoyed a quick sandwich in the warm, dappled sunshine in my backyard while the dogs romped around me.

After lunch, we went up to the shop, and the dogs promptly curled up on each other's beds. Apparently, the monograms I'd embroidered for them had failed to impress them.

Susannah could use overtime pay to help her hang on to her house. Accompanying her to the front door, I told her that Darlene's machine had returned to In Stitches. "Can you help me check it for damage tonight after the Threadville shops close?" I asked.

"Sure. Just don't ask me to join the fire department."

I grinned. "Don't worry. Also, could you come in tomorrow afternoon?" Susannah usually had Sundays off. "A couple of customers have dropped off their machines for routine maintenance, and you know how we all get when our machines aren't available."

She managed a tiny smile. "We suddenly have fifteen projects we absolutely *have* to work on that very minute. I'll come tonight, and tomorrow afternoon, too."

"In time for my lunch break?"

"Okay." She ran down the porch steps and across the street to Buttons and Bows.

13

It occurred to me, belatedly, that I should ask Chief Smallwood before I messed around with Darlene Coddlefield's sewing machine. As soon as I finished teaching the afternoon class, I called her.

"What's up, Willow?" As always on the phone, she sounded pleasant and helpful.

"Plug Coddlefield left his wife's . . . his *late* wife's sewing machine on my front porch."

There was a long pause. "So?"

I twisted the fingers of my free hand behind my back. "Dr. Wrinklesides told me that it fell on her."

"Busybody."

I had to defend him. "He wanted to know what the thing in her arm was, and why it was shaped like that."

"What was it, and why did he ask *you*?"

"He guessed I might recognize it. I did. It was part of a sewing machine needle."

Naturally, Chief Smallwood had to go on the offensive. "You're not trying to find the reason for a mysterious death on your own, are you, or accusing anyone of murder? Because this appears to be an accident."

Appears to be. She had doubts. I was curious about what could have gone wrong with the machine, but I gave Smallwood another good reason for examining it. "I would like to make certain it's in perfect working order again before we . . . I thought the proceeds of selling it could go to the Coddlefield family."

"I notice you didn't say to Plug Coddlefield." She sounded amused.

"You're right." Feeling like a tattletale, I blurted out that I'd seen him and his nanny in a clinch the day after Darlene died.

"People can act out of character under grief and stress. It's natural to offer consolation when someone's bereaved."

"I suppose so," I agreed. "But this was above and beyond consolation."

"Things happen. Why are you asking *me* if you can fix the killer sewing machine?"

"It arrived so quickly I thought you might not have had time to investigate it." Not a very subtle hint.

"We had a forensics team on the scene right away. They were thorough. You're not trying to tell me I should take the sewing machine as evidence, are you? I understand those things are programmable. Can you program them to slide off tables?"

Very funny, Chief. "Not last I knew. It was much heavier than other machines, though, so if someone who was extra strong picked it up and dropped it on her, it could have done a lot of damage."

"Where'd you get the idea that someone could have dropped it on her?" Her voice held an odd note, like she wanted me to tell her more.

"That machine is heavy, but her son lifted it. So did Isaac, the deputy fire chief. I can carry it, but only if I groan and make horrible faces." I figured I should get a turn to ask questions. "Did Darlene Coddlefield have life insurance? Who was the beneficiary?"

"All that's being checked." Her nails tapped the receiver. "You know what? I think that having sewing experts look at that machine is a good idea." It was probably the first time she'd ever approved one of my suggestions. "And I should be there when you take it apart."

Great. In person, she was usually impossible. Not like Felicity, but close. I told her we were planning to check out the machine after In Stitches closed at five. She promised to join us.

Threadville tourists, notorious for stretching their time in our stores, were still shopping when Susannah returned to In Stitches. She lent a hand with ringing up last-minute sales.

Chief Smallwood arrived but stayed near the front door, feet apart, hands on hips, staring at the cheerful crowd of Threadville tourists. Looking tough was difficult for her, despite the bulletproof vest she always wore over her navy blue uniform. Her blond ponytail and flawless skin made her appear girlish, but she had to be at least in her late twenties. No matter how much she scowled, she looked feminine and pretty.

Susannah sidled up to me. "Shall we postpone our investigations until after she" — Susannah pursed her lips to one side in an apparent attempt to keep Chief Smallwood from knowing who we were discussing — "after she goes? Or shall we look at that machine tomorrow, instead?"

"She wants to help us."

Susannah gave me an astounded look. Apparently, she harbored doubts about the ex-state trooper's knowledge of sewing machines. Avoiding looking at me or at Chief Smallwood, Susannah went back to waiting on customers.

Chief Smallwood's presence didn't seem to encourage our customers to go home. Maybe they hoped she'd let them embroider her bulletproof vest with sparkling metallic threads. If so, they were disappointed. Rosemary rounded them all up for the trip back to Erie on the bus.

Detective Gartener came in. He had been Chief Smallwood's partner when they were both Pennsylvania state troopers. He was still a state trooper, and had been promoted to detective. I suspected that losing him as a partner had made Smallwood apply to become Elderberry Bay's police chief.

Detective Gartener was tall, dark, handsome, and confident.

He was also, I had to admit to myself, slightly scary, with a way about him that made me fear he could wheedle a confession from the completely innocent. The last time Smallwood and Gartener had been in my shop together, though, they'd been very helpful. I couldn't help darting a glance at his left ring finger. Still no wedding band. Smallwood didn't wear one, either.

He shook my hand. "Willow! Nice to see you again." His deep, resonating voice always made me wonder why he'd chosen the dangers of police work when he could have gone into broadcasting, or maybe singing or acting. His usually wary brown eyes warmed infinitesimally. His hand was warm, too, and big and strong.

"Welcome, Toby," Chief Smallwood said sweetly.

I should have known she would invite him. I had nothing against him. He always seemed fair, and I was glad she had included him. I should have thought of it. Then again, why would I have needed to? Chief Smallwood *always* called for backup from the state police, including, no doubt, if someone ran a stop sign. She probably hoped, each time, that Gartener would be the one to respond to the call. Apparently, the night Darlene's body had been found, Smallwood had lucked out, and Gartener had been the detective on duty, and now he was the lead investigator into the somewhat unusual cause of Darlene's death.

Her head bent and her lustrous mane of dark curls hiding her face, Susannah backed away from the thread display, making it obvious that she was afraid of the officers. Why would she be?

I strode to her. "Let's get the Champion out."

In the storeroom, I whispered to her, "What's wrong, Susannah?"

Pressing her hands against her cheeks, she glanced toward the open storeroom door. "Nothing. Why?"

"You seem upset."

"I do?" She arranged her face into an obviously fake nonchalance. Panic lurked in her eyes.

"But —"

"They're waiting for us!" She appeared about to pick up that heavy carton by herself.

Resigned to finding out what her problem was after the officers left, I helped her carry the carton out of the storeroom.

Detective Gartener sprang forward, took it from us, and set it on the floor beside my bistro table.

Her eyes on us, Chief Smallwood crossed her arms over that under-embroidered bulletproof vest.

"How did you end up with this machine?" Detective Gartener asked.

As if she were looking for holes in my story that might show I was a liar at best and a murderer at worst, Chief Smallwood paid careful attention as I explained it all to Gartener.

Susannah squatted and stroked the top of the machine, still in its carton. I had sold Susannah a very good machine the year before, but it wasn't the top of anyone's line, and even with her employee discount, she probably wouldn't be buying a Chandler Champion anytime soon. Her voice harsh, she said, "Plug must have been awfully angry about his wife's death to give up a machine like this." She peeked underneath her eyelashes at Chief Smallwood, who didn't say anything.

From the flicker in Smallwood's eyes, though, I was certain she'd noticed that Susannah was trying hard to conceal her inexplicable nervousness.

Detective Gartener's gaze did not waver from Susannah's face. Uh-oh. When that man had a question, he didn't give up until he received an answer.

But I had never known him to be mean. I would have to convince Susannah that her worries were groundless.

For now, though, I needed to concentrate on the Chandler Champion. Plug hadn't bothered with the original packing material and had tossed the accessories and manual willy-nilly into the carton.

Detective Gartener steadied the box while Susannah and I lifted out the gleaming machine and placed it on the table. Except for the end dangling near where the eye of the needle should have been, the machine was threaded. It struck me as particularly sad that Darlene had not lived long enough to play with other types and colors of thread. The white polyester embroidery thread I'd sent home with the machine was still on the spool pin.

Susannah attached the foot pedal and plugged in the Chandler Champion.

Before I could touch the power button, the machine came on by itself.

That was bad enough.

It also started running at top speed, its nice, bright light illuminating the work surface as the fragment of needle in the machine pounded down with dizzying speed, again and again, on the plate covering the bobbin compartment.

14

Jouncing and crawling toward us on the slippery metal table, the machine seemed intent on destroying itself.

Susannah jumped up and shrieked. I pushed the power button.

The Chandler Champion continued its frenzied dance toward self-destruction.

I dove for the outlet.

Detective Gartener shouted, "Careful, Willow!"

I yanked at the plug. It didn't budge. Above me, the bistro table rocked.

Susannah screamed louder.

I pulled harder. With the disconnected plug in my hand, I rolled away from the table and stood up.

Susannah stared at me with her hand across her mouth.

Chief Smallwood was bracing the table, but the Chandler Champion was no longer on it.

Detective Gartener was clutching it tightly in his arms as if restraining a crazed animal. Carefully, he put it back on the table. "Willow why didn't you wait for one of us to grab the thing before you went flying for the plug?"

I tried to control the tremors rippling through me. "It was about to fling itself off the table. Stitching like that, it could have destroyed itself. It's not working right."

"That's putting it mildly," Smallwood contributed.

Gartener growled. "You should have let it destroy itself. I thought we were going to lose you, too."

I told myself to breathe quietly and not show how unnerved I was. "It's not likely to cause the same freak accident twice."

Gartener frowned, his dark eyes seeming to penetrate my brain.

Chief Smallwood stared at the machine. Her mouth turned down in distaste. "That thing's possessed."

Susannah whispered, "I think you're right."

"Nonsense," I said. "It must have suffered more from its fall than I expected." *Expected?* That didn't sound good.

I corrected myself. "More than I *would have* expected." I thought some very impolite things about Mr. Chandler, Felicity Ranquels, and everyone else associated with the Chandler Sewing Machine Company.

Chief Smallwood interrupted my silent but satisfying diatribe. "See anything wrong?" She poised her pen over her notebook. "Have you ever seen a sewing machine sew by itself like that before?"

I shook my head. "No. Let's get Haylee over here." I should have thought of it sooner.

When Haylee arrived, we told her what happened.

She grinned. "Show me?"

"No way," Detective Gartener said.

"Did the victim forget to turn off the machine before she unplugged it?" Haylee asked.

"The power switch doesn't work," I said. "Darlene was probably as frantic to unplug it as I was. Look at the damage it did to the stitch plate."

Haylee whistled. "You're not supposed to keep stitching after you break a needle. But Darlene should have known that, right?"

"Yep." I fetched a screwdriver and removed the sewing machine's casing. The machine was built of steel, and perhaps a few tons of the lead ballast I'd imagined, but the power switch was plastic. Sometime after Darlene took the machine home, the switch had snapped, and now no one could turn the machine off. It had probably chalked up less than two hundred hours of run time. So much for Chandler's claims of the best machines for the best price.

However, we should have needed to press the foot pedal for the machine to actually stitch. None of us had gone near the foot pedal. Was it poorly constructed also?

I got down on my hands and knees on the floor, which prompted Detective Gartener to issue more cautions about my safety. And to grab the table.

I carefully lifted the foot pedal, then dropped it as if it had burned me. Scrambling to my feet, I gabbled, "Somebody fooled with it. They stuck chewing gum inside the pedal so the machine would keep stitching even when no one was pushing it." *Premeditated,* I couldn't help thinking. Had someone deliberately broken the power switch also?

"Don't touch the chewing gum," Chief Smallwood warned unnecessarily.

She and Gartener squatted and pointed flashlights at the pedal. I steadied the table.

When they stood up, Gartener looked more serious than usual. "We'll have to take the pedal to the lab. It could be glue, or as you say, chewing gum." He turned to a new page in his notebook. Despite his tiny script, at this rate he was going to need a new notebook every few minutes.

Chief Smallwood, too. She didn't look up from her writing. "Didn't that woman have a whole tribe of kids?"

It was probably a rhetorical question, but I answered anyway. "Eight, and Susannah and I tested the machine before it left the shop. It worked perfectly. I've had no problems with the other Chandler Champion here, either."

Susannah reminded us in a soft voice, "Lots of people played with that machine here in the store, before and after the presentation. Maybe someone damaged it then."

Did she know who and was afraid to tell?

Gartener obviously wondered the same thing. "Who damaged it?"

Red blotched Susannah's neck. "No one. I mean I don't know. But something could have happened to it then. Like when we were serving refreshments — maybe someone dropped her chewing gum and it got stuck in the pedal." She held her hands out, palms up, showing she didn't have a clue.

I couldn't tell if she was acting. But I had to agree with her. "I'm afraid that lots of people did touch the machine then. But also, that afternoon the Chandler rep was supposed to give Darlene a lesson in using the machine. If it had misbehaved like it did just now, wouldn't Darlene and Felicity have noticed?"

Haylee laughed. "Darlene might have, but Felicity?"

Remembering Felicity's cardboard interfacing, I had to grin.

Smallwood asked Gartener, "Does the state forensics lab have a sewing machine expert?"

"They could find one. Meanwhile, can you three see anything else wrong?"

"The top of the broken needle is still in the machine," I said. "Most seamstresses would remove it and throw it out, but . . ." Darlene apparently hadn't had time. In her panic to stop the machine, she may have punched the switch with so much force that she'd broken it, leaving her with only one option — unplugging the machine. But before she could, it had jackhammered its way off the table, and there'd been no helpful detective nearby to grab it and save her.

"Okay, good," Gartener encouraged me. "Anything else?"

I asked, "Is it okay if I touch the shaft holding the needle fragment? It's coming out of the machine at an odd angle, and it dented the stitch plate in several places."

"It shouldn't have gone down that far," Haylee said.

Susannah spoke up. "Something's too loose, then, right?"

"Yes." Haylee was seldom this solemn.

Smallwood handed me a pair of cotton gloves. "Put these on before you touch any more of it."

I did, then opened the shield around the threading mechanism. The part of the machine that plunged the needle up and down should have been tightly fastened. It wasn't. I leaned aside to show the others. "It shouldn't wiggle like that." I looked up into Detective Gartener's intent brown eyes. "Any chance your crime scene investigators loosened this?"

"I don't think they took it apart, or anything like that. They dusted it for fingerprints." He and Smallwood raced their pens across their notebook pages.

Fingerprints. That had to mean that, all along, they'd been treating Darlene's death as possibly suspicious.

15

I asked Detective Gartener, "Did your crime scene investigators find fingerprints on the sewing machine?"

"The victim's."

Did Gartener mean victim of an accident or of murder? Maybe he didn't know.

Before I had a chance to ask, Smallwood said sternly, "And no one else's." As if she feared I might continue to interrogate Detective Gartener, she placed herself between him and me. "Would it be surprising if the owner of a new machine cleaned it before she used it, especially after all those people had been touching it?"

No, it wouldn't. It also wouldn't be surprising if Chief Smallwood knew things she wasn't telling us.

She pointed to the too-loose shaft. "Maybe it came like that from the factory."

"I'm sure it didn't. Let's check the other one." I led everyone to the Chandler Champion for sale in my shop and opened it. The plunger was firm. I turned the take-up wheel. The needle went up and down as it was supposed to, without damaging or denting the stitch plate.

We all moved back to the killer machine. Haylee pointed at the stitch plate. "That steel is thick. Darlene must have been very careless to let the needle hit that hard."

"The shaft of the needle probably did that," I said. "After it broke." Dents pocked the stitch plate around the slot the needle was supposed to go through to pick up thread from the bobbin. I explained, "The shaft was so loose that the needle must have been driven down at a slant."

Gartener and Smallwood looked at each other, probably thinking the same thing I was. If the needle hit the stitch plate at a slant, the fragment could have been deflected up into Darlene's arm. Then, in pain and panic, she had rushed to unplug her machine . . .

Detective Gartener spoke first. "So it looks like that plunger thing was loose before the crime scene investigators checked the machine?"

I agreed that was probably what happened. "Mind if I tighten it?"

They told me I could. I turned a screw,

and the plunger looked straight again.

How had it become that loose in the first place? Maybe the screw had come undone, and we should warn the Chandler company about that as well as telling them their on-off switch was dangerously flimsy. Phoning Felicity and suggesting a recall of all Chandler machines should be loads of fun. Not.

"Maybe Darlene caused all the damage by ramming her needle into a pin." Haylee didn't sound convinced.

Checking out the machine seemed to have had a calming effect on Susannah. "A huge pin," she said. "While she was running the machine at top speed." She no longer seemed to be putting on an act. She couldn't have sabotaged Darlene's Chandler Champion, but what had caused her apparent fear of Smallwood and Gartener, other than they could both be pretty scary at times?

To be certain the shaft was high enough and going in straight, I asked their permission to investigate more thoroughly. Cameras and notebooks ready, they agreed.

First, I turned the take-up wheel slowly. Everything seemed to mesh. I removed the bobbin. "Dented. Not surprising. It can't be used again and will have to be tossed."

Smallwood held out an evidence bag.

"Toss it this way." Good. She was taking all of this seriously.

"What about the part it fits into?" Susannah asked.

Shining a bright light, I turned the wheel slowly. "I can't see any problems." I asked Smallwood and Gartener if I could install a new bobbin, needle, and the foot pedal from the other Chandler Champion.

They said I could.

The killer Champion threaded the new bobbin like a . . . well, like a champ. I took out the needle fragment, gave it to Smallwood, slipped a needle into position and tightened the screw that clamped it in.

Still without plugging the machine in, I turned the take-up wheel. The wing needle went down into the slot where it was supposed to go, and brought bobbin thread up with it. So far, so good.

We attached the newer Champion's undamaged foot pedal to the machine. I grinned up at Gartener. "Mind if I plug this machine in again?"

What a warm smile he had, and what a pity he seldom let anyone see it. "Wait." He gripped the machine. Pressure whitened the tips of his fingers. "Okay," he said.

I crawled under the table and plugged the machine into the outlet. Because its switch was broken in the on position, it powered on. I was prepared for it to start its mad stitching, but with a new foot pedal, it remained unmoving, ready to sew.

I clambered out from under the table and lowered the presser foot onto a piece of fabric. Detective Gartener steadied the machine again.

I pressed the pedal carefully and started the default stitch, a plain straight stitch. It was fine. I pushed harder, and the sewing machine sewed faster. It didn't go out of control. I let it sew for a couple of inches, then lifted my foot. The needle obediently raised itself and stopped.

That was good, but the stitches were loose in places. The tension settings weren't right, which wasn't surprising after all the machine had gone through. We adjusted the tension on top, and finally decided that the bobbin carrier had been damaged. We tried a new bobbin carrier. The stitches were fine.

Susannah peered at the old bobbin carrier through a jeweler's loupe. "I can't see any damage. Maybe Darlene fiddled with the screw. She shouldn't have, since only a repair person can fix that." She got out the repair manual and recalibrated the bobbin carrier. She popped it into the machine.

I tried stitching again. The tension was

perfect. I took out the universal needle and inserted a wing needle.

"What's wrong with that needle?" Smallwood asked.

Haylee explained that the double-edged needle was supposed to make decorative holes next to stitches. "But you can only use it with certain stitches, or it would cut the stitches you just made, instead."

"I'll take your word for it," Smallwood said.

Haylee suggested, "Maybe Darlene put a wing needle into her machine, then switched to a wide stitch and forgot to turn on the override."

Normal needles could do the machine's widest stitches with no problem, but for needles that took up extra space, like wing needles, double needles, and triple needles, the stitches had to be narrowed or the needle would move too far to the side and plow into the stitch plate beside the slot they were supposed to go into.

"It's hard to believe she'd be so careless," I said. "The clothes she made seemed perfect."

Susannah frowned at the machine. "People forget things."

Yes, and Darlene could have been distracted by one or more of those children.

Or by catching her lovely young nanny in the arms of her husband.

I touched the screen to make the wing needle override come on. The picture of the stitch on the screen should have immediately looked narrower, but it stayed the same, too wide for a wing needle. Specialty needles were expensive, especially if they broke and damaged a machine. I turned the hand wheel slowly, and stopped the needle before it hit the stitch plate.

The wing needle override on Darlene Coddlefield's Chandler Champion did not work.

"Have I lost my mind?" I asked Susannah. "We checked this before we turned the machine over to Darlene, didn't we?"

"It was fine."

Together, Susannah and I worked our way through the manual. "Maybe she put something into the memory that she shouldn't have," I suggested. Like many computerized sewing machines, the Champion allowed seamstresses to place stitches and combinations of stitches into memory banks, one way of bypassing the factory default settings.

Sure enough, Darlene had set up the Champion to ignore the wing needle override. That had been more than careless, it had been foolhardy. From what I'd seen of Darlene, she'd been neither careless nor foolhardy.

We erased that portion of the machine's memory, and the Champion narrowed its stitches enough for a wing needle to move side to side and fit into the slot in the stitch plate.

I turned to face the two police officers. "Do you still think her death was an accident?"

"Probably," Detective Gartener said gently. "Even if someone maliciously sabotaged the machine, they could not have known for sure that their tampering would cause a death."

He had — pun intended — a point.

"Except," Smallwood blurted. At a look from Gartener, she closed her mouth.

Haylee and I demanded in unison, "Except what?"

"Nothing," Smallwood answered. "The death was very likely an accident."

Very likely. She had her doubts. Seconds before, Gartener had obviously stopped her from telling us something. What evidence about Darlene's "accident" were they keeping a secret?

And why?

Suddenly, I thought of a possible reason

and felt almost sick. Maybe they knew or suspected that one of Darlene's youngest children had messed around with the machine and caused a fatal chain of events. If so, I hoped the child would never find out the truth. How could he or she live with that?

Susannah asked, "Do any of the other memories have stuff in them?"

Good question. I fingered the touch screen. All of the banks were empty except one. The Champion had a memory bank called *Monograms,* with space for five large letters or eight small ones in each monogram. I leaned aside so the others could see. "*FR.* Felicity Ranquels put her initials in the monogram memory bank."

"What other initials are in there?" Gartener asked as if only vaguely interested, but I knew better. That man wanted to know everything.

I scrolled down. *DC* for Darlene Coddlefield, then other sets of initials ending in *C,* for her husband and children, probably. Then we came to one that said *TIFQRSC.*

"Tiffany?" I guessed. "Showing one of the little kids how to make letters appear on the screen?"

I scrolled down to the last monogram.

Actually, it was more like a signature.
  WILLOW.

16

How did my name get typed into the memory of Darlene's sewing machine?

Haylee and Susannah appeared as baffled as I was, but Chief Smallwood stared at me like she'd caught me harboring a skunk in my ponytail.

"Did you put your name into this machine?" Gartener's mild tones didn't deceive me. His voice could be warm, but the man was stronger than steel.

"No."

Susannah defended me. "It wasn't there before we gave the Champion to Darlene, and that's not how Willow signs her name in thread, either. She doesn't use a sewing machine and a plain font like that." She pointed at my nametag. "She uses an embroidery attachment and a script that looks like it's made of willow wands."

Smallwood dismissed fonts. "If you didn't program your name into the machine before it left the shop, you must have done it after it got to Coddlefields'."

I almost wished I did have a skunk, and could aim it at her. "I never set foot in the place until after Darlene died, when Edna and I took the family some cookies and a casserole and saw Plug and the nanny in a clinch."

Gartener nodded. Smallwood must have already told him about what Edna and I had seen and done that day.

I continued, "I didn't even see the sewing machine."

Susannah paged through the repair manual. "If the sewing machine's internal clock works, its computer will tell us when each monogram was entered."

Gartener became about as excited as I'd ever seen him. He leaned forward all of a quarter inch. "Can you tell when the wing needle override was turned off?"

"We erased that," I said.

"Let's check anyway," he said.

With Susannah reading the steps aloud to me, I found the time stamp. The wing needle override had been turned off at five p.m. on Wednesday. I turned in my seat and looked up at Gartener. "That was *after* Darlene took the machine home." I couldn't keep triumph out of my voice.

"And when were the monograms entered?" he asked. He couldn't possibly believe I would be foolish enough to put my name in a machine and then rig it to harm someone.

Somewhat deflated, I dictated my findings. "The *FR* and the *DC* and most of the other initials ending in *C* were put in between three and half past three. The one that looks like Tiffany and a child worked together on it went into the machine about four thirty. And my name . . ." I gulped. "Was entered at a minute after five, right after someone disabled the wing needle override." Behind me, the officers' pens scratched on paper. Now I was not only deflated, defeat weighed on my shoulders.

Haylee, always on my side, asked, "Can you tell if any monograms were erased?"

Did she guess the culprit may have erased his or her own monogram? It was worth checking. I reached for the machine.

Gartener stopped me. "I'd rather have a different expert investigate this. I'll take the machine to the crime lab."

A *different* expert. He didn't want me fiddling with that sewing machine's computer and memory banks and possibly destroying evidence. Did he expect to find evidence against me? "Okay," I agreed.

Smallwood bagged the original foot pedal. I disconnected the one we'd borrowed from the other Champion, and Gartener picked up the killer sewing machine as if it weighed nothing.

"Want the carton?" I asked.

"No, thanks." With Chief Smallwood and her bagged treasures following him, he carried the sewing machine outside to his cruiser. So much for selling it to benefit Darlene's children.

"He's cute," Haylee said.

I grinned.

Haylee quickly backed down. "Cute, but not my type. Too stern."

I jumped to his defense. "Not all the time."

Haylee smiled, no doubt remembering the last time he'd been in my shop with the two of us, and quite a few other people. "But who would want to date a state trooper? She'd have to drive under the limit all the time. And just generally . . . behave."

"You behave anyway." Susannah's manner was so encouraging that both Haylee and I burst out laughing.

"What?" Susannah asked.

"You've been around Opal, Naomi, and Edna too much," I said, "and their hints about what we should do and how we

161

should act."

"Opal and Naomi, anyway," Haylee corrected me. "Edna sometimes gets a little too wayward to suit the other two."

Yes, and so did Haylee and I, at times. But we weren't going to let Susannah in on our secrets. Even Edna might have a thing or two to say about some of our exploits, like walking the dogs at night near the homes of people we suspected of being up to no good.

"So, they're treating Darlene's death as suspicious," Haylee noted.

"They should," I said darkly. "Sewing machines don't go berserk."

"Or chew gum. See you tomorrow."

Susannah looked about to follow Haylee out.

I stopped her. "I need to talk to you." I waited until Haylee was out of earshot. "What's wrong? Why were you acting frightened?"

And possibly guilty.

Tears glimmered in the corners of Susannah's eyes. "I thought they might suspect me of breaking the Champion. I would never purposely break a sewing machine. I *fix* them." She raised her chin. "I just don't like police officers. They creep me out with their guns and everything. I know it's silly, but they remind me of the night our house burned down. A bunch of them were there. They scared me." She wiped her eyes. "But those two aren't as bad as I thought they'd be. I acted okay around them tonight, didn't I?"

Without waiting for my answer, she turned around and fled out into the evening. The door closed behind her, leaving my beach-glass chimes jangling.

The jingles slowed and stopped, and the only noise in my shop was the clock ticking high on the storeroom wall. Yes, Susannah had *acted* all right around Smallwood and Gartener. She had seemed almost like her-self.

But I was sure that it had mostly been an act.

What could I do? I wasn't her boss all the time. She was an excellent employee, repair-ing machines and always knowing how to help in the shop without being asked. I couldn't very well force her to tell me if anything was bothering her besides her childhood memories. And maybe she was already learning to cope with those old fears. Still, I was glad she was coming to In Stitches to repair machines the next day. If she needed to talk, I'd be available.

After the dogs and I had a good long romp

and some supper, I was ready for an evening of embroidery. I fussed with the trims I'd bought from Edna, but nothing gave me a reasonable, machine-embroidered semblance of candlewicking. I tied mini rickrack in knots. Why had I thought that might look good? I threw the strange-looking wad down in disgust.

My most successful attempt was with cord that looked like candlewick but was more flexible. Like the other trims, it would have to be tacked to the fabric first, then any zigzag machine could stitch it down, which hardly qualified as machine embroidery. Instead of entering IMEC, I'd have to enter a competition for strands of bumpy white stuff wandering over fabric. I didn't think such a competition existed.

I didn't *have* to enter IMEC or show off my work in the handcrafts booth at the Harvest Festival. The trouble was I wanted to.

However, no matter how long I stared at my embroidery software, my machines, and the heaps of discarded knotted-up trims, inspiration just wouldn't come.

Frustrated, I gave up and tromped downstairs with my dogs. We all went outside. Watching them run and attack each other in their play-fighting, I felt better. Again, I would have to let my brain work on the problem while I slept.

By morning, inspiration about my IMEC entry hadn't appeared.

But Chief Smallwood did.

17

Leaning against the cutting table in the middle of In Stitches, Chief Smallwood paged through her notebook. Apparently early morning made her grumpier than ever. "Yesterday when we were here, we spoke with you and Haylee and another woman, your assistant, what did you say her name was?"

Chief Smallwood had written Susannah's name down the night before, and was probably staring right at it.

"Susannah Kessler."

"How long has she worked for you?"

"Only a few months. Before that, she was one of our star students."

"How did you three zero in so quickly on everything that was wrong with that sewing machine?"

"We're all used to machines and how they should work. No machine should stitch unless the pedal is pressed by someone, not by some*thing*. And the needle plunger was so loose it wobbled and went down too far. Those led us to other, more subtle deficiencies. There could be more." Lots more. I grumbled, "I'm not impressed with this new sewing machine manufacturer."

"So where did you three get your expertise?"

"Haylee and I have been using sewing machines since we were little girls. Susannah probably has, too. In addition, we've all taken courses. Before Susannah began assisting in our shops, we made certain she was certified to repair all the machines that Haylee and I sell, and the quilting machines that Naomi has in Batty About Quilts."

"So this Susannah Kessler is the real expert?"

"In repair? Yes. She stays current on the latest machines. She also waits on customers and helps teach classes and workshops." I wasn't sure what we'd do without her. "Unlike Haylee and me, she's lived here in Elderberry Bay all her life. You can ask other residents about her."

"Do you know her ex-husband?"

"No. When I moved here, they were still together, but I never met him. I gather he moved out west somewhere."

"He doesn't have very nice things to say

about her."

Had the police decided Darlene's death was a homicide and Susannah was their prime suspect? Stepping back, I bumped into a bolt of linen. "You already got in touch with him?" I had to convince Smallwood that Susannah was innocent, and it was hard not to look guilty myself, since I suspected that Susannah had a secret reason for acting nervous around Smallwood and Gartener. I didn't know what it was, though, so I couldn't very well tell Smallwood about it. I managed, "Susannah's not a killer."

Smallwood actually smiled, though her smile was a crooked twist of her lips that put touches of red lipstick on her teeth. "Her ex got in touch with us, said that if anyone was killing people with sewing machines around here, it had to be her."

I spluttered, "But he . . . I'm guessing he doesn't like Susannah!" Which was probably putting it mildly.

"Don't worry, Willow, we know that some exes, male and female, can become vindictive."

"Could he have had a grudge against Darlene Coddlefield?"

"We're looking into everything, but we have corroborated that Susannah's ex was in Utah the night of Mrs. Coddlefield's death."

"A hit man," I began, then laughed at my silly conjecture. "No one hires hit men to gum up sewing machine pedals."

Smallwood pointed her pen at me like she agreed, then flipped through her notebook again. "The deceased got that sewing machine from you."

"Yes, and for the record, I didn't make a penny from it. My store is the closest Chandler distributor to the contest winner. That's why I had the good fortune" — I made a goofy face to show I didn't consider it to be good at all — "to host the Chandler representative and her presentation ceremony."

"And it was a national contest? How many contestants?"

"The Chandler company should be able to answer that."

She thinned her lips as if she'd already asked and saw no reason to share the answer. "Is the competition strong?"

"Very. Lots of my students entered, many of whom are experts at sewing and machine embroidering."

"And I have it on good authority that Darlene has won other sewing contests over the years."

I admitted that I didn't know anything about other sewing contests she could have entered and won. "But Felicity, the Chandler rep, said that Darlene had won Mother of the Year."

"Do they award that for having the most kids?" Smallwood opened her eyes in pretend astonishment.

I couldn't help grinning. "I think it was years ago, when Russ and the next child, a sister, I think, were little, before she had the other six."

Smallwood asked, "What was your impression of the older children?"

"Russ was obviously angry at his mother earlier that day, the day she died. He didn't want to attend the presentation, but she ordered him to, so he did, but he didn't stay for the whole thing. And he brought her back later to help her collect her sewing machine." I couldn't help smiling at the memory of his valiant face and bulging muscles. "He's quite strong for his age. So he was obedient even though he liked to pretend he wasn't. But that night — the next morning, actually, around two — I saw him driving recklessly and shouting out his truck windows like he was letting off steam. And on Thursday evening, he deliberately forced Edna's car off the road when we were returning from delivering the casserole and cookies."

"Were you sure it was Russ, not someone else?" Smallwood asked.

"Thursday evening, yes. At two on Thursday morning, I'm not positive, but it was a truck like his."

"At two Thursday morning, I was at his house. His mother had been dead for a couple of hours, and no one in his family had seen him since dinnertime." She tapped her pen on her notebook. "Would you say that Darlene Coddlefield was an expert at sewing?"

"Yes."

"She wouldn't have made mistakes using the machine?"

I spread my hands out. "People accidentally damage their machines all the time. They jump to conclusions and never question their logic. You probably see that type of behavior, too."

"Ooh, yes," Chief Smallwood agreed. "People who 'never' make mistakes make some real lulus. So you think Darlene may have caused all this damage to her machine, perhaps by accident?"

"The one thing I can't see any seamstress doing is putting something sticky in her foot pedal. That doesn't make sense."

"You're saying that someone's actions were deliberately malicious?"

I shuddered at the thought of people sabotaging sewing machines to harm their owners. "I'd like to be proven wrong."

"Any idea who might have done this?"

"Either a member of the Coddlefield household — Plug or Tiffany, maybe, because they had the hots for each other, or Russ, who seems unpredictable and maybe angry. Or the sewing machine company rep, Felicity Ranquels. On Wednesday afternoon, she was supposed to follow Darlene to the Coddlefield farm and train Darlene to use the machine. Do you know if Felicity found anything wrong with the machine when she was giving the lesson?"

Chief Smallwood snapped a fingernail against her notebook. "Investigators talked to her and to Tiffany again last night after we were here. Felicity said she didn't try a wing needle, but she and the deceased put in those monograms you found yesterday, except for the odd one that started with T-I-F. You guessed right about that one. Tiffany had been teaching the littlest girl her letters. Or trying to. But then —" She gave me a stern police officer look. "Someone typed in *your* name, too. Not Felicity and not Tiffany."

And if one of them had *done it, would she have admitted it?* "*I* didn't. That was around five, right after the wing needle override was turned off. What time on Wednesday did Felicity leave Darlene's place?"

"She claims it was around four."

"And she drove to Cleveland by herself. Did anyone see her? Did she buy gas? Was she stopped for speeding on the interstate?" The thought of sour-faced Felicity speeding made me want to giggle, but I maintained a solemn expression and asked, "Who was at the Coddlefields' at five on Wednesday? Tiffany? Plug? Russ?"

"Tiffany was with the four smallest children at the library. Plug and the four older children were working on an irrigation system in one of their fields. If anyone was home, it would have been Darlene."

"Maybe Darlene was going to monogram something for me," I hazarded, "as a thank-you for Wednesday's ceremony?" Stranger things had happened.

Smallwood rapped out, "Where were *you* around five on Wednesday evening?"

"In my shop, waiting on customers. You can ask Rosemary, the tour bus driver. She usually gathers her passengers around quarter past."

"Where were you the rest of the evening?

173

Anybody see you?"

I had to admit that, except for about a half hour around six thirty when I'd visited the other Threadville shops, I'd been home alone with my dogs.

"Could Felicity Ranquels have damaged the machine in all the ways you showed us yesterday?"

"Probably not on purpose. She didn't seem to know much about sewing." By the time I finished describing Felicity's homemade jacket and imitating her peeved expression, Chief Smallwood was obviously trying not to laugh, and I was beginning to like her. I asked, "Did you look into Darlene's life insurance policies? Were they large? Was Plug the beneficiary?"

"Would it be surprising for a husband to insure his wife for a large amount, especially when there are eight kids to look after?" Smallwood looked at me expectantly, like she knew I would draw my own conclusions from her rhetorical question.

"No," I answered.

Smallwood gave me a long, slow nod. Plug must have been the beneficiary on a big life insurance policy. Very interesting.

My first customer of the day came in.

"Thanks. You've been very helpful," Smallwood said. She trotted out like someone who had accomplished her goals.

What had those goals been? I hoped that she was strongly considering Russ, Felicity, Plug, and Tiffany as possible suspects and that she would pass those conjectures along to the lead detective in the case, her former partner, Gartener.

On Sundays, we didn't teach courses or give workshops, mainly because customers kept us busy. Halfway through the morning, a man marched into my shop. He was several inches shorter than I was, tanned and obviously fit. Who, besides Haylee, a trained tailor, would wear a neatly tailored suit in Threadville?

Another detective from the state police?

While I made change, bagged purchases, and chatted with customers, the man wandered around the store, picking things up and putting them down. He must have felt me watching him, because he occasionally glanced my way, but most of the time he was obviously eavesdropping on my customers.

If he wasn't a detective, he was a reporter.

I mentally rehearsed what I should say to reporters: *No comment.*

18

The stranger lingered over the lone Chandler Champion displayed in my store. He put his hand on it.

I quickly gave the last customer her embroidery hoops, appliqué scissors, and metallic thread.

The man's face was inches away from the Chandler Champion's needle. Maybe he wasn't a reporter. Maybe he was a professional saboteur of Chandler machines, about to harm this one, too. Where was Chief Smallwood when I really needed her?

I stumbled over my feet in my hurry to reach him. "Can I help you?" I asked.

"I'm looking for Willow Vanderling."

He didn't flash a detective's ID, so he had to be a reporter. *No comment, no comment, no comment.* "I'm Willow." I had to fight the friendliness a shopkeeper should show.

He reached into a pocket and handed me a card. *Jeremy Chandler,* it said, *President,*

Chandler Sewing Machine Company.

"You're . . . Mr. Chandler?" I managed. The boss for whom Felicity Ranquels had shown so much reverence when she came to In Stitches to present the Chandler Champion to Darlene? I had pictured someone older. This man was probably in his late thirties. In case he didn't like women looming over him, I backed up.

He flashed very white teeth at me. "Call me Jeremy."

Okay, I could do that, even if Felicity, his employee, hadn't. What was he doing here after missing the presentation Felicity had expected him to attend? "I thought you'd have been here on Wednesday." My inept words made me feel even more gauche.

"Couldn't make it." He stroked the Chandler Champion. "This wouldn't be the machine we presented to our winner, would it?"

Why wasn't he at the Coddlefields' asking that question? Did he know that Darlene's machine had made its way back to my store? "No," I said.

"Any idea where I could find it? I'd like to check it over, repair anything that might not be working. People are calling it a killer sewing machine. That's not quite the image we want to project." His tan was streaky, as if he might have painted it on.

"I believe the police have that sewing machine in their custody."

The blindingly white smile did not falter. "Police? *Custody?* Isn't that rather drastic?"

"Would you like the chief's phone number?" People were lining up at the cash register again.

"No, no, I believe you. I see you're busy. I don't have to be back in Cleveland for my flight to New York until tomorrow." He turned the full brilliance of those dazzling teeth on me again. "I'd like to talk to you about . . . this whole thing. Can I take you out to dinner this evening? Maybe you know of a place?"

Actually, I'd been looking forward to a quick supper with the dogs, then a companionable evening with my embroidery machines. But this man might divulge information about the Chandler Company and their quality control and safety checks. "Sure. How about The Sunroom, just a few doors down Lake Street, toward the beach?"

His frown didn't wrinkle his forehead as much as I'd have expected. Whitened teeth, tan from a bottle, *and* Botox? What else about this man might be an illusion? "I was thinking of something nicer," he said with practiced diction. "Should we drive to

Cleveland for a better class of restaurants? I have a rental car outside."

Like I was going to Cleveland with a complete stranger, especially one who might have manufactured a killer sewing machine. Besides, he had hired Felicity Ranquels, not exactly a point in his favor. "I hear The Sunroom is excellent. Five stars from . . ." I squinched up my face, trying to remember, and unsquinched it as quickly as possible. If I didn't already have wrinkles, I soon would, and then I'd need Botox, too, and I might end up looking like Jeremy Chandler.

The superior quirk of his upper lip said that a restaurant rating service that ventured this far from New York City wouldn't impress him, anyway. "Meet you there at . . . would seven o'clock be too late for farmers to eat their supper?" Again that superior quirk.

If he was going to insult everybody and everything in this corner of Pennsylvania, I didn't want to spend one more moment with him. However, I did have questions I wanted to ask him. "Seven will be fine."

Shoulders back, chin up, heels of his polished shoes hitting the floor like hammers, he strode out of In Stitches.

Customers streamed in and out all morning. After a large group of laughing women left, Tiffany walked in, trailing Darlene's smallest daughter and two little sons. All three children were damp, their sturdy little legs and feet covered in sand. The four-year-old boy clasped a green plastic shovel tightly in one hand. They'd obviously spent part of their morning at the beach. "We've come for their mother's sewing machine," Tiffany announced.

I didn't want to tell her in front of the children where it was. And maybe the police wouldn't want her to know, either. "Plug told me he never wanted to see it again."

For half an instant, I thought Tiffany was about to argue, but her expression went back to its usual bland polite interest, and I couldn't be sure what I'd seen.

The little girl piped up, "Tiffie's going to make me a new dwess."

Tiffany smiled down at the child, then gave me a clear-eyed look. "Plug acted out of grief. He would never come right out and say he was wrong, but he regrets bringing that machine back. He has four daughters, and although Darlene already had a sewing machine when she won that one, her two older girls love to make their own clothes, and the two younger ones . . ." She gave the small hand in hers a playful shake. "You want to learn how to make yourself pretty dresses, too, don't you?"

The little girl nodded solemnly. So did the boys. There was no rule, as Jeremy Chandler might attest, that only females could sew.

However, Darlene's sewing machine could be tied up as evidence in a maybe-it's-a-homicide case for years. But I had an idea I wanted to run past Jeremy Chandler. "You have your hands full. How about it if I get back to you tomorrow?"

Tiffany assessed me with those cool gray eyes. "I guess that will be all right." Her lips tightened as if she were chalking up my misdemeanors to toss back at me if she ever needed to. "The machine really should belong to the children, you know."

Obviously, she thought I was keeping it for myself. "It needs to be thoroughly checked by its manufacturer before anyone else uses it."

"Then maybe the manufacturer should replace it," she snapped, and I remembered the claw marks she'd put on Edna's arm.

The children must not have liked her tone. Wailing, they tugged at her to pick them up. She dragged them outside. She had a quick temper and wasn't always able to hide it. Had she lashed out at Darlene by tampering with her machine?

The visit from the two-faced nanny couldn't dampen my mood, however. Every time I pictured Jeremy Chandler and his bantam-like confidence, I wanted to laugh. The minute Susannah arrived at lunchtime, I ran to The Stash. Haylee took one look at the grin on my face and led me to a quiet part of her store. Patting leopard-patterned fake fur, I outlined my plans for the evening.

Haylee's eyes lit up. "You can gather clues about him and his sewing machine company. Have a great time!" The smile left her face. "But be careful. Don't go anywhere alone with him."

I promised I wouldn't, then sprinted back across the street and took the dogs outside with me so they could play while I ate. It was another hot day, but the breeze came off the lake, bringing humidity and haze with it. Farther to the north, tall clouds massed. If that storm was like others this summer, though, rain would fall into the middle of Lake Erie instead of on nearby fields where it was needed.

After lunch, I settled the dogs in their pen with the table that Susannah had set up. The shop's big back windows bathed her temporary sewing machine repair workshop in light. She was waiting on a customer, so I joined her at the cash register until the woman left.

With a troubled frown, Susannah whispered, "I have to show you what I found."

She led me to the storeroom and grabbed the carton that had originally housed Darlene's Chandler Champion. "Look what's in the bottom."

A scrap of candy pink fabric was wedged underneath one of the flaps. I yanked it out. I was almost positive that it matched the pink broadcloth Darlene had used for her twelve-year-old's dress and Russ's cowboy shirt. Using white thread, someone had sewn different stitches, some plain, some intricate, in equally spaced lines down the scrap. I ran the ornamental stitching between my fingers. "I wonder why we didn't see this earlier."

"That brochure must have been hiding it. I was looking for the screwdriver we were using last night, and pushed that brochure aside, and there it was."

The brochure advertised other Chandler products. Toasters weren't our prime interest in Threadville, so none of us had bothered to move the brochure before.

"Did you find the screwdriver?" I asked.

She grinned. "It was right in the tool box, where it belonged. I missed it the first time."

I shoved the scrap into a pocket and we

both returned to the shop. Cooing at the dogs, Susannah let herself into their pen and sat down to take a sewing machine apart.

Ashley, an avid fifteen-year-old customer, came in, picked up a bolt of heavy natural linen, and carried it to my measuring and cutting table. She had been attending classes in Threadville all summer. She wanted two yards for an embroidered wall hanging. "If it works out the way I picture it, I'll enter it in IMEC." She bowed her head as if embarrassed by her audacity in entering a competition in which most of the other contestants were adults.

I unrolled the fabric. "I can't wait to see what you come up with," I said. "You're so talented." She didn't own an embroidery machine but did very well with the ones in my shop. The freehand thread art she created with her mother's old machine at home was nothing short of amazing. I double-checked my measurements and gave her a little extra. "I still have to decide what I'm going to enter." If anything.

"I know what picture *I'm* making," she said. "It's in my head. Aren't you going to display them at the Harvest Festival next weekend?"

"Yep. I'd better hurry." It was Sunday. On

Friday night, I needed to set up my corner of the Threadville Booth. I gave her a student discount, and she left happy.

The rest of the afternoon, I waited on customers and tried, without success, to dream up a satisfactory method of making the candlewicking I'd envisioned. Susannah finished working on our customers' machines, helped me close the shop for the evening, and then went home.

I took Sally and Tally downstairs and outside. Watching them run around, I thought about what to wear to dinner with Jeremy Chandler.

Luckily, I didn't own any farmer's overalls, or Jeremy's comments about restaurants and farmers' dining hours might have tempted me to put them on. I considered jeans. A denim skirt.

I had to prove I wasn't a hick. After a luxurious shower, I put on a black pencil skirt and matching tank top, and draped a wrap around my shoulders. Edna had made it for me from black satin ribbons woven together and trimmed with tiny crystal beads. By the time I added strappy high heels and a black satin bag I'd embroidered with black silk thread in an allover design, my sophisticated look had to rival anything I'd ever seen on the sidewalks of New York.

I crammed the scrap of pink fabric into my bag and walked, head high, to The Sunroom to meet Jeremy.

The maître d' ushered me into the glassed-in balcony. I took one look around and nearly burst out laughing.

The room was almost full. Of people I knew.

19

Haylee and Clay waved at me from one table. I'd never seen Clay in a suit before. He looked, not surprisingly, gorgeous. And so did Haylee in a retro black linen sheath. As I came closer, I could make out a dried drop of white paint on Clay's ear. He'd cleaned up but probably didn't know he'd missed a fleck. It was endearing, and my smile had to be bigger than any I'd given him during the past few months.

At another table, Naomi and Opal raised their glasses and nodded at me. Naomi wore a long skirt and a jacket she'd quilted from patches of hand-dyed, jewel-toned silks. Opal was in one of her crocheted ensembles, this one a long skirt and top in coral.

In another corner of the glassed-in balcony, Edna, in her beribboned gown, didn't appear to notice my entrance. Her attention was locked on her dining companion, Dr. Wrinklesides. He could have worn that black suit on a concert stage. Was he about to burst into song?

Jeremy Chandler must have thought my ever-growing smile was for him. He beamed at me from a corner table overlooking the park, the beaches, the lake, and the river, then stood and pulled out my chair for me. For a heartrending second, I caught a heel, but managed to extricate it without ending up under the table — tablecloth, silver, crystal, china, and all.

Jeremy seemed pleasantly surprised by the menu. Consulting with our attentive waiter, he chose expensive wines to go with each course. Good thing I wasn't going to have to wobble very far on my stiletto heels to get myself home.

After we ordered, I excused myself, found the maître d', gave him my charge card, and arranged to pay for Jeremy's and my meals and the meals of all my friends — Haylee and Clay, Opal and Naomi, and Edna and Dr. Wrinklesides. They were giving up an evening to guard me and shouldn't have to pay for it. Besides, I didn't want to owe Jeremy anything. Except maybe a sewing machine. If he gave me one, though, it would be to replace Darlene's, which he and his company may have constructed so poorly that it ended up killing her.

Exchanging smiles and greetings with my friends, and trying to hide that I'd rather dine with them than with Jeremy and his pre-programmed smile, I returned to his corner table.

Discussing scraps of used fabric probably wouldn't be done in any of the superlative restaurants Jeremy undoubtedly frequented in New York City. However, I pulled the pink square out of my bag and unfolded it on the table between us. We needed something to talk about, and as far as I knew, our only common interest was sewing machines.

"What do you make of this?" I asked, all innocence. A straight stitch had been sewn in a line down the left side of the fabric. Next to it was a stretch stitch, then a series of zigzag stitches, and finally fancier and fancier stitches — flowers, hearts, quilting stitches, heritage stitches, all of them sewn neatly in rows about a quarter inch apart.

He glanced at it, then looked deep into my eyes. "Very nice," he murmured.

I smoothed the cloth. "Recognize the stitches?" Now he would definitely decide I was a country bumpkin. Fine, as long as he gave me answers.

He picked up the cloth and examined it by the light of the candle on our table. "Did you do this?" Again, he gazed at me instead of at the fabric.

Was Clay noticing Jeremy's apparent enchantment, and if so, would he become just a teensy bit jealous?

I managed a coy shrug and tilt of the head. A sane voice inside my head reminded me that Clay would undoubtedly recognize Jeremy as a fake. But maybe Clay would at least think I looked okay in my curve-hugging black outfit.

"Very nice, straight stitching," Jeremy began. Finally, he became interested in the stitching. "This was done with a Chandler Champion! I should have recognized our trademark stitches right away."

The rows near the middle of the fabric were various types of stitches known as entredeux, a sort of lacy stitch usually inserted between two panels, like the hemstitches I had discussed with Dr. Wrinklesides when he showed me the X-ray of the wing needle. The person trying out the machine's stitches had obviously switched to a wing needle for these rows, and it had punctured the fabric exactly the way it was supposed to. I pointed at the neat rows of tiny holes. "Wing needle." How very articulate. My attempt at a friendly smile came out more like a simper.

Jeremy must have liked simpers. He leaned closer. "You were following the manual, trying each stitch in sequence, weren't you? You did it just right. You even remembered to turn on the wing needle override. Good thing, too, or you might have broken a needle."

He really did think I knew almost nothing about sewing machines. Maybe my dunce act had been too good.

Beyond the hemstitches, the stitches became fancier and wider, with no tiny holes decorating them. Someone had replaced the wing needle with a universal needle. For the stitches to be this wide, the seamstress had to have turned off the wing needle override. Had she switched it off the correct way, or had she messed up the computer's memory?

I admitted that I hadn't done the stitching, then asked, "Does Chandler pack samplers like this with their machines to show what can be done?"

He shook his head. "We wouldn't want to discourage people who might not sew as straight a line as our technicians."

I prompted, "Maybe Felicity Ranquels packed it into the carton before I got the machine."

"We shipped the Chandler Champion

straight to you."

I slapped my forehead. "Silly me, of course you did."

Frowning his nonwrinkled frown, he accepted his garlicky-smelling escargots from the waiter. "I met Felicity for the first time yesterday, and I'm afraid I was disappointed. Judging by the outfit she wore, complete with a Chandler Champion motif embroidered on it, the woman can barely sew and would probably tug and pull at the fabric as it was being stitched, and would prevent the Champion from sewing its faultless straight lines." He had obviously memorized speeches extolling his namesake's features. "Felicity could not have sewn these sample stitches. And her people skills are almost nonexistent, even though she was trying to make a good impression on *me,* her boss." He gave me an attempt at a self-deprecating smile, to be certain, no doubt, that I recognized his exalted position. "Did she project the correct sort of image on potential Chandler customers at the presentation ceremony in your shop?"

I hedged, "Would it matter? What sewing enthusiast would pay attention to a company representative when a Chandler Champion was present?"

The approving smile Jeremy gave me

verged on adoring.

It was as good a time as any to bring up my idea. "Jeremy, today Darlene Coddlefield's . . ."

"Who's she?"

This could prove to be tougher than I'd expected. "The woman who won the Chandler Champion and died using it."

"Oh, her. Of course. I didn't catch her name before." Teeth glimmering in candlelight — did the man have to smile *all* the time? — he nodded encouragingly.

"Her nanny wants the sewing machine back for Darlene's four daughters."

"That makes sense." Melted butter dripped from a snail — an escargot — as he lifted his fork to his mouth. "But when I was in your shop, you said the police appropriated the machine."

I tasted my appetizer, fusilli diabolico. "Yes," I managed around spices searing my tongue.

"Maybe the police can deliver it to the nanny when they're done with it."

"That could take months." The heat in my pasta was perfect. My sinuses nearly burst into flames.

"Or days."

I doubted that. "Anyway, the Champion that malfunctioned should go back to your company when the police are done with it. As you said earlier today, you'll want to overhaul it and make certain nothing's wrong with it." My hinting was becoming almost unconscionable.

"It was in perfect condition when it left the factory. You've said it was fine when you had it."

Oho, we were being defensive, were we? Interesting . . .

"I thought I'd give them the one in my store."

He chewed. Closed his eyes and chewed some more.

"This," I said, "is delicious." It was. And the full-bodied red wine he'd chosen went with my spices perfectly.

He swallowed. "Tell you what. You give the family the machine you have, and I'll ship a new one to you."

I made a pretense of being surprised, but my gratitude was genuine. "That would be great. I'll make certain that the old one comes back to you when the police are done with it." If they ever would be.

He waved his fork dismissively. "Don't worry about it." He flashed me what he probably fancied was a sexy look from underneath his eyelashes. I was really glad

I'd made certain that I was paying for the meal.

We took our time through several courses. So did my friends at neighboring tables. What did Jeremy think about the way they all seemed to watch us? Probably that they were admiring the man from the big city.

I asked him why Chandler Champions were so much heavier than other sewing machines.

"Quality materials. We use a high grade of steel." The blazing smile might have torched through that steel.

"What about the plastics you use?"

"All first class. Those machines are designed to last."

"And they're tested thoroughly?"

He shook his head earnestly in a way that reminded me of Mona when she was agreeing with someone. "Every single one of them."

"Power switches, too?"

He glanced toward the lake. Looking for an escape? "Everything. Why do you ask?"

"The on-off switch on the machine we presented to the winner broke."

To give him credit, his amazement seemed real. "Broke? It couldn't have, not by itself. Someone must have tampered with it. Those switches are strong."

"If you wanted to break one, how would you do it?"

That brought his smile back. Sort of. "A sledgehammer."

20

A sledgehammer? Jeremy was undoubtedly exaggerating, boasting about his company's machines, possibly trying to avoid lawsuits. But if breaking the Chandler Champion's power switch would require any sort of tool, I had another clue, along with the gumming up of the foot pedal, that someone had actually intended to harm Darlene.

Jeremy didn't seem aware of my preoccupation with solving a mystery. He was happy to linger over after-dinner brandies. My friends departed in groups, Clay and Haylee first. "See you later, Willow!" Naomi called. I recognized the hidden subtext in her one raised eyebrow. *Don't worry. You won't be alone with him unless you want to be.*

Dr. Wrinklesides gave me a disapproving look, leaned over, and sang quietly, close to my ear. Although I knew very little about opera, and couldn't have understood Italian, the words of his song seemed to threaten a deep, dark revenge. I couldn't help laughing. His message was as obvious as Naomi's had been. He would get me back for buying his dinner.

Threats from him were particularly scary, and would most likely take the form of a dinner invitation. He and Edna left.

Jeremy and I sipped our brandy. He bent forward with his back straight, which made him seem unnaturally stiff. It also put his face closer to mine. Fortunately, the table was between us. "Before I hired Felicity, I should have flown her to New York for a personal interview. She impressed me over the phone with her encyclopedic knowledge of embroidery competitions. She knows them all, including who won them, going back years! But as I mentioned before, her people and sewing skills are, I fear, lacking." He placed a hand, palm up, on the tablecloth with his fingertips just stretching onto my side of the table. Such a subtle invitation.

I swirled my brandy while leaving my free hand resolutely in my lap.

His voice became smoother and lower. "I feel I know *you* much better than I did her when I made the mistake of offering her the job. You can sew, you obviously love sewing machines, you understand why our Chandler Champion is the best machine for the money."

I did?

He smiled and added his clincher, "And people like you."

I saw where this was going, and gave my head a little shake.

"They do! Most of the people in this restaurant seemed to know and like you."

There was a reason for that. They all came here to spy on you. I didn't say it aloud.

We finished our coffee and Jeremy asked for the bill. The maître d' said what I'd rehearsed with him. "It's all been paid for, sir."

Jeremy asked who had paid for our meals.

"Another gentleman did, sir."

Jeremy seemed to color under his painted-on tan. "Who, that old man who came to our table *singing*?" He didn't need to speak in derogatory tones about my friends.

"I'm not at liberty to say, sir. The lady has, should we say . . . many admirers." The maître d' nodded and headed back to his post.

Muttering about restaurants in Cleveland undoubtedly being superior to this one, Jeremy shoved back his chair.

I quickly stood before he could help me out of my chair and maybe, if I caught my heel again, onto the floor. Not that I was very good at standing after that meal and the accompanying drinks, anyway.

Taking my arm as if I were delicate china, Jeremy steadied me.

As soon as we were out on the sidewalk, he went on with the pitch that had been interrupted by his discussion with the waiter. "The job of Midwest representative is yours if you want it."

"Oh, no," I said. "I love my shop and I love living in Threadville."

"You could continue to run your shop, at least for a while, until Chandler becomes really big. Of course, we'd expect you to discontinue representing other lines of sewing machines right away."

I might have been teetery on my feet, but my mind wasn't *that* badly affected. "I have contracts."

"Break 'em! It would be worth it to you."

Nice guy.

"I'm quite confident," he added, "that in time, you'd work your way up to national rep. Then you'd get to come live in New York City! How would you like that? Imagine — the Manhattan lifestyle! SoHo lofts! Nightlife!" He gave my arm a squeeze.

I wanted to laugh aloud but managed to keep it down to a breathless chuckle. "I lived in New York City for about ten years. I moved here because I preferred Thread-ville."

That silenced him for a moment. Behind us, waves splashed. The night had cooled, and the air felt fresh.

"We'd pay for your move, of course," he purred. I suspected he'd made similar promises to Felicity Ranquels, though maybe not quite in that tone of voice, and certainly not in person. Now he was ready to fire her.

"No," I said more firmly. "I really like it here." And I preferred the other sewing machines I sold to the ones his company made. None of my favorites had, as far as I knew, gone on rampages and thrown themselves onto their owners.

We passed Mona's home décor shop, Country Chic, on our side of the street, and Naomi's Batty About Quilts on the other. Both were dark, as was the apartment above Naomi's shop. The Ironmonger was closed up tight, but across the street in Edna's dimly lit Buttons and Bows, Edna and Dr. Wrinklesides, standing close together, looked out through her glass door and waved at us. Haylee's spies were everywhere.

I couldn't see lights in Haylee's or Opal's shops and apartments. Jeremy and I turned toward my porch.

Rocking chairs squeaked. Picturing a paint-daubed ear, I imagined Clay waiting for me.

Opal stood up from one of the chairs. "There you are, Willow!"

Naomi emerged from another chair. "We ate way too much and are more than ready for our nightly walk with you and the dogs."

Nightly walk? This was news to me. I had to fight impending giggles again. "Great!" I turned to Jeremy. "Thank you so much for dinner and the offer of the sewing machine for poor Darlene Coddlefield's daughters."

"Think about my other offer. Midwest rep." His syllables had become clipped. Opal and Naomi must have surprised him.

"I'll let you go," I said. "You have a long drive to Cleveland."

He turned on his heel and marched down the sidewalk as if he couldn't leave quickly enough.

I suspected I would be giving Darlene's family a Chandler Champion all by myself with no help from him. It had turned into an expensive night. But an entertaining and perhaps informative one.

I let my two friends into In Stitches and

locked the door behind them. Jeremy was out of sight. "Thanks, you guys," I said, finally letting the laughter out.

"Smarmy." Protective of members of her extended family, Opal lowered her eyebrows in what she probably believed to be a very fierce expression. "I didn't like his looks."

"He was okay to look at." Naomi always had to be fair. "We hope you don't mind our interference, Willow." Naomi also liked to apologize.

"Not at all." I eased my feet out of the shoes. "He offered me a job that might one day allow me to live in New York City and enjoy its lofts and nightclubs."

"Willow," Naomi gasped. "You wouldn't go back there, would you?" She spoke as if Manhattan were the worst possible den of iniquity.

"Nope." Sally-Forth and Tally-Ho were whimpering at the door to the apartment. "Want to come outside with us?"

Naomi nodded. "Sure." She patted her waistline. Slender, she didn't carry an ounce of extra weight. "We did eat too much."

Offering me another of her fake glares, Opal really resembled Haylee. "And some *mystery* person paid for our dinner."

"It was delicious," Naomi said. "Thank you, Willow. We'll have you over to one of our apartments for a feast one of these evenings."

I opened the door to the stairs leading down to my apartment. "I'd love that, but there's no need to. You gave up your evening, and I really appreciate it. And thanks for being here when I got back, too." I could always count on my sisters-in-thread.

The dogs ran up and down the steps about a hundred times to make certain we were following them, which, of course, slowed our progress. I put on comfy flats and we all went outside. Naomi, Opal, and I toured my fragrant, night-lit garden and made fusses over the dogs whenever they returned to us. Eventually, the humans walked, with the dogs running circles around us, to the gate near the street. Opal and Naomi left for their apartments, and Sally, Tally, and I went back into ours.

Haylee phoned. "I gather you sent the new man away quickly."

"Yes, and Naomi and Opal were extremely helpful. Thank you."

"Actually, thank *you* for dinner. Clay feels like he owes you. That can only be good."

Someday, I hoped to renovate Blueberry Cottage with Clay's assistance. The paint on his ear had been cute, but I wondered how charming he'd find *me* if I were covered in sawdust, paint, and I was afraid to think what else. He had looked hot at the restaurant, and I had tried to. Had he noticed?

Haylee asked, "Did your date bring a swatch of fabric for you to admire?"

"I brought that." I explained about the sampler that Susannah had found. "If Darlene worked from left to right, she switched from a universal needle to a wing needle and back again, and turned off the wing needle override, all without a problem. The machine had to have been functioning properly when she did all that."

We went over the evening, every single course, our friends in the restaurant, everything that Jeremy had said, including his somewhat dubious promise to send a replacement sewing machine for Darlene's children. By the time I got off the phone, my face and sides were hurting from laughing. Not fair, I knew, but Jeremy deserved it, just as he and Felicity deserved one another and (if anyone were to ask me) their inferior line of sewing machines. And toasters, too, and whatever else the Chandler company sold.

I pulled Darlene's stitch sampler out of my bag and examined it, front and back, under strong light.

No bloodstains, strange holes, or stitches gone wild.

What had she been working on when her power switch broke?

21

Could Plug or someone have thrown out whatever Darlene was working on when her machine went berserk? Maybe Gartener's investigators had taken Darlene's project with them. Smallwood wouldn't be anxious to fill me in on that, but I did have news for her, so first thing in the morning, I called her and told her I had more evidence. It was Monday, the day our Threadville shops were closed.

Smallwood said she'd be at In Stitches in about an hour. She must have been busy. Either that or she was bringing Detective Gartener along again.

Sure enough, both of them arrived at the shop together. I told them that Jeremy had said a sledgehammer would have been required to break the power switch.

"Doesn't sound like he has much regard for the truth," Smallwood said.

"Maybe a screwdriver, used as a lever,"

Gartener suggested.

"Did the lab find evidence of that?" I asked him.

"We don't know yet," Smallwood said quickly as if to quell Gartener.

Gartener stared back at me with his dark, inscrutable eyes. I took it as confirmation that he believed that someone had used a screwdriver to tamper with the machine.

Attempting to ignore the chills needling their way up my spine, I showed them the stitch sampler stitching. "After that, someone disabled the wing needle override, loosened the needle shaft, damaged the power button, and put sticky stuff in the foot pedal."

"We don't know that someone actually *intended* to hurt her," Gartener reminded me.

Barely hiding a gasp, Smallwood looked up questioningly at him. I could almost hear her asking, *We don't?*

I became more certain than ever that these two knew something I didn't, some evidence they weren't making public.

Outside, a yellow VW drove slowly down Lake Street. Susannah was at the wheel. She peered toward the two cruisers parked in front of In Stitches, then sped away.

Gartener asked me, "Do you have any

idea who might have wanted to hurt the deceased?"

"Most likely, as I said before, it was someone in Darlene's household. Her husband, Plug, so he could be with the nanny, Tiffany. Or Tiffany so she could be with Plug."

Gartener wrote in his notebook. "People don't usually go to such lengths to carry on affairs." He didn't look at either of us and said it drily, like someone who had been unceremoniously dumped.

I asked, "Aren't murders frequently committed by those closest to the victim?"

Gartener kept writing, so of course I went on talking, as he probably expected me to. "And then there's their oldest son, Russ. His mother humiliated him in public the morning they were both here, and the night she died, he went roaring around the village in his truck, shouting out the windows."

Chief Smallwood shook her head. "You said that was around two. His mother was already dead, but he hadn't been home all evening. From what you told me about him running you and Edna off the road the next evening, that boy has a habit of reckless driving. I'll catch him at it one of these days, never fear."

Before he hurts someone, I thought. I

asked, "How did he find out about his mother's death?"

Smallwood looked to Gartener for an answer.

"His father told him," Gartener said. "No state troopers were present."

"And no one has questioned the boy?" I asked.

Smallwood glowered at me. "The investigators are looking into everything. Including . . ." She clammed up.

Including me? Susannah? I tried a different line of questioning. "When was Darlene found, and who found her?"

Smallwood didn't answer.

Gartener pointed at the pink fabric with the neat lines of white stitching. "May I take that with me?"

"It's yours," I said.

He placed the scrap into a brown paper bag, then folded the top of the bag as precisely as if he'd first measured and marked it with a ruler. "Could this have been what she was working on when the sewing machine fell on her?" he asked.

I straightened linen hanging from a bolt beside me. "If that machine was sewing madly like it did here on Saturday, the needle's shaft would have punched holes in the fabric and probably torn it. When she was found, whatever she was working on should have been in or near the machine."

Smallwood lifted one delicate eyebrow and one delicate but bulletproof-vested shoulder. She looked up into Gartener's face.

"You were on the scene before I was," he said to her in that warm voice that contrasted with his usually distant demeanor. "Did you see anything stitched like Willow just described?"

Smallwood shook her head firmly. "There was no fabric anywhere near that machine. Maybe whatever she was working on slipped out when the machine fell?"

"Only if someone cut the thread from both the spool and the bobbin," I said. "Maybe she had a habit of turning her sewing machine on before she collected what she was going to sew, but this time, with the pedal gummed up that way, the machine started stitching crazily and broke the needle. The fragment pierced her arm, and she dove under the table before she had a chance to get out whatever she was about to sew."

"Very likely," Smallwood agreed. Admonishing me to let them know if I found or thought of anything else, she left with Gartener.

I ran errands, shopped for groceries, prepared meals to freeze for the week, and baked cookies to serve in my store. I kept thinking about Darlene and the people who might have wanted to harm her. Chief Smallwood didn't seem to want to imagine a sixteen-year-old as a murderer, not even one as fond of dangerous pranks as Russ, and I didn't either. I suspected that Russ usually spent his time as far from his parents as he could, and wouldn't willingly venture anywhere near Darlene or her new sewing machine.

Darlene had humiliated most of her older children in my shop, from Russ to the other brother who hadn't worn his cowboy shirt but had cooperated enough with his mother to hold it out for everyone in the audience to see, to the twelve-year-old daughter who had been forced to wear a dress that was too tight and made her look silly. The fifteen-year-old girl had obviously been coached to photograph her mother accepting the certificate, and she had done as asked. Parents often angered their kids without the kids taking physical revenge. Darlene's children must have been used to her bossy ways.

My hair was in my eyes, and my hands were floury. I brushed at my forehead with the back of my wrist and rolled out more cookie dough. I was certain that neither the eight-year-old girl nor any of the three smallest children would have harmed their mother on purpose. I smiled again at the little girl's pronunciation. Dwess. She was adorable.

Tiffany had promised to make her more dresses.

Was Tiffany offering empty promises, or did she know how to sew? She'd obviously learned enough about the Chandler Champion to program a monogram into it, and she'd learned that very quickly, as if she'd sat in on the lesson Felicity gave Darlene. Tiffany wasn't a Threadville tour student, which wasn't surprising. Darlene hadn't been one, either, and if Tiffany was looking after the younger Coddlefield children, she didn't have time to come into the village for sewing lessons.

However, if Tiffany *did* start coming to our courses, we would be able to learn more about her . . .

It was possible that no amount of suggesting that she start attending Threadville classes would make her come, no matter how motivated she was, unless we suggested she bring the children. Could we cope with that? There were enough Threadville tourists in our classes to help look after all the kids.

Uh-oh. I was thinking too much like Haylee's mothers. If I was unconsciously imitating them, what else might I do? I was already making most of my own clothes. What would be next? Knitting my own lingerie?

I eased my sewing-machine-shaped cookie cutter into the rolled-out slab of dough. There was a lot about the Coddlefield family that didn't quite add up. Like having a nanny. Had Darlene worked outside the home?

Susannah had said that Darlene had volunteered as a fund-raiser for charities. Volunteers didn't get paid, and winning sewing and embroidery contests wouldn't put much food on the table, either. The Coddlefields needed a nanny now, but how had they justified having one before Darlene died? And how had they afforded it? Was farming that profitable?

I dug out Thursday's newspaper and reread Darlene's obituary. She'd been a "devoted stay-at-home mother." In lieu of flowers, donations should be made to charities — Koins for Kids, Kompassion for Kids, Kiddies' Korner, and Cure the Children. I'd never heard of any of them.

When the first batch of cookies was in the oven and the second batch was waiting on cookie sheets, I searched the Internet. All four charities had similar websites, with lists of donors. The three charities that seemed overly fond of the letter K used the same post office box in Erie. The same telephone number, too, but the exchange was a local one, not in Erie.

I called it.

A woman answered on the first ring. Unless I was mistaken, it was Tiffany. I hoped she wouldn't recognize my voice or do a reverse look-up, but just in case, I didn't pretend I was someone else, like a reporter. I didn't give my name, either, but blasted ahead with a question. "Can you tell me what Koins for Kids does?" My voice came out like candlewick rubbing against burlap.

"We . . ." There was a pause as if she had to think about the answer. "We provide funds for needy children. Totally."

How enlightening. "What do they use the funds for?" Great question, too.

"Food, clothes, housing." Another pause. "You name it."

"Is this for children all over the world?"

"All over America."

"How do I send a donation?" Having no

intention of making one, I crossed my fingers.

Tiffany rattled off the address.

I thanked her and hung up. She'd had trouble naming the charity's goals and mission, but could spiel out the P.O. box number and zip code.

I was tempted to call the other two charities that shared the Koins for Kids phone number, but Tiffany would undoubtedly answer and figure out who I was.

The fourth charity, Cure the Children, had a different phone number and post office box, but the phone number was also an Elderberry Bay exchange. I'd heard of people disguising their voices by draping a tissue over the receiver. I tried a lightweight piece of linen instead, and dialed the number.

"Cure the Children, Miss Quantice speaking." Tiffany, again, sounding annoyed. I hoped she didn't have number recognition.

I pitched my voice higher than believable for anyone larger than a squirrel. "Sorry, wrong number."

She slammed her phone down. The nanny Darlene had hired was running children's charities during the hours I'd have thought she'd be looking after Darlene's children. Had Darlene been scamming people, obtaining donations for fake charities? And Tiffany had taken over. Strange.

I phoned Chief Smallwood. "I heard that Darlene volunteered for charities," I told her.

"And this is pertinent because . . . ?" Smallwood was always so helpful.

"I called two of those charities."

"Whatever for?" Smallwood exploded.

"They're listed in Darlene's obituary for donations instead of flowers, and I wanted to know more about the charities before I donated."

Apparently, I didn't fool her. "You're to keep out of this investigation, hear?"

"Yes, of course." I crossed my fingers. "But it got interesting. I recognized the voice of the woman who answered the calls. It was Tiffany, Darlene's nanny." And then just to be certain that Smallwood knew who I meant, I added. "Darlene's husband's *girl*-friend."

"Would it be strange for Darlene's nanny to take over some of the volunteer jobs that her boss — her *late* boss — had been do-ing?"

"Not if those charities are real. I suspect they aren't." It was my turn to put her in the hot seat. "Are they?"

"We're looking into everything." Some hot

seat. I had a feeling she knew the answer and was only being difficult. "Do me a favor," she said.

I hated it when she spoke to me like I was a slightly amusing child. "Okay." Smallwood was going to tell me to butt out.

"Look at the list of donors for Koins for Kids." She sounded a little too pleased with herself. "Tell me if you recognize any of the names."

I stared at my computer screen. One name jumped out at me.

I skimmed through the list again. There was no point in lying. I admitted in a small voice, "The only name I recognize is Susannah Kessler."

"Isn't that funny?" Smallwood obviously enjoyed being sarcastic. "That's the only name on any of the lists that I recognize, too."

22

Susannah's fear of the police on Saturday night had seemed to stem from something in addition to memories of a childhood fire, and she'd been nervous at Opal's storytelling on Friday when she'd disclosed that Darlene had raised funds for charities. Had she been afraid that someone might discover she'd been one of the donors? "Susannah would never hurt anyone," I told Smallwood.

"Being that certain about others can be dangerous, you know." Smallwood's stern personality overcame her usually friendly telephone manners. "Trust me on this. The police know better than you do. And we will do the investigating. All of it."

"So you're checking into all of the charities, and *all* of the donors? Any of them might have borne a grudge against Darlene if they thought they had donated money to Darlene instead of to a charity."

"We're looking at everything," she again told me. "*You* keep out of it." She hung up.

I reread donor names on all four sites. I didn't recognize any other names. Only Susannah's.

Baking the rest of the cookies, I thought about Susannah. What did it all mean?

I could imagine Susannah being sad if she discovered that Darlene's fund-raising was fraudulent. But angry enough to arrange Darlene's death? I'd never seen her show the slightest annoyance, even about her ex. Only an overwhelming despair about a husband who didn't love her, after all. Worse, he was now accusing her of possibly harming Darlene.

I still suspected Russ, Tiffany, and Plug. And maybe Felicity, too, though I couldn't figure out why she'd damage one of her employer's sewing machines.

When I'd called Smallwood just now, she'd already known about the charities. Grudgingly, I admitted to myself that she was right. I should leave the investigating to the police.

Besides, if I didn't concentrate on my IMEC entry on my one day off, I probably wouldn't finish it in time to display it along with the others at the Harvest Festival. I still hadn't come up with an easy way of replicating old-fashioned candlewicking embroidery stitches.

I went up to In Stitches. Across the street, Haylee was rearranging the front windows of The Stash. I loved the natural fabrics I sold in my shop, but sometimes I just had to touch other fabrics.

Maybe they could be the solution to my candlewicking problem. What about using a nubby fabric, corduroy, for instance, and creating a very narrow appliqué in a winding shape? Wouldn't that resemble the lumps of knotted candlewick that had been used in place of embroidery floss?

I ran across the street. Haylee was, as always, happy to have me browse through textiles with her. I chose mid-wale corduroy in a perfect shade of off-white.

Folding my purchase, she grinned. "You're copying something made of candle wicks, and my mothers are using quilting, knitting, and weaving ribbons to copy something like fiery embroidery."

"Flame stitch," I supplied. "Otherwise known as bargello." I held one index finger up. "I could program my embroidery software to create a bargello-type pattern, and then frame it with my meandering white 'candlewicking' frame!"

Eager to begin, I didn't stay at Haylee's,

even though she offered coffee and cookies.

I ran to Naomi's shop. In her front room, surrounded by handmade quilts and haloed by light from her windows, she sat at a long-armed quilting machine and stitched free-hand over her colorful bargello quilt. Calm seemed to radiate from her as she concentrated. Her narrow fingers expertly guided the stitching.

It took her a while to realize I was there, and when she did, she jumped and apologized in her soft, kind way. "I was in a different world."

I asked if I could borrow the colored diagram she'd made for the quilt.

She sent me to her desk in the back room. I picked up the paper, admired her work, thanked her, then dashed back to In Stitches, where I scanned her drawing into my favorite embroidery software program.

The rest was easy. I clicked on the icons that told the software to transform the picture into an embroidery design. In only minutes, my screen showed what the flame stitch pattern would look like when "painted" in thread.

Naturally, I had every shade of embroidery thread I would need to match Naomi's multi-hued drawing. The stitching and thread-changing took a while, but the end result was beautiful.

Flame stitch, candlewicking . . . I'd been trying to put the next night's firefighters' training session out of my mind. Apparently, I wasn't succeeding.

I could carry the theme to extremes, too. Another age-old embroidery stitch, fire stitch, resembled flames. Simple curved lines were open at the bottom and closed in points at the top. I saved my bargello design under a new name and superimposed bright orange fire stitch "flames" on it.

Next was my attempt at candlewicking, actually a very thin appliqué framing the colorful part of the embroidery. Appliquéing was easy with embroidery machines, software, and hoops.

Ordinarily, the first step in machine embroidery appliqué would be causing the software to stitch the shape of the finished appliqué on the base fabric so I could see where to place the appliqué fabric. For this project, though, the appliqué would frame the entire base fabric, my colorful bargello pattern with the orange "flames" embroidered on top. All I had to do was cover my entire design with a piece of corduroy. If I placed it straight up and down, I'd have short ridges and furrows on the top and bottom of my corduroy frame and long stripes of corduroy on the sides. I turned the corduroy on the diagonal.

Then I had the software stitch a wavy line around where I wanted the outside of the frame to be, and a slightly smaller wavy box just inside the first.

When I was done, the stitched corduroy still covered Naomi's bargello design. Careful to keep the fabrics tight in the embroidery hoop, I removed the hoop from the machine. I clipped out the inside of the corduroy close to my stitching, then snipped the excess away from the outside of my thin white frame, and I had it — a narrow, twisty, bumpy, off-white decoration around the outside of the colorful flame stitch design.

The final touch was reattaching the hooped design to my embroidery machine and outlining both the inner and outer edges of my corduroy "candlewicking" with satin stitching that was just wide enough to hide the corduroy's raw edges.

Flame stitch, fire stitch, and candlewicking, all on one small wall hanging, almost like an embroidered pun. I wasn't sure it would win any IMEC prizes, but it had been fun to create. And wasn't that what hobbies were all about?

Fire. I couldn't put off getting ready for the next night's firefighting session much longer. I dragged out the manual Isaac had given me and studied it on the patio in the seemingly never-ending summer afternoon.

After supper, I leashed the dogs and took them out the back gate to the riverside trail. Ordinarily, I might have simply walked, but failing the physical fitness part of the fire-fighters' exam could be embarrassing, so we jogged, south, away from the lake. Leashed jogging was apparently very exciting. We frequently tumbled to the ground in heaps of leashes, arms, legs, and paws. It worked, more or less, as exercise, and I may have run as much as two miles. Crisscrossing back and forth in front of me, the dogs probably ran twice as far. When we arrived back at the gate leading into our yard beside Blueberry Cottage, I was panting at least as much as Sally and Tally were.

We'd had so little rainfall during the summer that the only water in the river was a narrow stream meandering down the middle. We would be able to hop over that stream now, but rain could fall again any day, and we might never have another chance to cross the river here, conveniently close to home. We had never explored the state forest on the other side.

Hanging on to the dogs' leashes with one hand and to tree trunks with the other, I sidestepped down the bank to the river bed.

The earth was not as solid as it looked.

I ended up on my rear in thick, oozy mud with a fragrance that was more attractive to the dogs than to me. The leashes were in my right hand, and I didn't dare let go for fear my dogs would take off. I rolled over onto my hands and knees and pushed myself up until only my hands and feet were in the mud. My hands sank up to the leashes looped around my wrists. Wet clay plopped off my bare knees. My feet went in up to my ankles.

Sally and Tally liked nothing better than mud wrestling, and now, as far as they were concerned, I was joining them. They barked and danced, coating themselves and me in grime. Instead of crawling up the bank like a sensible person, I collapsed laughing, in the mud.

"Pull me home," I gasped.

They barked faster. Sally had a way of running her yips together until she was almost howling.

I laughed so hard that anyone hearing me could have believed I was howling, too. Luckily, no one was anywhere near.

"Willow!" A man, shouting nearby.

Oops.

It was all I could do not to truly howl.

And not with laughter. I recognized that voice.

Clay.

23

"Shhh!" I told the dogs. "Pretend we're not here."

No luck. Sally and Tally recognized Clay's voice and accelerated their barking so he could find them. And me.

My gate clanged. Clay must have come from Lake Street, climbed over the locked gate into my side yard, run down my sloping backyard, and now he'd gone through the gate beside Blueberry Cottage. He had to be on the trail above the river. "Sally, Tally!" He sounded tense.

I didn't want him to find me in my mud-covered predicament. I lowered my head. At closer range, the mud didn't smell any better.

My two sweet doggies strained up the bank toward their hero, but they were attached to a wallowing monster. Me.

They almost got away. Their leashes slipped from my wrist to my hand as my fist popped out of the mud. I tightened my fingers on the leashes, and the two doggies pulled me, with horrible sucking and burbling sounds, free.

I willed Clay not to find me. Mud weighed my eyelids down. If I couldn't see him, maybe he couldn't see me.

But it would have been hard for him to miss the gleeful dogs. Warm fingers extricated the leashes from my hand.

I muttered, "Don't touch me. I'm filthy." He didn't obey.

The next thing I knew, I was being dragged unceremoniously by the wrists up the bank. A truly romantic man would have picked me up and carried me all the way home.

A truly romantic man would have done all that without noticing my mud or having any of it transfer to him.

On the other hand, a truly romantic woman would not have rolled around in a distinctly soggy riverbed.

Soft cloth rubbed mud from my eyes and face. I peeked between my sodden eyelashes. Clay had taken off his T-shirt and was using it as a washcloth. I had never seen his bare torso before. Distracting. Then again, I needed to be distracted, or I'd have slunk away and hidden for two hundred years.

"Are you okay?" Oh, no, his usual question again. Maybe I should have convinced the mud to swallow me whole. "What on earth happened?"

"*Earth* happened. Muddy earth." A giggle slipped out.

"Are you hurt?"

I shook my head.

He leaned back on his heels and looked me over.

"I didn't break anything. The landing was rather soft." I bit back another giggle.

Brows together, Clay helped me to my feet.

My sneakers had stayed on, but had become giant paws, more mud than shoes, and I was at least an inch taller than I'd been before I fell. To conquer an onslaught of giggles, I asked Clay, "What are you doing here?"

"I was driving up Lake Street from the beach and heard your dogs barking." He cocked his head and grinned. "It sounded pretty exciting."

For them it was, and they were still bouncing around and licking our hands.

"The lake's nice and warm," he said. "Maybe we should all go for a swim." He was already in damp swim trunks.

I looked down at my mud-caked shorts

and T-shirt. I was hopelessly encrusted. "Is the beach crowded? I'd prefer not to be seen by anyone." Including the man at my side, but it was kind of late for that.

Muscles twitched around his mouth. Okay, so I wasn't the only one trying not to laugh. "No one would recognize you." That helped. Not.

However, putting this unwanted mud in the lake, where it should have been heading eventually, did seem like a better idea than carting it home.

Clay and I each took a leash and jogged with the dogs the short distance along the trail to the beach. As we passed The Sunroom, I averted my face. Maybe no one on the glassed-in balcony would see that last night's sexy sophisticate had turned herself into a grubby waif.

At the beach, people were still lying on towels in the warm sand or finishing their evening barbecues. Several strolled along the water's edge. Clay threw his T-shirt down, then all four of us plunged into the water. It was heavenly, almost bath temperature. Mud billowed from me. Suddenly, a wall of water hit me in the face. Still holding Tally's leash, Clay splashed me. I ran the flat of my hand across the water and reciprocated, then took a deep breath and ducked under. I came up to find Sally swimming close to my face and looking extremely worried. "I'm okay, Sally," I gasped. I swear she smiled.

As clean as possible under the circumstances, I waded onto the sandy beach. Clay dipped his T-shirt into the waves, wrung it out, and passed it to me to use as a towel. I wiped my face and gave it back. My hair hung in wet strands. How very becoming. Clutching the leashes, we ran back up the trail. My sneakers made rude squelching sounds.

I didn't even want to think what a truly romantic woman would do.

There was one saving grace. The bra underneath my wet T-shirt was pretty and lacy, and *not* the hand-knit one I'd imagined while worrying that I was becoming too much like Haylee's mothers.

I opened the gate next to Blueberry Cottage.

Clay asked, "Need help cleaning the dogs?" He looked like he was about to use his T-shirt on them.

"They have their own towels," I said quickly. "If —" Panicking, I reached into the pocket of my shorts. "Whew. I still have my keys."

Clay accompanied us up the hill to the

sliding glass door leading to my great room. The evening was balmy, and our clothes had already begun to dry. I worked my feet out of my sneakers and tiptoed inside for doggie towels, red to contrast with Sally's pretty black and ermine coat, tan for my handsome brindle and white Tally. I had embroidered their names and doggie paw prints on their towels.

I tossed Sally's towel to Clay. Sally loved being rubbed. Tally was more businesslike, and considered himself to be clean and dry long before Sally was willing to give up Clay's attention, which gave me time to go back inside and fetch a plate of cookies and two big glasses of lemonade. Outside, dusk softened the air, but after weeks of heat, the dampness in my clothes was refreshing. We sat on Adirondack chairs overlooking Blueberry Cottage and the riverbed beyond it. The dogs flopped down at our feet.

"Did the dogs pull you into the river?" Clay's tone was very polite, giving me the chance to save face.

I couldn't blame my dogs. "It was all my doing. I wanted to see if we could cross the river and go hiking in the state forest, but we sank into more mud than I anticipated."

"The bridge is easier." His voice was still mild, but he was obviously on the verge of laughter.

"I found that out. Wouldn't it be nice if we could just cross the river from my backyard?"

He finally let the laugh out. "I suppose."

"I guess I was a pretty funny sight."

He took a deep breath in the darkness. "Actually, you weren't. I'd heard you laughing, but by the time I saw you, you were silent."

Because I'd been hoping you wouldn't discover me . . . "You didn't think I was dead, did you?" What was I thinking? A truly romantic woman would never have said such a thing.

"I didn't know what to think."

"Thanks for rescuing me. Us."

"You'd have gotten out on your own."

I wasn't so sure.

Not only did he always seem to have to help others, he always followed up. He asked, "Did the light that Russ Coddlefield changed for you keep working?"

"Yes."

"What did you think of him?"

"He's . . . unhappy, I think. His mother was mean to him after you left. That appeared to make him mad." I decided that Clay didn't need to know that Russ had gone joyriding through the village before he was told that his mother had been killed by her sewing machine, or that he had forced Edna's car off the road.

Clay frowned. "Poor kid. He was probably still angry at her when she died, and now he'll have to live with regret." He took a long drink of lemonade. "Russ wants to come work for me. He wants to drop out of high school with only a year to go. I hired him for the summer, and now he thinks he doesn't need his diploma and can just keep working for me year-round."

I guessed, "So you told him to finish school and reapply next summer?"

"You got it. But he just stomped away. He needs to work on his temper."

"When was this, before or after his mother died?"

"Before," Clay said.

Russ's mother had treated him like a baby in public. His father may have already been pursuing a young nanny. Russ had legitimate reasons to be angry.

"He wants to be an electrician," Clay said. "He's shown me some of his work. Computerized light shows for holidays, things like that. He's good."

Maybe Russ would figure out that Clay's suggestion about completing high school would help him in the long run. I was glad that The Three Weird Mothers weren't part of this conversation. They'd be planning the kid's life, maybe offering to supervise his homework.

Clay was being so nicely companionable that I took a chance on acting the damsel in distress. Again.

However, telling him about the peculiar outlet in my shop had to be more professional than needing to be dragged up the bank of a river.

"I'm a licensed electrician," he said after I finished my tale of woe, "and I supervised the wiring in your place. Let's go see."

The dogs went with us. I was afraid I wouldn't be able to replicate the problem, but I jiggled a plug in the outlet, and lights flashed.

"Sorry, Willow, I had no idea I'd left it like this. I've got tools in my truck." He always did. He went outside, then came back in with the supplies he needed. He knelt in front of the outlet. The dab of paint was gone from his ear. I kind of missed it.

However, it was almost gratifying that he or one of his employees may have installed a faulty outlet and failed to test it. If Clay wasn't completely perfect, maybe he could overlook some of my flaws. After he replaced the outlet with a new one, no amount of wiggling a plug caused trouble.

We went back outside, plunked ourselves into the lawn chairs again, and watched the dogs' antics. I'd been selling lots of high-end sewing and embroidery machines and had put away a nice sum toward the renovations I wanted to do in Blueberry Cottage. I asked him when he would be available to supervise.

"How about next spring?"

"Sure."

"I'll put it on my calendar." He levered himself out of his chair. "Thanks for the cookies and lemonade."

"Thanks for the rescue. And for repairing the outlet. And for the bath in the lake."

He bent until his face was close to mine.

24

Was Clay leaning in for a kiss?

I couldn't help a tiny quiver. A tiny, *unthinking* quiver.

Away from him.

A truly romantic woman would have quivered toward him.

He peered at my face in the darkness. "You may want to scrub a little harder at that mud."

I clapped a hand over my mouth and backed farther from him. I must have looked as wretched as I felt. And considerably dirtier.

"It's not that bad," he said. "You look fine."

A truly romantic man would have taken me in his arms and sworn undying love despite the mud. Somehow, I wasn't liking the image I was building of the truly romantic man, so it was just as well that Clay wasn't fitting it.

"I climbed over your front gate to get in," the truly unromantic man said. "Do you have a key to let me out?"

I gabbled something agreeable, and the dogs and I went with him up through the side yard. I unlocked the gate.

Clay left, carrying his damp T-shirt and whistling.

We were friends again. He'd forgiven me for the mistakes I'd made. The dogs were delighted. They loved Clay. Maybe they'd see more of him.

They'd like that.

And so, I had to admit, would I.

I didn't know if the dogs had sweet dreams that night, but they didn't howl or cry, and I didn't exactly have nightmares.

But in the morning, a nightmarish thought returned. I had promised Isaac I'd go to the volunteer fire department training session that evening. I didn't want to become a fire-fighter, and I also didn't want to fail the tests in public. I only wanted to find out more about Plug. If I could prove he had damaged the sewing machine in a way that killed his wife, the police could stop snooping around Susannah and me. I also didn't want In Stitches to have a reputation for providing malfunctioning sewing machines.

While I was teaching the morning embroidery class, Jeremy Chandler called to assure me that he had arrived safely home in New York. I'd barely given him a thought since Sunday evening after Naomi and Opal made it clear he would have no time alone with me.

He had talked to his insurance company and was authorizing a new Chandler Champion to be sent to my store. "Meanwhile, why not take the one you have to the bereaved family?" he suggested.

I said I would.

"And think about my offer. I don't think I can keep Felicity Ranquels on my staff much longer. I fear she's not making friends for Chandler."

I didn't point out that manufacturing possibly lethal sewing machines was also not very beneficial to his company's image.

Susannah arrived early to give me my midday break. No customers were in the shop, but she pulled me toward the back of the store. "Those police officers were back here yesterday."

"I saw you drive past."

She blanched. "I was just running errands and saw their cars. What did they want?"

Why did she want to know? "I called them. I told them that the Chandler company president said that it would have taken

240

a sledgehammer to break a Champion's power switch."

"Not true. That plastic was flimsy." Color rushed back to her cheeks. "I saw it when you opened the machine. It looked like someone had prodded at it with . . . well, not a sledgehammer."

"Maybe a screwdriver?"

She nodded.

We still had no customers. "Susannah, on Friday night at storytelling, you mentioned that Darlene volunteered for charities. What do you know about them?"

Susannah evaded my gaze. "She collected money for them."

"Do you think those charities were legitimate?"

She shrugged.

"You donated to one of them."

She still wouldn't look at me. "How do you know?"

"The charities list the donors on their website."

"That's horrible! I didn't say they could use my name."

I pressed harder. "Chief Smallwood is checking on those charities and everyone who contributed to them. She found your name."

Susannah studied her feet for a couple of

heartbeats. When she raised her head, panic struggled with horror in her eyes. "Oh, Willow," she whispered. "I'm so afraid the police will find out what I did."

25

Susannah wasn't the only person who couldn't hide her emotions. Her confession had shocked me. "What did you do, Susannah?"

She darted a glance toward my row of sewing machines. "I didn't hurt a machine or anything. I didn't hurt Darlene. But I threatened her."

"How?" I needed to sit down. I leaned back against a shelf of lightweight linens.

"Those charities Darlene wanted money for? They weren't charities. The money was going right to her. That's how she could afford a nanny and all those expensive sewing machines and everything. I . . . I wrote to her and demanded my contribution back." She sounded and looked absolutely wretched.

"What did she say?"

"Nothing. I only mailed the letter the day

before she died. I wish I hadn't sent it at all."

There was only one thing she could do. "You're going to have to tell Chief Small-wood."

She shook her head. "I can't."

"Detective Gartener, then. He's not as scary as he looks."

She repeated, "I can't. They'll think I killed her, and I didn't."

"What did you say in the letter?"

"I didn't blackmail her or anything. I should have said I would report her to the authorities if she didn't repay my contribution. But I didn't know which authorities to threaten her with — the state police? The IRS? The FBI? So I just said I would take action. That could be read the wrong way."

It certainly could. "That's why you have to talk to the police before they find the letter. Tell them what you said and what you really meant."

She kept shaking her head. "Maybe they've already read it."

"You should still tell them about it."

She pulled a strand of her long, curly hair into her mouth, clamped her lips around it, and shook her head.

I pointed out, "You might not be the only donor who was upset at giving money to a fake charity, and someone else may have been more than upset." Might have gone into a murderous rage? "Tell the police what you know about the charities. It could be important."

"I guess you're right." She was saved by the bell, or at least by my front door chimes. She rushed off to greet customers, and I went downstairs to share lunch outside with my dogs. It was another glorious, if rainless, day.

When I went back to In Stitches, Susannah headed for the door. I caught up and murmured to her, "Call Smallwood. She's not an ogre."

She gasped. "I'm supposed to be back at Batty About Quilts right this very minute." She ran out the front door.

If she didn't confess, what could I do? Should I do? Other than keep my eyes open for that letter when I delivered the Chandler Champion to Tiffany . . .

After the Threadville shops closed for the day, I phoned Edna, who was, of course, eager to help deliver the Chandler Champion. She offered to drive, but I said that, no, it was my turn. I wasn't certain I ever again wanted to be a passenger in a car Edna was driving.

We'd barely made it out of the village

when I heard the distinctive keening erupt from the siren on top of the fire station. Fields on both sides of the road were still parched. Off to the south, dark smoke rose. That had to be where the fire trucks would head.

We drove down the Coddlefields' long, winding driveway. No fire chief's SUV. Russ's truck wasn't in front of the house, either.

I parked behind a small black sedan. Preferring to be certain that Tiffany was home before we lugged the heavy sewing machine to the house, Edna and I walked up the gravel driveway past the sedan. Its engine ticked.

Ever the sleuth, Edna said, "Someone else has just arrived."

We climbed the porch steps. Inside the house, children screamed with despair.

Edna and I looked at each other. "This is too much," she muttered under her breath. "Those kids are not being well cared for."

"It's probably hard to keep them from crying," I reminded her.

Heaving a sympathetic sigh, she knocked on the screen door's wooden frame.

No one came, and the children continued bawling. I pushed the button for the door bell.

Tiffany sprinted down the hall from the back of the house and opened the door wide. Her face was flushed. "Thanks for . . ." She looked down at our feet. "I thought you were bringing my . . ." She turned redder. "Um, bringing the kids their sewing machine."

I explained, "We wanted to make sure you were here before we got it out of the car. That sewing machine is heavy."

She nodded twice, a decisive gesture. "I'll carry it."

Edna flung her arms straight out like she was flying. "No. You —" She paused, then repeated the word emphatically. "*You* go comfort those children."

Edna undoubtedly thought she was being subtle.

I turned quickly so that neither of them could see my horrified amusement. Calling over my shoulder, "We'll be right back," I trotted toward my car.

Edna followed me. "Shall I take one side of the carton and you take the other?"

I remembered being pulled around by a hot lasagna. "I'll carry it. Can you open and close doors for me?" I tugged the carton across the backseat until I got both hands underneath it.

"Good idea," she crowed. "We can be in

the kitchen with those kids before she returns to the front door."

Carton in my arms, I staggered toward the porch. Edna slammed my car door, then flitted ahead of me. Before I got anywhere near the screen door, she had pulled it open slowly, minimizing its squeaks. I walked into the foyer. No one, I was glad to see, had taken down the framed antique linens that Darlene must have loved.

Tiffany rushed toward us from the direction of the kitchen. "Sorry, I should have gotten the door for you." She must have succeeded in comforting the children. I didn't hear even the tiniest sob.

"Where would you like this?" I managed not to drop the thing. I was beginning to fervently dislike Chandler Champions.

"Leave it on the table in the dining room. I'll carry it up to the sewing room later. It's way up on the third floor."

"We can take it," Edna offered.

We could?

Edna added another of her subtle hints. "You have those kids . . ."

Tiffany brushed hair from her face. "They're fine. I sent them to the basement to watch TV. It's the only thing that takes their minds off" — she made a sad little moue of her mouth — "you know. Their

248

mother."

"Oh, dear," Edna said. "We do know."

The Chandler Champion must have gained three hundred pounds since I removed it from the car. "I don't think you can carry it upstairs by yourself, Tiffany," I cautioned her. "Maybe you should leave it for Plug."

That did it. Tiffany suggested that she and I could carry it together. She slid her hands underneath the carton. Edna zipped around us and up the stairs as if she hoped to uncover important clues to Darlene's death, like maybe a written confession.

We passed bedrooms. Pink frills and bunk beds in one, blue trucks and bunk beds in another. All of the beds were covered in quilts that Darlene must have made. She'd outdone herself with the intricate quilt on the king-sized bed in a large corner room.

Edna pounded up the flight above us. With determination, gritting of teeth, and tensing of muscles, Tiffany and I carried that five-ton sewing machine up the top flight of stairs without tumbling back down.

The sewing room took up the entire south end of the attic, with high, sloping ceilings, and windows on three sides, plenty of storage, and a dressmaker's dummy in Darlene's size.

I could barely wait to set the sewing machine down, preferably at table height, but apparently, no one had tidied away Darlene's work. All three tables were loaded — a top-of-the-line sewing and embroidery machine from a reliable manufacturer, a serger, fabrics, patterns, cutting mats, notions, and the pieces of a small dress cut from pink calico with tiny lavender flowers printed over it. Would anyone ever finish the little girl's dwess? Again, I felt sorry for the woman whose life had ended too soon. If she'd lived to a ripe old age, she would have had plenty of time to finish all of these projects and begin many more.

Breathing heavily after the climb, Tiffany stared at a bare corner. "I forgot! They took the table the machine was on."

Edna bunched fabrics together and made room on another table. "Who took it?"

"The investigators."

Edna's eyes widened, and I could see she was wondering the same thing I was. *Why would the police take a sewing table as evidence?*

26

Fearing that Tiffany would pick up on Edna's and my silent communication about the police removing Darlene's sewing table for evidence, I looked away from Edna. I hoped that Darlene had appreciated her sewing room, a dream of natural light, plenty of space, work tables, and built-in cabinets.

Tiffany and I eased the carton onto the table Edna had cleared, then rested, huffing and puffing, against the table. Edna trotted to the cut-out dwess. "Adorable!"

"I'm going to finish it," Tiffany said.

A phone rang in a room in the northern end of the attic. The room's door was open enough for me to see a cluttered desk and at least two phones. Was this where the charity work was done? Would police investigators go through all those papers on the desk, or had they already taken away what they wanted? If only I could spend a few minutes in that room, maybe I could find the letter Susannah had sent to Darlene . . . And do what with it?

Following my glance toward the phone, Tiffany flapped a hand in dismissal. "The answering service will get it." Maybe it was just as well that I wouldn't be tempted to remove evidence.

Edna asked, "Why did the investigators take a sewing table?"

Because something about it was wrong. Gartener and Smallwood had hinted that they had evidence of murderous intent besides the obvious sabotage of the sewing machine. Like maybe they knew that someone had sawed the table's legs partway through and . . .

"It collapsed," Tiffany said, as if collapsing sewing tables were a common occurrence. "That's how the sewing machine ended up on top of Darlene."

"Did you see it on her?" Edna was apparently abandoning every attempt at subtlety or tact.

"I was away, at my apartment. I've moved here now so I can be here evenings and nights if Plug gets called out to a fire, but then I was only here days." She blushed.

"So this happened in the evening?" Edna asked her.

"Yes. That day, I took the little kids to story-telling at the library at four thirty. I brought them home to Darlene around six. Plug got home around ten."

The blush deepened as if Plug had been with Tiffany that evening. Maybe they'd told the police they were together to establish their alibis.

"Plug found Darlene. He was, like, devastated. I asked the kids who put them to bed that night. They said that Darlene did. She usually tucked them in around eight, then headed up here to sew."

Edna continued her cross-examination. "Do you know who else was here that evening?"

"As far as I know, only Darlene and the five youngest kids. The three little ones were sleeping and the eight-year-old and twelve-year-old were in the basement watching TV. They didn't hear anything. Which reminds me. I'd better get downstairs. I can't hear the little ones from up here."

Edna offered, "While you're with them, want us to set this machine up for you and test it?"

"No, that's fine." Tiffany engaged me with her clear-eyed look. "A manual should be packed with it, right?"

"Yes," I agreed. "I checked. And this is a

floor model, and has been working perfectly." *And it should continue to . . .*

Tiffany herded us downstairs.

In the foyer, Edna made another attempt to stay. "Is there anything else we can do? I used to play games with our daughter." That would be Haylee. "We could entertain the children for a half hour or so while you —" She glanced toward the dining room. "Set the table and prepare dinner."

Tiffany edged us toward the front door. "That's all under control, and they set the table. It's always been their job. I try to keep up their routine as best I can."

"Have you been with them long?" Edna made her interrogation into a polite, sympathetic conversation. I had to admire her persistence.

"I've been their au pair for two years."

With a hand on her wrist, I urged Edna toward the porch. "They're lucky to have you." I wasn't sure I came across as sincere. If Tiffany had caused their mother's death, the children weren't lucky at all.

Edna was probably thinking the same thing. She didn't move despite my tugging. Was she trying to manufacture more ways for us to stick around and snoop?

"Hurry," Tiffany said. "Plug's gone to a fire. If he comes back and sees you here, there will be questions. It's better if he doesn't see your car, either."

Edna jutted her chin out. "He'll see the sewing machine."

Tiffany ran her hand across her forehead, letting a couple of fingers wipe her eyes as if tears had leaked out. "He's not likely to go into the sewing room again, ever. Being up there to pack that sewing machine nearly killed him. He swore he'd never go back." She bowed her head until her straight blond hair curtained her face. "Darlene's daughters deserve the machine. Like totally."

I tightened my fingers around Edna's wrist and hauled her outside.

On the driveway, Edna pulled out of my grasp. "What got into you, Willow? Every time we come here, I end up black and blue."

"Let's go," I muttered. "I don't feel safe here."

She showed me her wrist, the bruises that Tiffany had made last time, and the pinkish marks from my fingers just now. "Me, neither, but you seem to be the greatest danger to me." Her eyes twinkled. She loved teasing Opal, Naomi, and Haylee, and as far as she was concerned, I was a member of their family, too.

We got into the car. Edna asked, "Are you

afraid Russ and Plug might come back?"

I drove down the driveway "That, and Tiffany was lying about something."

"Murdering Darlene, most likely," Edna contributed drily.

"Or these daughters of Darlene's who *must* have a sewing machine. In a sewing room that is too painful for their philandering father to visit. He exchanges an old wife for a younger model, and the two older daughters, who didn't seem very happy with their mother, to put it mildly, are going to ensconce themselves in their mother's sewing room beside her dressmaker's dummy and take up her hobby?"

"None of it adds up, does it?" Edna asked.

"It adds up to Tiffany selling that machine and pocketing the proceeds. Plug and his kids won't even know." I drove back to our shops and apartments.

I ate outside on my patio while the dogs romped around, but trepidation about the adventure in store for me — learning how to fight fires — nearly spoiled my dinner. Fortunately, Haylee was going, too, so maybe the whole thing would be bearable. Or, knowing us, we'd be kicked off the force for laughing too much.

It might be a good idea.

The evening was hot, without a whiff of a

breeze. I changed into old jeans, a T-shirt, and comfortable running shoes. The dogs looked woebegone when I told them to stay. Kissing them good-bye, I promised to return before long.

Haylee and I got into her bright red pickup truck, and she drove to the ball field.

The first thing I saw there made me want to ask Haylee to turn around and drive home again.

A red truck. Not the fire truck, although that was there, too.

Clay's pickup.

27

Surely, even though Clay and I seemed to be on friendlier terms again, he wouldn't think I was chasing him.

Isaac waved at us from a group of men next to the fire truck, but Clay strode to my side of Haylee's pickup. He asked through the open window, "Are you two okay?"

When would he stop believing I was always in dire straits?

I gave him a confident smile. "We're here for the training." That would show him that I didn't need help *all* the time. "Are you, too?"

"I'm already on the force. You two aren't by any chance trying to solve a murder, are you?"

I climbed out of Haylee's truck and stood facing him, nose-to-nose. Nose-to-throat, actually, since no matter how much I stretched, he was taller. I backed up and tilted my head until I looked him in the eyes. "No one has said it was a murder. Mona thought that a couple of Threadville proprietors should become firefighters, and she . . . um, volunteered us. This was before Darlene died."

Isaac called, "We're ready to start."

The three of us walked toward the group near the fire truck. Tall brown grasses swished against our jeans.

Plug Coddlefield's terse nod contrasted with Isaac's wide and welcoming grin. Russ Coddlefield shuffled his feet and didn't look at Haylee or me, though his gaze did flick toward Clay. Four other boys about Russ's age, dressed in jeans, ball caps, and T-shirts, stared at Haylee and me like we were from outer space.

Haylee and I introduced ourselves, but no one else did. Maybe they already had, though we weren't late.

"We're all here —" Isaac began.

Plug stepped in front of him. "I'm running this, not you."

Isaac backed away, hunched his shoulders, and flapped his hands, palms up. "Whatever."

Plug threw his cigarette butt onto the grass and ground it out with a boot. "All you applicants, line up in front of me."

We did. Russ, the four boys, Haylee, and me.

"Not behind each other," Plug thundered. "Beside each other."

Where were we, in elementary school? We rearranged ourselves.

"Shoulders back," he ordered. "Feet together, hands behind your backs."

I did all that, adding chin up. Defiantly. Although Clay was facing us, I couldn't tell what he was thinking. So far, Haylee and I were keeping up with the other recruits, except that we didn't squirm and grumble, at least not noticeably.

"The fire department must work as a team," Plug barked. "Anybody who doesn't want to do that can leave right now."

Isaac rubbed his hands together as if hoping that Plug might take his own advice and quit the force. Plug scowled at him. Isaac shoved his hands into the pockets of his baggy cargo shorts.

The teens surrounding Haylee and me rustled. One of them was breathing quickly. No one left.

Plug jerked his head toward the fire truck. "Elderberry Bay has two of these. Many of our calls are rural, far from fire hydrants, so both trucks have huge water tanks. Isaac and Clay will demonstrate putting on gear.

Teamwork, folks, if you learn nothing else this evening, learn that. You must act as a team. Isaac, you suit up. Clay, you show how to help someone else." Plug's eyes seemed to bore into me. "If they need it."

Clumsy boots, suspendered pants, a heavy jacket, a mask and respirator, an oxygen tank, gloves. Who wouldn't need help?

When he was all dressed, Isaac stomped his feet. I could barely hear the "Ta-da!" through his mask. He resembled a lanky, amiable alien.

Plug showed us how to turn on Isaac's respirator and radio, then told him to remove it all and assigned the new recruits to don the gear quickly and to turn on our respirators and radios.

All suited up, I was sweltering. Plug told us to run laps around the ball field. Uh-oh. I was going to flunk out. I could barely move in the huge boots, and Haylee's pair didn't seem to fit her any better. The boys started jogging. Haylee and I followed.

Although I lifted my feet, the boots stayed on the ground, doing little besides making rubbery flop-flopping sounds. With each sliding step, I had to resettle my feet into the boots. I rounded second base. Footsteps pounded beside me. I turned my head to see out of the fogged-up mask.

261

"Put these on," Isaac panted. He had found smaller boots for Haylee and me.

They were an improvement, but by the time Haylee and I scrunched our feet down into them, the other applicants were far ahead of us.

One boy fell. I thought he would get up, but he just lay there. The other boys kept running, getting farther and farther ahead.

Haylee, Clay, and I all reached the prone applicant at the same time. Clay knelt and took off the boy's mask. The kid was breathing, but pale. He looked even younger than Russ.

I threw down my gloves, ripped off my mask, and squatted beside the boy. Haylee did the same.

Plug and Isaac lounged against the fire truck.

Clay shouted at them, "He's fainted!" Clay unfastened the boy's heavy jacket. By the time Plug and Isaac joined us, the boy's eyelids had begun fluttering open. He was going to be very embarrassed. I stood up and backed away. He, Haylee, and I had probably failed firefighters' school in our first ten minutes. Fine.

Plug glared at Haylee and me and adjusted a dry stem of grass from one corner of his mouth to the other. "Laps," he reminded us.

Haylee and I donned our gloves and masks, then jogged off. We started our second lap. The others were near the end of their third lap, detouring around their friend.

Maybe I should have stayed home and run with the dogs on the riverside trail. Clay could have joined us. Haylee, too.

Clay, Isaac, and Plug helped the recovering boy out of his gear and carried it off the ball field for him. Clay escorted him to an old gray pickup truck. The boy climbed into the driver's seat and sat with his head in his hands.

Plug waved all of us off the ball field.

Russ pointed at Haylee and me. "They didn't do three laps. The rest of us did."

Huge hands balled into fists, Plug stomped forward and put his face next to his son's. "Who's runnin' this department, you or me?"

Russ mumbled, "You."

" 'You, *sir,*' " his father corrected him, staring him down until Russ repeated it. I didn't know quite what I expected to learn about Plug at this training session. He would hardly announce to all of us that he had killed his wife. I did, however, confirm my earlier impressions of the man. He seemed constantly on the verge of rage. Had he been like that before his wife died, or only after?

"I should fail you all," he said. "Those two for being slow and the rest of you for not helping your fallen comrade. You're a team, remember? The first thing I teach you, and only the *girls* get it." I should have guessed he would pronounce "girls" in a demeaning way.

I didn't say anything, although I was tempted to fling off the outfit and stalk to Haylee's truck. But I had to prove that a woman could learn firefighting as well as Russ and his buddies could. Haylee's chin was raised at what the men should have recognized as a dangerous angle.

If Opal, Naomi, and Edna had seen Russ trying to get us thrown off the squad, would they still want to help the boy?

Probably. Not only that, they'd cheer him on. They wouldn't want Haylee and me fighting fires or even going along to watch someone's field of soybeans smolder into ashes. They wouldn't want us to cart defibrillators to heart attack victims if it meant riding in a fire truck. Fire trucks would go too fast to suit them, though the drivers couldn't be worse than Edna.

Next, we had to learn how to unroll and carry empty fire hoses. We were told that water spraying through them would make maneuvering them much more difficult.

Susannah passed slowly in her yellow VW. She was driving away from the center of the village, where she lived. More errands, or trying to save Haylee and me from the fire department?

By the time we rolled up the hoses and took off the cumbersome equipment, the boy who had fainted had driven away. At least I wasn't the first applicant to quit or be fired — though maybe that was a little too appropriate a word.

Plug fanned a handful of papers. "Here's your test. Go over to the bleachers to do it. You have a half hour."

None of us had pens or pencils. Clay retrieved some from his truck, and we trooped to sagging wooden bleachers that threatened to give us splinters and chiggers.

Haylee and I sat about two yards apart. Russ plunked down one row above us.

"Spread out!" his father yelled across the field. "No cheatin', son!" His voice was so freighted with weariness and resignation that I heard unspoken words at the end of his command — *no cheatin', son, for once . . .*

Muttering, "Yeah, yeah," Russ clomped

upward a couple of levels. The bleachers shook.

The questions were multiple choice, and the first few were not difficult.

From across the river in Elderberry Bay, the siren on the fire station's roof swelled into its wail. The siren was quieter out here near the state forest, but it was still impossible to ignore.

Plug, Isaac, and Clay leaped into the fire truck and roared away.

Russ and his friends laughed. "I guess *somebody* gave us more time to finish," one of them drawled. "Hey, miss, you got a smoke?"

I shook my head.

"I don't smoke," Haylee said.

One of the boys had a pack of cigarettes. They put their feet on the seats and lit up. "What'd you get for number ten?" one asked.

Haylee looked at me and raised an eyebrow.

"I'd better go home to my dogs," I said.

Haylee stood up and dusted the seat of her jeans. "I'll take you." Together, we started across the infield.

Susannah drove past again, this time quickly, and in the direction the fire truck had taken. Maybe she'd see the firefighters at work and lose some of her fear of fires.

One of Russ's friends hollered, "Hey, where do you two think you're going?"

I turned and gave them a dried-up grimace that resembled a smile, but only slightly. "Home."

They seemed to think that was excruciatingly funny. We climbed into Haylee's truck.

The three young men tossed their cigarettes into dry weeds — apparently fire prevention wasn't one of their major concerns — and charged across the ball field toward us.

Haylee started her engine.

Russ poked grimy fingers into the gap at the top of my window. "Give us your exam papers and we won't tell that you left early."

"Go ahead and tell," I said.

Haylee eased the truck away from the gangly youths surrounding it.

As we approached the road leading to the center of Elderberry Bay, another siren started. Behind us. Gaining on us.

A blue light flashing from the dashboard, Russ's pickup truck tailgated us.

Russ was not yet a full-fledged firefighter, but Haylee pulled over, anyway. If she hadn't, he could have rear-ended us.

Ignoring the stop sign, he sped onto the highway. In their own trucks, his buddies stayed close behind him.

Haylee pulled onto the road. "Working with those guys could be dangerous."

I folded my unfinished test paper. "We're not likely to find out."

28

By the next morning, I regretted failing the fire department's entrance exam. I'd lost the opportunity to spy on Plug and Russ.

As always, my students cheered me up, but halfway through the morning, Mimi looked at her watch and cleared her throat. "It was last Wednesday, only a week ago, that you had that nice presentation here and gave Darlene Coddlefield that prize sewing machine."

Georgina, dressed all in lemony yellow, commented, "Too bad we can't go back in time and do something to prevent the death." Her eyes glistened.

My eyes blurred with tears, and Mimi's eyes must have also. Though she'd been embroidering her latest design beautifully, when she threaded her machine with the next color, green, she must have done it wrong. The thread snapped. She rethreaded the machine, then forgot to tell the embroidery software to retrace its steps, and ended up with a gap in the design. Before I could suggest she could start again where the green thread began, she removed the design from the hoop and threw it out.

"Time for a do-over," she said.

We couldn't go back a week, as Georgina had wished, and have a do-over that would prevent Darlene's death, but I owed it to Darlene to find out what really happened. I also needed to exonerate myself, Susannah, and the care we took of the sewing machines in my store.

Susannah didn't make it easy. Coming into In Stitches around one to give me my break, she blushed and trembled and stared toward the front of the shop as if afraid that Smallwood and Gartener might pop in and question her. Handing a customer change, she sent coins spinning to the floor.

I waited until the customer departed, then asked Susannah, "Did you tell Chief Smallwood about that letter yet?"

She gulped. "Maybe the letter was lost in the mail. Maybe, since it was to *her,* no one read it. They just threw it away."

"Don't count on it. Look at it this way — if Darlene was scamming the public and if Tiffany is still collecting money for charities that don't exist, you'll be doing everyone a favor by reporting the fraud."

"I suppose you're right."

I followed her gaze to the front door. No one was there. "The longer you take to explain the whole thing to the police, the worse it could look for you."

She heaved a tremulous sigh. "I know. And I've *already* taken too long."

And so had I — for the dogs' outing. Tally-Ho whimpered.

After the dogs had their run, Susannah was more like her old self. Browsers milled around us, though, and I couldn't ask if her better mood was due to a determination to confess about that letter. She returned to The Stash for the rest of the afternoon.

My afternoon students put finishing touches on their IMEC entries. Ashley had made great use of the linen she'd bought from me. She had disabled the feed dogs in her mother's sewing machine so those little pointy teeth couldn't push the fabric forward or backward. Then she had hooped the linen in a regular old-fashioned embroidery hoop and carefully moved the hoop while her mother's sewing machine stitched. She had created a misty moonlight scene showing a wistful unicorn standing alone in a forest of bare trees. She called the piece *Waiting for True Love*. Hmmm. Autobiographical embroidery? Sweet.

And my entry was *Flame, Candle, and Fire.* Very original. And not autobiographical, I hoped, especially since I hadn't finished the firefighters' exam.

However, after the last customer of the day departed, Isaac tiptoed in. "I came at lunchtime, but you weren't here."

"Sorry I missed you." Apparently, he hadn't frightened Susannah too badly — she hadn't been quaking with fear when I'd returned, and she'd forgotten to tell me he'd been looking for me. "How did the firefighting go last evening when you all had to dash away from training?" I asked him.

"We were too late. The barn burned to the ground."

"Anyone hurt?" My mouth went suddenly dry. I managed to croak, "Animals?"

"Nope, nobody hurt, and the barn was used for storing machinery. Most of the tractors and stuff seemed to be elsewhere, however."

"That was lucky."

He combed his hand through his hair, making it spikier than ever. "Yes, very."

"Very convenient, too?" I asked. "Is it being investigated as a possible arson?"

"Plug says it wasn't."

"So what caused it?"

"Plug says faulty wiring." Isaac toed at the floor and ducked his head. "You didn't turn in your test paper last night."

"I didn't finish."

"The guys did."

"Haylee and I left earlier." About a half minute.

"I'll wait while you finish it now."

I wanted to refuse. I definitely preferred sitting at a sewing machine to broiling in heavy clothing at a fire. Besides, what if Russ and his friends were as wild with their firefighting as they were with their driving? Haylee and I might end up in a heap of coals.

Maybe we didn't need to learn more about Plug and his son, anyway. Darlene's death could have been a freak accident.

My hesitation must have shown on my face. "We need you," Isaac pleaded.

Gartener and Smallwood didn't seem to believe that Darlene's death had been an accident. And neither did I. Someone had tampered with the sewing machine and maybe the table it was on as well. Someone, possibly her husband or her son, had planned to at least injure her. If I passed the test, I'd have more opportunities to watch those two, maybe catch them in a lie about Darlene and her sewing machine.

Isaac urged, "Those kids may work out, but maturity is helpful on the force."

I admitted, "I've seen Russ Coddlefield do some pretty crazy and dangerous things in his truck."

Isaac stepped closer. His eyebrows went up. "Like?"

Maybe I shouldn't have mentioned it. "Oh, you know, the sort of careless driving lots of teenagers do." I hadn't been a model teenager, but I had never run anyone off the road.

Isaac leaned against my cutting table and fiddled with my scissors. "Thing is, his dad wants him on the force. Thinks he can make a man of him, but I'd rather we had people who were already men . . . er . . . adults."

Isaac slouched around the store, touching fabrics. Maybe I could turn him into a fabriholic. He backed against a row of homespun linen, faced me, and folded his arms across his chest. "Plug says the boys passed the written test with flying colors but he wouldn't listen to me when I pointed out that no one monitored them."

An undercurrent of distrust always seemed to run between Plug and Isaac.

Isaac controlled his obvious anger with a loud gulp. "The boys each missed one question. With the same wrong answer."

Not wanting to tattle on Russ more than I already had, I tried to keep my face neutral. I was certain that Russ had originally positioned himself to read Haylee's and my answers, and all four boys had been comparing answers when Haylee and I got up from the splintery bleachers. After we all drove away, Russ and his friends could have collaborated.

Isaac whipped another test out of his pocket. "C'mon, Willow, give it a try." He nodded across the street. "Haylee passed it."

Okay, I had to take the exam. Not only that, I had to pass, or I'd never hear the end of it from Haylee.

"She got all the answers right," he said. "And I was watching her. She didn't cheat."

I laughed. "Of course not. She wouldn't."

A boyishly eager look on his face, Isaac advanced on me. "If you choose the same wrong answer the kids did, maybe we can give them the benefit of the doubt." He frowned. "Not that Plug isn't already giving it to them, anyway." His voice was dark with frustration or with the anger I'd glimpsed earlier.

Those teens and their careless and possibly dangerous pranks — if Haylee was on the force, I needed to be, too, so I could watch her back.

My fingers shook only slightly as I accepted the exam from Isaac.

29

As Isaac had warned, the questions on the firefighting test were harder than "What is a fire truck?" Circling *a*s, *b*s, and *c*s, I kept thinking about Plug on Thursday, standing by his SUV, his hand underlining the words "fire chief," and the threat that Edna and I had inferred — if we wanted our shops and apartments to be safe from fires, we'd better leave him and his family alone.

Chief Smallwood lived in Elderberry Bay. Was she afraid to investigate Plug for fear of reprisals? She seemed too confident to consider such a thing, but maybe her reluctance to suspect him stemmed from a subconscious need to protect herself.

I circled my last *b* and checked my answers.

Isaac was sitting at one of the Chandlers but not touching it. The dogs kept his hands occupied. He stopped petting them to take my exam paper and pull a sheet of paper from his pocket.

I'd expected him to mark my exam later, somewhere else. Failing the test could be embarrassing. On the other hand, passing it could be, too.

"You only missed one." He stood up and shook my hand. "Congratulations. And welcome to Elderberry Bay's volunteer fire department."

I had a feeling I was supposed to be enthusiastic, not burdened by dread. "So what do I do?" I asked. "Like when the fire siren goes off?"

"Drive to the station. If you get there in time, hop on the truck with the rest of us. If not, you'll see directions on the message board. Don't speed, though, before you get yourself one of those flashing blue lights. You could be pulled over and miss most of the fire."

I had visions of Chief Smallwood lurking near the fire hall in hopes of catching speeding firefighters. What had I gotten myself into?

Isaac went on, "The first few times, you'll be observing and learning. We'll expect you for training drills at the old ball field the next three Tuesday evenings. After that, you'll be full-fledged, whether you attend fires in the meantime or not."

My dread began to resemble panic. "Did I give the same wrong answer the boys did?"

"Nope. You missed a different question." He showed me my error and told me the correct answer. Not *millions* of pounds of pressure per square inch in those hoses — it would only feel like that. He gave me an encouraging nod. "And I'll bet you'll be better than they will at actually coming to fires."

"I won't be able to fight fires when my shop is open," I warned him.

"You can help out nights and Mondays when your shop is closed."

"There've been a lot of fires recently, especially at night. Do you suspect arson in any of these fires?"

He looked down at his feet. "Plug says none of them are arson," he mumbled.

"What about you?"

"He doesn't look at the evidence, says he trusts his gut." He shrugged, displaying the palms of his hands. His fingers were long and narrow. "Gut. Ha. That's no way to investigate fires. But as he points out, if someone throws a cigarette from a car when the fields are dry, is it arson? Or litter with unintended results? What about careless use of candles or do-it-yourself wiring? Are those arson, or unfortunate circumstances?"

I asked, "Have you seen any of those things causing fires?"

"Yes. And sometimes we get investigators in from the state to verify it. There are so many ways that fires can start." He threw his arms out to his sides like he was measuring something huge. "And they can go out of control. This happens in rural areas. Firefighters sometimes have to travel far."

"These field fires. Have they been close to each other, or spread out?"

He tilted his head. "Spread out. Not to the north, because that's the lake." He flashed me a goofy grin. "You've given me an idea, though. I'm gonna plot this summer's fires on a map. If they're clustered near one particular farm . . ." He flushed.

Was he thinking about Russ Coddlefield and his friends? One of them had said that *somebody* had given them extra time to finish the exam — had he meant the teen who left the training session early? Had they expected their friend to cause a diversion? I asked, "Can some of our training sessions be about things like detecting arson?" Maybe I could actually be useful to the fire department.

"Plug likes them to be more about physical things, like, you know, actual practice. People donate wrecked cars, and we practice cutting them open, then we torch the cars, then we put the fires out." His eyes shone with a glee he probably didn't know he was showing.

"What about obvious arson? Can't investigators tell by the way the fire burned if someone used gasoline or another fuel?"

"Could be, but who's to say someone didn't accidentally kick over a can of gas? Someone could ignite a pile of oily rags and say the rags caught fire by themselves. Or they could light a match to old, dry timber in their shed and drive off to town. By the time we respond, the matchstick would be long gone, along with the rest of the shed."

So much detail, like he'd spent a lot of time thinking about it. "Have you ever suspected anything like that in fires you've fought?"

His eyes lit up as if from fires within. I was obviously asking questions he'd been hoping to hear. "Not *fought.* No."

"Or seen after it was too late to fight?" I prompted.

"There was one like that. Last summer. Plug lost a barn. Got quite an insurance settlement out of it, too, judging by the two bigger barns that replaced it. Strange, huh?"

I nodded. Plug had also, if I'd understood Chief Smallwood's hints correctly, purchased large amounts of insurance on his wife's life, and then she had died under suspicious circumstances.

Isaac went on. "Now that you're on the force, you'll want to be sure not to miss a fire except when your shop is open. Tell you what. I recently installed a system that automatically dials volunteers whenever there's an alarm. Very handy for firefighters who live out of town or who sleep too heavily to hear the siren on the fire hall. We've got your phone and cell numbers, of course, from your application. Want me to add you to our system?"

His enthusiasm was contagious, so I agreed, though I wasn't thrilled at the prospect of being awakened by both a siren and an insistent phone.

"Great! Plug says the phone system won't do a lick of good, but we'll show him!" Judging by the width of his smile, he was overjoyed. "And can we depend on your help setting up the firefighters' booth at the Harvest Festival on Friday evening?"

"I can help for a few hours, but the Threadville store owners have a booth, too, and we'll be putting it together at the same time."

"No problem. Our booth is next door to yours."

"In the handcrafts tent?" Did rummage qualify as handcrafts?

"It's a big tent." He beamed. "When I found out that you and Haylee might join the firefighters, I pulled some strings so our booths would be together. It will be easier for you two."

His innocence was boyish and charming. To hide my grin, I bent over to leash Sally-Forth and Tally-Ho. "That was very thoughtful." I pointed at the leashes. "The dogs need a walk." We all went out the front door.

Isaac got into a black pickup truck, made a U-turn in the middle of Lake Street, flashed his blue light, waved at me, and then sped away.

I half expected Opal, Edna, and Naomi to trot out of their apartments to ask what Isaac had been doing in Haylee's and my shops, but they didn't. The dogs and I took a leisurely trip to the beach and back. After supper, I played with them in the backyard before we finally went to bed.

It seemed like only minutes later that Sally and Tally woke me up. They bounded out of the bedroom and raced to the back windows. I jumped up, followed them, and turned on floodlights. No one was out there.

The dogs ran to the door to the stairway

leading up to the store. We all barged into the shop. As far as I could tell without opening the front door and going outside, no one was anywhere near.

"False alarm," I told the dogs. They trotted downstairs and pointed their noses at the cupboard where I kept their treats. "Yes, you deserve these," I said. Wagging their tails, they took the treats in their soft, gentle mouths.

We all went back to bed. I awoke to the sound of thunder. I got up, hoping to see rain. Nothing.

I fell asleep, but apparently the night was destined to be an interrupted one. Another noise socked me out of a deep sleep.

The fire siren howled, calling volunteers to rush to the station and clamber onto the truck for a wild ride. At two in the morning.

I leaped out of bed. My cell phone signaled that I had a text. *Fire,* it said. I threw on jeans, a sweatshirt, and sneakers, then patted the dogs good-bye and jogged down the street to my car. The fire station was close, but if the trucks had already left, I'd need to drive. Besides, I wouldn't actually be fighting the fire, only observing, and I could come back whenever I wanted.

The fire hall doors were rolled all the way

up, and both trucks were gone. I ran to the chalkboard.

I would have no trouble finding the place. The Coddlefield farm.

The ominous word *House* was scrawled beneath the address.

30

A house fire at the Coddlefields'. Eight children, four of them under the age of twelve. Hardly aware of anything besides my fear for the kids, I sprinted to my car and sped south.

The smell of summer-dry grasses blew in through the open windows. To the east, another siren's call rose and fell. A fire truck from the next township? The sound dwindled, and the orchestra of insects took over.

I half expected to see other volunteers, their blue lights flashing, rushing with me to the fire, but I was alone with the night, the stars, and the dry, crackling lightning between distant clouds.

Headlights came toward me. As a car whooshed past, I caught only a glimpse of a light-colored vehicle shaped like Susannah's VW. What could she have been doing out at this time of night near a fire?

Ahead, bright lights spangled trees surrounding the Coddlefields' farm. No flames, no orange glow, but smoke burned my nostrils.

I passed a dark sedan parked on the right shoulder. A fireman in full gear opened the passenger door and reached toward the seat. His casual, unhurried pose reassured me. The worst of the crisis had to be over. The children must be fine.

But I needed to be certain. I drove farther and parked on the shoulder beside the Coddlefields' rural mailbox. Its door gaped open, but I didn't take time to investigate. I scrambled out of the car and pelted up Plug's driveway toward his house. Pickup trucks had been left helter-skelter on the lawn. I recognized Clay's truck, red with *Fraser Construction* printed in white on the doors. Plug's fire chief SUV and Russ's truck were parked in their usual spaces, close to the house.

I had to find those children.

All I could see nearer the house were firefighters, fire trucks, and water pouring from hoses into the top of the dark house. The tallest firefighter would be Isaac or Clay. The short, wide one, made even wider by his bulky jacket, had to be Plug.

Smoke, panic, and running made me gasp

287

and wheeze.

No flames.

Also, no children.

I had to dodge a tanker racing down the driveway away from the fire. Would nearby ponds yield enough water, or would the truck have to go all the way to Lake Erie to fill up? Russ was driving, with his fourteen-year-old brother as passenger.

Surely, they wouldn't have left if any of their brothers and sisters had been hurt.

Then I heard the familiar crying and made out the other six Coddlefield children huddled in blankets on the lawn. I'd have seen them sooner if my eyes hadn't been dazzled by lights from the tanker still on the scene.

I stumbled to the mass of blankets.

The twelve- and fifteen-year-old sisters sat cross-legged on the ground, each with a quilt-wrapped child on her lap and another in the shelter of one arm. The tiny girl and the two little boys bawled. The eight-year-old sobbed. Their faces startlingly devoid of emotion, the two older girls stared at me. I could have been a tree.

I squatted and asked the oldest girl, "Can I do anything?"

She shrugged, looked away, and pulled the eight-year-old closer.

The littlest girl shouted at me, "Nasty lady in my house!"

The oldest girl corrected her. "Darla, no one's in the house. We're all here."

"Is, too!" She pointed at her own little chest. "Darla seed her. Sleeping in Tiffie's room when Daddy carrying me and blankie. *Nasty* lady."

Smoke drifted out of the front sewing room window. Men shouted. The tall fire-fighter who could be Clay or Isaac helped two shorter men aim a hose. Near them, Plug stared through his mask toward the water arcing into a hole in his roof. I ran to him and grabbed his arm. He shook me off.

I screamed, "Your little girl says there's someone in the house."

He made a backhand gesture at me. If I didn't leave him alone, he would swat me.

I dashed to the taller firefighter and waved my arms in his face. The man was Isaac, not Clay. I yelled that there might be someone in the house.

Isaac shook his head vehemently, glanced toward Plug, and motioned with his head for me to go away.

Where was Clay? And why was Plug so insistent on not hearing about someone in his own home?

Darla had said there was a nasty lady in

the house, sleeping in Tiffany's room. Tiffany had told Edna and me that she now lived here. Tiffany took the littlest kids on excursions, like to the beach and the library. She'd used Darlene's sewing machine to help teach little Darla her letters. She'd promised to make the girl new dwesses. She wouldn't abandon her charges in the middle of the night after a fire broke out.

The black car that Tiffany drove was in the driveway, more or less in the way of the firefighters and fire trucks. Tiffany had to be here. However, Darla seemed very fond of Tiffany and called her "Tiffie," not "nasty lady."

Where was Haylee? Had she come to the fire? Her pickup wasn't here, but what if she had hitched a ride with other volunteers on the fire truck, then had helped evacuate the children, and had not made it out of the house? If Plug had indoctrinated his children to believe that all of the storekeepers in Threadville were nasty, would the youngest child refer to Haylee as a nasty lady?

Sleeping in Tiffie's room . . .

Sleeping?

It felt like a door in the base of my heart unlatched. I sprinted to the other side of the fire truck where the firefighters' outfits were stored.

I did not have enough training to fight a fire or to pull someone from a burning house, but I knew how to don the gear. And I had a fierce determination to rescue my best friend. Besides, the house was not actively flaming, and the damage, from what I could see, was mainly to the roof. A lightning strike?

Plug and the others would surely explore the house later, but all I could think of was Haylee, perhaps injured and unable to escape or call for help.

Sleeping . . .

I pulled on the pants, boots, and jacket. I loaded an oxygen tank onto my back, adjusted the mask, tightened my helmet's chinstrap, and made certain that both my respirator and radio were on and functioning.

I didn't dare go in the front way. Plug might see me and stop me.

Pulling on gloves, I clomped through the woods to the back of the house.

The back door wasn't locked. Lights were on in the kitchen, and everything looked normal. The basement door was open. Lights were on down there, too, and voices came from a radio or TV. The fire must have been in another part of the house; probably, judging by what I'd seen from outside, in

291

the attic above the original part of the house, near the sewing room. Using a flashlight, I checked the dining room, playroom, and living room. I found no apparent fire damage, and no ladies, nasty or otherwise.

Where was Haylee?

She would not have stood around wondering if I were trapped inside a smoke-filled house. She would have searched for me. I would never forgive myself if I could have saved her and didn't.

The child had said the nasty lady was in Tiffany's room. When Edna and I delivered Tiffany's sewing machine, I'd seen bedrooms one flight up. The floor beneath my feet seemed sturdy.

Heartbeat accelerating, I grasped the railing with one gloved hand and carefully climbed the stairs. Water dripped through the ceiling. Wet plaster might break off and cascade down on me, but my helmet would protect my head, and I refused to think about the possibility that the house might collapse around me.

On the second floor, I shined my light into bedrooms. The pink frilly quilts and blue race car quilts were now outside, wrapped around kids. Fleecy blankets trailed across the floor from the beds as if trying to crawl out of the bedrooms by themselves. In the master bedroom, the fabulous quilt covered the king-sized bed.

Little Darla had to have been wrong. No one had remained in the house.

A mostly closed door might lead to a bathroom or closet.

Something thumped behind that door. I rammed it open with my shoulder and stumbled into a small bedroom. Tiffany's?

I aimed my light down.

Felicity Ranquels lay in a heap on the shiny oak floor.

31

"Felicity?" I said.

No answer. She simply lay there dressed in the jacket she'd worn to the presentation in my store, and matching pull-on pants. The day after Darlene's death, little Darla had referred to Felicity as a nasty lady who had taken her dwess. Darla must have been referring to Felicity this time, also, not to Haylee.

Smoke swirled. A few seconds before, Felicity must have been conscious enough to kick the floor with her sturdy shoes. Now she wasn't moving.

Either something was still smoldering or leftover smoke was trapped in the house, shadowing and blurring everything. I had to get Felicity outside where she could breathe fresh air.

I didn't dare take time to radio for help. Even a second's delay could harm her more and might prevent me from escaping, too. I bent over, grabbed her by the armpits, and pulled.

The bed came, too.

I shined my light. A strip of pink fabric was tied tightly around Felicity's wrist, with an extra loop that went around the leg of the bed. The fabric was printed with tiny lavender flowers, matching the dwess that someone had cut out for little Darla.

Determined to get Felicity out of the house as quickly as possible, I didn't let myself think about how she'd ended up in this predicament. I lifted one corner of the bed, toed the loop of Darla's dwess fabric out from under the leg of the bed, then grasped Felicity's upper arms again. This time, the bed stayed put. I hauled the woman out of the room and down the stairs. Her feet bumped on each step. My clumsy firefighter's gloves and the wet carpeting didn't make the job easier.

The back door was too far away. I heaved Felicity out the front door and onto the porch.

Uniformed firefighters gazed at the water they were spraying at the roof. I couldn't move Felicity one more inch. Where had the strength come from to bring her all the way down from the second floor?

We could still be in danger from collapsing roofs. I looked for Clay, wanting his help although knowing he would give me a much-deserved lecture about safety.

My muscles hot enough to ignite a new fire, I stooped and reached for Felicity.

She scrabbled away from me. "Help!" she screamed. "He's trying to kill me!"

She was conscious again, at least. What made her think I was trying to kill her? Was she remembering something that had happened before she conked out? Someone had tied her to that bed. Had that person been wearing a fireman's uniform, and now she was mistaking me for him?

Her shouts brought Plug running. He bellowed for help. Isaac dashed to the porch. Between the three of us, we carried Felicity farther from the house.

Plug stared at my mask as if trying to see my face. Felicity had called me "he." With any luck, Plug also thought I was a man. I didn't know what he might do if he discovered I had invaded his house, and I didn't want to find out. Plug had a temper, and for all I knew, he had murdered his wife. And it appeared that somebody had tried to murder Felicity by tying her to a bed in a burning house. If that person guessed I'd seen the fabric tethering Felicity to the bed, I was in danger. I hunched my shoulders to keep anyone from seeing my face.

Plug dropped to his knees, removed his own mask and put it on Felicity's face. She tried to squirm away. Isaac helped Plug hold her down. Plug and Isaac never seemed to get along well. Neither of them would dare harm Felicity, would they, with the other one present as a witness?

I couldn't stay there to protect Felicity, though. I would come back, but first I needed to make certain that Haylee was safe. I should have called her earlier, but as things had turned out, I was glad I'd rushed headlong into the house, instead.

Russ and his brother had apparently filled the second tanker truck and brought it back. I ran to the other side of the nearest truck, checked to make certain no one was watching, then took off my mask, undid my jacket, reached into my pocket for my cell phone, and pressed the button for Haylee.

I was about to put the mask on again and dash into the Coddlefield house when she answered.

Relief reduced my bones to chiffon. "Where are you?" I blurted.

"At home. I was asleep. Why are you call-ing at this hour?" She yawned.

"I was afraid you had come to the fire. I couldn't find you." I didn't tell her I'd linked her — possibly — to little Darla's words, *nasty lady.*

"Fire? What are you talking about? Where are you, Willow? And are you all right?"

"I'm fine. There was a fire at the Coddlefields' house, but it didn't amount to much." Except that someone may have tried to kill Felicity. "I'll tell you about it in the morning."

"Want me to come?"

"No. Everything's fine."

I had to reassure her several times and tell her I was about to go home before she would break the connection.

Next, I needed to tackle that little matter of what looked like attempted murder . . .

I called 911. Hanging on to the phone, I clumsily shed the rest of the firefighting outfit and stowed it in the truck while telling the dispatcher that Felicity had apparently been overcome by smoke at the Coddlefield fire. I said that, last I knew, the fire chief was giving her oxygen, and she was apparently healthy enough to fight his ministrations.

The dispatcher told me that the nearest ambulance wasn't available, but should be free soon.

Even though the whole idea seemed preposterous and unreal in the noisy, artificially lit night, I blurted my suspicion that Felicity had been deliberately harmed.

The dispatcher agreed to send the police, and asked me to stay on the line.

Holding the phone to my ear, I peeked around the fire truck. The children were still sitting on the ground beyond the driveway.

I couldn't pretend I had just arrived. The children knew I'd talked to them earlier. Plug and Isaac had seen me, too.

Felicity's attacker could be sneaking up on me, about to silence me. Having a 911 dispatcher on the line gave me courage. If anyone attacked me, the dispatcher would know. Besides, the police were on the way. Soon I, and everyone else near the Coddlefields' house, would be safe.

I crossed the driveway to the children and squatted to their level again. I asked the fifteen-year-old girl, "Would you like to bring the children to sit in my car?" I wished I could offer hot chocolate.

"My father's the fire chief," the eight-year-old girl said.

"And he told us to stay right here," snapped her twelve-year-old sister.

The two little boys regarded me with tearstained eyes. Darla popped a thumb into her mouth. At least they'd stopped screaming.

"Where's Tiffany?" I asked.

Darla started bawling again.

The fifteen-year-old girl growled at me, "Now look what you've done!"

Phone still to my ear, I closed my eyes and rocked back on my heels. What *had* I done?

I remembered hearing a siren while I was on my way here. Its sound had diminished, as if it had been speeding somewhere else. The dispatcher had told me that an ambulance should be available soon. Had the area's only ambulance taken someone away before I arrived? I opened my eyes. "I'm sorry. I should have asked sooner. Was anyone hurt?"

The oldest girl handed Darla and the smaller boy to her twelve-year-old sister, then strode across the driveway. I caught up with her.

She spat, "It's none of your business, but, yes, my dad went back into the house and carried Tiffany out, and she wasn't moving and he tried artificial respiration and CPR and everything and an ambulance came and got her, and one of the firemen went with her, and I have to look after the little ones. Got it?"

I nodded, though I was reeling, trying to

make sense of it all. "Will Tiffany be all right?"

"I don't know, and personally, I don't like her and don't care, but my mother was always too busy with her stupid sewing and charities to look after the little ones, and now she's gone, and they depend on Tiffany, so you just shut up about her around them."

"Do you know where they were taking her?"

"The hospital. In Erie, I guess."

"Who went with her? Clay Fraser?"

"How would I know? Some man."

"Was he tall?"

"What is this, twenty questions?"

She was right. I was being overly nosy. "Sorry, I'm just learning to be a volunteer firefighter and am trying to ask the things a seasoned firefighter might."

If Clay hadn't gone with Tiffany, where was he?

Fear clawed at the back of my neck.

No, I told myself, Clay couldn't be lying injured inside the house. I asked the girl, "Did you see anyone else go back into the house?"

"What do you care?"

"Your dad's working on someone who was stuck inside, and I'm just checking to make sure that everyone else is out safely."

"That's my *dad's* job, not yours." She stalked away, jerking like a puppet on a string, her knees and elbows jutting out.

32

The 911 dispatcher asked if I was all right and how the victim was.

"I'm fine," I answered, though judging by my shaky knees, I wasn't telling the truth. "And the victim —"

Uh-oh. A tall firefighter was helping roll up the fire hoses. Isaac had left Felicity alone with Plug. Phone clasped to my ear, I stumbled to Felicity. She was scratching at the mask Plug held over her face as if trying to remove it, and although he was pinning her down, he did seem to be trying to help, not harm her.

Where were the police? They had to arrive soon so I could show them the strip of fabric tied to Felicity's wrist. The police could take over keeping Felicity safe. And keeping me safe, too.

I asked Plug, "Where's Clay?"

Plug stood. His eyes were like wild things in his soot-blackened face. "What do you think you're doing here?"

I staggered back, away from his anger. "I thought I was supposed to respond to fire alarms so I could learn . . ."

"Why this fire? At *my* house?"

"I didn't know where this fire was until I got to the fire station."

"Sure you didn't." He stomped away, then turned and shouted, "Get off my property. And stay away from my children."

I yelled, "Where's Clay?"

Plug waved a dismissive hand and collared a burly fireman, who rushed to Felicity and thrust an oxygen mask toward her face.

She pointed at the phone I held to my ear. "Hey, you" — she never remembered my name — "you have a phone. Call the police! Everyone here is trying to kill me."

Looking pained, the burly fireman held the mask inches from her face as if ready to clamp it over her mouth and nose.

"The police are on their way," I said as soothingly as I could. "The rest of us are trying to help you. You must have inhaled too much smoke."

Felicity was not the most soothable person on the planet. She glared at me. "And don't you come near me, either. I know what you did. And I'm trained in self-defense."

What I did? Maybe I was a little rough,

dragging her to safety, but I didn't have the energy to argue with her about it. "Try to rest," I said. I wasn't leaving her. I didn't want her or anyone else removing that strip of fabric from her wrist until a police officer saw it. I should have brought a camera.

Hugging myself, I sank down near Felicity, not close enough for her to wield her alleged self-defense on me. If I'd known it would be this chilly at three a.m. in August, I'd have worn a sweater. I asked the burly fireman, "Do you know where Clay is?"

He shook his head. "Haven't seen him all night."

A far-off siren became louder. I hoped it was Chief Smallwood or a state trooper. I would show them the fabric on Felicity's wrist and tell them she'd been fastened to a bed in a smoke-filled house. Sharing the dangerous information should make me safer. My shoulders slumped in relief.

My relief didn't last long. Plug came back. "I told you to go away."

The burly fireman made a startled reply, got up, and headed toward the fire truck.

Plug shouted after him, "Not you, you idiot, her." He turned to me. "Get off my property."

"I can't." I pointed to the phone still clamped to my ear. "I called the police about Felicity, and they told me to stay with her until they get here."

He must have heard the siren, too. Obviously steaming, he strode to the firemen rolling up hoses and shouted instructions. Rude ones.

The dispatcher asked me again if I was all right. I told her very nicely that I was. I hoped their recording equipment was good enough to capture everything people were saying to me. Some of it might come up in court one day.

"What were you doing here tonight?" I asked Felicity.

"None of your business," she snapped.

She was about as much fun as Plug.

"Who attacked you?" I asked.

She shot me a look filled with suspicion. "I'll tell the police when they get here."

I heard firemen's boots behind me. "Willow!" Coat flapping, Isaac ran to join me. "What did you do to make Plug so angry?"

Great. Now Isaac was about to lecture me. "He ordered me off his property, but I'm staying here with Felicity until the police arrive."

"I've got a thing or two to tell them," Felicity said.

Yes, probably all the wrong things, like how someone tried to kill her by dragging her out of a smoke-filled house, then how other men tried to kill her by forcing some much-needed oxygen into her.

Isaac snapped his suspenders. "Plug has no business sending volunteer firefighters away."

Maybe in daylight, things would start making sense again. I massaged my neck with the fingers of my right hand, but they were clumsy and useless. I managed a grim smile. "He's fire chief, and this is his house. I guess he can send me away. I'd just as soon go, but . . ." I pointed at my phone again. "The 911 dispatcher is staying on the line with me."

"I sure am, honey," the calm voice in my ear said. "I can tell you're having a tough time of it. You just hang in there and keep on doing what you're doing. An officer is almost there."

I nodded as if she could see me, then asked Isaac, "Are you sure everyone is out of that house?"

"According to Plug, everyone is accounted for. His boys did a pretty good job tonight. This morning. Whatever. I guess we'll have to let the younger one join the department, too."

"I saw Clay's truck, but he's not here. Where is he?"

Isaac sat on the ground beside me. "He went to the hospital with Plug's girl. His what-d'ya-call-it."

"Nanny?"

"Some French word."

"Au pair?"

"Oh pare. Right, that's it. But if you ask me . . ." He didn't go on.

"What? I'm asking you."

The burly fireman looked distinctly uncomfortable, like he'd just as soon not know about romances between fire chiefs and their younger au pairs.

Isaac thinned his lips. "Nothing."

"You almost said girlfriend, didn't you?"

"Yeah, well, I'm not sure, but, well, you know, sometimes it's hard to tell."

And sometimes it wasn't. I had nothing against Tiffany, or Plug, either, unless they'd been causing and almost causing deaths. I asked in gentler tones, "Is Tiffany going to be all right?"

Isaac glanced at the children. They were too far away to hear us, but his caution sped my pulse. "Don't say anything," he murmured. "When they left here, they were trying to get her to start breathing again."

Ignoring the angry glare that Felicity focused on me, I asked Isaac, "Why did Clay go with her?"

He took off his gloves. "Clay asked if Plug was going with her, and Plug said he was fire chief and couldn't go, and the ambulance people could look after her. I said I could manage the fire. I'm deputy chief. Plug's stubborn. It was his house, and he was going to fight the fire. The oh pare must have been trapped and gotten overcome by smoke. But Clay said that he wasn't letting her go to the hospital without someone along who cared, and he hopped into the back of the ambulance."

Clay . . . cared for Tiffany? Or he was merely being a caring person?

Merely?

I pictured Clay's face, and the concern in his dark eyes whenever he thought that someone — frequently me — required rescuing, and the way he always pitched in and followed up. His dragging me up the riverbank suddenly began to seem romantic, more romantic than not being near him. If only I could see him and know for sure that he was all right . . .

To distract myself, I asked Isaac, "Do you have any idea how the fire started?" What would the 911 dispatcher think of my trembling voice?

"Honey? You okay?" she asked.

"Yes," I mumbled into the phone.

"What?" Isaac asked.

"Just talking to the dispatcher. Do you have any idea what caused the fire tonight?"

Isaac flapped his hands. "Nope. We'll wait until daylight, and make certain the structure is secure enough to enter it, and then we'll do our investigation."

"Think you might get outside help?"

Isaac scowled with one corner of his mouth, then the other. "If I have my way, we will, but Plug's the chief." The frustration behind his eyes silently added, *if Plug started that fire, he won't want anyone else investigating it.*

The siren was close now. Lights bounced off trees near the road.

Elderberry Bay's police cruiser pulled into the end of the driveway. I told the dispatcher that the police chief had arrived. Putting my phone back into my pocket, I asked Isaac, "How come Chief Smallwood wasn't here all along?"

Isaac probed at the extra-deep wrinkle that his helmet had engraved on his forehead. "She doesn't come to fires unless she's on active duty. She must have only been on call tonight, and no one requested her services."

Until I did.

Plug marched toward the cruiser. Was he planning to send Chief Smallwood away?

33

I jumped up. "Stay with Felicity," I commanded as if I were Isaac's and the burly fireman's boss. "Make certain that no one hurts her." I ran toward the cruiser.

Chief Smallwood stepped out of it and gazed at the scene in one of her calm assessments.

Plug's fireman outfit hampered his progress, so it was easy for me to dodge around him. Panting, I told Chief Smallwood, "Come see something before anyone removes it."

Her mouth dropped open. She was used to giving orders, not taking them. I didn't particularly like my newly aggressive personality, either. She tilted her head in question.

"Evidence," I blurted, "of attempted murder."

Expecting her to follow me, I turned around.

Hands on hips, Plug blocked our way.

"What're you doing here?" he asked Chief Smallwood.

She got into his face and raised her chin. "Why didn't you call me sooner?"

Instead of answering her, he growled at me, "I told you to leave."

"I don't want *anyone* leaving," Smallwood said directly to Plug.

Cursing, he shambled away. His boots were too big.

Smallwood spoke into the radio in a pocket on her shoulder. "Where are you? There's too much going on here for one person."

Backup from the Pennsylvania State Police? I hoped so.

She turned to me. "Okay, show me your evidence."

I murmured, "See that woman sitting on the ground, there, with Isaac? When we get closer, have a good look at her left wrist."

We trotted to Felicity.

"Ma'am," Smallwood said to Felicity, "show me your wrists."

Felicity held her wrists out, gaped at her left one, and yelped at me, "Why did you put that thing on my wrist?"

Why was she blaming me? "I didn't."

Her legs still straight out in front of her, she shot up to a sitting position and tore at

313

the pink and lavender calico tied tightly around her wrist. The loop attached to it flopped around. "Ouch," she shrieked. "Cut it off."

"Leave it alone," I said. "It's evidence that someone tried to hurt you."

"*Someone?* You." Felicity plucked at the cloth. "Or that fireman."

Smallwood gazed at the trucks and volunteer firefighters milling around them. "Which fireman?"

"The one who attacked the nanny, then came after me and dragged me out onto Darlene Coddlefield's front porch."

I gasped. "A fireman attacked Tiffany?"

"What did he do to Tiffany?" Smallwood asked. It worried me that her notebook was still in her pocket.

"He hit her!" Felicity yelled as if we weren't right beside her. "And when she fell, he grabbed one of the pieces of a little dress that Darlene had cut out. He ripped off a strip of fabric." Felicity thrust her arm toward Smallwood. "Like this. Take it off."

"Not yet." Chief Smallwood spoke in a surprisingly calm voice. "I'm sorry it hurts. Let me have a look." Smallwood aimed her flashlight at the pale pink calico, then handed me her flashlight and took out her notebook. "Shine this so I can see to write,

314

please, Willow. Felicity, first of all, what were you doing here tonight?"

Felicity glared at me. "*Some*one had to find out who sabotaged the sewing machine I gave to Darlene Coddlefield."

Smallwood let that pass. "When did you arrive here tonight, Felicity?"

"I don't know. I couldn't sleep. I was worrying about someone" — again, she turned an evil eye on me — "getting off scot-free while a Chandler was being blamed for a death. So I drove here. I must have gotten here around one."

"Where did you leave your car?"

Felicity waved toward the south. "On a farm road just past the driveway."

"Okay, Felicity, you arrived around one, snuck into the house, and you saw a fireman rip a piece of fabric off a child's dress —"

"The dress wasn't sewn together yet."

Smallwood continued her calm questioning as if Felicity hadn't interrupted her. "What did the fireman do with the strip of fabric?"

Felicity gave Smallwood a look like she should have understood. "He tied it around the nanny's wrist and to the leg of a sewing table. Then he lifted the heap of fabrics off the Champion —"

"Whoa," Smallwood said. "Run that past me again."

"The fabrics!" Felicity waved her arms as if she could clear smog from Smallwood's brain. "The nanny had been smothering the Champion with a pile of fabric."

"Smothering a *champion*?" Smallwood was clearly at a loss.

"Sewing machine," I explained. "A Chandler Champion like the one we examined together in my store."

"That's what I'm trying to tell you." Felicity was more impatient than ever. "The Champion had caught fire. That nanny was trying to put the fire out. But after this fireman tied her to a table leg, he took the fabric off the Champion and it burst into flames." Talk about bursting, Felicity's eyes glimmered like she was about to weep. "I was about to rescue it —"

"Not Tiffany?" I demanded.

Smallwood shushed me with a quick flip of the hand holding the pen.

But Felicity was off on another tangent. "A *Chandler Champion* was on fire! In case you don't know anything about fire, you have to put the fire out before you can rescue anyone."

Clamping my lips together, I managed not to say anything.

"But I couldn't rescue the sewing machine *or* that nanny. The fireman saw me, ripped another strip of fabric off the dress piece, and started toward me. I ran down to the second floor. That fireman rushed down from the attic and pushed me into a small room, and the next thing I knew, I was lying on the porch outside and the fireman was coming after me *again.*"

Felicity was missing a big chunk of time.

Smallwood wrote quickly. "Did you recognize him?"

Felicity pointed at me. "I think it was her."

"You said it was a fire*man,*" Smallwood reminded her.

"Well, a fireman can be a woman. And she" — she pointed at me — "is tall, like a man. And when she chased me down from the attic, she had that piece of fabric in her hand. She must have tied it on my wrist. My hand will get gangrene. *Now* will you take it off me?"

"Can you bear to wear it for a few minutes more while I talk to Willow?" Smallwood spoke surprisingly gently.

Kneeling, Isaac patted Felicity's shoulder with a large but gentle hand.

Felicity flinched away and shouted at Smallwood, "Arrest everyone. They've all been attacking me."

317

Smallwood held up her hand. "Give me time." She beckoned me a few paces away. "Okay, Willow, let's hear your side. First of all, how did the nanny — Tiffany — get hold of another sewing machine like the one we took as evidence?"

"She wanted a replacement, for Darlene's kids, she said. I gave her the one in my store. Jeremy Chandler, the company president, told me he would send me another one."

"Now tell me what happened here tonight. This morning."

"The littlest girl said that someone was still in the house." I described putting on firefighter's gear, going into the house to look for the person, finding Felicity tied to the leg of a bed, lifting the bed off the loop, and dragging Felicity out of the house. "She came to and started yelling, 'He's trying to kill me.'" I added quickly, "I don't think anyone else knows I was the one who dragged her out, and I don't want them finding out."

"Ashamed of endangering yourself and possibly other firefighters by entering an unsafe house?"

"Yes, and . . . I haven't told anyone else that she was tied there. But her attacker — the mystery fireman — knows, and I'd just as soon he didn't find out that I know what he did. Also," I added somewhat lamely, "I didn't think you'd want me broadcasting the culprit's methods."

"You were wrong to go into the house without clearance," she scolded, "but right not to tell anyone besides me what you found."

"I didn't attack *anyone.*" I probably sounded like I had, though.

"Did you by any chance see this mystery fireman?"

I slapped my forehead. "I did see *a* mystery fireman. I don't know if it was the same one. He was leaning into a car parked out there on the road." I pointed. "Beyond those trees."

"Did you recognize him?"

"No. He was about Plug's height, but not as big around."

"His son, maybe?" she asked.

"No. I saw his two older sons only seconds later, in the tanker truck."

She looked up from her notebook. "So where'd this guy go?"

"Maybe he's still out there near that car?" I suggested.

"I only saw one car out on the shoulder when I came in. Yours. Everyone else parked in the driveway. Describe the car the fireman was near."

"It was a dark sedan. Four-door, I think."

A vehicle, its headlights blinding, jolted down the rough driveway toward us. Smallwood pointed her flashlight at its windshield. "You just turn around and get out of here, buddy," she muttered. The driver couldn't have heard her. "I've got enough to handle without sightseers in my way."

The driver killed the headlights, and we could make out the red pickup truck. Haylee jumped out and ran to us. "Willow, are you okay?"

"Great," Smallwood complained. "All of Threadville is about to show up and destroy evidence."

"We'll be careful," I promised.

Haylee grinned. "As far as I know, my mothers are sleeping in their apartments and not about to interfere."

Smallwood sighed. "Where is my *backup*? Look, Willow, I'm convinced that you rescued the victim and didn't harm her."

That was quite a concession. "Thank you," I said. "I didn't attack anyone, but I understand why she might see being dragged down a flight of stairs as an attack."

Smallwood shook her head. "She's obviously confused."

"She's not the only one," Haylee said.

"What's going on?"

Smallwood brushed her question aside. "You two are going to have to help me. Make sure no harm comes to the victim while I get a camera. Don't let her take off that strip of fabric. I want Detective Gartener to see it."

"Victim?" Haylee demanded.

"Felicity Ranquels, the Chandler representative," I told her.

"What's she doing here?"

I filled her in as we hurried to Felicity.

"My hand's swelling up," Felicity wailed. "I'm going to sue you."

"Who?" Haylee asked.

Felicity pointed her other hand at me. "Her."

Haylee crouched beside Felicity. "Why?"

But all Felicity would say was, "Get that policewoman back here."

An unmarked cruiser pulled in behind Smallwood's and a man got out. Even in the dark, I recognized his height and military bearing. Detective Gartener. He was good at figuring everything out. I felt safer than I had since I'd arrived.

Her camera in hand, Smallwood brought him to us. She shot pictures of Felicity's face and hands. Objecting, Felicity reached for her right lapel. Unlike her left one, stiff with cardboard, it was limp. "Oh, no," she said, "I lost my —"

"Interfacing?" Haylee, the accomplished tailor, suggested.

"Yes. I must have lost it at *your* —" Felicity glared at me.

"My place?" I suggested. Now I was confused, too, which seemed to be a normal state for most of us during that dark and horrifying night. Felicity had dropped her interfacing, made of corrugated cardboard, on my porch the day of Darlene's presentation, but she had shoved it back into her jacket immediately.

Felicity let out one of her little shrieks. "I've got to go find —" She struggled to stand, but her eyes lost focus, and she went limp.

34

Gartener caught Felicity, eased her to the ground, and placed his fingers on her neck. "Her pulse is good, but the back of her head's bleeding." His rich voice was unusually sharp. "She's been hit hard. Have we called an ambulance?"

"One's supposed to be on its way," I said.

"See if we can speed it up," Gartener said to Smallwood. "Let's get her to the hospital. Possible smoke inhalation and . . ." He didn't finish, didn't have to. His dark eyes locked on mine.

Smallwood was already on her radio.

"I dragged her down the stairs and out of the house by her upper arms," I told Gartener. "I don't think her head touched anything."

"Even if it had, it wouldn't have caused this injury. This was a severe blow." I'd never seen Gartener so rattled. Usually, he kept that sort of conclusion to himself.

I explained, "She said she saw a fireman hit Tiffany — the woman who has already been taken to the hospital — and knock her out."

After I summarized the rest of Felicity's accusations, Gartener directed Haylee and me to stand at the end of the driveway and keep anyone from driving out. "Unless there's another fire. If there is, you can let the firemen and fire trucks leave, but not Plug. He'll have to stay here. We need to talk to him."

Gartener stayed with Felicity. Slapping her leg with her notebook, Smallwood marched purposefully toward Plug.

Haylee and I walked to the end of the driveway. I filled her in on nearly everything that had happened that night.

"And those children just have to sit there?" She was more like her mothers than she realized.

"The smaller ones are cuddled in quilts on their big sisters' laps."

We'd barely reached the end of the driveway when a pickup truck came roaring toward us from the vicinity of the Coddlefield house.

Gartener had told us to prevent anyone from leaving. I stepped forward and tried to flag the driver down.

Russ tore past us in his maroon and white pickup truck. At the road, he turned south and accelerated. I couldn't tell if he had any passengers.

His fifteen-year-old sister screamed at him to come back. The smaller children began crying again.

Haylee dusted off her sweater. "We're not doing a good job of keeping people from leaving."

I stared down the road at Russ's taillights, two red pinpricks in the distance. "At least he didn't ram into us. For once, he didn't seem to be trying to."

"He was in too much of a hurry."

"I wonder why," I said.

"It seems kind of suspicious, doesn't it?"

I agreed. "But he's only sixteen. And he's not the fireman I spotted near a car out on the road when I arrived. I saw Russ right after that."

"The fireman you saw may not be the fireman who attacked Tiffany and Felicity."

Haylee was right. Felicity was confused about my role in the entire thing. What else did the cranky woman not understand?

The fire trucks' headlights illuminated the scene near the house in a smoky, eerie glow. Chief Smallwood strode to the younger Coddlefield children, knelt beside them, reached for little Darla, and took the child in her arms.

An ambulance trundled up the driveway toward us. Gartener waved it closer, then left Felicity to the paramedics' care and headed toward Plug.

A state police cruiser pulled in off the road. The trooper driving it seemed to take a mental snapshot of Haylee and me before he drove down the driveway toward the action. A second state police cruiser had been following the first, but it turned around and sped south, the direction Russ had taken. Smallwood or Gartener must have radioed them about Russ driving off without permission.

Haylee folded her arms. "They'll catch him."

Smallwood bundled the youngest Coddlefield children into Plug's SUV with their big sisters, but the SUV didn't go anywhere. Plug gestured angrily at Gartener, who was apparently asking questions and taking notes.

The ambulance headed down the driveway toward the road. The light inside showed a very pale-faced and apparently unconscious Felicity with a blanket strapped around her. Strobes flashing and siren silent, the ambulance turned south, toward the interstate, the quickest route to Erie. At the rate it was going, it might overtake the state police cruiser pursuing Russ.

It was still dark when Chief Smallwood told Haylee and me we could go home. "I'll want you back here, Willow, after they determine the house is safe to go into. You'll have to show me where you found Felicity."

Haylee picked up on one word. "Safe?"

I had conveniently not found time to tell her about the risks I'd taken.

To avoid a scolding, I waved good-bye. "Tell you later." I ran to my car. Smallwood had been right about the dark sedan I'd seen on the shoulder beside the Coddlefields' woods. It was no longer there. I drove back to the village. Haylee followed me in her pickup.

The attempts on Tiffany's and Felicity's lives had unnerved me, so instead of parking on Lake Street near the beach as I usually did, I pulled into the lot behind Opal's, Edna's, and Naomi's shops. Haylee parked behind me, hopped out, and as I feared she might, accosted me. "Safe?" she repeated. "You went into that house without knowing it was safe?"

"It *was* safe." It had turned out to be, anyway. "The kids told me that a lady was in the house, and I was afraid it might be you."

"What would I have been doing there in the middle of the night?"

"Observing how fires were fought, like I was."

"Is that what Felicity was doing?"

"She said she was trying to figure out who damaged the first Chandler Champion, though it seemed more like she was trying to prove that *I* did it."

"That woman," Haylee declared, "is not the sharpest needle in the pack."

"And her head wound didn't help. I hope she and Tiffany both recover soon."

"Me, too," Haylee said. "And that they catch the person who did this to them."

"They," I repeated, "can do the catching. We will stay out of it."

Haylee gestured toward the apartments where her three mothers were undoubtedly asleep. "And we'll keep them out of it, too."

Easier said than done.

Haylee's lopsided grin told me she was thinking the same thing. We parted, urging each other to be cautious.

I was afraid the dogs would think it was time to get up, but when I let myself into our apartment, they raised their noses and sniffed. Tally growled, probably at my smoky

328

aroma. I spoke, and they plunked their heads down onto their front paws.

I threw my clothes into the wash, showered, crawled into bed, and lay there, still wired.

Who had assaulted Felicity and Tiffany, and *why*? Although I'd assured Haylee that I'd been perfectly safe going into that house, I admitted to myself that in my panic about Haylee, I hadn't been thinking clearly. I should have let someone know where I was going.

But if I had, the wrong person might have followed me inside, and Felicity and I could both be dead. I had done the right thing, I told myself. Besides, in the future, I would always think and plan carefully.

Next thing I knew, my cell phone was performing its wake-up-bright-and-early song. Yawning, I let the dogs into the backyard.

A piece of brown corrugated cardboard lay in a flowerbed near the door. Even at first glance, I knew what that cardboard was.

Felicity's missing "interfacing."

35

That's what Felicity had meant about leaving her interfacing at my place? Had she been in my yard last night before she went to the Coddlefields'? She must have felt that her mission was so important she had to climb over one of my gates — quite a feat — and peek in through my windows. No wonder the dogs had barked.

I almost picked up the piece of cardboard, risking adding my fingerprints to it. I left it among the marigolds, took the dogs inside, and phoned Chief Smallwood. She didn't answer. I left her a message.

At midday, she walked in behind Susannah, who rushed to help Ashley frame her IMEC entry. Had Susannah been driving away from the Coddlefields' early that morning? I was certain she wouldn't want me asking her about it, not with Chief Smallwood right there.

Smallwood's face was sooty. Wisps of hair

escaped from underneath her chief of police cap. Her eyelids and the corners of her mouth drooped. She must have come directly from the Coddlefield farm.

Sorry for her, but admiring her dedication, I led her down to my apartment and outside, without the dogs, who gave me reproachful looks through the glass door.

I showed Smallwood the cardboard beneath my window. "That's the interfacing Felicity Ranquels said she was missing this morning. Remember, she said she lost it, pointed at me, said 'at your,' and then clammed up?"

Smallwood held up a hand. "Whoa! How much sleep did *you* get last night?"

I grinned sheepishly. "Not much."

"Me, neither. So take it slowly." Heaving a sigh that was just short of a yawn, she opened her notebook.

"Felicity mentioned the interfacing right before she fainted and Detective Gartener said her head was bleeding. How is she? And how is Tiffany?"

"Both of them will be in the hospital for a while."

I gulped. They must have been in worse shape than I'd feared. "Why?"

"Concussions. Both of them appear to have been clobbered with a wooden thing we found in the house. It looked like a toy wooden ironing board, but with one end sharpened to a point. Maybe you know what it is. I certainly don't."

"That sounds like a point presser. It's used for pressing small areas when an ironing board or sleeve board is too big. I have one." Where was it? In my guest room closet? "Haylee probably sells them, and like any other tailor, she would have one of her own, as would an avid seamstress like Darlene." I didn't remember seeing one in Darlene's sewing room, but she may have kept it out of sight in one of her many enviable cabinets. She'd had a great sewing room. Was it and everything in it now ruined? Sad. Sad for all the plans she'd made, projects she'd hoped to complete, children she'd wanted to see grow up, grandchildren she would never know.

"Maybe you can show me your point presser after you enlighten me about Felicity leaving cardboard in your yard."

"Okay." I didn't want to take time for a complete sewing lesson. "Lapels need more body than fabric has by itself, so we insert a stiffer material we call interfacing between the layers of fabric."

Fingering her shirt collar, Smallwood nodded.

"Felicity used corrugated cardboard to stiffen her lapels."

Smallwood scratched her head, dislodging more of her ponytail. "How do you know that?" I couldn't blame her for being skeptical.

"When she was in my shop last week, a piece of corrugated cardboard fell out of her lapel. It was the same shape as this one."

"And you're guessing she dropped her cardboard again? In your backyard?" Smallwood removed an evidence bag from a pocket and stepped into my flower garden. The marigolds released a pungent odor that made me sneeze. Smallwood's hand was just big enough to grab the cardboard by its edges. She began slipping the cardboard into the bag.

She couldn't see the side that had been facedown in the flowerbed, but I could.

Someone had written on it.

"Turn the cardboard over!" In my excitement, I came across as bossy and aggressive again.

With another dramatic sigh, Smallwood complied.

It was definitely Felicity's interfacing. Around the edges, stray marks from a blue ballpoint pen showed where she'd traced around the lapel pattern. But she'd also printed a message on the cardboard, pressing down so hard that her pen had repeatedly punctured the cardboard, like a spray of minuscule blue-ringed bullet holes, which made it difficult to decipher the words: *The Chandler Champion never hurt anyone. Somebody tampered with it, and I'm going to prove it if it's the last thing I do. If anything happens to me, check out that woman who owns the embroidery store. She'll stop at nothing to put down Chandler machines in favor of her other machines.* Felicity must have felt really adamant. She'd jabbed her pen down hard on the period at the end of that sentence, punching an even bigger hole into the cardboard. Then she'd added a sentence fragment, with no period after it at all, as if she'd been interrupted in a thought: *That woman who wins all the embroidery contests . . .* What, if anything, had Felicity meant to add to that?

Smallwood slid the interfacing with its hand-printed note into the evidence bag. "Ooooo-kay, this looks like some sort of evidence, all right." Of course she had to remind me of Felicity's accusations. "She obviously suspected *you* of tampering with that first machine."

"Before I knew Darlene was dead, Felicity called and accused me of killing her."

"When was this?"

"Last Thursday, about eight thirty in the morning. I don't know how she knew about Darlene's death that soon, unless she'd been at the Coddlefields' that morning, too. And if Felicity *was* at the scene of that crime . . ."

"She wasn't. She saw it on the morning news."

"You're taking her word for that?"

Smallwood sighed again, showing me she didn't really have to answer. But she did. "Don't forget that we know for certain that someone tried to harm *her.* How likely is it that two people are playing these deadly pranks?"

"So you're ruling out Felicity. And Tiffany, too. That leaves Plug and Russ." I thrust my hands into the pockets of my khakis.

"And a couple of others. *You* must be the woman who owns the embroidery store. There aren't any others for miles around, are there?"

"I don't win all the embroidery contests." It came out like the sullen defense of a desperate person.

Smallwood folded the top of the bag. She was not as precise with pleats and tucks as Gartener had been. "Maybe Felicity was talking about someone else winning embroidery contests. Any idea who?"

"The only person I can think of was Darlene Coddlefield, since she won the Chandler Champion competition, but Felicity can't be accusing Darlene of causing her own death." I opened the door. "Come inside and I'll find my point presser." I was hungry, but I'd worry about lunch later.

"How many embroidery contests *are* there?"

I fended off my welcoming dogs, then led Smallwood to my guest room. "Probably hundreds, all over the world, though we can probably narrow it down to machine embroidery contests in this case. But there would still be hundreds." The dogs curled up on the carpet. I gestured to the armchair beside the window. "Have a seat."

"No, thanks. I'm all smoky and would smudge your upholstery. White, when you have dogs. You're brave."

"They don't get up on furniture." They'd been surprisingly easy to train. I'd told them "no" once, and they'd been good about it ever since. Keeping the guest bedroom door closed most of the time helped, too.

Smallwood asked, "Have you won any embroidery contests?"

I opened the closet door and ran my fingers down labels on plastic boxes. "Small ones. And I was one of many runners-up in the previous IMEC contest."

Smallwood smiled with her lips, not her eyes. "So according to the note Felicity probably wrote — we'll check her printing, by the way — I should ask you where you were last night when she was attacked."

Of course the box with the point presser would be on the bottom. "I don't know when she was attacked."

"Don't be difficult."

I suppressed an annoyed sigh of my own and began removing the top boxes. "The fire siren woke me up. You can check with the fire department what time that went off. My clock said it was two. When I was on my way to the Coddlefields', I heard another siren, probably the ambulance with Tiffany in it. I must have arrived at the Coddlefields' shortly after two thirty. You can check what time they rushed Tiffany to the hospital."

Smallwood pulled a plastic box containing fabric remnants out of the closet for me and set it on the floor. "And you found the victim when?"

"Between ten and fifteen minutes later."

"Did anyone see you during this time?"

"I spoke to the Coddlefield children. The oldest girl must be about fifteen. The youngest girl, Darla, told me a lady was still in the house. Actually, she said that a 'nasty lady' was in the house. She had referred to Felicity Ranquels as a nasty lady before, but it didn't occur to me that Felicity, who lives in Cleveland, could be there at that time of night. Haylee's also a new volunteer in the fire department, and I hadn't seen her at the fire. I can't imagine anyone calling Haylee nasty, but what if Darla had meant Haylee? I needed to find out if Haylee was trapped in that house."

Her eyelids closed to slits, Smallwood appeared to be half asleep. "I'll give the cardboard with the note on it to Gartener." Planning to see the handsome detective again seemed to perk her up. "Would you have called me if you'd seen what she wrote?"

The neckline of my T-shirt was trying to strangle me. I tugged at it. "Of course. Felicity is rabidly protective of her company's machines. She was going to rescue the machine last night *before* she rescued Tiffany. Who set that sewing machine on fire in the first place, the mystery fireman?"

"How did you know it was set?"

"I didn't." Had Chief Smallwood just let me in on a clue? Did she *know* that arson had been responsible for the fire? "But why knock people out and tie them to furniture

338

unless he planned to destroy all the evidence in a fire? He probably planned that Felicity's and Tiffany's deaths would appear accidental. Darlene's death could have passed as an accident."

"We were almost certain that Darlene's death was *not* completely an accident, even before last night. There had to have been malicious intent."

I frowned. "That's what I thought, too, based on the number of things that went wrong with the machine."

"And the table it was on."

I held my breath in hopes she'd give me more information.

As if resigned to filling me in, she explained in a weary voice, "We took the table as evidence. The bolts fastening the legs were held on with wing nuts. The front two wing nuts were so loose that when the sewing machine started going top speed, the bolts worked themselves out and the front legs fell, bringing the table and the machine with them. If Darlene had been sitting at the table instead of lying on the floor trying to unplug the crazed machine, she may have ended up only with some bad bruises on her thighs. From the look of the bolts, those wing nuts had once been quite tight. Someone must have unscrewed them."

Malicious intent. Why would anyone do such a thing? Feeling sick, I knelt and lifted the lid off the box that, according to my labeling system, held my point presser. I pulled out a tailor's ham, some pressing cloths, and a box of small pressing aids. And finally, my point presser. I hauled it out. "Is this like the weapon you found?"

36

"Yes," Smallwood said. "Tiffany and Felicity were hit with something just like that. You seamstresses own a lot of lethal tools."

I nestled the point presser back in its place. "Using a wooden weapon before setting a fire shows premeditation, doesn't it?"

"It could. And many killers expect a fire to burn up all the evidence. Fires don't, and this one didn't come close. The good thing about amateur criminals, if there is a good thing, is that they make mistakes and are easier to catch."

I tried to keep a neutral expression on my face, but she shook her pen at me. "You were *lucky* that other time. Don't think of yourself as a detective, amateur or professional. Let us do the investigating."

"Yes, ma'am." I nearly saluted.

She glared at me.

Maybe she didn't want me investigating, but even she might admit that I could come up with plausible theories. They might not be the right theories, but they could lead her and other investigators down paths that would yield results, couldn't they? "Did you ever find Felicity's car?" I asked.

"Yep. It was where she said she'd left it, in a farm lane south of the house, tucked among the trees. Tell me this, Willow — Felicity reported that she saw the firefighter attack Tiffany on the third floor, and then Felicity went to the second floor, where we know she was attacked. You said that the little girl told you she saw the nasty lady sleeping in Tiffany's room when her daddy was carrying her and her blankie outside, right?"

I nodded.

"Okay, here's the thing — Plug had his fourteen-year-old son report the fire while Plug and his two oldest teenagers evacuated the little kids. Which means that Felicity saw a firefighter inside the Coddlefields' house *before* the fire was reported. How could that be?"

"Maybe Tiffany had already called it in?"

Smallwood shook her head decisively. "Nope. We checked with 911. No one had."

I shoved the plastic box containing the point presser back into my closet. "If one was going to set a fire, wouldn't wearing a firefighter's uniform, complete with respirator and mask, be a sensible precaution?"

"I suppose."

"Maybe the actual attacker wasn't wearing a firefighting outfit. Felicity was stunned and could have been confused about what happened before she was hit. I didn't clobber her, anyway." I only dragged her down a flight of stairs. "And there was that mystery fireman who must have left early, while smoke was still coming out of that house and the others were spraying water on the roof. Maybe he arrived early, too." To attack people and start a fire? Why would someone do that?

And had Susannah been at the Coddlefields'? The mailbox door hadn't been closed, but it wouldn't have made sense for her to rifle through people's mailboxes hours after the mail should have been delivered. Unsure who had been driving the car that resembled Susannah's, I didn't mention it.

Smallwood had kept track of the boxes. She handed them to me in order so they'd end up where they'd been before. Her thoroughness and helpfulness despite her lack of sleep impressed me. I thanked her, shut the closet door, and added, "Maybe the mystery fireman wore a firefighter's outfit as a disguise."

"It could be difficult to clomp around in someone else's house and not be noticed," she said. "Especially dressed as a fireman."

She had a dry sense of humor that I was only beginning to recognize and appreciate. "Unless it was a common occurrence," I contributed. "Maybe Plug and his sons strut around in those uniforms frequently." At the look on her face, I quickly added, "Maybe they do fire drills, teach the little kids about fire safety, or something."

"Or something," she repeated drily. "Whatever it is, I don't think I want to know about it."

"It's your job."

"Thanks for reminding me, Willow."

Yes, she definitely had a sense of humor.

"No problem. And anyway," I said, "someone besides Felicity did see that fireman. Tiffany. Where was Plug when Felicity saw Tiffany and the fireman having their encounter?"

"He claims he fell asleep in the basement watching a baseball game."

"I did hear a TV or radio in the basement when I ran inside. Presumably, the smaller children were sleeping in their bedrooms on the second floor when the fireman, or whoever, crept in. Where were Plug's older kids?"

"Russ and his two teenaged siblings, a boy and a girl, had been out driving around. They came home and saw flames shooting from the sewing room window on the third floor."

Or at least they *said* they'd been out. "So Tiffany's attacker was able to creep up to the sewing room without anyone noticing, except Tiffany, who could have been up there working on a project. And Felicity's entry went unnoticed, too. Even if Plug heard someone walking around upstairs, he might have figured it was Tiffany or one of his kids. But you'd think he'd have heard his smoke detectors. Not that they were making any noise when I arrived." With all that smoke still billowing, shouldn't they have been beeping?

"They were out of batteries."

I clapped my hand over my mouth and squeaked through my fingers, "The fire chief? Neglected to replace his batteries?"

She waved her hand in front of her face as if trying to blow smoke away. "Someone in that household — Plug says it wasn't him — took batteries out whenever the detectors warned that the batteries were low.

They probably *intended* to put new ones in."

Maybe as volunteer firefighters, Haylee and I could go around reminding people to replace batteries in smoke and carbon monoxide detectors. We could even help them do it, and no one would accuse us of being snoopy.

My stomach growled. I asked Smallwood, "When did you last eat?"

"Supper last night."

"Come on, then." I led her to the kitchen and set out bread, peanut butter, grape jelly, knives, spoons, and plates. We dug in and made thick, gooey sandwiches. Grapes weren't good for dogs, so I left the jelly out of theirs.

Smallwood asked me to give her a more detailed description of the firefighter I'd seen out on the road.

"He was wearing full regalia, including a mask, I think, which would have been odd, since those things aren't comfortable and he was so far from the fire. I couldn't see all of his face. He was about Plug's height."

"Why are you making that face?"

I had squeezed my eyes and mouth closed as if someone were blowing smoke at me. "I wouldn't want to rule Plug Coddlefield out of any of this. But I don't think that firefighter was as heavy as he is."

"Why don't you want to rule him out?"

"He seems mean enough to hurt his wife. And he may have had a girlfriend while Darlene was still alive."

"The girlfriend was also attacked." Smallwood cut her sandwiches into cute triangles. "And according to Felicity, the mystery firefighter encouraged the fire in the sewing machine. Would a father do that when his children were asleep on the next floor down?"

"I hope not! But Felicity was wandering around inside his house in the middle of the night. I'm not sure I'd blame him for attacking an intruder he found near his children's bedrooms."

"His teenagers — except for Russ, whom I haven't yet managed to interview — have separately corroborated that he was asleep when they got home and saw smoke and flames. If Felicity's story is correct, the fire began *before* she was attacked." She shook a forefinger at me. "And don't tell me the teenagers started a fire in the house where their younger sisters and brothers were sleeping, either."

She was probably right. The mystery fireman must have started the fire and attacked both Tiffany and Felicity. As far as we knew, the Coddlefield teenagers had behaved well. The boys had fought the fire while the girls had looked after the small children. It was possible that none of them, except Darla, had known that Felicity was there.

We took the dogs and our lunches outside. I patted one of the Adirondack chairs. "You can sit here. It's washable, so leave all the smudges you want."

"Thanks." Smallwood sat, grunting as if she'd been on her feet for hours. She probably had. "This is great."

"Peanut butter and jelly is comfort food, sometimes."

"Nearly always," she agreed.

The dogs charged to the bottom of the hill, then raced back up. I gave them each a piece of their special, peanut-butter-only sandwiches, then turned to Smallwood. "You know, the would-be murderer last night probably expected other evidence besides the wooden point presser to burn up completely. Felicity said he tore two strips off a piece of an unmade little dress. The fabric on Felicity's wrist was cotton, so I'm guessing that Tiffany was tied up with cotton, too. Cotton burns into fine ash hardly distinguishable from other types of ash, but artificial fabrics melt, leaving telltale beads."

"How do you know all that? And how would someone intent on harming Tiffany and Felicity know?"

I rubbed my fingers against my thumb as if touching fabric. "I can usually recognize cotton by the way it feels. If I'm not sure, I light a match to a scrap. Cotton burns. Polyester melts."

Smallwood looked about to accuse me of lighting matches to fields of soybeans and empty barns.

I defended myself. "Most people who sew know the flame test. A chemist would know. An arsonist might know. The husband or children of a seamstress might have heard about it. All of my boutique-owning colleagues should know."

"If you Threadville ladies are lighting up your fabrics all the time, it's no wonder we have so many fires around this village."

I blustered, "We don't!"

"JK," she said with a grin. "Just kidding. Does *any* of this make sense to you?"

I had to admit that it didn't. "Felicity was wearing polyester, so the cloth used to tether her wouldn't have mattered, and maybe her attacker didn't know about the flame test. The fireman I saw beside the dark car could have been a teen, maybe a friend of the oldest Coddlefield son, Russ.

He couldn't have been Russ, though," I reminded her. "I saw Russ driving a tanker truck seconds after I saw that other fireman."

Smallwood shook her head. "But later, that kid tore away last night after we said no one was to leave."

"We tried."

"I know, and we didn't want you endangering yourselves. You were right to dodge out of his way. I radioed the state police and they went after him but didn't find him. They will. We have a few questions for that young man." She polished off her second sandwich. "Fleeing the scene. If there's a way to make oneself look suspicious . . ."

"He's only sixteen," I reminded her.

"Huh," she said as if nothing could surprise her, though she wasn't old enough to have worked in law enforcement, or anything else, for more than about six years.

37

I asked Smallwood, "Have they figured out why Tiffany was trying to use a heap of fabrics to put out a fire in a sewing machine?"

She bit into her apple. "What did you want her to do, blow on it?"

"I mean, why was the sewing machine on fire?" Felicity had said it was the Chandler Champion, and she would have known.

"Why do you think?" Smallwood asked.

I gripped my apple tightly. "Please tell me this Chandler Champion didn't malfunction and start a fire."

"Sure, I'll tell you that if you like."

I would have to accept the inevitable. "Tell me the truth," I said. "Go ahead. Tell me my shop gave away two killer sewing machines in a little over a week."

"Okay," she agreed. "Here it is, unsugared and unembroidered. Yes. No one, not your mystery fireman or anyone else, set that fire.

The second killer sewing machine shorted out and caused a fire."

I still wanted to blame something besides a sewing machine that had come from In Stitches. "But if Felicity's memory was right, a mysterious fireman was conveniently on the scene."

Smallwood leaned back in her Adirondack chair and closed her eyes against sunlight filtering down through leaves. "And he very nicely restarted the fire after Tiffany almost managed to smother it."

"That was considerate." I was punchy from lack of sleep.

"Very. If you think of anything that could help us identify the firefighter you saw beside the car, please call me." She yawned. "I'd better go or I'll fall asleep right here listening to those birds."

We went inside and took the dogs upstairs to In Stitches. Smallwood and I went through the dogs' pen, then I shut the gate so the dogs wouldn't make nuisances of themselves or escape through the front door.

Women sewed, embroidered, chattered, and laughed. It was still my break. Susannah was busy with customers.

On the way to the front door, we passed my row of bright new sewing machines. Smallwood gave them a grim look. "Maybe

I should take up sewing," she muttered.

"We have classes Tuesdays through Fridays. If you miss a morning session, attend an afternoon one."

She frowned at me like I had no clue, which was close to the truth.

It seemed that every woman in the store was watching us with keen interest. "Step outside with me," Smallwood muttered. The door closed behind us. Smallwood asked, "That sewing machine you gave Tiffany, the one that shorted out. Had you tested it?"

"No, but I'd been using it in some of my classes. Lots of other people saw it working perfectly."

"How can they know one sewing machine from another, especially if they're the same model?"

"That was the only other Chandler Champion I had here. You can check that with the Chandler company."

"Have any of your machines besides the Chandlers ever harmed anyone?"

"Other than people sticking their fingers under needles at the wrong time, no."

She glanced through my huge front windows at cheerful women buying embroidery supplies. "Maybe you shouldn't use, sell, or give away any more Chandlers until they're inspected."

"Please, take my other Chandler models and have them tested."

Smallwood nodded. "We may do that."

Two customers ran up to my porch and greeted me. Any minute now, a crowd would gather in and around my rocking chairs and I'd never pry more information out of Chief Smallwood.

Maybe she wanted to learn more from me, too. When I suggested a walk down the street, she agreed. We passed her cruiser. Waving at Sam inside his hardware store, The Ironmonger, I asked Smallwood, "Did you learn anything more from Felicity?"

"No, unfortunately. She's still unconscious. They had to operate right away to relieve pressure on her brain from internal bleeding. She's being kept in an artificial coma." Smallwood was still carrying the evidence bag. She raised it to eye level. "All we have until she wakes up is what she wrote on this cardboard and what she said early this morning — a fireman attacked Tiffany, then pushed Felicity down and dragged her out of the house. Apparently she doesn't remember someone breaking her skull and tying her to a bed."

Mona peered out Country Chic's door as if hoping to lure customers to visit her home decorating boutique. We waved at her, then strolled silently past The Sunroom.

Bashing Tiffany and Felicity with a point presser hadn't been enough for their attacker. He had been determined that neither of them would escape before the smoke or fire finished them off. What did the two women have in common, other than that they both had some experience, maybe, with sewing, and both had known Darlene? Presumably Tiffany hadn't harmed herself, so maybe she hadn't engineered Darlene's death, but the culprit almost had to be another member of the Coddlefield household.

I didn't like Plug and wasn't about to absolve him of fatally harming his wife, but I could not believe he would allow a fire to rage in a home where his children were sleeping. His daughters had said he'd found Tiffany and carried her out of the house. Maybe he did that to make himself look like a hero, but why tie her up, and why leave the fabric evidence on her wrist when he carried her out?

We climbed the stairs to the bandstand in the park where the river met the lake. The bandstand's recent coat of white paint nearly blinded me in the afternoon sunshine. "Did Tiffany see anyone?" I asked

Smallwood. "Hear anyone creep up behind her?"

"Tiffany's concussion was worse than Felicity's. She needed the same emergency operation. She's still unconscious, too." She squinted at me. "Could Felicity have attacked Tiffany, then blamed a fireman?"

I bit my lip. "It's possible, but she wouldn't have tied herself to the leg of a bed, unless she wanted to commit suicide and make it look like murder, but why drive all the way here to do that? She could have stayed in Cleveland. And how did she bash herself in the back of the head with a point presser, by falling on it? Did you find it on the second floor, or upstairs in the sewing room?"

"Second floor."

"That fits with what she told us about the fireman following her down there," I said. "How do you police officers manage to keep this all straight?"

She waved her notebook at me. "Notes. I'll meet with Gartener and the others and go over all this. Thanks for your help."

I couldn't remember her ever being this grateful before.

She quickly undid the goodwill by adding, "Don't leave the county without telling me first." Head high, she trotted down the

bandstand steps and strode toward her
cruiser, leaving me gaping after her.

38

I reminded myself that Chief Smallwood hadn't said I needed her permission to leave the county, only that I had to *tell* her if I was going. It was a small distinction, and an even smaller consolation.

I returned to In Stitches only seconds before Susannah was supposed to be back at Tell a Yarn. I walked out to my front porch with her and asked, "Did I see you driving around early this morning about the time of the Coddlefield fire?"

"What were you doing out then?"

Not really an answer . . . I said, "I went for on-the-job firefighting training."

She shuddered. "I wish you wouldn't do that."

I asked boldly, "Why were *you* there?"

"I wasn't sleeping. But I didn't go to the fire." She pleated the hem of her shirt between her fingers. "I didn't set it, either."

"Have you told Smallwood about that letter yet?"

"It's too late. She must already know about it. Or it was destroyed in the fire." She put on a faked hopeful smile.

"Not much was destroyed in that fire. Tell her, anyway."

"Okay, okay!" She stormed off my porch and across the street.

The Threadville shops closed at six on Thursdays. When my last customer left, I let my dogs out in the backyard. I couldn't help smiling at the way they attacked each other, gnashing their teeth in play, but neither of them ever got hurt.

Had the police found Russ yet?

Maybe Clay would know. I called his cell, but he didn't answer. Was he still at the hospital with Tiffany? I texted him to call me.

I phoned Isaac. He didn't know where Russ was, either. His voice took on foreboding overtones. "Plug's looking for him."

"Why?"

"He *said* he was going to kill him. But you know how fathers can be."

Mine had not said anything remotely like that, even in teasing, when I was a teen. On the other hand, as an adult, I had gotten into a lot of trouble for making a threat like Plug's. I hadn't meant it, though. Had Plug?

I called Smallwood and told her what Isaac had said.

"That could explain why the boy hasn't shown up," she said. "Some parents! We'd like you to show us where you found Felicity, now, Willow. Meet you at the Coddlefields' in fifteen minutes?"

I agreed, though I really didn't want to return to that smoke- and water-damaged house, didn't want to be involved in anything to do with the Coddlefields' life or the investigation into Darlene's death.

It was a little late to stay out of it, however.

Maybe, I told myself as I shut the dogs into my apartment, the police were on the verge of solving the crimes and would soon tell me they'd arrested a culprit, and I would be able to leave the county if I wanted to without telling Chief Smallwood first. Not that I particularly wanted to. I loved Threadville.

I drove south into the countryside. The golden haze hovering over fields would have been lovelier if I hadn't been on my way back to the Coddlefields'. I slowed to turn into their driveway. A car coming from the opposite direction stopped to let me go first. Detective Gartener lifted one finger from the steering wheel in greeting.

He followed me down the driveway and

parked behind me. The Coddlefields' farm-house looked empty and forlorn with that gaping black hole in the roof and glass missing from the third-floor windows. Yellow police tape was draped from tree to tree. Everything reeked of smoke.

Chief Smallwood's cruiser was near Tiffany's car, but Plug's SUV and Russ's pickup were nowhere in sight.

Smallwood, Gartener, and I got out of our vehicles. Gartener wore a T-shirt and jeans, so it was easy to tell he wasn't wearing a Kevlar vest, but he walked with his usual take-no-nonsense bearing.

Smallwood had found time for a shower and a fresh uniform. Maybe a nap, too, but she always glowed when Gartener was around. She greeted him first, then me. "Willow, we want to see where you found Felicity Ranquels tied to a bed . . ."

One of Gartener's eyebrows rose.

"The leg of a bed," I corrected her. "She was on the floor."

Smallwood waved her hand in front of her face. "Wherever."

"Retrace your steps for us," Gartener said in that warm voice that didn't go with his wary eyes. "From the moment you arrived here last night."

"I parked out on the road, then ran up

the driveway." I showed them where the children had been sitting when I talked to them, and where I'd collected firefighter's garb from the fire truck. They had me lead them through the woods the way I'd gone to the back of house. We ducked under the yellow tape. Unlike the night before, the kitchen door was closed. Smallwood had a key.

The smell of smoke was worse inside. They wanted to know how I knew my way around the house, and I felt like a museum guide. Here was where the children were crying instead of eating their snack. Here was where Edna and I saw Plug kissing Tiffany. Here was the late Darlene Coddlefield's collection of framed antique linens, now stained by smoke and water.

And . . . I balked. There were the stairs that Tiffany and I had climbed, huffing and puffing under the weight of the second killer sewing machine, the same stairs I'd dragged Felicity down in the dark of night, with smoke billowing and water dripping. I asked, "Are these stairs safe?"

"You weren't worried about that last night," Smallwood scolded.

"The local fire officials" — Plug and Isaac? — "have said they are," Gartener assured me. "And state fire investigators concurred."

"Lead on," Smallwood ordered, a little too cheerfully.

Bracing my shoulders, I trudged to the second floor. I pointed through open doorways to bedrooms, the pink frilly one and the blue cars-and-trucks one, with quilts missing from bunk beds and blankets pulled onto the floor. The quilt was still on the bed in the master bedroom. Everything was wet. "I checked these rooms, first."

I didn't have to touch the tiny bedroom's door. It was open, the way I'd left it. "Did you fingerprint this door?" I asked. "Felicity was lying there, on the floor, early this morning."

"Everything was checked for prints, right, Toby?" Smallwood asked the tall detective.

He looked down at me. "Did you touch the door last night?"

I thought back. "I was wearing firefighter's gloves."

Smallwood pointed behind the door. "Those?"

Two firefighter's gloves, with the letters EVFD stenciled on them in red, were almost out of sight under the bed. I stared at the gloves in bewilderment, and then at my bare hands. "I don't think so. I'm sure I left them on, even when I was dragging

Felicity out. I put mine away where they belonged on the fire truck. Those must be —"

Gartener was one step ahead of me. He scooped up the gloves and dropped them into an evidence bag. "Felicity said her attacker was dressed as a fireman."

But I'd discovered a new horror. Thickened blood. I backed away. "Felicity's head was just about there," I managed.

"We figured," Gartener said.

"The loop around her wrist was under this leg," I said.

Smallwood took photos and made notes.

Except for the bloodstain and a tiny, yellowed scrap of paper on the floor near where the gloves had been, Tiffany's room was sparse and neat.

"What's that piece of paper?" I asked Gartener.

He picked it up. "A return address label for Darlene Coddlefield."

"Think it matches that small rectangle of glue on the weapon?" Smallwood asked him.

"We'll find out." He placed the sticker in an envelope.

"Let me guess," I said. "Darlene Coddlefield put return address labels on her sewing things."

"Bingo," Smallwood said.

"So the point presser you found was hers?"

"Two for two," she said.

"Did you find her point presser in this room?"

"Three for three," Smallwood said.

"Ever think of joining the state police?" Gartener asked in that voice that might have made me consider doing all sorts of uncharacteristic things.

But maybe not becoming a cop. "I'll leave investigating to you experts."

"Good," Smallwood snapped. "It's about time you learned that. We're done here." She started down the soggy, carpeted stairs.

Following her, I asked, "How are Felicity and Tiffany?"

"Still being kept unconscious," Smallwood said.

"Is anyone with them?" I asked.

Behind me, Gartener answered, "State troopers."

"Is Clay Fraser still with Tiffany?" I asked.

I couldn't see Gartener's face, but he sounded surprised or amused. "No."

Where was Clay, and why hadn't he returned my call or text?

Smallwood led us out the back door and locked it, and we walked around the side of the house beside zinnias and petunias, still blooming and mostly, except for a few trampled ones, undamaged by firefighters.

At our cars, I asked, "Have you found Russ Coddlefield yet? The sixteen-year-old?"

Smallwood and Gartener exchanged looks that I couldn't read. "No," Gartener answered.

"If you find out where he is, or think of anything you haven't told us, let us know," Smallwood added.

I drove home and let the dogs have an extra-long romp in the backyard. Clay didn't return my call. He'd been up most of the night, then could have worked all day.

Maybe he knew where Russ was and didn't want to be put on the spot about it.

I would have to leave Clay alone.

39

The next day was Friday, Susannah's day to help in my shop. She came in early with a spring in her step, and smiled with obvious relief. "I don't have to tell Chief Smallwood about the letter."

"She knew?"

"She has a suspect." Susannah lowered her voice as if we already had customers in the store. "Not me. Russ Coddlefield, Darlene's son. He ran away from home, and the police are looking for him."

The morning's students bounded into the store, so we couldn't continue the discussion.

Watching Susannah patiently explain why the correct stabilizer and tension were crucial to machine embroidery, I couldn't believe that anyone ever could have suspected her of harming Darlene. I still worried that her refusal to confess about the letter would come back to bite her.

It was hard to concentrate on anything for very long. All day, our customers were excited about the Harvest Festival, which would begin later that night. Susannah confessed that she was a fall fair junkie and could hardly wait for lights, music, and rides. "And the fireworks," she crowed. "Tonight at nine." It was great to see her acting like herself again.

I tilted my head. "You like *fire*works?"

She pushed her hair back. "I know. It makes no sense. Fire scares me, but fireworks don't. Maybe because they're more controlled."

I raised my eyebrows.

She laughed. "Well, they're pretty, anyway."

I had to agree with that.

Opal had canceled her usual Friday storytelling so we could all set up the Threadville booth. The Harvest Festival would be a mini-holiday for all of us, complete with yummy food, games, shows, and other booths to tour. Haylee, her mothers, and I planned to work in our own stores on Saturday and Sunday, but we had notified everyone that we would close early so we could spend evenings at the festival. We had hired Susannah and Georgina to assist visitors in the Threadville booth during the days we couldn't be there.

As soon as our last customer left In Stitches at a quarter past five, I badgered Susannah again about confessing to the police about the letter she'd written to Darlene. She said she would after supper if she had time before the fireworks.

"Make time."

Promising she would, she left.

I loaded my car with IMEC entries and embroidery supplies, then took off for the festival.

A few miles south of Elderberry Bay, I came upon fences surrounding acres of recently mown hayfields where dozens of white vinyl tents and several ovals of bleachers had sprouted up. A tall Ferris wheel, its colorful lights glittering even in the daylight, dominated the fairgrounds.

I smelled popcorn. Suddenly hungry, I pulled up at the festival's entry gate. A smiling teenager wearing a bright red vest with the words *Harvest Festival Volunteer* on it — silk-screened, not embroidered — handed me a map. "The Threadville booth is in the handcrafts tent, right here on the corner of Brussels Sprouts Boulevard and Cabbage Court."

I thanked her and drove off, bumping over furrows until I found Brussels Sprouts

Boulevard. Haylee's pickup truck, Naomi's SUV, and Opal's and Edna's sedans were parked behind the tent. Clay's truck wasn't there, but one of Elderberry Bay's fire tankers was. An ambulance crew and state trooper were supposed to be on the grounds, too, on standby, at least when the festival was actually open.

I wondered if Tiffany and Felicity were conscious yet and able to give the investigators new details. If so, maybe the state police had already arrested a suspect. Determined to enjoy the festival no matter what, I parked and got out.

The handcrafts tent was big, probably about forty by eighty feet, with entrances at both ends.

Snickering, two teenaged boys galumphed away from the nearest entryway. I recognized them. Russ's friends. I called, "Do you two know where Russ is?"

"No!" They laughed harder and ran faster.

I didn't believe them and was tempted to chase them, but if I caught up, would they tell me the truth about Russ? Did they know who had attacked Tiffany and Felicity?

Inside the vast tent, a wide walkway separated the two long rows of booths. Booth was not quite the right word, since the only walls, except for barriers that exhibitors brought with them, were the tent walls around the perimeter.

Threadville's booth was the first one on our right, in a corner formed by the tent walls. I couldn't see beyond Naomi's quilts into the next booth, which should be the firefighters' flea market.

The second she saw me, Opal wanted to know why I'd asked the two boys where Russ was.

Edna stepped in front of her taller friend. "We overheard those boys talking in the booth next door. They said Russ was hiding, and it had something to do with the fire at his place. They said his father told them he's going to kill Russ if he ever finds him!"

I nodded. "I heard that, too."

Naomi shook her head and looked about to cry. "Imagine saying that to your kid's friends. No wonder Russ doesn't want to go home."

I asked, "Did the boys say where Russ is? The police want to talk to him."

Edna clapped her hands to her cheeks. "The *police*! What has he done?"

"Nothing, as far as I know," I answered, "besides leaving the scene of the fire before they told him he could."

"The boys didn't let on where Russ is,"

Naomi said. Her kind and caring voice always calmed the situation. "But I got the impression that they know."

Opal straightened a package of knitting needles hanging on a display rack. "That's what I thought, too."

"Me, too," Edna said. "Let's help Willow get organized."

Haylee and her mothers had already arranged their sections of our booth. They all went with me to unload my car. We quickly carried everything inside.

Setting up the glass-fronted case displaying the IMEC entries, I couldn't help admiring the gorgeous embroidery my students had created. Georgina had drawn, all in thread, a simple yet elegant vase. Susannah had created a dreamy girl with metallic stars glimmering in her flowing hair. Mimi had surrounded a hummingbird in flight with intricate vines and flowers and had backed the piece — meant to be a doily, I guessed — with canvas, which made the doily bulky, and even a bit lumpy in places. Rosemary had embroidered a pair of kittens tangling each other in a ball of yarn. My favorite was Ashley's wistful unicorn. That girl would go far with her thread art. I locked the case.

"Done?" Edna asked.

I nodded. Edna, Opal, Naomi, Haylee, and I trooped into the center aisle and turned around to see how the Threadville booth might look to strangers.

We all agreed that it was lovely, with Naomi's quilts guarding us from the firefighters' booth, Haylee's fabrics lining the wall of the tent nearest the doorway, Opal's knitted and crocheted clothing and blankets sharing the front with Edna's bling-bedecked garments. And finally, samples of embroidery across the back. The glowing rainbow hues in the matching flame stitch quilt, afghan, sofa pillow, and my embroidered wall hanging unified the display. Haylee had used the same color palette in the garments she'd tailored for the show.

We weren't planning to sell anything at the festival. Instead, we would hand out brochures and schedules for our fall classes. We would also show potential customers and students what could be done with a little imagination, creativity, determination, and supplies — many of them displayed here in our booth — that could be purchased at the Threadville boutiques.

It was nearly seven. The opening ceremonies were due to start in less than two hours. Opal, Edna, and Naomi wandered off to explore the fair and pick up something to eat.

Haylee and I hoped to finish setting up the firefighters' booth before the fireworks at nine. We peeked around Naomi's wall of quilts. Books, glassware, dishes, kitchen gadgets, and toys covered every flat surface in the firefighters' booth.

"Someone has already done a lot," I said, surprised and pleased.

"Isaac was here, working with Russ's friends," Haylee told me. "But he had to check on the fireworks and left the boys to work alone."

"*Isaac*'s setting off the fireworks?" I asked.

"No. They brought in professional pyrotechnic artists."

Just as well. Our sweet but cautious deputy fire chief would probably feel he had to douse the fireworks with water before lighting them.

Apparently, the boys had given up before unpacking all the cardboard cartons. They had piled obviously full ones in one tall stack next to a tarpaulin hanging in the corner farthest from the Threadville booth. I could hear Mona muttering to herself on the other side of the tarpaulin.

Haylee frowned at the precariously balanced cartons. "I'll have to get the ladder out of my truck again so we can finish unpacking and pricing."

Before we could take one step, Mona raced in from her booth next door and stuck a round red sticker on a love seat. "I'm buying this for Country Chic!"

Haylee pointed out, "The upholstery's torn."

Mona shook her head. "I'll have . . . I'll refinish and reupholster it."

To keep from laughing, I carefully did not look at Haylee. Mona always expected us to believe, against all evidence to the contrary, that she could sew, refinish, and upholster.

Mona slapped a sticker on a scratched-up bookcase. "Just tell me the prices." She claimed a lamp, a set of dishes, and a copper pot. "How much? How much?" Shaking her head in her usual way, she never stopped talking long enough for us to answer.

Eventually, Haylee managed to show her the price tags and stickers. Mona wanted to haggle. Haylee and I refused to sell anything for less than what we thought the fire department might get after the handcrafts tent opened for business in the morning. Deciding that some of the pieces couldn't be worth as much as we were asking, Mona removed many of her red stickers. She did, however, pay for the love seat, several lamps, a wing chair, and an urn that looked like it might contain Uncle Herbert's or Great-Aunt Alicia's remains. Glad to make space so we could unpack more cartons, Haylee and I helped Mona cart her loot into the Country Chic booth.

Finally, Haylee and I went out, retrieved her ladder, and set it up next to the leaning tower of cartons.

Mona huffed and puffed as she arranged her purchases in the next booth. The tarpaulin between the two booths bulged, increasing the size of her booth and decreasing the size of the firefighters' booth.

The stack of cardboard cartons swayed.

Mona screamed.

40

The top carton tumbled over the makeshift barricade into Mona's booth.

She shrieked louder.

Haylee leaped over a stool and grabbed the ladder. I squeezed between a table and the bulging tarpaulin separating the firefighters' booth from Mona's, but I was too late to steady the tower, even if I could have.

The second carton tilted toward Mona's booth, then fell. It bounced off the frame holding the tarpaulin and came straight at me. I fended it off. It crashed onto the table beside me. China and glass flew everywhere.

More cartons cascaded over the table, the ladder, and me. They knocked Haylee down. I couldn't see her. She had to be somewhere behind furniture and the remains of what had once been sets of dishes.

"Haylee, are you okay?" I yelled.

Haylee shoved cartons away and rose, somewhat disheveled, from among them.

"I'm fine. That was exciting." Boxes settled onto the packed earth around her. She pushed hair out of her eyes. Her smile turned to shock. "Willow, you're bleeding."

Blood welled out of a cut on my right hand. I put my hand behind my back. "It's nothing."

She scrambled toward me between up-ended boxes, furniture, and broken dishes. "Let me see," she ordered.

"It's nothing."

"Help!" Mona shouted. "Come help me!" At least I thought that was what she yelled, but her voice came out oddly muffled.

Haylee and I raced around the tarpaulin hanging between the firefighters' booth and Mona's.

Mona sat on the ground in the back corner of her booth. A cardboard box was upside down on her head. About a zillion men's ties covered the rest of her.

The box wasn't stuck. We lifted it off easily. Ties poured out of it.

"I could have suffocated," Mona gasped, looking daggers at us.

I opened my mouth to tell her that we'd also been attacked by falling boxes, and that she could have removed the box from her head by herself.

And then I saw Haylee's face. She'd

stopped plucking ties off Mona, and was gazing in apparent rapture at the ties in her hands. "One hundred percent silk," she breathed, "every one of them. I'll take the whole lot."

Mona struggled to rise. "Whatever for?"

I tried to help Mona stand, but she saw blood on my hand, avoided touching me, and levered herself up by leaning on the love seat she'd crammed into the corner. Silk ties slithered from her to the love seat to the ground.

I was afraid that Haylee might ruin one of the ties by using it as a tourniquet on my arm. My hand wasn't bleeding heavily, but the cut stung.

Haylee, however, seemed to have forgotten my wound. She murmured, "Beautiful silks, cut on the bias. I can turn them into seam binding and piping."

"But they fell into my booth," Mona whined. "Finders, keepers."

"What would *you* do with all these men's ties, Mona?" I asked. *Put an ad in a singles' column — forty-something woman, complete with a box of expensive silk ties?*

Mona shrugged, sending even more ties onto the floor. "If Haylee can use them for piping, I can, too."

Haylee lost some of her dreamy expression. "You're going to start making your own clothes?"

"For upholstery."

Haylee raised her eyebrows. "Silk won't last a month as piping on upholstery. Besides, there's only enough fabric in one tie to embellish a few short seams. It would work for clothing, not love seats."

Mona didn't seem to know that a bright red and green striped tie was looped over her chignon. "Sofa pillows, then." With both hands, she sketched out a large pillow.

"Smaller," Haylee corrected her.

She wrinkled her nose. "Ugh. Not trendy. I guess they won't be much use to me. You buy them. If I need one, I'll come over to your place for it."

Haylee asked me, "How much should I pay the firefighters for the entire box?"

"Let's ask Isaac when he comes back," I suggested.

One end of the tie on Mona's head must have touched her ear. She brushed at it and missed. "Hundreds of dollars' worth of ties." She looked like she expected to benefit from the proceeds herself.

Haylee and I put the ties into the carton. By unspoken agreement, we did not tell Mona about the one dangling from her head. She would dislodge it soon enough with her usual head-shaking.

As a respite from trying to control my Mona-induced giggles, I went with Haylee when she carried the carton to her truck. She remembered my injury. "Willow, raise your hand over your head. I have a first-aid kit in my glove compartment."

A few minutes later, we'd both indulged in a fit of laughter, my hand had been thoroughly disinfected and bundled in gauze and covered in extra-large adhesive bandages.

"I hate to complain," I said, "after your first-rate care, but didn't you have any plain Band-Aids?" Haylee's were covered in cartoon characters.

"Afraid not," Haylee said. "You needed a bit of whimsy in your outfit."

I was dressed the same way she was, in jeans and a black T-shirt. Suddenly, I remembered what had been odd about Opal, Naomi, and Edna. "Your mothers aren't wearing handmade clothes tonight," I said to Haylee. "I've never seen them in jeans before."

Haylee groaned. "Cowboy boots, too. They figured that a Harvest Festival called for Western dress."

"It could have been worse," I said. "They could have worn bandanas over their faces."

"Don't even *think* it."

Not many people were in our tent, but we did manage to borrow a broom and a dustpan from a woman in the scrapbooking guild's booth and were able to sweep up shards of china and glass. After we took the broom back to the scrapbooker, I unpacked a box of mismatched teaspoons and banged-up colanders.

Haylee opened a box and whistled. "Come see this, Willow."

I couldn't believe my eyes. Old linens. The pair of tea towels on top were decorated with hand-embroidered candlewicking, the real kind, made with genuine candlewick. Gently, I lifted the towels and peeled back the edges of linens below them. Heritage linens. I could buy the whole box. My students and I could copy some of the old-fashioned embroidery techniques and designs with our software and embroidery machines.

Mona joined us in our booth to see what we were oohing and aahing over.

She and Haylee helped me remove folded linens from the box. Luckily for me, some of them were stained. Mona shook her head. "Ugh. Old things. You can have them."

At the bottom, we found a cross-stitched

family tree. The earliest dates were in the 1700s.

"This could be an antique," Mona exclaimed. "I could get a nice price for this in Country Chic." Naturally, as she spoke, she shook her head, and the end of the tie she didn't know she was wearing tickled her ear again.

Before Mona could snatch the supposedly antique linen from me, Haylee pointed at names and dates in the top branches. "Look — triplets born in 1994. Anderson, Sam, and Mary."

Mona said, "Someone in 1736 could have been predicting the future."

I pointed at the lower corner. "She signed it in 1995. Marian Hartley." The name seemed familiar. Someone I'd met in or around Elderberry Bay?

Mona was not easily dissuaded. She fingered the lace ruffle sewn around the sampler. "This lace could be antique, maybe from 1736. I could remove it and have my seamstress — I mean *I* could sew it onto a pillow."

Hiding a grin, I put the family tree into the box and covered it with tea towels, guest towels, dresser scarves, doilies, and napkins, all hand embroidered. "I'm buying the whole box." I left no room for argument.

A wily look came into Mona's eyes. "You two better make sure Isaac charges you good prices for the stuff you took."

I nodded. To keep her from rifling through my treasures, I balanced the carton on my good arm, carried it to my car, and locked it in.

I returned to the firefighters' booth in time to hear Mona ask Haylee, "Which one of you two pushed me?"

"Pushed you?" Haylee asked Mona. "When?"

"Right before that carton fell on my head. Someone pushed me."

Haylee and I looked at each other, mystified. "We couldn't have," Haylee said. "You were in your booth." She sidestepped a couple of paces. "I was right here, and Willow was over there, two feet from the tarpaulin." Two feet from where the tarpaulin continued to intrude on the space that was supposed to be occupied by the firefighters' booth, in fact.

Mona brushed at the end of the tie again, then folded her arms. "Someone pushed me. I felt it."

"Show us where you were in your booth when this happened," I suggested.

She led us to the back corner where we'd found her sitting with the carton overturned on her head. "I was right here, putting this love seat in place, and someone pushed me." She pointed at the wall of the tent. "From there."

I said, "Whoever it was had to be outside." I nodded at the frame holding the tarpaulin. "We were inside the tent, next door in the firefighters' booth."

Mona stared at where the tower of cartons had been, then at the side of the tent. "I suppose you're right." She shook her head. "AAAAACK! What *is* it?" Swatting at her ear, she cavorted like she'd been stung. "A snake? Get if off me!"

"Stop dancing around," Haylee, ever the diplomat, suggested.

With my unbandaged left hand, I lifted the tie off Mona's head and gave it to Haylee.

Mona, however, was still frantic. "Someone was outside the tent pushing me? Who? Go see if they're still there and tell them not to do it again."

I hadn't seen anyone in that vicinity moments ago when I put the box of linens in my car, and the person who had done the pushing, if any pushing had actually been done, would be long gone by now. However, to placate the nearly hysterical Mona, Haylee and I ran outside and around to the tent wall near Mona.

No one was there. "Mona?" I called. "I'm touching the tent. Can you see where my hand is? Is this where the push came from?"

"Yes!" She slapped the tent. Fortunately, I'd been using my uninjured hand.

Haylee and I went back inside.

"Who was it?" Mona demanded.

Haylee said, "No one was out there."

"Why did they push me?" Mona asked.

"Your guess," I said, "is as good as mine." Better, probably, since I was picturing her distending the tent with her rear end and believing the tent's natural resistance was a push. If she'd wanted a larger booth, she should have rented one instead of ramming the tarpaulin and tent walls in directions they didn't want to go.

I was still trying to figure out where I'd heard Marian Hartley's name. The more I thought about it, the more I realized I hadn't *heard* her name. I had read it.

On a computer screen. When I was skimming through names of donors to Darlene Coddlefield's charities?

I took out my phone and logged onto the Internet.

Marian Hartley had donated to Koins for Kids several years ago.

I showed Haylee. "She must live around

here," Haylee said.

"Who?" Mona asked, shaking her head.

I pocketed my phone. "The woman who embroidered that family tree. Marian Hartley. Do you know her?"

"Never heard of her. But I haven't lived around here as long as you two have."

"And neither of us have been here very long, either," Haylee said.

She was undoubtedly thinking the same thing I was. Chief Smallwood had said that investigators were checking on donors to those charities. If they didn't make an arrest soon, I would nudge them, especially about this donor. Then again, maybe all of the donors were from around here, people Darlene had known.

Music started nearby. Then a voice. A square dance? And the roar of engines.

"What's all that racket?" Mona asked.

Haylee and I raced out of the tent and up Brussels Sprouts Boulevard to an outdoor arena surrounded by bleachers.

The square dance was unlike any I'd ever seen or imagined. All eight of the dancers, guys and gals, were driving red farm tractors from the 1950s.

Skirts, crinolines, bloomers, and long hair flying, the four women wheeled their tractors around, braking, turning, reversing in speedy but careful choreography with their partners, who wore cowboy shirts matching the women's full-skirted dresses — the head couple in chartreuse, a couple in royal blue, a couple in orange, and the fourth couple in purple.

The "women" had beards, mustaches, hairy arms, bony knees, uniformly large busts, and wigs in colors that would have inspired Edna in the best of her hair-dye experimentation days.

Eight tractors going full speed in a small space, and no collisions? I'd spent some quality time on lawn tractors, but had never had to worry about other tractors. With the gathering crowd, Haylee and I laughed, clapped, and cheered them on.

"Promenade around the hall!"

Two by two, the tractors circled.

Haylee gasped, nudged me, and jerked her head to one side, a sure indication that I was to look beyond her but not make it obvious.

What was Jeremy Chandler doing at Elderberry Bay's Harvest Festival?

41

I hadn't thought about Jeremy since he'd called to assure me that he'd arrived safely in New York. He hadn't seemed enthralled by this corner of Pennsylvania, and I hadn't expected him to return soon. Or ever.

Haylee and I clambered out of the bleachers and caught up with him near the handcrafts tent.

"Willow!" What a phony, acting surprised to see me on my home turf. He'd gone native, sort of, in designer jeans and a blue button-down chambray shirt with neat creases showing that it had been removed from its packaging only minutes before. "Have you thought more about my offer?"

"What are you doing here?" I asked ungraciously.

"What happened to your hand?" he countered.

I put it behind my back. "Nothing. How come you're back so soon?" Had he been visiting Felicity?

He leaned toward Haylee and me like a conspirator. "Don't tell anyone." He pressed a finger to his lips. "I'm one of the judges. I meck."

It took me a second to understand. Jeremy wouldn't know that my students and I jokingly pronounced the initials for the International Machine Embroidery Competition "I make."

"I'm checking things out beforehand," he confided.

How odd.

"Excuse us," Haylee blurted. "We need to talk to someone."

We did?

She grabbed my good wrist and hauled me toward the square-dancing tractors.

"See you later, Jeremy," I called.

Sauntering down Cabbage Court toward the brightly lit carnival area, he waved over his shoulder without turning around.

It hardly seemed fair for the judge of an international contest to preview the entries from one small village. Would he guess that the flame stitch embroidery that matched other Threadville designs in our booth was my entry? Did he think he could coerce me to work for him by giving me high marks? He didn't know me very well. I wouldn't accept an unfairly awarded prize.

Still pulling at me, Haylee tucked us in among square dance fans. "Look," she commanded.

Russ's friends, the two teenagers I'd seen running from the handcrafts tent, were now slouching toward it. Actually, they were staggering.

A stern look on his face, Isaac followed them.

"Swing your partners high and low!"

Those drivers made their tractors appear to swing each other, four pairs of tractors circling in tight, and very noisy, formations.

I hated to leave the fun again, but Haylee and I tiptoed after Isaac and slipped into the firefighters' booth behind him and the two teenagers.

"Why didn't you unpack all of the boxes?" I asked the boys.

The taller one answered, "They were full of old clothes and garbage like that. Besides, we didn't have space."

"Hey," drawled the other. "What happened to all the stuff we did unpack?"

I smelled beer.

Haylee tapped her foot on the bare earth. "Your tower of cartons fell down and broke most of the dishes."

"But there was, like, more chairs and

stuff." The shorter boy looked at everything besides Isaac, Haylee, and me. He was so unsteady I was afraid he might do a face plant on a table of ashtrays.

I didn't take my eyes off him. "Some of us already bought some of it."

"Cool," said the first boy, tripping over a lamp.

Isaac caught it. "You two fellows are done here, but don't go driving anywhere until you sober up." He dangled keys in their faces. "I have your truck keys, but I left your doors unlocked. Go sleep it off."

Again, I asked them, "Have you two seen Russ?"

"Nope. Not since we helped put out the fire at his dad's place." Hands in pockets, heads down, they slunk away.

After they were out of earshot, I tilted my head at Isaac. "Did you find out where Russ is?"

He spread his hands. "No."

"Isaac!" Mona called in an artificially husky voice. "I need your help!"

Isaac loped around the tarpaulin to her booth.

Haylee murmured to me, "Maybe she's *tied* up again."

I had to run outside to vent another case of the giggles. Haylee came, too, which didn't help. The two boys weren't in sight.

Mona and Isaac, each carrying one end of Mona's recently acquired love seat, came out of the tent. Puffing with exertion, Mona said, "If you two girls aren't doing anything, you can help us put my purchases in Isaac's pickup."

Isaac had probably brought everything here in his truck in the first place, and now he had to drive some of it back to Elderberry Bay. But he was good-natured about it, and we helped carry, too, even though we would have rather watched the square dancing, and Mona didn't want me touching anything with a possibly bloody hand.

"Where's all this stuff going?" Haylee asked as we helped Isaac pack boxes, stools, and lamps in the bed of his truck.

"My shop. My upholsterer . . . I mean *I* will reupholster and fix it all up."

As soon as we'd removed everything Mona wanted, she turned to Isaac and demanded, "Follow me home." She actually batted her eyelashes at the poor guy. "And help me stow this all in my workshop." She shook her head more emphatically than usual.

"Sorry, ma'am, I can't." He twisted his hands like a bashful schoolboy. He was putting on an act, maybe using "ma'am" to show he wasn't interested in a woman ten or more years his senior.

"Sure you can," Mona encouraged with a sultry voice.

"No, ma'am, I'm sorry, but as deputy fire chief, it's my job to stay at the festival with the fire truck until after the fireworks." He looked at his watch. "I have to take the tanker to where they're setting them off." He loped to the fire truck.

Pouting, Mona watched him drive away over the furrowed ground. "He could have given you girls the keys to his pickup so *you* could drive my belongings to my shop."

"We're firefighters, too," I said before Mona could rope us into moving her purchases from Isaac's pickup to Haylee's. "Remember, you wanted us to join? We also have to stay until after the fireworks."

Haylee added, "Especially now that the other recruits are out of commission."

"No one should set off fireworks tonight," Mona said. "It's too dry. If anything goes wrong, this place could go up like that." She snapped her fingers to show us how fast. Her vision of a roaring inferno was enough to send her scooting to her own car. She slammed herself in and drove toward the exit.

Where was Clay? Ever since I'd texted him

to call me, my phone had been stubbornly silent. Just to be sure, I pulled it from my pocket. The battery was fine. I had no messages.

I turned to Haylee. "What would you like to do next?" The square dance music had ended and the tractors were silent, but there had to be something equally entertaining, beginning with finding something to eat. I was starving.

"Yoo-hoo! Willow! Haylee!" Waving white plastic shopping bags in the dimly lit night, three peculiar creatures charged down Brussels Sprouts Boulevard toward us. We were about to be accosted by a short clown with two bright red spots on her cheeks, a tall giraffe with a serious crick in its neck, and a purple furry creature resembling an overgrown teddy bear.

Beyond the amusement area, someone spoke into a PA system. The Harvest Festival's opening ceremonies were beginning.

Haylee and I could probably have listened to the speeches from where we stood, but the clown, the giraffe, and the teddy bear herded us into the Threadville booth.

Haylee didn't seem surprised at her mothers' appearance. "Where did you three pick up those costumes?" she asked them. "From someone's trash?"

The crook-neck giraffe answered in Opal's voice, "We found a very nice man who makes and rents costumes. He's interested in opening a shop in Threadville."

I couldn't help pointing out, "That giraffe costume is not exactly rentable anymore." In addition to having a broken neck, its dark brown patches were threadbare.

Edna, the short clown, waved my complaint away. "He knows that. He said we could keep it. And besides, we think he might be a good customer for our shops."

The purple furry creature bopped in a typical mascot dance and answered in Naomi's sweet way, "And for the courses we teach."

I laughed. "He could use a few pointers."

Edna raised a finger in the air. "Exactly."

"Why," Haylee asked her mothers, "are you wearing costumes?" She took a step back as if she dreaded their answer. I prepared to run away, too.

Edna raised a hand in a signal for silence, then darted out into the aisle. We heard her run the length of the tent on the hard-packed earth, then back again.

Brushing red yarn hair out of her eyes, Edna beckoned us closer. "We found Russ's truck," she whispered.

42

"You found Russ's truck?" Haylee repeated.

As if she expected a crowd of eavesdroppers to materialize, Edna shushed her.

"Where?" I asked Edna.

"In a parking lot near the rides and games. We figure he's working as a carnie."

Opal, the threadbare giraffe, added, "If we spread out and search that area, between the five of us, we should find him."

"Russ might recognize me," I began.

Despite those bright red circles on her cheeks, little Edna managed to look earnest. "We have a plan."

I might have known.

Opal took off the giraffe head, fished in one of the bags, brought out two black Stetsons, and handed them to Haylee and me. "You can hide your hair under these."

Great. But we'd still be two women, considerably taller than average.

Naomi took off her purple furry mitts and

dug in the other bag. "Look what else we bought." Cowboy shirts. When had The Three Weird Mothers begun channeling the late Darlene Coddlefield? Or had they been watching the square dancers? However, these shirts were not pastel like the ones Darlene had made for her sons, or bright like the square dancers had worn.

Haylee spluttered, "Black? You three always tell us not to wear so much black."

"You'll blend into the night." In her polka-dot, ruffled clown suit, Edna obviously had no intention of blending into anything less rowdy than a three-ring circus.

Opal the giraffe tore into the plastic around the shirts. "We bought them big so you two could pass as men."

We knew better than to argue. While her mothers fussed about my bandaged hand, Haylee and I buttoned the black cowboy shirts over our T-shirts.

"Thank goodness Willow's fingers work," Naomi said through purple fur.

I was glad of that, also. Haylee and I tucked our hair underneath our hats.

Opal complained, "They still look like women."

Edna cast a speculative glance around our booth.

Knowing the mothers' penchant for involving me in preposterous schemes, I quickly said, "There's no law against women wearing black shirts and hats, blending into the night, and wandering around the fairgrounds."

They paid me no attention.

"I should have brought batting," Naomi apologized. Her purple fake fur costume couldn't fit into the booth.

Edna's and Opal's costumes could. The clown and giraffe swooped down on a couple of bolts of Naomi's quilt fabrics — pastels printed to resemble cloth that had been painstakingly hand-dyed.

Outside, the PA system squawked out opening night speeches.

Inside, despite our complaints, Haylee and I developed batik beer bellies. And batik beer *backs*.

"There," Opal, the improbable giraffe, said after Haylee and I were thoroughly bound in fabric. "You two don't look like women anymore."

That figured. Underneath our cowboy shirts, each of us had been padded in an entire bolt of cotton batik.

"How gratifying," Haylee said drily. "We don't look like men, either. We look like beach balls wearing cowboy hats."

"All the better for blending," Edna said,

unfolding a map of the festival. "Here's where Russ's truck is parked, in the lot off Wheatfield Way, nearest where they're going to shoot off the fireworks. We can loiter there. Not together, or we'll be obvious — Haylee, that fake cough isn't fooling anyone. We can tell you're laughing at us. But this is a really good plan! We can pretend to watch the fireworks while we're really observing Russ's truck."

Applause came over the PA system. Was the first speech over?

Edna urged us all to hurry.

"Wait!" Naomi rumbled through purple polyester fur. "They can't carry those feminine handbags."

Haylee's and my simple, square bags could have been carried by cowboys if one of them liked plastic-laminated geometric prints and the other one leaned toward embroidered abstracts. We shoved our wallets and phones into pockets, then locked our bags in a display case.

Edna hustled us all out to Brussels Sprouts Boulevard and pointed down Cabbage Court toward the brightly lit Ferris wheel. Wheatfield Way and the parking lot where Russ's truck was supposed to be were beyond the amusement area.

"Walk like men, you two," Opal instructed.

She put the giraffe head back on. If she said more, we didn't hear it.

In our sneakers, attempting to walk like men, Haylee and I easily outpaced the other three, who couldn't have been accustomed to wearing cowboy boots covered by clown shoes, giraffe hooves, or purple fake fur paws.

"How do men walk?" I asked Haylee.

"Think of Isaac." She kind of rolled from one foot to the other. I was too polite to tell her she didn't walk a thing like Isaac did. He never looked dead drunk. I bent my knees slightly, let my shoulders droop forward, and dangled my hands. Very Isaac-like, I thought.

Haylee giggled. "Good gorilla."

I stuck my hands into my pockets and tried swaggering, but it came out more like swaying.

"Your padding's showing," Haylee warned. Unfortunately, the bolt of cloth the women had wrapped around my waist was pale yellow, not a nice blendy black. I tucked the loose end into my jeans.

Haylee pointed ahead. "Walk like that man."

I knew that walk. I knew that man. "No," I breathed. I'd been wanting to talk to Clay for the past two days. Now he was striding toward us.

And I was a hideous pear shape.

43

Maybe Clay wouldn't recognize Haylee and me in our cowboy outfits.

"Just keep going," Haylee muttered out the side of her mouth in a nicely masculine way.

So we did. Right past Clay without looking at him. I held my bandaged hand out of his sight.

I heard him come to a halt right behind us. "Willow and Haylee, what are you two up to now?"

A miracle. For once, he hadn't greeted me with his usual question — *are you all right?* The best policy might be to follow Haylee's suggestion. I strode on as if he couldn't have been talking to us.

Haylee, however, stopped and informed him, "If you walk between us, maybe we can pass as men."

But Clay was laughing too hard to walk. He looked behind him. A clown, a giraffe with a floppy neck, and a giant purple fake fur teddy bear picked their way toward us between worn-down furrows. Clay stopped laughing. "Those are your mothers, aren't they, Haylee? Don't tell me you five are trying to solve murders and attempted murders."

"How's Tiffany?" I should have asked sooner.

"They say they're about to let her wake up and she's going to be fine. State troopers are with her. Investigating is *their* job."

I asked him, "Did you hear about Felicity Ranquels, the sewing machine rep who was also hurt at the Coddlefields'?"

"They expect her to recover, too. And maybe one day, the gaps in her memory will fill in, and she'll be able to say what really happened. I heard you pulled her out —"

Before he could scold me for my part in her rescue, I fired another question at him. "Have they arrested anyone for attacking those two?"

"Not last I heard." He frowned. "You two —"

I interrupted, "Do you know where Russ Coddlefield is?"

Clay's eyes filled with concern. "No. Last time I saw him, he was still at the fire. I left early, but Isaac told me he zoomed off in his truck after the fire was out, and the police are out looking for him. Poor kid. He must be frightened."

"Come with us," Haylee demanded. "My mothers think he's in danger from his father. They want to rescue him, but they're afraid he'll recognize them and run away, so we're all in disguise and about to go where we can watch his truck."

Clay offered us each an arm.

I whisked both hands behind my back as best I could, considering my strange balloon shape. "We can't walk arm-in-arm with you. We're trying to pass as men."

"And not exactly succeeding." Clay was very close to guffawing again. "I'm surprised Haylee's mothers didn't make you wear fake beards."

"Shhh." Haylee giggled. "They might hear you."

Knowing them, they were already on the lookout for improvements to our costumes. Failing beards or bandanas, they would rub dirt on our faces where five o'clock shadows might be. We sped our pace.

Clay pointed out that he didn't have a disguise, and that Russ might see him and run the other direction.

I didn't warn him that at that very moment, a short and energetic clown, a tall giraffe with potential swallowing problems, and a huge purple teddy bear were probably discussing which rent-a-mascot costume would suit him best. Instead, I said, "If Russ runs away from you, maybe Naomi, Opal, and Edna will catch him." I'd been around Haylee's three mothers so much I was beginning to think like them, which, considering their fondness for costumes, didn't bode well for my future wardrobe choices.

Behind us something slapped on the ground. "Yoo-hoo! You two cowboys and Clay!" Edna's voice. We turned around. The clown ran toward us, her oversized shoe coverings hindering her every step. "Wait," she called, and promptly foundered in a furrow.

She didn't fall. She leaned forward, yanked the shoe coverings upward until the elastic around their tops was above her knees, picked up her clown hat and its attached yarn hair, clapped it on her head, and hurried toward us with her big clown shoes, toes pointing outward, flapping near her brightly polka-dotted thighs.

"Glad I caught you," she gasped when she reached us. "We had an idea."

And I had a sinking feeling.

But the idea that she and her best friends

had come up with wasn't too terrible, after all.

"We don't have time to camouflage Clay." Edna smiled an apology up into his face.

"That's okay," Clay said, ever the gentleman.

"So it will be your job, Clay, to look like yourself and flush Russ out. We saw his truck in the parking lot, so he may be hanging out at the carnival. Soybean Street cuts through the center, so you case Soybean Street. Haylee and Willow, you two stroll down the next street, Corn Alley, and watch for Russ to pop out between tents while fleeing Clay. Naomi, Opal, and I will go down Rutabaga Row to grab Russ if he goes that way."

My hand throbbed. I continued hiding it and its cartoon character bandages from Clay. "What if we don't find Russ?" I asked.

Edna had a plan for that, too. "We'll go back to our original idea. We'll all meet on Parsnip Place. It runs along the ends of Rutabaga Row, Soybean Street, and Corn Alley. Then we'll wander to the parking lot near Russ's truck and wait for him to appear."

Great. We could spend most of the night in uncomfortable outfits and still not find Russ.

"Hurry," Edna urged, wiping red yarn hair out of her eyes. "We don't want to miss him. Someone needs to set that kid on a safer path."

Opal and Naomi, mincing along in their strange footwear and even stranger costumes, were catching up. Haylee, Clay, and I hurried off in the direction Edna had sent us.

"You don't have to participate in their schemes," Haylee told Clay.

"I'd like to help the boy," Clay answered. A red firework umbrella unfurled overhead, lighting the planes of his worried face.

Regretting my earlier refusal to take his arm, I had an almost overwhelming desire to whip my bandaged hand out of hiding and go into damsel in distress mode. Instead, I said calmly, "He's more likely to trust you than the rest of us."

Clay's jaw tensed with determination. "He could be afraid I would turn him in to the authorities. Or to his father."

Maybe, I thought, *we should all be afraid of* Russ . . .

With a quick nod good-bye, Clay turned down Soybean Street and disappeared among the lights, noise and crowds. Haylee and I started along Corn Alley.

About three booths down, a rifleman in a

red cowboy hat shot at plywood ducks bob-
bing on plywood waves. The teenaged girl
running the game looked flustered. No
wonder. The rifleman was a good shot, and
the girl would soon be out of prizes. Tall,
with a muscular build, the rifleman didn't
look like a collector of stuffed toys. He
looked like . . . like . . . oh, no!

He *was*.

Detective Gartener. Out of uniform.

No, that didn't sound right. In plain
clothes. Apparently, he was on duty. Some
of that "muscle" was a bulletproof vest he
wore underneath his cowboy shirt. Was he
also searching for Russ? His cowboy shirt,
unlike ours, was red plaid.

Haylee must have recognized him, too.
She turned her head away from him, then
stopped in her tracks.

On the other side of Corn Alley, a cowgirl
wore an ankle-length denim skirt with
police-issue boots peeking out from under
it. She was making a disgusted expression
at the huge fluff of pink candy floss she held
as far as possible from her face and from
the white cowboy hat perched on her head.

Chief Smallwood.

She didn't notice us, either.

Were they both looking for Russ?

As one, Haylee and I sped our preassigned

saunter in an attempt to get away before Gartener or Smallwood saw us and figured out that we might be dressed oddly so we could snoop in an investigation they'd told us to stay away from. *Walk like a man,* I reminded myself, still having no idea how to accomplish that feat.

It occurred to me that we could go back and tell Detective Gartener and Chief Smallwood that Russ's truck had been spotted nearby.

But I had some pride. It was bad enough that Clay had seen us in our peculiar garb. He knew us — and that Haylee's mothers were the ones who usually put us up to such antics — and had never suspected either of us of murder. Gartener and Smallwood, on the other hand . . .

Besides, Opal, Naomi, and Edna would be very disappointed and unhappy if police officers swooped in and falsely arrested Russ before they did whatever it was they thought they could do to set him on a safer path.

It was hard not to be drawn into the carnival atmosphere — fireworks, laughter, bright lights, and the smells of candy floss, caramel popcorn, and hot cooking oil. Booths sold deep-fried chocolate bars, ice cream, butter, pickles, and, of all things, strawberry gelatin.

"I'm hungry," Haylee said.

I was, too, but not for deep-fried gelatin. "French fries?" I suggested. "Or fried jalapeño mozzarella balls?"

Haylee had a great solution. "I'll get the fries. You get the cheese."

Standing in line, I glanced up Corn Alley. No sign of Detective Gartener or Chief Smallwood.

But . . . was Jeremy Chandler in line for the bumper cars?

What was Jeremy really doing here? Last I knew, IMEC judges didn't go around the world prejudging entries. I couldn't remember seeing his name on the list of judges. I would have noticed because of the Chandler Challenge.

Carrying our hot snacks, Haylee and I met in the middle of Corn Alley and continued our slow inspection of booths.

We were almost at the end of Corn Alley when we spotted Clay.

With Russ.

44

One hand on Russ's shoulder, Clay leaned down, his face serious as if he were trying to convince the boy of something. Even if they'd been closer, I wouldn't have heard their discussion over the whistling, popping fireworks and the clashing music of the merry-go-round and the Ferris wheel.

Clay and Russ headed down Parsnip Place toward the parking lot where Russ's truck was supposed to be.

Clay was a particularly nice and caring person. I looked down at my outfit. Ugh. Maybe someday I would look decent, not muddy or in a strange costume, when I was with Clay. With *him* and not only in the same restaurant.

Haylee said, "I guess we don't have to stake out Russ's truck after all." We stopped and shared our yummy fried treats.

Two figures pushed through the crowd around us. Detective Gartener and Chief

Smallwood were on a mission heading toward the spot where Russ and Clay had been only moments ago.

Haylee and I traded horrified glances. Smallwood and Gartener must be after Russ. And they were wearing bulletproof vests and police boots underneath their cowboy outfits. They were probably armed, also. What if Russ did something foolish and endangered himself and Clay?

His red cowboy hat askew on his head, Gartner picked up speed. Chief Smallwood held that giant pink ball of candy floss away from her face and clothes. The two officers dashed around the corner onto Parsnip Place and disappeared.

A crook-necked giraffe, a short clown, and a purple furry bear bumbled along Parsnip Place toward the parking lot.

Haylee muttered, "If they don't recognize Smallwood and Gartener, they might interfere and get themselves into trouble."

We stuffed the last of the French fries and jalapeño cheese balls into our mouths, tossed the paper containers into a trash barrel, jockeyed around a group of seniors wearing matching straw boaters with headbands that said *Erie Mystery Tours,* and rounded the corner onto Parsnip Place.

Beyond the giraffe, the clown, and the

purple teddy bear struggling along in their ungainly costumes, Parsnip Place dead-ended in a vast parking lot. Roofs of cars and trucks reflected fireworks.

I didn't see Gartener and Smallwood. Or Clay and Russ.

Haylee and I caught up with her mothers and jogged beside them.

Edna's clown shoes were above her knees again, pointing forward this time. "Run faster," she yelled.

Opal swung around, endangering Naomi with the giraffe head swinging from the bent neck. "They turned left."

From inside the purple fur, Naomi yelled something. Mmmmpfhl?

Haylee and I dashed ahead and turned left at Wheatfield Way. Several rows into the parking lot, Clay's head and Gartener's red cowboy hat showed above the roof of a van.

We zigzagged around vehicles until we were in the same row as Clay and Gartener. Slowing, we tiptoed toward them, although the sound of our approach had to be masked by the fireworks.

Next to Russ's truck, Russ and Clay were being held at bay by a police chief wearing a white cowgirl hat and brandishing candy floss, and a tall detective wearing a red cowboy hat and brandishing . . . a baby?

Clay leaned against Russ's truck in a casual pose, but his arms were folded and a muscle twitched in his jaw. Trying not to laugh at the strangely rotund cowboys, the red-haired clown, the jolly purple bear, and the pathetic goose-necked giraffe creeping up behind the two unsuspecting police officers?

Russ, however, stood stiffly with his back pressed against his truck, his ropy teenaged arms angled out from his body, his palms flat against the fender, as if the hard metal gave him comfort. He shook his head. "I didn't do anything," he wailed. "Someone's trying to kill me! I had to run away." In his rumpled jeans and dirty white T-shirt, he looked about eleven years old. A lock of his hair covered one eye.

Gartener asked in his made-for-radio voice, "Why do you think someone is trying to kill you?"

Bang! A rocket spiraled up into the night sky.

Russ flicked the hair out of his face, jutted his chin, and became sixteen again. "That sewing machine didn't just fall on my mother. Someone slammed it down on her." His voice broke and his chin trembled.

Smallwood started to respond, but Gartener interrupted her. "Did you see this happen?" He spoke with empathy and without talking down to the boy.

"No, but . . . dude, that thing was heavy, but not that heavy."

"It wasn't so much the weight," Gartener told Russ, "as *how* it fell."

Plus, I thought, all the trouble someone took to make certain that it did fall, making it run at top speed and partially detaching the front legs of the table it was on.

Russ looked bilious, possibly because of the green fireworks opening with a deafening crash above us.

Smallwood must have wanted to distract Russ from the images he must have been seeing of his mother. She asked, "Are you the one who loosened the front legs of the sewing table?"

Russ tilted his head. Lines appeared between his eyebrows. "What are you talking about? I made that table. I put those legs on nice and tight."

"How were they fastened?" Gartener asked.

Russ shrugged. "Bolts. And this'll sound dumb, but it worked. The bolts were held on with wing nuts."

Red fireballs exploded like crazed popcorn.

Gartener moved closer to Russ. "Could

the wing nuts have come loose if the table was jiggled a lot, say by sewing?"

"No way! I do good work. I tightened them really, really tight."

Clay reached out and squeezed the boy's shoulder as if agreeing that Russ's carpentry was good.

"With your hands, or a tool?" Gartener asked. "Pliers?"

Russ stared at his palms. "With my fingers. But I'm strong."

Gartener suggested, "So someone strong came along and loosened them."

"Guess so."

"Who is that strong, besides you?" Gartener asked.

"I don't know," the boy said wretchedly. Tears glistened in the corners of his eyes. "My . . . my dad's *girlfriend* didn't like my mom."

Gartener waited for a quiet moment between fireworks. "Do you think she did all those things that caused your mother to die? On purpose?"

Russ went back to shaking his head. "I don't know."

Smallwood apparently couldn't let Gartener do all the questioning. "And who tampered with the second sewing machine so that it shorted out and caused a fire and nearly killed your dad's . . . er . . . your family's nanny?"

Russ shook Clay's hand off his shoulder and yelled, "I didn't do it! And I don't know who did! Just because I ran away doesn't mean I *did* anything! Whoever killed my mother and tried to kill Tiffany and that other woman could have been after me."

I knew Russ was good with electricity and could have figured out how to reconnect wires in a sewing machine to make it catch fire. I wanted to ask him if he ever used sewing machines, but I didn't want Gartener and Smallwood to realize we were there. They might send us away and we'd never know what really went on.

Bang! A spangled white sphere bloomed above us.

When all was quiet again, Smallwood tapped the ground with the toe of one of her police boots. "And you don't know anything about other fires that have been mysteriously cropping up on farms all around yours?"

Russ looked off to his right. "No. The fields are dry. And there's been lightning."

"And arson," Smallwood said firmly. "And you and some of your friends have shown up at nearly every fire. Very quickly."

"We're firefighters, dude!"

"This goes back to last summer, before any of you joined the force," she told him.

Russ again remembered how to sneer. "Well, don't ask me. We didn't set those fires. And don't think I ran away because I was afraid you would accuse me of that, either. Someone killed my mom and almost killed Tiffany and that old broad who tried to show my mother how to use her new sewing machine. How do you know they weren't trying to kill me, too?"

Behind me, Edna's voice rang out, "Who would want to kill you?"

Smallwood jumped and whirled around, smashing her candy floss into Haylee's black cowboy shirt. "Hold that for me," she ordered.

Haylee complied, though she didn't need her hands. The candy was stuck to her shirt.

Flares lit the sky with painful white light.

With Smallwood no longer blocking his escape, Russ slipped behind his truck and dashed away.

Smallwood chased him.

Detective Gartener thrust a blanket-swaddled baby doll into my arms and took off after both of them. Obviously anticipating that Russ might turn the other way, Clay ran around the front of Russ's truck.

Haylee peeled the candy floss off her shirt.

Hanging on to its paper cone and pointing the gooey ball like a weapon, she sprinted after the officers and Russ. Not knowing what else to do with Gartener's baby doll, I cradled it in my good arm and ran after Clay.

Behind us, Edna exclaimed while Opal and Naomi mumbled into their fur masks.

Then all I could hear were fireworks, bursting forth in a noisy and brilliant grand finale.

Smoke, sharp with the tang of gunpowder, blurred everything. I kept Clay's head in sight as I skidded around cars and trucks.

Echoes of the last fireworks died away. Far behind me, the merry-go-round played its hurdy-gurdy music and the Ferris wheel tinkled out its bell-like tones. I kept running.

Shouts erupted in front of me. Had someone caught up with Russ?

The smoke became thicker.

I could no longer see Clay. I ran toward the shouts.

The fire truck blasted noise through the night. The smoke in front of me turned a ghastly yellow, and I understood what people were shouting.

Fire.

45

The fireworks must have ignited the hay stubble beyond the parking lot. I kept running, searching for Russ.

Clay was near the tanker truck, pulling on boots. Another tall man was already suited up. That had to be Isaac. With the help of a couple of shorter firemen, he aimed a hose at burning grasses. The wind was blowing toward the parking lot. If any of the vehicles caught fire, the firefighters would have a huge problem. They? We. I was a firefighter, too.

Maybe this was the time for me to don the outfit and help. One of my hands was fine.

A third short firefighter joined the others. Russ? With only one tanker truck, they'd soon run out of water.

Clumsily balancing my cell phone in my bandaged palm, I dialed 911 and was told that the other tanker was on its way.

To my left, Chief Smallwood was keeping rubberneckers at bay. Purple furry teddy bear ears, a black cowboy hat, the angle of a broken giraffe neck, and the lime green pompom at the peak of Edna's conical hat showed up above heads in the crowd milling around the chief.

To my right, two more short firefighters had joined the crew. Russ's friends? It must have been more than an hour since Isaac had sent them to their pickup truck. I hoped they were sober enough to help the firefighters, not hinder or endanger them.

Wind blew flaming wisps toward me, cutting me off from the fire truck and gear. Gartener didn't seem to be anywhere around, and Smallwood needed help with crowd control. That was something I could do despite wearing a bandage around my hand and a bolt of batik around my middle.

I dashed around vehicles toward Chief Smallwood.

Its siren howling and horn blasting, Elderberry Bay's other tanker truck, with an enraged-looking Plug at the wheel, made its way toward the fire. People scurried out of the way. A floppy-headed giraffe, a short clown, and a purple furry bear toddled away from the group around Smallwood. In her clown suit, Edna pointed ahead and up, at the Ferris wheel. Its lights twinkled against the night sky.

I texted Haylee and asked what her mothers where doing.

She answered that they were planning to search for Russ by riding the Ferris wheel. Haylee was following them to keep them out of trouble.

I looked back at the fire. The evening's breeze fanned it toward the parking lot, not toward the Ferris wheel, but I didn't blame Haylee for her caution.

Keeping an eye on the fire's spread, I hurried toward Chief Smallwood.

A firefighter skulked away from the fire.

He was about Russ's height. His hands were bare, but he was wearing the rest of his uniform, including mask and respirator.

That was odd. Was Russ so afraid of his father that he wouldn't take time to remove the unwieldy gear before fleeing? The outfit had to be slowing him down, and it certainly made him stand out in a crowd.

But most people were too busy gawking at the fire to notice him.

He didn't head toward his pickup truck, which made sense considering the way the fire was going.

My breath caught in my throat. Unless I was mistaken, he was following Haylee.

Furiously, I sent her a warning text. I turned my phone to vibrate, and stalked after him. I stayed in shadows, but probably didn't need to. He was obviously concentrating on Haylee.

He'd seen Haylee and me a few minutes before. We were dressed alike, with our hair hidden under our hats, and our waistlines curving in the wrong direction. Did he know which one of us he was following? Not that it mattered. I couldn't let him harm her.

Finally, I was close to the Ferris wheel. Its calliope music blared above the merry-go-round's organ ditties. The giraffe, clown, and the fuzzy purple bear, crammed together in one swaying seat and facing forward, ascended.

Russ disappeared into a tent at the base of the Ferris wheel.

An empty seat rose above the tent, and then Haylee, alone in her seat, moved upward. At the top of the wheel, her mothers waved at the world in general, three peculiar creatures having a great time. Haylee looked down as if scanning the grounds below her. The Ferris wheel carried her up to the top.

A blue flash and a loud pop came from inside the tent where Russ had gone.

I froze. A gunshot?

I no longer heard music from the Ferris wheel, and the merry-go-round was blaring again. The Ferris wheel's passengers shrieked. Silhouetted against the sky, Haylee and her mothers waved at each other. The great wheel had stopped turning, and its lights had gone dark.

That "shot" I'd heard must have been Russ shutting off the power to the Ferris wheel. I was sure he'd seen Haylee board it. Maybe he didn't want her to disembark until after he made his getaway.

Now, would he take off for his truck?

I flattened myself next to the tent flap. Haylee and her mothers were immobilized on the Ferris wheel. Clay and Isaac must be hosing down the smoldering remains of a hayfield. It wasn't a life-or-death situation, so there was no point in phoning 911, and I hadn't programmed Smallwood's non-emergency number into my phone.

I would stay put. When Russ came outside, I would watch where he went, then go find Chief Smallwood and tell her.

Where was Russ?

I heard no sounds inside the tent, which wasn't surprising, since people on the Ferris wheel were yelling and the ride's operator was shouting at them to sit still.

Haylee texted that she had seen someone creep out the other side of the tent and head west along Cabbage Court. That would be away from the fire and toward the handcrafts tent.

Was it Russ?

She didn't think so.

Was he wearing a firefighter's uniform?

He wasn't. *Be careful,* she added. *Acting sneaky. Like staying out of sight of people on ground.*

So who had just left the tent? Could someone else have been in the tent when Russ entered? Had this other person found a way of silencing the boy in the fireman suit? Cautiously, I peeked into the tent. I caught a whiff of ozone. Shadows moved when I pushed at the flap, allowing light from beyond the Ferris wheel to seep in.

A fireman was lying, all jumbled up, in the middle of the tent.

46

I managed not to scream. The fallen firefighter lay beside thick electrical cables running along the ground from the tent wall nearest the Ferris wheel to a large electrical panel mounted on a pole.

Schooling myself not to go anywhere near those cables, I tiptoed to the firefighter and nearly wept in relief.

The "firefighter" was only a pile of firefighter's gear, apparently dumped in haste. No one else had been in here with Russ. In fact, Russ probably hadn't been in here at all, and I'd been following someone else. Who?

Wednesday night, someone wearing a firefighter's outfit had left a fire while it was still going. Could the same person have done something similar just now?

I set down the baby doll that Detective Gartener must have won with his sharpshooting and picked up the firefighter's jacket. EVFD was stenciled across the back of the jacket. Hadn't I seen those same initials on the gloves we'd found where Felicity had been attacked? I'd been too rattled to question it then, but the gloves and the jacket were missing a letter. They should have been stenciled E*B*VFD for Elderberry Bay Volunteer Fire Department. I shined my cell phone at the label inside the jacket. *Property of Emblesford Volunteer Fire Department.*

Maybe Elderberry Bay had bought used equipment. The person who had left this gear here had been wearing a full firefighter's ensemble except for gloves.

Because he'd accidentally left the gloves behind after he clobbered Felicity?

I texted Haylee that I was going to follow — very carefully, I added to myself — the person she'd seen creeping away.

I rushed outside. Only the tent I'd left, the Ferris wheel, and a few of the games and rides near them were dark. The rest of the Harvest Festival continued as if nothing had happened. Smoke lingered from the grass fire, but no flames licked up toward the cloudy night sky. The merry-go-round played its organ-grinder tune. Bumper cars bumped. People laughed and shouted. Carnies delivered their spiels.

I turned west on Cabbage Court.

Far ahead, near Brussels Sprouts Boulevard, a figure edged along, staying close to tent walls.

He wore jeans and a light shirt. Russ had been dressed that way. So had Jeremy Chandler.

There was something feminine about the way the person moved.

I couldn't imagine either Jeremy or Russ masquerading as a woman, especially in a poufy blond wig.

The person's furtiveness slowed him down, and I gained on him. That was no wig, and the person wasn't a man. I recognized that fluff of platinum hair.

Mimi.

47

Mimi?

Was I following the wrong person?

I turned around and scanned Cabbage Court and the tents lining it. No one was behind me. Most of the people attending the fair were either watching the firefighting or enjoying the rides, games, and food.

Quickly, I texted Haylee. She confirmed that I was following the person who had dodged out of the tent near the Ferris wheel. She agreed that the person was blond and did resemble Mimi.

Mimi had been fighting the fire but stopped to follow Haylee? When Haylee boarded the Ferris wheel, *Mimi* had ducked into the tent and disconnected the ride's electrical power?

Mimi, not Russ?

Russ might have had a good reason to flee Plug, and I could have understood if he had gone after Haylee in hopes of keeping her from turning him over to the police. Slowing her progress by stranding her on the Ferris wheel would have worked for a while, especially if she hadn't ended up at the top with her cell and a clear view of most of the fairgrounds.

Why had Mimi been wearing a firefighter's outfit and apparently helping fight the fire? She didn't belong to the Elderberry Bay Volunteer Fire Department.

Where was Emblesford?

Why had Mimi fled when *Plug* arrived? Other firefighters besides Plug could have recognized that she was an intruder. Maybe she simply didn't want to be around when the firefighters started taking off their outfits.

Mimi couldn't have known where Haylee was heading, so she couldn't have pre-planned turning off the Ferris wheel and marooning Haylee on it. That must have been pure luck.

What did she hope to accomplish while the power was out?

Haylee would keep close track of me from her perch on the Ferris wheel and she'd phone for help if I got into trouble. I tiptoed after Mimi, who was several tents ahead of me.

When I had dragged Felicity outside, she

had yelled for help, saying that I was trying to kill her. And she'd thought I was a man, probably because of the firefighter's equipment and mask hiding my identity. I was about six inches taller than Mimi, but that might not have been obvious to Felicity, lying half conscious on the floorboards of the porch.

A few minutes ago, I had mistaken Mimi for Russ.

In her gear, Mimi had been close to the size of the firefighter I'd seen ducking into a car as I'd arrived at the fire at the Coddlefields'. I already suspected that person of having attacked Felicity and Tiffany.

Mimi would know that cotton fabric would burn away to ash.

But why would she have wanted to murder Tiffany and Felicity?

Because they knew or might figure out something about her, something worth killing over. Like that she had been responsible for Darlene Coddlefield's death.

Mimi could have expected to ambush Tiffany at the Coddlefields'. If Felicity had remembered correctly, Felicity had surprised Mimi attacking Tiffany and encouraging the Chandler Champion to flare up. Mimi might have thought she had no choice besides putting Felicity out of commission, too.

Ahead of me, Mimi edged along tent walls. I stayed near the tents, too, clambering over ropes and stakes, but the tents were white and my outfit was black. If Mimi turned around, she would see me.

But she didn't, and with my longer legs, I closed more of the gap between us.

When Darlene had received the certificate announcing her as the winner of the Chandler Challenge, she had cast a look of malicious triumph toward people in the back of the audience.

Lots of us had been in that vicinity, including Mimi.

Mimi knew enough about sewing machines to disable the first Chandler Champion. And she'd helped Georgina figure out that an outlet in my shop had a loose connection, so she probably understood wiring well enough to cause the second Chandler Champion to short out and start a fire.

And I was positive that, a few moments ago, she had shut off the Ferris wheel's power.

In the clue on her cardboard interfacing, Felicity had accused me of tampering with the first Chandler Champion. She had also mentioned "that woman who wins all the embroidery contests." Smallwood and I had assumed that Felicity had been referring to me, even though I hadn't won any major ones. Jeremy had said that he hired Felicity because of her encyclopedic knowledge of embroidery competitions. Maybe Felicity had suspected *both* me and Mimi.

Mimi's machine embroidery ability had been inconsistent. The day after Darlene died, Mimi had been the only student in my classes besides Georgina and Rosemary to have no problem transforming a photo to an embroidery design, but later in the week, when we were practicing hooping and re-hooping to create allover embroidery designs, Mimi hadn't been able to line up her work, though other students had managed the feat easily.

During another lesson, she'd been doing an expert job with her embroidering, then had made a show of threading a machine wrong and throwing out embroidery that she could have easily fixed.

She had turned in excellent embroidery as her IMEC entry. What her hummingbird and flower design lacked in originality, it made up for in perfect tension and stitching. She hadn't clipped her seams well when she attached the backing, though, and the resulting doily was bunchier than it could have been.

Maybe some of her intermittent incompetence had been an act. Maybe she had tried, when she remembered, to hide her skills from the rest of us. So we wouldn't guess she'd held a grudge against Darlene for beating her in contests?

Mimi crossed Brussels Sprouts Boulevard, turned left, and disappeared, either into the handcrafts tent or behind it.

I texted Haylee, but she couldn't see the entrance to the handcrafts tent and wasn't sure where Mimi had gone, either.

Beyond the tent, a car started.

If Mimi drove off, I had no hope of catching her unless I hopped into my car and chased down country roads after her. And then what would I do, follow at a discreet distance until the police caught her? With a bolt of fabric wrapped around my waist, I wouldn't fit behind my steering wheel.

Maybe I was letting Mimi get away, but as various people, including Clay, had told me, I was supposed to leave the investigating, chasing, and catching of suspects to the police.

Well, maybe not the investigating.

There were methods that wouldn't involve confronting suspects.

The Internet. And I had my phone.

I slunk to the doorway of the handcrafts tent. It was dark inside. Nothing stirred, and there were no sounds except a car bumping away from the parking lot behind the tent.

48

Haylee texted me that a dark sedan had left the parking area behind the handcrafts tent. On Wednesday night, the mystery firefighter, who could have been Mimi, had been near a dark sedan.

I eased into the handcrafts tent, tiptoed to the back of the Threadville booth, and sat down in a low folding chair.

Haylee texted that the Ferris wheel still wasn't lit or moving, but she had seen Clay, Russ, and the amusement ride manager enter the tent beside it.

That was a relief. Russ was found again, and I was certain that Clay would stay with him and help him talk to the police and to Plug, if necessary. Haylee's mothers could stop following the boy around the festival. Knowing them, they wouldn't be in a hurry to chuck their disguises. They loved costumes. I asked Haylee to come to the handcrafts tent as soon as she got off the Ferris wheel.

The jacket I'd found had belonged to the Emblesford Volunteer Fire Department, and the chances were excellent that the gloves that Gartener and Smallwood had removed from Tiffany's bedroom were also Emblesford's.

I logged on to the Internet and found several Emblesfords. One was in Pennsylvania, near Erie. Mimi had said that after she began renting a cottage in Elderberry Bay, she learned she could have commuted from Erie on the Threadville tour bus.

I looked up Emblesford's volunteer fire department. The first name on the list of members was Anderson, Mimi. When Georgina had introduced Mimi to me, she'd told me Mimi's last name. If I recalled correctly, she'd said it was Anderson.

Mimi could have crossed the wires in the second Chandler Champion anytime after Edna and I took it to Tiffany on Tuesday. But how had she gotten into the house?

At the presentation in my shop, Darlene's malignant glance could have been directed at Mimi. If the two women had known each other, possibly other people in the Coddlefield household knew Mimi, too, and might have welcomed her into their home.

Outside the tent, something scraped against bare dirt. Furtive footsteps? I turned my phone over in my lap to smother its light and bowed my head so that the brim of my black hat would conceal the pale glimmer of my face. I didn't move. I was not about to reveal my hiding place unless I knew for certain that the newcomer was a friend.

Someone crept through the tent's doorway and went into the firefighters' booth next door. Light from his or her flashlight reflected off the white vinyl tent ceiling.

There was the sound of a carton being moved, then another, and then the cautious clearing of a throat.

It was a sound I'd often heard Mimi make. Somebody had driven a dark car away from the lot behind the handcrafts tent, but it must have been the scrapbooker or another handcrafter. It hadn't been Mimi. She was in the tent with me.

I slumped down lower in my seat. I'd been standing when Opal and Edna wound the bolt of fabric around my waist, but now the fabric cut into me, and I couldn't have taken a deep breath or gasped even if I'd dared.

I heard a distant, almost metallic, "Hello?"

"Mona?" Mimi's voice.

Only a few quilts and fabrics separated

439

her from me. My heart pounded.

She went on, "Do you have any idea where that box of linens I donated to the firefighters is? I must have goofed and given away a family tree sampler I embroidered for my mother. She needs it."

Mimi didn't tell Mona she was rooting around in a booth at the Harvest Festival in the dark when no one else should have been around. Mimi obviously wanted that family tree sampler very badly. Why?

That box of linens was locked securely in my car. I closed my eyes and pictured the sampler. It had been signed "Marian." Mimi's mother? Not likely, since Marian was also shown on the branch below the triplets as their mother, and they'd been born only eighteen years ago.

Mimi had mentioned that she had three children who had all left the nest and gone off to college orientation this year. I didn't think she'd used the word triplets or freshmen, but all of them, orientation the same year? One of the triplets on the family tree sampler had been named Anderson. The triplets' last name had been Hartley.

That sampler had been trimmed in tatted lace. I would need to examine the lace more closely to be certain, but I suspected that it was the pattern that Mimi had been tatting at Opal's storytelling night. Mimi had said it was the only lace pattern she knew. She'd learned it from her grandmother, though, so other family members might tat identical lace.

The lace wasn't conclusive proof that Mimi Anderson and Marian Hartley were the same person, but for my own safety, I needed to assume that Mimi was dangerous. I measured the distance between me and the longest knitting needles in Opal's part of the booth.

"Willow put it in her car? You're sure?" Mimi asked into her phone. "Thanks."

Thanks, Mona, I echoed silently, wanting to shake my head like she always shook hers.

Mimi said good-bye to Mona and tore out of the tent.

Why was she so determined to get that sampler back? The telltale lace around it and the names Anderson and Hartley on the same piece?

If Mimi had attempted to murder Tiffany and Felicity, she would be desperate to keep her secrets. I was going to stay put, out of her way, hidden in a dark corner of a tent.

I sent a quick text to Haylee to call 911 and have them radio Smallwood and Gartener to come to the handcrafts tent immediately.

Meanwhile, I would be able to continue my silent Internet investigation. I searched for sites combining Mimi Anderson, Darlene Coddlefield, Marian Hartley, IMEC, and names of other well-known contests.

Outside, metal clanked against metal. Glass broke. Great. Mimi was armed with something that could shatter a car window.

I had to fight the desire to go out and protect my car. However, a knitting needle, or even a pair of them, would not be a great defense against a rock or a tire iron.

Hoping that Smallwood and Gartener would be here soon and catch Mimi rifling through my car, I focused on my phone's little screen.

Mimi Anderson had come in behind Darlene in many sewing competitions. In one of them, there had been a scandal. Mimi Anderson had won a first-time contestant's prize, and then had been disqualified because she'd entered the contest other years under a different name — Marian Hartley.

The prize had been taken away from Mimi/Marian and awarded to Darlene Coddlefield.

According to the date on the sampler, Mimi's children would have been about four the year that Darlene won Mother of the

Year. Someone with triplets that age might have also entered that contest.

She had.

Marian Hartley had come in second as Mother of the Year, right behind Darlene.

And there was a picture.

Mimi/Marian hadn't changed much in fourteen years. The fluffed-up platinum hair was the same. Darlene, holding her trophy, beamed into the camera. Mimi's mouth and chin were tight with disappointment. For at least fourteen years, Darlene had beaten Mimi at contests.

Mimi — as Marian Hartley — had also donated to at least one fund that, if Susannah was right, went straight to Darlene's personal bank account.

For fourteen years, Darlene had won, every time.

Mimi had gotten even.

Outside, a car door slammed. Maybe Mimi was driving off with the box of linens. With any luck, Gartener could mobilize state troopers to catch her before she destroyed that family tree wall hanging.

But she wasn't driving away.

Clearing her throat, carrying a carton, Mimi came into the tent.

She tripped and landed on her face.

Spewing linens, the carton went flying.

49

Mimi, a possible murderer, was sprawled on the dirt floor of the tent only a dozen feet from me. She must have tripped over a tent stake and knocked herself out.

Smallwood and Gartener would find her there. I was safe. I allowed myself to breathe again, cautiously and silently.

Mimi cursed.

I peeked under the edge of my hat brim. Her feet were tangled in something. A rope?

She got up on her hands and knees. Something brushed against the leg of my jeans, the faintest of touches, similar to one I'd felt and ignored only moments ago when Mimi tripped. I'd also felt a tug at my waist, and had ignored that, too.

Now I had to face the awful truth. The fabric wrapped around my waist must have been coming undone when I slipped into the tent. I'd left a tail of pastel yellow batik that crossed part of the doorway, and it had thrown Mimi.

Maybe she wouldn't see the fabric. She had come in from outside, where the wan light that helped her break into my car could have blinded her to the gloom inside the tent.

I'd been in denial when I ignored the touch on my pant leg and when I ignored the tug at my waist, and I was obviously still in denial.

Of course Mimi noticed the fabric around her ankles.

I couldn't continue watching her, though. She might see my face, which by now must be so pale it would almost glow in the dark. I lowered my head farther.

Why hadn't she simply packed the carton into her car and driven away? Why had she come back in here with her loot?

Maybe she'd still go away.

Denial.

Clothing rustled. Suddenly, the fabric around my waist tightened and I was yanked up out of my seat. My phone slithered off my lap and landed at my feet.

Struggling to catch my balance, I pretended to have been awakened. "Mimi?" I tried to sound groggy, but couldn't completely keep fear out of my voice. "Where are we?"

"What are *you* doing here?" she snapped. "Why are you sitting in the dark?"

I yawned. "Napping. Waiting for Haylee."

"How did you get here so fast? You were . . ." She clamped her lips shut.

Haylee and I were dressed identically. *You thought I was stuck on the Ferris wheel, didn't you?* I didn't say it.

In the distance, music played, discordant and with odd rhythms. The Ferris wheel had started again, and its tune clashed with the merry-go-round's. Haylee and the others would be here soon. Mimi would leave. Smallwood and Gartener could find her, and I could stay here, completely safe.

Denial.

With one fist gripping the fabric attached to my waist, she looked down at my phone. I followed her glance. Oh, no.

My phone had landed with its screen up.

Maybe she wouldn't see the photo on the tiny screen, the one of her and Darlene Coddlefield fourteen years ago, minutes after Darlene was named Mother of the Year.

I'd become *really* good at denial.

Mimi swooped down, dropped something that landed with a heavy *thunk,* and picked up my phone. Mouth screwed into a knot, she studied the screen. She hadn't let go of

446

the batik. Maybe I would be able to twirl my way out of it, but the back corner of the Threadville booth didn't have space for pirouettes.

"What are you doing with this?" Mimi asked.

I didn't think it would help my case if I pretended she was talking about my phone. "I was looking up Darlene Coddlefield for something to do while I waited for my friends" — *hint, hint, leave before they get here, Mimi* — "and I guess I fell asleep before the picture came up." Maybe she'd believe I hadn't seen the picture, hadn't connected Marian Hartley from fourteen years ago to this wrathful — and patently dangerous — woman in front of me.

"You think you're smart, don't you."

Yes, actually, I did.

"You think you can solve mysteries, don't you. Solve murders."

"No." Carefully, I did not look toward the knitting needles hanging near me. I'd have to brush past her to get them, not something I wanted to try.

She shook my phone in my face. "This means nothing. Has nothing to do with me." She threw the phone into the corner. It bounced off a tent wall and landed underneath my display case of IMEC entries.

She might as well have admitted she was the woman in the photo with Darlene.

Where were Haylee and her mothers? More importantly, where were Smallwood and Gartener? Didn't Haylee tell the 911 dispatcher my call was urgent?

Tugging at the batik with her right fist, Mimi stooped for the object she'd dropped near my feet. She stood again. Her eyes became mean slits. She raised her left hand in the air.

"Don't," I managed, ducking, which was exactly the wrong reflex near a shorter assailant, but the tight quarters gave me no choice.

Something hard hit my head. My Stetson protected me a little, but the blow knocked me off my feet. I tumbled down in a boneless heap.

50

Both Tiffany and Felicity had been knocked out and then tied to furniture and left to die. If I had to, I would jump up and defend myself, but my head hurt, and I felt like I was stuck in translucent sludge and unable to do much besides watch this strangely surreal movie unwinding in front of my eyes.

The others would be along soon, anyway.

If Mimi hit me again, I would be even less capable of moving.

She didn't. She sneaked to the door of the tent.

I peeked at her between too-heavy eyelids. She picked up the tail of fabric that had tripped her and knotted it around a tent pole. Most of the bolt was still around me, so tight that it might as well have been tied.

She returned to the carton she'd brought into the tent. She tossed the beautiful heritage linens into the box as if they were garbage, without smoothing them, folding them, or brushing off the dirt.

As if that weren't villainous enough, she asked me, "You saw me outside the Coddlefields', didn't you, when you were driving to the fire? I hid my face, but you figured out who was inside that firefighter's outfit, didn't you?" She waited as if expecting me to answer.

I would. Later, maybe, when the sludge cleared from my brain.

She muttered, "That Darlene. Always throwing her weight around. Mother of the Year when she only had two children, singles, and I'd been raising triplets on my own. Then asking me what other contests I was entering, and she entered them, too, and beat me, every time, even taking that first-time contestant prize from me after *she* told the judges I'd gone back to using my maiden name. So I rented a beach house in Threadville and pretended I was her friend, just like she acted like she was my friend all those years." Mimi raised her voice to a whine and parroted what Darlene must have said to her. " 'What contest are you entering now, Mimi? Let's enter *together.*' " She lowered her voice again. "And then she won, every time. She had no right to act like she deserved to win that Chandler Champion. That's what really got me. *I* wanted that

450

machine."

Mimi stood and felt around her pants pockets. "While I was staying near Darlene, I visited her often, including the afternoon she brought home that Chandler Champion. I timed it wrong that day and arrived a little too soon. That sewing machine rep, Felicity somebody or other, was driving out of Darlene's driveway. I was on the road with my turn signal on. I waited to turn into the driveway until Felicity left, but obviously, she saw me."

Mimi kept talking, and I kept lying there, watching and listening but uninterested in moving.

"Darlene took me up to her sewing room. She was gloating over her new machine and ignoring her other expensive machine. Some people have it all and don't deserve it, right, Willow?"

I didn't answer, and wasn't sure I could.

"No one else was home. Plug and his older kids were out in the fields and the nanny had taken all the younger kids to the library. Darlene started saying it was time for her to fix dinner. Between hinting for me to leave and the nasty look she'd given me when she collected her award certificate, it was easy to tell that she didn't like me. She must have hated me for years. Pretending to be my friend, she'd stolen prizes that should have gone to me.

"Then she got a phone call. Yelling good-bye to me, as if she expected me to go home, she went to the next room to answer the phone. I eavesdropped. She gave a fake name, pretending to be someone else."

I'd seen that room and the phones, and had guessed that was the office Darlene had used for her charities.

"While I listened, I hunted up the screwdriver that came with her Chandler Champion. First I loosened the shaft holding the needle. Sooner or later, needles would go in crooked and break. She had put in a wing needle, so I had the great idea of disabling the setting that told the machine it had a wing needle in it — another surefire way of breaking a needle and annoying the seamstress. I loosened the screw on the bobbin carrier, too, so none of the machine's stitches would work well."

I was wrong about Mimi not smoothing the old linens. She had that family tree sampler in her hands and was straightening the lace around it, pressing it between a finger and thumb. She turned toward me and went on, smoothing that lace and making a confession she probably didn't expect anyone to hear or remember. "To make certain it looked like *you* goofed up the machine, Willow, I put your name in one of the memory banks. They're going to blame you for everything, including what happens to you here tonight."

Still caressing that sampler, she used a foot to nudge the carton toward the quilts lining one side of our booth. "Meanwhile, Darlene was still gabbing away on the phone, telling her latest victim all about the poor children her charities helped. As if! I was getting tired of chewing my gum, and found a great place to put it — in her foot pedal so her machine would sew whether she pushed the pedal or not. She went on babbling her sales pitch, so I decided to make her next sewing adventure with her new machine even more interesting. The legs on her sewing table were fastened with wing nuts. Appropriate, right, Willow?"

Yes, for Mimi.

Not surprisingly, Mimi had given up on hearing answers from me. "I loosened the front two legs, not enough for them to fall off right away. But when that heavy machine started stitching, like it would with the chewing gum in the pedal, the table could shake a leg off. Then I realized that Darlene would be able to turn the machine off, and all the excitement I'd caused would be over too soon."

She tossed the sampler she'd been holding into the top of the box. "She was going on and on about helping supposedly needy children, so I opened the sewing machine. With a jab of the screwdriver, I distorted the plastic on-off switch. With any luck, she would hit it too hard when the foot pedal was stuck down, and she wouldn't be able to turn it off. Or if that didn't work, the switch might break when she tried to turn on her machine, and it wouldn't work at all. That would have served her right, too."

Mimi's voice took on dreamy overtones. Or maybe I was the one who was dreaming.

"I closed up the machine just in time. Darlene came out of the next room and seemed surprised that I hadn't gone when she first answered the phone. 'I'll walk you to the door,' she said. That's what she was like. Mean."

If I wasn't having nightmares then, Mimi's rant would probably give them to me later. "What I did to her machine was only mischief," she whined. "There's no *way* I could have known she'd die. Everyone said it was an accident. But that sly Tiffany — slinking around all the time poking her nose into things. Wheedling another sewing machine for herself. She was the only one

454

besides the little kids who knew I sometimes visited Darlene. Sooner or later she was going to figure out that I had caused Darlene's death. So I had to get rid of Tiffany. Visiting her so she'd show me her new machine was easy, and so was fiddling around with the new machine. She was always distracted, often by the kids, and sometimes by those phones Darlene had for her charities. When Tiffany went to answer a call, I crossed the wires in the sewing machine, and after that it was simple. All I had to do was wait in my car out on the road at the time of night that Tiffany told me she usually sewed, and if I saw a fire start, I could go inside and make certain Tiffany didn't survive. I always keep my firefighter's gear in my trunk, so I put it on. No one would know who I was."

Maybe I was waking up. I told myself not to attempt moving, though, unless I could escape.

Mimi's tale became even more nightmarish. "And sure enough, I saw a flickering orange glow through the third-floor windows. I put on my mask and went into the house through the back door. No one saw me until I got to the sewing room. Tiffany played right into my hands. Instead of calling for help, she had nearly smothered that fire. She saw me, and I was afraid she recognized me. I grabbed Darlene's point presser and took care of Tiffany quickly. For some reason, that sewing machine rep showed up again. I dealt with her and was back outside, hiding in the woods, in a flash. Darlene's older kids came roaring up the driveway, and before I knew it, the siren at the fire station was going off. And I was dressed as a firefighter. After everyone else arrived, *you* drove right past and didn't stop," she crowed. "It was the perfect disguise. It came in handy tonight, too."

She crammed the carton against the quilts separating our booth from the firefighters' booth.

Something in her hand made a snapping noise.

Mimi had thought quickly when Felicity had appeared in the sewing room early Thursday morning, and she thought quickly this time, too.

But just like when she'd entered those mothering, sewing, and embroidering contests, she never did anything as perfectly as she thought. She'd expected the evidence she'd left in the Coddlefields' house to be reduced to ashes. But it hadn't been. And she probably hadn't realized until tonight that she'd left her firefighter's gloves at the Coddlefields'.

And minutes ago, she had stunned me, without, thanks to the cowboy hat that Haylee's mothers had foisted on me, knocking me out completely. So I'd heard her horrific confession. I only hoped I'd be able to remember and repeat it. And make someone believe me. They'd be here soon, wouldn't they?

This time, Mimi was taking extra care. She wasn't messing around with shorting out electrical circuits to cause a fire.

Mimi had a faster method.

She had a lighter.

51

Mimi was planning to incinerate those heritage linens. And also, I suspected, the quilts that Naomi and her students had slaved over for weeks, months, maybe years. The quilts could set the entire tent on fire.

How could I lie there, semiconscious and silently whimpering?

I couldn't. With a roar of outrage, I leaped up off the dirt floor.

Mimi didn't seem concerned about what I was doing. She was squatting next to the carton, flicking that lighter. A flame erupted.

One end of the fabric around me was still tied to a tent pole. Grabbing at my huge sash to loosen it while also twirling to unwind it, I yelled at Mimi to stop.

I was going to become dizzy and end up on the floor again.

One flap of the cardboard carton flared up.

I unwound enough of the batik to throw

myself toward the carton. Mimi could burn her antique linens if she wanted to, but I had to move that flaming carton away from Naomi's quilts.

Mimi tried to head butt me in the stomach. I put my hands out to stop her, but her momentum drove her shoulder into what was left of my batik padding and knocked me down, with her on top of me. My black Stetson went flying.

I was younger, stronger, and taller. Barely aware of my injured hand, I flipped her over so that I was straddling her and holding her down by the upper arms. My hair covered my face. Both of us were screaming, but neither of us probably made any sense.

She managed to scoot out from under me. I steamrollered her and held her arms down again.

She yelped and tried to twist away from me.

"Stop or I'll shoot!" Smallwood commanded from the doorway. She wouldn't be able see what was going on inside the dark tent.

"No, don't," I shrieked. "I've got things under control."

Smallwood's voice was deadly serious. "Put your arms above your heads."

Heads, plural. Both of us.

Strange things went through my mind, like what, exactly, did above my head mean when I was lying on a squirming she-devil?

"We're not armed," I called back.

Mimi's knee went into my thigh. She rolled onto me.

"Stand up and let us see your hands." Gartener was now giving the orders in his calm, firm, resonant voice.

"We can't," I screeched. I was on top again. "Can you please come over here and grab this woman's hands so she won't scratch my eyes out?" *I* thought it was a reasonable request.

"Why can't you stand?" Smallwood asked.

"We're tied together." Our rolling around had wrapped the middle of the bolt of batik around both of us. One end was tied to the tent pole and the other end was tighter than ever around my waist.

Large, warm hands touched my shoulders. "It's okay, Willow." Gartener.

Mimi lay still and gave him a girlishly innocent and tremulous smile. "Don't let her go. She attacked me."

I slid away from her, levered myself up from my hands and knees, unwound the rest of the bolt of batik from my waist, and piled it onto the yardage that Mimi had inadvertently wrapped around herself while wrestling with me.

Smallwood stood in the doorway, feet apart, hands hovering over holsters she wore outside her long denim skirt.

Suddenly, I understood why I could see her. The cardboard box was now blazing, threatening Naomi's quilts more than ever.

I darted to the box and kicked it into the tent's center aisle.

Mimi managed to get her feet underneath her. Stooping, she ran toward the tent's entrance.

But the center section of that bolt of batik was still wrapped a few times around her, with one end tied to a tent pole and the other end, the one that had been around me, loose in the dirt.

Chasing her, Gartener tripped on the fabric tail and rolled into Smallwood's feet. She crashed down onto him.

Unfortunately, the two police officers couldn't enjoy the moment. Mimi was dragging them behind her in her bid for freedom.

Clay, Isaac, Plug, and Russ swarmed into the tent and stomped on the blazing carton of linens. I wondered why Isaac was carrying a firefighter's jacket instead of wearing it. And why he had Gartener's prize baby doll in his other hand.

From inside her purple furry teddy bear costume, Naomi yelled at Mimi, "Where do you think you're going with the quilt fabric I lent Willow?" Calm, sweet Naomi, shouting? I almost felt faint again.

Mimi didn't make it very far before she reached the end of her yellow batik tether, the one she'd tied to a tent pole and then had accidentally wrapped around herself. With the help of Haylee, passing as a tall but strangely pear-shaped cowboy, Edna, the short, red-cheeked clown, and Opal, the crick-necked giraffe, Naomi tackled Mimi and threw her to the ground. Naomi was not only salvaging her now unsalable quilt fabric, she was also protecting me, a member of her extended family.

Clay left the smoldering carton, grasped my elbows in gentle hands, and asked his usual question, "Willow, are you all right?"

Biting my lip, I nodded.

Smallwood and Gartener untangled themselves from the fabric. They sprinted to Mimi, but she was covered in costumed Threadville proprietors. Calmly, Detective Gartener helped the rounded cowboy, the giraffe, the teddy bear, and the clown stand up.

Mimi screamed at the officers to arrest

me for killing Darlene and for attempting to kill Tiffany, Felicity, and Mimi herself.

52

Gartener turned her facedown and snapped handcuffs on her. "Sorry, ma'am, but we heard the end of your confession."

"That was her," Mimi argued. "Willow confessed how she sabotaged Darlene's machine and loosened the wing nuts on Darlene's table, then caused a fire at the Coddlefields', knocked Tiffany and Felicity out, and tied them to furniture with strips of cotton calico so they'd die in the fire."

"Ma'am," Gartener said in a polite but dangerous voice, "we know Willow's voice. She didn't say all that. You did."

Actually, Mimi hadn't said all that, either. In her mutterings to me, she hadn't mentioned the fabric strips, their fiber content, and the way she'd used them. Only a few of us knew about them. Mimi had just pointed her finger directly at herself.

"You can't put me under arrest without reading me my rights," she snapped.

Gartener rattled off the Miranda warning, then asked Smallwood to hold Mimi while he went off for his cruiser.

"We'll help you hold her." Edna was, of course, a very enthusiastic clown.

"I can do it," Smallwood said, patting a holster. "You civilians stay away."

Gartener hopped onto one of two golf carts parked beside the tent's entrance, turned the cart around, and tore away at its highest speed, probably all of about a half mile an hour.

"Golf carts?" I asked Clay. "Is that how Smallwood and Gartener got here?"

"Haylee, Opal, Naomi, and Edna had already commandeered the golf carts. The officers caught a ride with them."

"But weren't you all near the parking lot? That's where the fire was. Why didn't the police officers drive here in their cruisers?"

Mischief flashed in Clay's grin. "Chief Smallwood and Detective Gartener hid their cruisers near the administration building so no one would recognize them. They're in plain clothes tonight."

I turned my face away from Smallwood so she wouldn't see my smile. Who was I to carp about insufficient disguises?

Clay must have guessed what I was thinking. He winked.

I bit back a laugh. "How did you, Plug, Isaac, and Russ get here?"

"We ran."

Isaac had found a fire extinguisher and was pumping foam onto the carton of linens. Those beautiful heritage linens, including some that Mimi had created, were ruined. Even if they weren't, they'd be taken as evidence. However, my machines and I could make modern versions. The quilts and the rest of the tent's contents, including the humans, were okay.

More than okay. Plug had an arm around Russ and was telling him how worried he'd been about him. Plug was gruff, but if I could hear the love in his voice, Russ should be able to, as well. "Never run away again, son," Plug said. "If things get bad, just talk to your old man."

Russ ducked his head, but I thought I saw tears glimmer near his eyes. "Okay."

"And no more setting fields on fire."

"We didn't . . ."

"Don't lie, son. Your mother would be so sad."

"We won't do it again, sir."

"Dad."

"We won't do it again, Dad."

Isaac finished putting out the fire in the carton of linens. Leaving the baby doll in

466

the dirt, he carried the firefighter's jacket to Plug. "Chief," he said, "where did this jacket come from? Inside, it says *Emblesford Volunteer Fire Department.*"

"Then it came from Emblesford," Plug answered.

"Mimi's a member of the volunteer fire department there," I said.

Mimi mumbled that we'd all be made to pay for our false accusations.

Smallwood chastised Isaac for disturbing possible evidence.

He held his hands out. "I'm sorry, ma'am. I didn't know. Want me to put the jacket back where I found it?"

"No," she exploded. "Don't go back there. Leave everything alone. Later, I'll get your statement about where you found it."

And she'd get my statement, too, about where I saw it and the rest of the gear Mimi had removed. And Haylee's statement about seeing the firefighter sneak into the tent and, after a loud bang, the power going off and Mimi slipping out of the tent.

Poor Isaac didn't seem to know what to do with the jacket. He wadded it between his hands, then let it go, nearly dropped it, and caught it in midair.

Something white peeked out of one of its pockets. I edged up to Isaac for a closer look. A white cloth hankie trimmed in Mimi's signature tatting was about to fall out of the Emblesford jacket.

I took the jacket, hankie and all, from him, showed it to Smallwood, and explained.

"Put it on the ground beside me," she directed, never taking her eyes off Mimi. "I'll take it with me when we go."

Jeremy Chandler must have tired of bumper cars. He drifted into the tent. "Willow?" he asked. "I almost didn't recognize you in that black shirt. I like your hair that way."

After being crammed underneath the Stetson, my hair probably had a fresh-out-of-bed look. "Thanks," I faltered, not particularly in the mood for compliments about mussed hair.

"You're sure you don't want to become the Midwest rep for Chandler? You'd get to work for *me.*"

"I'm sure," I said.

He turned to Haylee, still in her cowboy disguise, including hat and extra padding. "You're good at sewing, aren't you?"

Shaking her head, she backed away from him. "I'm staying in Threadville with my mothers and my friends."

"Your rep is expected to get better," Clay told Jeremy in unyielding tones.

Jeremy sidestepped toward the tent's entryway. "That's good to hear." He could have *tried* to sound sincere.

Naomi was back to being her sweet self, even if she was a bit purple and fuzzy. She pointed out, "She's been through a lot."

In her clown suit and her usual, sturdy way, Edna backed Naomi up. "The least you can do is keep her on."

Opal would have towered over Jeremy even without the help of a tall and floppy giraffe neck. "Doing work she loves should help her get over her trauma," she informed him.

"Okay, well, see you all later." Jeremy melted into the night.

Good riddance. Had I said it aloud?

Behind the tent, a car door slammed. Jeremy leaving? Or Gartener returning?

But Gartener, broadcaster's voice and all, had never, in my hearing, sung opera.

53

What was Dr. Wrinklesides doing here?

"We could use some light in this tent," I said to no one in particular.

"Son?" Plug asked. "You got the Ferris wheel running. Think you can turn on a few lights?"

"Sure." The boy strode away.

Edna, her smile so wide it went with the clown costume, trotted to Dr. Wrinklesides. "Thanks for coming, Gord. I called you because Willow hurt her hand."

He gave her a peck on one red-painted cheek and sang something like, "I always answer your call, my little chickadee." He strode to me. "Let me see that hand, young lady."

"It's fine," I said.

Nevertheless, he took my hand gently in his, examined the bandages, and boomed out his hearty laugh. "Nice bandages. Cartoons. Who bandaged you?"

"Haylee."

He cast her an admiring grin. "She did a slick job of it." He peered at the side of my head. "Who hit you?" Without waiting for an answer, he ran gentle fingers over a very tender lump. "I'm calling an ambulance. That needs to be checked out in a hospital."

"No."

"Yes." He got out his cell and punched in three numbers.

Smallwood continued to stand over Mimi, who would have trouble fleeing, anyway. Lying on her stomach with her hands cuffed behind her, she would have lots of trouble disengaging herself from the confining bolt of batik.

Lights came on in the tent. Grinning, Russ returned to his father.

Another car door slammed in the parking lot behind the tent. Susannah ran toward me, but Smallwood stopped her. "Thanks for the evidence you gave us."

Susannah looked down and mumbled, "You're welcome."

"Evidence?" Mimi squawked.

Smallwood stared at her as if she were a particularly repulsive beetle on the ground. "Something about Darlene's charities not being legitimate."

"They weren't," Mimi said. "I could tell

you —" She clammed up.

Susannah sidled to me. "Willow, while I was wandering around the carnival after the fireworks —"

"There was a fire!"

She pushed the mane of hair from her face. "I know, and it hardly scared me. So those fireworks were good for something besides looking pretty. Anyway, I thought of something, and it could be important." She glanced at Mimi. "But maybe it's already taken care of." She gave me an earnest look. "Mimi's entry in the IMEC contest was thicker on one side than the others, with some odd stitches. Let's get it out and look at it."

With Dr. Wrinklesides watching my every move, I unlocked the display case and Susannah took out Mimi's entry. I'd already noticed the bulge on one side of the doily, and Susannah pointed at a line of hand-sewn stitches near the seam. We turned the doily over, unpicked the seam, and peeked inside.

Candy pink piping had been stitched to the fabric, too close to the embroidered design to be cut off. Instead, Mimi had tucked it inside and pulled too hard at the fabric, puckering it, when she closed the seam with hand stitches. Another of her mistakes.

Luckily, Threadville's assistant, Susannah, had questioned the shoddy work.

Isaac strode to Susannah and placed his bony hands on her shoulders. "Good job, Susannah. You really should join the fire department."

She looked up into his face. "You know I'm too afraid of fire." It was a good thing she didn't appear to know about the sparks twinkling from her eyes.

Isaac put both arms around her. "Even after tonight?"

"I'm no longer terrified of it, just scared."

He pulled her closer. "I'll protect you."

She let out a long, heartfelt sigh. "Fine, but I'm not going near any fires."

"Okay," he agreed, his voice muffled in her hair.

So that's why Susannah had been hanging around the firefighters' training? Had she dropped Isaac off at the Coddlefields' the night of the fire, and she'd been too shy to tell me he'd been at her place, possibly without his pickup truck, in the middle of the night?

Isaac peered at Haylee and me over her head. "You two are staying on the force, right? Elderberry Bay needs you."

"Sure," Haylee said.

He tightened his arms around Susannah. "Good, because I've accepted the job of fire chief down near Butler. And Susannah's coming with me."

Haylee, her three mothers, and I gazed at each other in dismay. We were losing our assistant already?

Finally, Naomi broke the silence. "We hope you'll both be very happy."

All of us agreed.

Although still goggle-eyed about the romance that must have been going on almost in front of my nose the whole time, I realized that something about the embroidery design in my hand was familiar. I turned it over. "I should have recognized this embroidery motif!" I started to clap my good hand to my forehead, but immediately rethought giving myself another blow to the head. "It's stitched white on white, but it's identical to the designs that Darlene sewed on her children's outfits. Darlene must have been practicing, with the piping and everything, and then decided to use pastel embroidery thread instead of white. Mimi stole her work to enter in IMEC."

"Ridiculous," Mimi snapped.

My thoughts, exactly. How desperately could one want to win a contest?

I added the embroidery to the growing

pile of evidence at Smallwood's feet. "When you're not so busy, you'll want this for evidence. Also Darlene Coddlefield's computer and Mimi's computer. You're likely to find this design in Darlene's software, not in Mimi's. I can help you look."

"I could have deleted it," Mimi said. "I don't keep everything I make."

She lay with her cheek in the dirt, her hands cuffed behind her, and bits of straw poking out of her flattened platinum hair. Despite the pity I couldn't help feeling, I had to point out, "Most people would keep a copy of the embroidery design they enter in a contest, in case there are questions."

She shrugged. "I'm not 'most people.' "

Smallwood echoed my thoughts. "Thank goodness."

Gartener pulled up in an unmarked cruiser and got out. Smallwood's police radio made a noise. Somebody started talking. I heard the name Tiffany. Smallwood smiled, asked the person on the other end to repeat what he'd just said, and turned the radio up. "Listen, everyone," she whispered.

The voice said, "Tiffany Quantice became conscious and was able to tell us the name of her attacker. It was a friend of her late boss's, someone named Mimi Anderson.

Anderson is renting a cottage in Elderberry Bay for a couple of months. We're sending a team there now."

"You can search the cottage if you want to," Smallwood told her radio. "In fact, that would be great. However, with the help of some good citizens, we have already apprehended Mimi Anderson."

She and Gartener lifted Mimi to her feet, unwrapped the batik, and guided her into the cruiser's backseat. I rescued the baby doll from the dirt floor and wrapped its blanket more tightly around it. Gartener headed toward the driver's door.

Silently, I offered him his baby doll. He stared at it for a second, then burst into a deep, warm laugh.

Gartener, laughing? Wonders never ceased.

Leaving me holding the doll, he folded himself into the driver's seat.

Smallwood told us she'd be around to talk with each of us in the morning. She pointed her finger at me. "Especially you. You did a great job." I thrust Gartener's baby doll at her. Wearing her cowgirl skirt, shirt, and hat, she cradled the doll. The goofiest maternal look flitted across her face.

But she quickly regained her stern solemnity and clambered into Gartener's passenger seat. With Mimi scowling behind them, they bumped away over the former field's ancient furrows.

A laugh from Gartener and a compliment from Chief Smallwood. I nearly fell over. But I couldn't have.

Not only was I standing right beside Clay, I was leaning into him, and he had an arm around my shoulders. Although I hated feeling or acting needy, just this once I deserved a little comfort.

"I'm coming with you to the hospital," he said.

"I'm fine."

"I'm coming with you." He tightened his arm around me and brushed a gentle kiss across the good side of my forehead. "I went in the ambulance with someone I didn't know at all, why wouldn't I go with someone I —" He broke off and buried his face in my hair.

Obviously there was no arguing with him, even if I could have spoken at that moment.

And there was no arguing with Haylee and her mothers, either. Opal removed her giraffe head, and Naomi took off the purple furry teddy bear face. Edna, her red wig with its attached hat still crooked, snuggled against Dr. Wrinklesides.

They all beamed proudly at Clay and me.

Dr. Wrinklesides began to sing an operatic aria. No doubt it was about undying love.

WILLOW'S DIAPHANOUS FIRE STITCH SCARF

You will need:

Water-soluble stabilizer
Water-soluble adhesive spray
Bits of thread, lace, ribbons, yarn, and/or fabric in fiery colors
Straight pins
Embroidery thread in fiery colors

You don't need an embroidery machine for this project. You don't even need a sewing machine — you can do all the stitching by hand, and it still won't take you very long!

You may have seen scarves like these in upscale gift or dress shops. They look lighter than air and can be very elegant.

1. Lay out the stabilizer in the shape of the scarf you're going to make. You can use small pieces of stabilizer and overlap them. Spray adhesive on the pretty bits and stick them to the stabilizer in an appealing pattern. Make certain that each piece is touching at least one other one.

2. Pin more stabilizer over the top of the scarf.

3. Carefully stitch up and down the length of the scarf in a fire stitch pattern (curved lines open at the bottom and pointed at the top to resemble fire) several times, then back and forth across the scarf. Do diagonals, too. Change thread and bobbin colors whenever the urge strikes you. Make certain you catch *every* teensy bit of thread, lace, ribbons, yarn, and/or fabric at least twice.

4. Soak the scarf in warm water to dissolve the stabilizer.

5. Lay flat to dry.

There! You have it! A beautiful, one-of-a-kind scarf! Send a photo to Willow@ ThreadvilleMysteries.com, and I'll put it on my website: ThreadvilleMysteries.com.

Note from Haylee: Do you ever cut off selvedges? If so, you can wind the cut-off selvedges over the stabilizer like ribbon.

Note from Opal: For a heftier, warmer scarf, use yarn instead of thread, lace, ribbons, and/or fabric.

Note from Edna: I like to string little beads or sequins on yarn or cord before I make one of these scarves, but you must be careful not to hit a bead with your needle and (shudder) break the needle. Sequins could damage needles, too, and probably look best without needle punctures.

Note from Naomi: You don't have to use a fire stitch. You can sew straight, zigzag, or curved stitches. You can incorporate free-hand designs like hearts and stars if you want. It's like quilting . . .

TIPS

1. I learned to sew from my grandmother. Her sewing machine was fastened to the top of a little desk. The table legs forced me to station myself at the middle of the sewing machine. Haylee, who tailors perfectly, came into In Stitches one day and saw me making a tank top for myself (I'd already embroidered the fabric, of course). When she stopped laughing, she pointed out that if I sat directly in front of the needle, my stitches would be less likely to stray off to one side or the other. I tried it, and she was right!

2. Today's sewing machines go at incredible speeds, just because they can. Embroidery machines stitch at top speed. Let them. But when you're sewing or tailoring, take it slowly and stitch it right the first time. If you have a lead foot on your sewing pedal, or are teaching beginners, especially chil-

dren, to sew, check your sewing machine manual. You may be able to lower the machine's top speed. You can always reset it later.

3. Take your sewing and embroidery machines to a reliable repair person for check-ups annually, or more frequently if you use them a lot, like I do.

WILLOW

CPSIA information can be obtained
at www.ICGtesting.com
Printed in the USA
FFOW031111210113
738FF